DÌLSEACHD

A STOLEN CROWN

ALSO BY CHEYENNE VAN LANGEVELDE

BETWEEN TWO WORLDS

DÌLSEACHD

A STOLEN CROWN

PRINCESS OF THE HIGHLANDS TRILOGY
BOOK ONE

CHEYENNE VAN LANGEVELDE

"Beautifully written with tender moments and heart wrenching scenes, I fell in love with this story. Most definitely one of the best books I've read this year. Highly, highly recommend!"

~ CAITLIN MILLER; AUTHOR OF *THE MEMORIES WE PAINTED*

"Dìlseachd – A Stolen Crown is a compelling, gripping tale of loyalty lost and regained that will captivate readers of all ages. Van Langevelde authentically captures the culture and the beauty of ancient Scotland and quickly draws reader into Fiona's journey from imprisoned orphan to warrior princess. It's the historical novel readers have been waiting for!"

~ GRACE A. JOHNSON; AUTHOR OF *HELD CAPTIVE*

"With descriptive, poetic prose, Cheyenne van Langevelde weaves a tale of Scotland sure to please lovers of historical fantasy."

~ KRISTINA HALL; AUTHOR OF THE *KENTUCKY MIDNIGHT* SERIES

TABLE OF CONTENTS

To Mrs. Feia

For believing in this story from the very first draft
And telling me it needed to be published

It took six years, but it has come at last

Thank you

AUTHOR'S NOTE

THIS story began as a simple idea, based on a couple of images from Pinterest—which is a great place to find inspiration for stories none of us have time to write. There are only so many that can be penned, but I am glad to say that *Princess of the Highlands* is one of them. In fact, it was the very first original story I wrote that was longer than a few thousand words.

I typed out the first chapter at my aunt's house in Florida, where we were vacationing back in 2016. I finished the first draft a year later at some 34K words. I deeply apologise to whoever read that first draft, where thirteen-year-old me didn't know what she was doing. This book has since grown to 99K words in several rounds of serious edits over the years as I've grown in both age and skill as a writer. Thanks to my friend, Sary, this story also became not just one book, but three, with more stories set in the same full tale playing around in my head. But all these explanations regarding this book's origin are boring.

The story, while based on a general time of the Danish occupation of Scotland, around 800 A.D., is not set in any particular era. None of the people, places, or events existed or happened—to my knowledge, anyway. For those of you who have read my debut, *Between Two Worlds*, if you're expecting a very particular, historically detailed novel, you may be disappointed. Consider this instead to be a type of mediaeval period drama. Which brings me to the other important point of accents.

Yes, this book has plenty of Scots English, and it varies from character to character. Those for whom it is a second language, it is not as thick. Most of the Danish characters, on the other hand, speak in plain English, for which I imply they are speaking in their own tongue.

This book and the characters in it mean more to me than anything else I've ever written. It is a tale full of tragedy, but also joy and hope and love and the beauty of life. If you finish this book and its accompanying novels, I hope you are touched in some way.

But I digress.

Come. A princess without a crown, a harper without his sight, and a boy tortured by the past are waiting for us.

PRONUNCIATION GUIDE

*Most names in this book are of Scottish or Welsh origin.
The pronunciation of trickier words and names are below.*

*Tip: a common sound in both languages is a soft guttural sound in the
throat, marked by a ch. A c is almost always pronounced like a k, and a
g as a hard g sound as in "get."*

Athair-cèile — ah-har kay-luh
Annag — ahn-nugk
Carbinenth — car-bih-nehnth
Cymraeg — come-rige
Cymreig — come-rayg
Cymru/Cymry — come-ree
Daibhidh — day-vee
Dìlseachd — jeel-shochg
Eachann — ae-chahn
Fionnuala — finn-oo-la
MacClydno — mac-klid-no
McCurragh — mic-kur-rah
Nuith — noo-ith
Sabhal — sa-val
Sioned — shee-on-nid

Maps

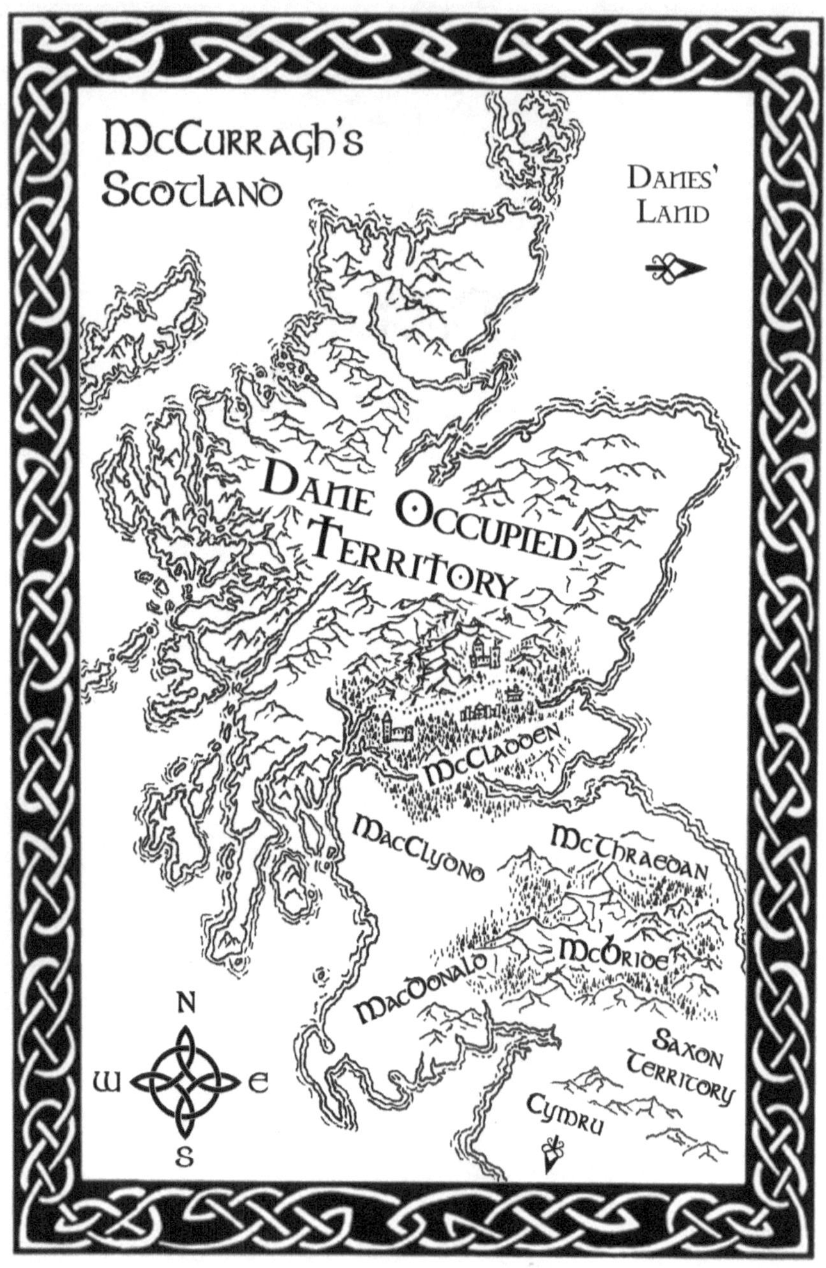
McCurragh's
Scotland
Danes'
Land
Dane Occupied
Territory
McCladden
MacClydno
McThraedan
McÐride
MacÐonald
Saxon
Territory
Cymru
N
W
E
S

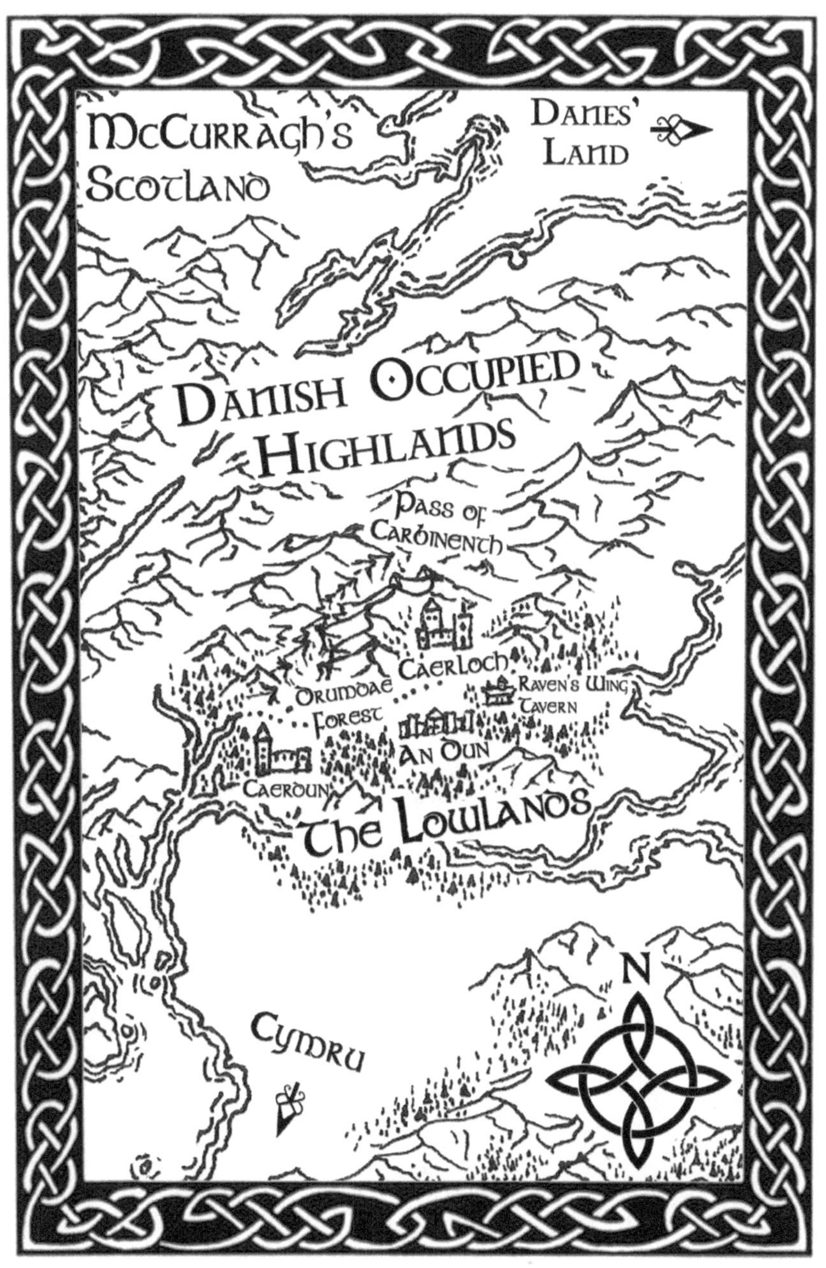
McCurragh's
Scotland
Danes'
Land
Danish Occupied
Highlands
Pass of
Carðinenth
Caerloch
Ðrumðae
Forest
Raven's Wing
Tavern
An Ðun
Caerðun
The Lowlands
Cymru
N

"Faithless is he who says farewell when the road darkens."
~ J.R.R. Tolkien ~

~ PROLOGUE ~
CRIMSON DAWN

THE sun rose over the sloping Highlands, tainting reddish-gold the swathes of fog that lay in the valleys. The bittersweet smell of salt rolled in on the chill morning breeze, and one could hear faintly amidst the silvery birdsong the distant murmur of the sea. Emerald hills glowed in the warm light, and when the war host crested the rise, the northern horizon twinkled like dazzling gold as the sun glanced off the rippling waves.

Douglas McCurragh inhaled the tangy air, relishing his first sight of the sea. It was odd how peaceful the scene was. For he knew, with a heaviness in his chest, that this tranquillity would soon be shattered with the clash of steel upon steel and the cries of dying men.

It had only been a few hours since their scouts had brought word of Danish warships in sight of this beach. Only a few months since they had known of the threat—of the burnings and the carnage of animals, fields, and human beings that the Danes left in the bloody wake they called victory.

It would be cowardly to stand back and wait until the Danes came to them. Divided, they would fall, clan by clan. Mere pride and self-assurance would do nothing against the Danish numbers. Unified, though, they stood a chance against the raiders from the sea; thus the sending out of the Cran Tara, the king's call to a war hosting, the like of which had not been seen since the days of their forefathers. That was why the Scots were here now, assembled on horse and foot to defend their country, their homes, and their families.

But Douglas had no wife and children of his own. He was only a few moons past sixteen years, scarcely of age to fight in a war, though he had been trained well. As young as he was, he did not feel a special passion for his country as the men beside him did, even if he would one day be king of Scotland when his father went beyond the sunset.

No, he would fight only to protect his sister, whom he loved more than anyone else in the world.

The wind whipped his brown hair into his eyes as the Scots descended the hill. Ahead of him, he could see the company of horsemen trotting ahead of his own band of foot soldiers. He shut his eyes tightly for a moment, not wanting to be distracted from his purpose as they marched. But the remembrance of his sister was more poignant in the early hours of this dawn, which perhaps would be his last.

A bouncing lass with springy red curls and a smattering of freckles across her small face, she was the only one who could always make him smile, no matter how tired he felt after training. Despite her eight short years, she had already attained a realistic view of the world, and her thoughts and comments on the happenings of Scotland often astonished him. He wondered now what she would tell him at this moment...probably to be courageous, and make her and their father proud.

Douglas smiled, and then it faded away as the memory of their parting came unbidden to his mind.

"Keep yerself safe, Fiona, and donnae forget the footwork I taught ye." He grinned, trying to make light of the seriousness of it all. He kissed her on her forehead. "And keep yerself free until I get back. I must make sure tha' yer future husband is acceptable," he added with a wink.

They laughed, the merry sound ringing off the cobblestones of the castle courtyard.

"I donnae think I'll be wed yet, brother," she returned, still giggling. "I'm only eight."

He stuck out his tongue teasingly. "Jist to be sure." Then his face sobered as he turned to their father and stood, head bowed, as King Daibhidh repeated the ancient blessing:

"May the road rise to meet ye and may the wind be always at yer back."

Fiona added, *"And may the road bring ye back safely to us; but till then, keep yerself safe, my brother."*

He had replied with a laugh—such a stark contrast to his current mirthlessness, *"I will, sister, dear."*

His breath hitched in his chest and he swallowed hard, looking with wide eyes at the spreading grey sea before them. Even from this distance, he could see the black ships and their black sails, full and flowing in the morning breeze. The sun caught on the gory scarlet embroidery, fearful ravens and dragons and other mythical beasts seeming to fly in the wind toward the Scottish war host. Soon, men with axes and garishly painted shields would disembark from those ships and pour themselves like an ink stain upon the beach, leaving crimson wreckage in their wake. Who knew whether the Scots would prove victorious that day or not? Whether they would keep Scotland safe from this threat of invasion. Whether he would live to see Fiona again.

Douglas glanced up at the sky, an anxious tingling shooting through his fingertips. He had only ever practised with swords against straw-stuffed figures. Would he weaken at the sight of blood? Would he turn coward in the inevitable fight?

These thoughts had tormented his mind since they had first heard of the Danes' arrival in Scotland, since his father had said he could go with the war host. He remembered how he had longed to go, longed to prove his worth as a man, longed to defend his country with the rest, and how Fiona had looked at him with a quizzical expression on her innocent face and asked him why he would want to leave her and die far from home.

Her question had startled him. Why would she ask such a thing? It was never guaranteed that one would die in battle, though it was never said one would survive it, either. But the swiftness with which she had jumped to that conclusion.... Even now, the memory sent a chill racing up his spine, and he shivered.

Glancing at the beach opening before them, he inhaled sharply, determination striving against the fear that those incoming ships bore in on the tide. He had made a promise to his little sister, and he meant to keep it as best he could. Yet, in the battle that was before him, how would it be possible to do so?

Blade against blade, the battle swiftly descended into chaos. Douglas hardly remembered the order in which they had marched towards each other just a short time ago. Everything in him deadened itself to the world, and he was only aware of his beating heart and any nearby threat to his life. He thrust as if into straw and tried to ignore the softness of sword plunging into flesh, the hardness of hitting bone, and the sticky warmth of blood on his hands.

The two armies struggled for dominance on the body-strewn beach as all the while, the sun climbed hot in cloudless skies.

A cold sickness twisted in Douglas' belly, and his grip on his sword hilt kept slipping. His arms were tiring—he wondered how much longer he would be able to keep on fighting. Snarling faces pressed close on every side and the din of the battle deafened his ears, ears that longed to hear only the peaceful sound of the sea and birdsong that had rung out over these hills just that morning.

He let out a choking sob as someone rushed in from behind, ramming their shield into his elbow. His sword flew out of his hands and landed several paces away. His chest tightened in panic, the air too thin to breathe. He would not be able to regain it in time, not before someone saw his helpless state and came to his destruction. He was only a boy; few would hesitate to finish him off.

Douglas reached for his dirk, the only weapon he had left. He glanced around frantically, his heart hammering in his throat, ready to spring at the first sight of danger.

He did not wait long.

A mountain of a man with a beard that matched his bloodied blade came at him, harsh laughter echoing in his eyes.

Douglas' chest tightened in rising panic, nearly suffocating him. He was surrounded on all sides by Danes, any Scots near him dying. He was separated from the host, armed only with a dirk, and facing certain death. But in that moment, instinct kicked in. Years of training came rushing back. The panic ebbed away like the bloodied tide, leaving clear-headed calm in its wake.

The Dane shouted something in his own tongue—a challenge, perhaps—but Douglas understood none of it.

A memory came to him in a fleeting instant: his sister waving goodbye from the top of the battlements, held up by her nurse, worry written on her face as the sun shone fiery red on her hair.

A tear slipped down his face. *I am so sorry, Fiona.*

Without waiting for the other to attack, Douglas let out a cry and rushed in, thrusting his dirk into an opening in the man's chainmail, underneath his armpit.

The Dane let out a howl of pain and instinctively swung his sword, plunging it deep into Douglas' stomach.

It was cold, at first, like winter's breath. Then it flamed.

The Dane withdrew his sword, moving onward to shed more lives for the red harvest before he bled out himself.

Douglas sank to the crimson sand, gasping for breath. How it hurt! He had never in his life felt pain like this! Burning and burning, as if someone had lit a fire within him.

He reached down to where the pain spread out over his abdomen and his fingers met hot, sticky blood.

Sobs wracked his frame, not only from the pain of the wound but because of how much he had failed. Failed his country, failed his father, failed his sister. As a prince, it was his duty to protect the kingdom. As a chieftain's son, it was his duty to defend his land and honour. And as a brother, it was his task to keep his sister safe from harm.

Douglas closed his eyes, tears streaming down his face, broken moans escaping his lips. The sounds of the battle were fading away. The skirmish must have moved on, or perhaps it only seemed so because he was dying. He knew he was dying. Men did not receive such wounds as this and live. Not even in the legends.

A sharp *tran-tara* was heard, a horn's call breaking across the beach filled with dead and living men. But Douglas scarcely gave it thought. It was not meant for him. It did not matter what the signal meant now.

It was getting harder to breathe. Every intake felt like dragging a cart over rough stones, and the burning only grew more intense, drowning out his senses, drowning out his thoughts.

The end was coming fast.

Douglas McCurragh closed his eyes in agonising pain as the last cold tears spilled down his dirtied cheeks.

"I am so sorry, Fiona," he whispered. "I am so sorry…"

~ 1 ~
A FORGOTTEN PRINCESS

FIONA McCurragh reined in her horse and paused at the top of the rolling hillside, looking out over the treeless glen. A misting rain fell from the clouded heavens, hiding Tor-na-Cruithne in the distance behind a silver veil. The rain was as soft as snow—though not as cold—and the fitful wind tossed Fiona's flaming curls about, carrying with it a hint of the bygone summer.

She fiddled with the bright sword at her waist, her fingers finding their position on the familiar hilt. But she did not pull it out. Not yet.

It was an old habit of hers to wait a few moments before she performed the stunt that her only sibling had once patiently taught her. Ever since he had passed away six years ago, she had relentlessly practised it—practised it to perfection, as if somehow she kept alive the memory of her beloved brother by doing so.

The rising foothills to the southwest lay dark blue and dim, dense drifts of fog hiding their peaks. Her horse, Sgàil, a grey *gearran*, tossed her silvery mane and gently played with the bit between her teeth. The mare's velvety nostrils twitched at the rain and heather-scent hanging between the heavens and the earth, the air heavy like the sense of fear and danger always lurking within Fiona's breast.

She pursed her lips, looking out at the vast, empty moorland. The ever-present bitterness, the longing for the old days that seemed only to be put at rest when she escaped into this verdant wilderness, threatened to overwhelm her senses before she rode on down into the glen.

Even now, she could hear her brother, Douglas, saying, "No' yet, Fiona! If ye let it out now, ye willnae hae any left fer facing yer enemy!" No one had been willing to teach her weaponry as her brother used to.

She smiled grimly, the memory painfully precious, as all memories of her brother were.

Fiona clenched her eyes shut for a brief moment. The mere remembrance of her family's fate brought back so much grief that she hardly dared to think of them, and yet she had nothing else worth thinking of. She alone was left, the sole survivor of the McCurraghs, once the rulers of Scotland. The Danes had destroyed her family, slaying her brother with the sword and her father with grief; her mother, farthest from her mind, had died at Fiona's birth. And soon, unless Fate decreed otherwise, Fiona would join her family beyond the sunset.

Her eyes fluttered open as a warm gust of wind blew into her face, scattering wet droplets of mist on her dampened cheeks. Lady Nuith was only waiting until the right time to seize her crown by disposing of its last living threat—Fiona—thus carrying out in full the treachery begun by the Danes six years ago.

Fiona barely remembered it, barely remembered her father's marriage to the Danish woman, his attempt to bring peace to the war-torn country. She had been so distraught over her brother's death that everything else had only been a tear-stained blur. But she remembered the whispers, the concerned looks, and she remembered her father's death and what followed after.

Three years since then, she had been locked up in the east tower at Caerloch, once the capital of her father's kingdom, save when she was occasionally let out to ride on the moors where no one dwelt. She had no friends, and even the servants that she had known from birth had been sent away or silenced in ways she could only imagine.

Her crown stolen, her family murdered or conveniently dead, her existence forgotten by the Scots once loyal to her, Fiona had little hope of survival. Once Lady Nuith had a child by which to claim the throne instead of the Scottish princess, whom Nuith insisted was not the late king's daughter, it would be over. And since Nuith's marriage to the Danish Lord Erland, it was only a matter of time before the threat became tangible.

Life was never so precious as when one would soon be dead.

Fiona swallowed, banishing the morbid thoughts. She must focus, even as her brother had always said, and not let her bitterness get the better of her. Flipping her thick locks of hair behind her shoulders, Fiona leaned forward on her horse and whispered a few words in the mare's ear. Then she sat up straight and dug her heels into Sgàil's flanks, spurring her forward. Together, they raced onward towards a few scraggly and barren bushes beside a small burn, which still flowed this late in the year.

As they darted across the fading emerald landscape, Fiona unsheathed her sword and, leaning nearly parallel to the racing ground, began to veer to the left. Sgàil, who was familiar with this, swerved to the right as they drew near the small burn.

At the last instant, Fiona straightened, swinging her right leg over her saddle with one fluid motion and diving headlong off her horse. But instead of falling to the ground, she somersaulted through the air and landed on her feet, her sword held firmly high above her. The strange calmness of battle frenzy flooded her veins, every movement seeming clear and yet distant, only her rapid heartbeat disturbing the windswept silence.

She had practised this move countless times, but it was her first attempt while wearing a dress instead of one of her brother's kilts. She was glad she had managed it without falling, not only for her own sake, but also for her brother's, as it was Douglas who had taught it to her. In some unexplainable way, succeeding in doing it right was the only way she could cope with his death, for he had died before he had seen her do it perfectly.

Having caught her breath, she swung her sword behind her smoothly and brought it in front of her in a whistling arc before proceeding with other similar moves that Douglas had taught her at this very burn so long ago. Each stroke, each turn of the blade thrust back the murky fear that edged on her conscience, familiar repetition of practice bringing reality clearer into focus. Perhaps one day, this same swordplay might save her life.

The lass swung her sword around once more—save this time the blow was blocked by something behind her, a metal *clang* shattering the peace of the moors.

Fiona whirled around in sudden panic, meeting her opponent:

a lad roughly her age, with hair as dark as peat and eyes as piercing blue as a cloudless September sky.

He looked at her with something akin to a wry smile. "Excellent," he said, startling the silence. His low, melodic voice had a pleasant ring to it, but still Fiona kept her guard, her eyes wide in terror. Before he could say anything else, she swiftly slid her sword off of his with a harsh grinding noise, stepping back and centering her weight. Heart hammering in her throat, she waited in suppressed terror for his next move.

Had Lady Nuith sent this lad to threaten her into never leaving Caerloch again?

Fiona swallowed against the panic rising within, anticipating this stranger to advance, a quick movement that might end her life forever.

But the lad only slammed his blade home into its scabbard in one fluid motion.

Slowly lowering her sword arm, Fiona likewise sheathed her weapon as they both stared at each other for several moments without speaking.

"Ye almost lopped my head off," she sputtered at last, her eyes never leaving his face.

"Nae, I had nae such intention," he replied soberly. Then he grinned, the swift change seeming like mockery. "Well, ye're a bonnie lass."

The blood rushed to Fiona's face, but she did not smile back. "I thank ye," she returned in a cold tone of voice. She was not used to anyone complimenting her these days, especially complete strangers in the middle of uninhabited moorland.

She scrutinised him more closely as he leaned against a leafless tree on the banks of the gurgling burn. He gazed back at her, his silence almost intimidating, as if he dared her to judge his appearance. His clothing was clean and finely-woven, that of a chieftain's family, not a lower-ranking clansman. And his sword, what little she had seen of it, was a good blade, not a dented relic from the last war, but something to be cherished, the sort handed from father to son. Unless he had stolen it.

Her throat tightened. He seemed young to be an outlaw, but it was possible. If he was so skilled a thief to be well-clad, what sort of threat did he pose to her? Perhaps she should not so quickly have sheathed her sword.

But that was not the only thing that struck her as outlandish. Of all the times that she had ridden upon the uninhabited heaths of the Highlands, this was the first time she had seen another human being. Few other individuals from Caerloch ever came this way.

The grin slowly vanished from the lad's face and he stared, not at her face, but at the plaid which was draped over her left shoulder, as was the custom. Then he said, "I noticed tha' the brooch ye're wearing on yer plaid is that of the McCurraghs' emblem. And I also recall tha' that clan was ended about three years ago, was it no'?" An unspoken challenge rang out in his words, a challenge that sparked in his bright blue eyes.

Fiona glanced down at the silver pin with its small boat delicately carved into the metal, a mark of her clan as much as the tartan pattern woven into her plaid. Her thoughts raced, her mouth dry as she scrambled for an answer.

Wherever this lad came from, he was surely no Dane. None of Lady Nuith's people could speak the Gàidhlig without a trace of accent. If he was a thief, he was still a Scot. Perhaps he still had some shred of honour. At the worst, he would simply turn her in to the Danes for a reward. At best, her name would have no meaning to him—but she doubted that. Any dignity her ancestors might have had was squandered when her father married Lady Nuith, losing all respect in the eyes of the Scots. McCurragh was now a byword, used for speaking of someone who had abandoned honour.

"I am Fiona McCurragh, the last of tha' line," she said at last, a note of despair hanging in her words. "And who might ye be?" she added nervously, her eyes searching to see how he would respond to all she had said.

No emotion crossed his face, whatever he might be thinking inside. He only bowed his head slightly, saying with a note of grandeur, "Angus McCladden, son of Donald McCladden, High Chieftain of the Lowlands."

Fiona's eyes went wide in surprise. So his father had given him that sword after all.... When the War against the Danes ended in failure and succeeded in tearing Scotland apart, the McCladden clan had become the rulers of the Lowlands. Down south, they had managed to keep some semblance of order like there had been before the War, but in the Highlands, the Danes were the rulers and the Scots their subjects—or in some cases, such as hers, their prisoners.

"I heard tha' the line of the McCurraghs was dead," Angus repeated, snapping the lass back to attention.

The challenge was still afire in his eyes.

Fiona glanced up quickly. "Nae, nae. The present laird wishes it so."

"Why?" he questioned, the challenge now married with curiosity.

Sgàil trotted up, having attempted to graze despite the bit in her mouth, and nudged Fiona lightly in the shoulder. The princess's gaze flew to the ground, the words sticking bitterly in her throat. "Would ye wish to hae any possible threats to yer throne kept alive?" When Angus did not reply, she continued, "They donnae hae any real claim to the throne as they still lack a born heir. They cannae jist murder me without threat of reprisal from any loyal to the true throne of Scotland. So they keep me in hiding." She swallowed hard against the fears threatening to resurface. "My one solace in my imprisonment is that I may sometimes ride alone out on the moors. Does that satisfy ye?"

He shrugged carelessly, his eyes never leaving her face, seeming to study her closely despite his air of nonchalance. "I suppose so. Yet I still wonder how a lass like ye, wi' yer story, ends up riding in the northern reaches of the Lowlands, especially armed wi' a sword. Lady Nuith and her husband hae their realm in the Highlands, unless places hae changed since my father spoke to me about it."

Fiona was flustered. "They donnae ken I am armed; I keep it hidden in a dry bank a league from the castle.... But the Lowlands? I had nae idea tha' I was this far south." Panic set in the depths of her heart. If Lady Nuith found out....

Angus looked up from his musings. "Aye, ye're in the Lowlands. Is tha' such a bad thing?"

Fiona backed away into her horse, a knot entangling itself in the pit of her stomach. "I must be gang."

"Why?" Angus' dark brows drew together in confusion. Or was it fear? She could not see past any expression he chose to wear.

"If Lady Nuith discovers I hae been down this far south, she willnae hae mercy. And she will ken if I return too late to Caerloch."

"But—" He began to walk towards her, attempting to lay a hand on the mare's bridle.

"I cannae stay longer!" Without another word spoken, she swung herself onto her horse and rode off, her fiery locks of hair streaming out behind her in the autumn wind.

The brown and parched moorlands raced by as the leagues vanished beneath Sgàil's hooves. The sky had swiftly turned to dark grey, and a chill breeze began to rise, harsh and gusting. Fiona paid no heed.

I must get back. I must get back. I must get back.

She did not know for certain what Lady Nuith would do if she discovered Fiona had ridden to the Lowlands—let alone armed and talking to the son of the Danes' most powerful rival in Scotland besides herself. She might excuse the first thing, for Fiona only ever rode to this burn that Douglas had shown her long ago, but as for the second? She had little hope of mercy. It all reeked of rebellion, and Fiona feared what consequences that might incite. But it was not a rebellion, was it? Exchanging a few words with someone who was a complete stranger to her did not exactly mean revolution, did it?

As the leagues sped away, her heart was filled with confusion and mystery. It was not rebellion in any logical sense, but fear did not follow logic, and if Lady Nuith was afraid that Fiona had become too dangerous, the princess's life would be over—with or without another heir.

At the same time, a small shred of hope kindled itself in the depths of her heart. Surely this meeting with the son of McCladden was no accident? Surely there was something more to this whole encounter that was significant, something meaningful, something that would have impact at some point in the future, even if she did not know what it was yet. For, even though her father and brother could never return from the grave, she yearned to no longer remain a slave to Lady Nuith's wishes and in constant danger of being swiftly and silently murdered. Perhaps a rebellion was truly coming, and she would be freed.

Fiona shook her head, blinking against the wind in her face. It would never happen. As Angus had said, the line of the McCurraghs had ended, and she with them. She was not even a figurehead, only a lost princess doomed to fade out of memory. Her people had forgotten about her—such a rebellion would never happen in her lifetime, if it ever did at all.

For after the disaster that had followed the War, no one would attempt to overthrow the Danes now.

~ 2 ~

SHADOW OF THE PAST

CAERLOCH rose dark and ominous against the stormy horizon as Fiona and Sgàil drew near. The growing winds and the pounding hooves beneath Fiona did nothing to soothe the questions in her mind. The grey clouds loomed threateningly above the bleak and imposing towers that sprawled around the thick castle walls. Guards paced on the battlements, their black armour dim spots against the paler stone. But they did not take special notice of the red-haired princess approaching the gates; perhaps Lady Nuith had not realised Fiona's long absence after all.

As Fiona crossed the bridge running over the deep and muddy moat, the guards slowly raised up the creaking iron portcullis, permitting her to pass without asking questions. She exhaled softly, some of the worry sliding off her shoulders and remaining outside the castle walls. Perhaps it would be all right.

But then the dim daylight caught on the crimson raven emblem on the guards' shields, drawing Fiona's gaze and sending a familiar fear whispering across her skin.

Whether Lady Nuith knew of that afternoon's happenings or not, it did not lessen the danger the princess was in.

Fiona spurred Sgàil onward, shutting away the image of those bloody ravens as she glanced up out of habit at the dark murder holes in the stone arch above her head. While grim reminders of Caerloch's double function as both a residence and a defensible fortress, she never knew when something might be hurled through those holes intended for her. She did not think Lady Nuith would stoop so low as to have her murdered in such a way, but she did not know how or when Nuith would dispose of her. That fear of the unknown constantly wormed its way into her thoughts whenever she was enclosed behind the walls of Caerloch; it was only on the moors that Fiona felt truly free. And who knew how long those tastes of freedom would last.

A cold gust howled across the courtyard and Fiona shivered as she dismounted; she had forgotten to bring her cloak. A scowling stable hand came forward and led her horse away without saying a word to her. Fiona was used to being ignored and took no notice.

The courtyard was mostly empty, save for a group of white doves pecking at some grain left on the ground for them. Thin tendrils of smoke drifted up from the open windows of the kitchens, which were below ground, but that was the only sign of life. Even the blacksmith's forge remained oddly silent, and Fiona shivered again, though this time not because of the wind.

Whether Lady Nuith was waiting for her or not, Fiona walked across the echoing courtyard and entered the foot of the tower, the remaining daylight vanishing behind the closed door. It was dim inside, the only light coming from the small slits in the wall meant for archers. There were no windows on the ground floor, and the torches in their respective brackets were not lit. It all gave a horrible, oppressive feeling, and Fiona ran up the spiralling stairs as if she could escape it if she went fast enough.

Inhaling deeply to better prepare herself for whatever encounter with Nuith awaited her, Fiona entered her apartments, stepping into a small, narrow corridor. The torch on the wall was not lit here either, and a cold draft came through unseen cracks in the stone.

The princess hesitated.

Lady Nuith rarely came here, preferring instead for Fiona to go to her. But an air of waiting hung about the whole place, as if something were about to happen. It was not just in the empty courtyard, but in the unlit torches, the dark hallways, and the onerous silence.

What was going on?

Without further hesitation, Fiona opened another door to her chambers, a much broader room with oaken panelling along the walls and high windows that revealed the fading light outside. There was not much else save her bed, a sturdy chest that contained her clothing and other belongings, and a few chairs. A fire burned in the small fireplace in one wall, lighting and warming up the room as the evening chill approached and filling the place with the welcome scent of apple logs.

Fiona blinked in surprise. The Danish woman was not waiting for her. Her shoulders loosened with the breath she had not known she had been holding, the tension fading away.

But the relief did not last long.

Stepping farther into the room, the floor creaking slightly beneath her step, she saw someone sitting in the gloom by the window.

"Fiona?" It was a male voice, not a young one, and certainly not one she recognized.

Her heart leapt into her throat, nearly choking her with panic. Had Lady Nuith sent an assassin to kill her? But then, he would have already struck and not simply sat there and asked her name. Unless it was all a trick. None of it made sense.

Fiona stepped closer, gripping her dirk so tightly she feared she might break the handle. She wished then that she had her sword with her, not left behind in its hiding place, but a sword would do little good in combat this close.

The man remained seated, as if waiting for her. Dried mud caked his boots and the hem of his cloak, as if he had journeyed far. She could not see his face, which was mostly obscured by the hood of his large cloak, but she noticed that he bore no weapon. Unless it was the strangely shaped bundle beside him. No, that looked like a harp within its carrying cloth; no blade was shaped like that.

Faint memories came to Fiona's mind, a character who was only a shadow in her mind, a ghost from the days before the War.

"Rhiada?" she asked, daring to speak and yet not letting down her guard. Her hand still clenched the dirk at her side.

The individual in question smiled and flung back his hood, hair the colour of a raven's wing falling to his shoulders, though grey laced a beard she did not remember him having before. The flame-light danced across his face, harshened by exposure to the elements, shadowing empty sockets where his eyes should be.

Fiona stared in horror at his face, biting back the exclamation that screamed to escape her throat.

"Aye, Fiona McCurragh, 'tis the same." He spoke her tongue well, though with an accented lightness that almost seemed harsh despite his warm voice.

"What happened to yer eyes?" she forced out at last in a hollow whisper, not wanting to offend, but unable to repress the longing to know.

Rhiada hesitated. "Ye would no' remember; it was so long ago. But in the days before the War, I was a messenger between yer father and the king of my country, Cymru. Yer father hoped they would ally against the Danes, should they ever invade Scotland. When on a mission in the Highlands, I was caught and blinded as a spy. I was fortunate to be left alive at all."

"I am sorry," Fiona murmured at last, not knowing what else to say. She pulled up a stool and sat down by him, unsure whether she should stare at the fire or at Rhiada's mutilated face. Of course, he would not know either way, but she found it rather disconcerting to look at.

Smoothing out the wrinkles in her skirt, she gazed into the depths of the fire, the flickering light gentler to her eyes than Rhiada's scars. "Why did ye come back to Scotland? My father has been dead fer three years and his second wife has long since remarried. There is nothing left fer ye here, unless ye would play the part of a traitor to my father's cause." Her words were morose on her tongue.

"Wheesht, Fiona!" Rhiada cried. "Donnae assume evil of every stranger who seeks food and shelter beneath yer roof." He shifted his position on the hard wooden chair before he leaned back and continued in a lower tone. "Fiona McCurragh. First of all, I am to teach ye the harp, and aye, I hae Lady Nuith's permission. In return, ye will play fer them and earn more worth in their eyes than jist being their prisoner."

Fiona swallowed, confused by the sudden turn of events. Rhiada was almost a stranger to her; what did he mean by this, to be her teacher? "Lady Nuith wishes me to become a harper?" She looked from the fire to his face, searching for any sign of dishonesty and finding none.

"'Tis an honour to be one, especially in a king's court. In my country, harpers—good harpers—are in high demand." He sighed and said something in his own native Cymraeg tongue. "Lady Nuith cares little whether ye play well or no', but the guise of a teacher is the only way I can speak to ye. Ye might even take a fancy to it; 'tis a beautiful instrument." He smiled, a strange sight on the face of one so disfigured. "But I hae my own reasons fer wanting to speak wi' ye." He leaned closer to Fiona. "I hae been recently down south in the Lowlands. They are talking of rejoining the throne of the Highlands and reuniting together to be Scotland once again."

Fiona stared at him, hope and disbelief mingling in a shockwave that left her stunned in its wake. Surely it could not be mere coincidence that she had run into the son of Chieftain McCladden that very day! "W-wha'?" she stammered. "How is tha' even possible? They swore never again to reunite under the throne after wha' my father did! Why are they changing their minds now?"

"Aye, I didnae believe it when I first heard about it either. But they are serious about this, though they hesitate. They donnae believe that any of the McCurraghs are still alive."

Fiona started, her foot scuffling against the floor. No, it could not be mere coincidence after all. That meeting had been intentional. There was no other explanation—there could be no other explanation. The only question was whether it was all some great, evil trickery....

"Ah!" Rhiada exclaimed. Perhaps he had heard the scuffle. "Something has happened. Tell me."

"Sometimes Lady Nuith permits me to ride out on the moors since I promise only ever to go to one burn, far from human habitation. My brother—ye may remember him—taught me first how to use a sword there."

"Sa ha, I remember him. But come, what happened?"

"I stumbled upon a lad, whom I found out later to be Angus McCladden."

The briefest of smiles passed across the harper's face, though perhaps it was only her imagination and the uncertain light of the fire. "I ken the lad and his family."

Fiona waited for him to say more, watching him closely for any tell-tale sign of deception, but he was silent. "Angus asked me who I was and I told him the truth, and wha' had happened since the War."

"Excellent," Rhiada said under his breath, but she still heard him. "Fiona," he began again, a strange edge of excitement in his voice. "The sooner Scotland kens that ye are alive, the sooner Scotland will be one country again and ye will be queen, ruling o'er yer father's throne."

Fiona's eyes widened in surprise. Her heart skipped a beat; surely she was dreaming! Either this was an elaborate, wicked scheme to harm her worse than the Danes could or an unbelievable reality—the former seemed more likely. "Wha' do ye mean?"

"I told ye that Scotland wants to become one again; Donald Mc-Cladden was the one who spoke up fer all those in the Lowlands. And, more importantly, they want ye, if ye're still alive, to be placed back on the throne that is rightfully yers. They willnae hae their country ruled by a Dane. However, I'm a-thinking that it will take more than the lad's word of seeing ye fer them to believe ye are still alive." He leaned back in his chair. "Aye. We'll hae to smuggle ye down there."

"But how? And when?" Panic crept into her voice as an overwhelming wave of new changes and possibilities swept over her, dragging her along with its heavy surge.

"Och, Fiona! All things in their due time." He rose to his feet. "I will speak wi' ye on the morrow. A servant should be bringing ye supper soon; 'tis getting late," he added as he made his way to the door with the help of his carved wooden stick.

"Rhiada?" Fiona questioned before he left, her voice under control once more.

"Aye, Fiona?" He turned towards her, his empty sockets black holes in the dimness.

"Forgive me fer saying this, but how do I ken if I can trust ye?" She paused. These were difficult words to say, exposing her vulnerability to someone little better than a complete stranger, even if she had known him in the past. "I ken my father did, but wi' all the mistrust of the Danes and traitorous Scots, I am afraid to trust anyone anymore—let alone a forgotten acquaintance from my past. How did ye even remember me?"

He approached her, his soft footsteps matched with the gentle *thump* of his walking stick. He reached out with his hand, floundering for a moment before resting it on her shoulder, as he was a head taller than her. "I saw ye many years ago when I still had my sight. Ye were but a wee lass then. Yer brother always spoke of ye fondly and was always asking King Daibhidh to be excused from council meetings so he could be wi' ye." His hand left her shoulder and grasped her hair gently. His voice whispered, as if to no one in particular, "Still a flaming gold?"

Fiona fumbled for a response, wondering what this had to do with answering her questions.

"Aye, I remember," he continued nonetheless. "Flaming hair and shining golden-green eyes; one of the bonniest lasses in Scotland." He sighed softly. "Of course, that was before it all happened." He was silent for several minutes, as if his empty eyes could see the past as vividly as if it had happened yesterday. "Fiona, I cannae convince ye to trust me. Nae sound argument would ever succeed in doing that fer anyone, nae matter how sceptical they might be. But I will ask ye to trust me, if only to escape certain inescapable death if ye stay. How much ye trust me is another question. I never failed yer father, and I will most certainly no' fail ye. Ye hae my word: I willnae let harm come to ye if I can help it."

"Fer that I thank ye," Fiona murmured back, despite the uncertainty in her heart. She did not feel afraid of him—that was the odd thing—but she remained as fearful of the future as ever.

Hope, as fleeting and faroff as it was, had arisen out of the darkness, but she was too timid yet to take ahold of it.

A knock sounded on the door before a servant girl entered, bringing Fiona a bowl of stew. She left it in the princess's hands without a word, her footsteps fading away in the silence.

"Now get some rest," Rhiada said once he was certain the servant was out of hearing. "Things always seem clearer in the morning." Then he was gone, and only the crackling of the wood on the hearth disturbed the silence.

That night, Fiona's dreams were filled with rain-stained hills awash with morning fog. Scarred harpers whispered in her ear of fates yet unrealized. Dark-haired lads mirrored her fear in their blue eyes. And hope rose like a golden sunrise, chasing away the anxiety of deathly shadows—hope for a future that might still be hers.

If she could stay alive long enough to see it.

~ 3 ~

GROWING DANGER

FIONA awoke to the skirling of pipes. She sat up in surprise, her heart stirring with long-forgotten emotion; she must still be dreaming. It had been years since she had awakened to that sound. How she had missed it!

Throwing back the covers of her warm bed, she gasped as her bare feet met the icy stone floor. She stepped gingerly to the window, trying to discern who was playing. It must be very early in the morning, for the eastern sky paled towards dawn and fog lay in a thick curtain upon the ground, hiding all below. Still, she could not espy who was playing the lilting music.

Someone rapped on the door, startling her. A man's voice, muffled by the wood and strangely accented, called out, "Fiona! Get dressed quickly and meet me in the Great Hall." His words were followed by footsteps shuffling away, echoed by the thump of a wooden staff hitting the stone floor. It could be no other than Rhiada. No other man would dare come near her rooms, let alone one with a staff and a voice like his.

There was no use trying to understand what it was all about, for thinking would take far too long, and Rhiada seemed to think his plan was a matter of urgency.

Pushing away her sleep-befuddled confusion, Fiona dressed hurriedly. She tied off the loose plait she pulled her hair into, pausing to glance at her distorted reflection in the piece of polished bronze hanging on the wall. She looked presentable enough, she mused. Not that Rhiada would notice, anyway.

Closing the door behind her, she walked swiftly through the empty corridors, lit torches leading the way. The air was chill and damp, as always in draughty Caerloch, and she clenched her hands tight to keep from shivering.

The large, oaken doors of the Great Hall greeted her, and she glanced down the hallway before pushing against the heavy frame. The hinges, stiff with cold, squealed like a pig about to be slaughtered. Fiona froze where she stood, straining her ears to hear any sound that might indicate someone coming to inspect the cause of the sudden noise.

But she only heard Rhiada's voice saying gently, "There's nothing to fear. No one is awake yet except the servants. Come, there are several things that we need to talk about."

Fiona closed the door with more care than she had used to open it, before walking across the darkened hall.

Rhiada sat on one of the lower steps of the dais, no longer cloaked but dressed in the usual woollen tunic and breeks worn by those who were not Scots. Nonetheless, his boots were still caked in dried mud as if he never cleaned them. She wondered, with a smile, whether Lady Nuith would approve of such dirt upon her dais.

The early morning light shone cold and grey through the tall, narrow windows, a strange, uncertain gleam resting upon the ornaments of war and of the hunt hung upon the walls. The polished blades of swords and spears, as well as the metal inlaid on shields, glittered in the pale dawn, sending a shiver down Fiona's spine.

No fire burned in the vast hearth, no heat to drive out the damp nor provide a warm, comforting light. The two long tables and benches running along either side of the wall cast elongated shadows on the floor, seeming more monstrous than they truly were. Fiona felt small and insignificant in this room, whose arched ceiling extended far above her head. Her footsteps, quiet though they were, echoed eerily in the waiting silence.

She had rarely been to this hall. Her father had never sent for her, and after her brother died, she had no reason to come of her own will. Lady Nuith likewise rarely called her here, and she had always taken her meals in her own room. To come now, at such an hour, for a reason yet unknown, and after she and Rhiada had whispered of rebellion last night.... This place seemed far more foreboding than she remembered.

When she reached the dais at last, Rhiada motioned her to sit next to him and she complied, staring at the strange bag he had slung over his shoulder. Was that the covered harp she had guessed it to be last night? Was she to receive her first lesson now, before breakfast?

As if in answer to her unspoken questions, he opened the bag and pulled out the most beautiful harp Fiona had ever seen. Interlacing carvings embellished the polished wood, and the strings glimmered in the faint light as Rhiada positioned it against his left shoulder and plucked a few notes.

The delicate sound reverberated throughout the hall, mesmerised awe and wonder filling Fiona's mind with images of sunlight on bubbling burns, touching budding leaves with gold. But Rhiada did not play anything more, only laid his hands on the strings to still them. The thoughts of cheery sun and the freshness of spring faded away, the dimness of the hall taking its place as reality returned to her.

Rhiada put the instrument back in its protective covering, much to Fiona's surprise. Did he not mean to teach her after all? "I suppose there are a few questions ye wish to ask me?"

"Aye." Fiona nodded, that strange clashing of hope and fear stirring again in her breast.

"Well then, ask away. We hae time before the others awaken," he replied with a smile. The light coming from the windows illuminated the dark hollows in his face where his eyes had once been, and Fiona looked away, the sight still eerily uncomfortable.

"First," she began, "who was the piper I heard this morn?"

"He is one of the few loyal to the true heir of Scotland. He came wi' me to Caerloch as my guide, as I cannae see the way myself." Rhiada chuckled slightly, but Fiona did not find it amusing to jest about the loss of one's eyesight. "I asked him to play the pipes this morning," Rhiada continued, "hopefully to awaken ye."

"I thank ye, Rhiada; 'tis long since I heard them last." The wistfulness in her voice fled at her next words. "But surely ye hae endangered his life!" Her voice rose higher and faster as fear overtook rationale. Her hands trembled wildly in her lap as her thoughts spun out of control. "If Lady Nuith finds out what he has done, she willnae let him gae unpunished. And she will trace him to us and then 'twill all come to naught, and she will kill me anyway!"

"Nae, nae, Fiona; calm yerself. He came wi' me to Caerloch as I cannae ride very well, being blind. I couldnae come by myself to this place, else Laird Erland and Lady Nuith would ne'er believe me when I offered to simply teach ye the harp." He gestured something like a shrug with his hands. "'Twas the only way I could get past the guards to ye. Besides, he is here to see the way the land lies, to find out the Danish plans if he can."

Fiona sighed, her fears not quite put to rest. "Well then, wha' is his name?"

"Cameron MacClaerthun."

"I donnae ken his name."

"Didnae think ye would." Rhiada smirked. "But perhaps it shall become important soon. Who kens wha' the future holds."

The doors to the Great Hall swung open, resounding with an echoing bang.

Fiona jumped and turned towards the entrance to see Lady Nuith enter as any stately queen of old. Fiona attempted to avert her gaze, fear and disgust creating a bitter taste in her mouth at the sight of that woman, but Lady Nuith was the sort of person who demanded one's attention. Not because she was especially tall or beautiful—for she was not much taller than Fiona herself, and her face was rather ordinary—but everything about her bespoke command and control. The tightly plaited crown of hair, the close-fitted bodice, the hands clasped in front of her as she walked, each brisk step brought her ever closer to the Scottish princess.

Unable to look entirely away, Fiona focused her attention on the shimmering gold thread on Nuith's luscious, crimson skirt that swished with every movement, afraid to look up into a face that had only ever gazed on her own with deep, intense hatred.

Coming to an abrupt halt before them, Lady Nuith questioned in that clipped voice of hers, "Well, harper, has that child learned anything yet?"

Fiona tensed when she heard the epithet Lady Nuith called her. Since her brother—and likewise her childhood—had been lost in the War, Fiona could claim that title no longer. But when her father had married the Danish woman who now stood before her, such a nickname had followed Fiona's steps, ever reminding her of what she had lost and filling her with shame. She was no child, not anymore.

Rhiada replied after a moment, his controlled, melodic voice soothing her, and she relaxed even if she did not completely let down her guard. "Nae, I hae only just begun to instruct her on the various details of the harp. It takes a wee bit of time to learn this instrument."

"Well then, it cannot take too long. We shall be entertaining some important guests in about a month and I intend to have that child play for them."

"We shall see if she can play then. If no', I can play in her stead. And one more thing, m'lady." He leaned forward, seeming to stare at her from empty eye sockets. "Fiona McCurragh is nae a child."

Fiona gasped, shocked at his daring. She glanced hurriedly at Lady Nuith, gauging her response.

Nuith, who had turned to leave, checked when she heard the Scottish princess's full name. The silence seemed as sharp as a knife blade. Then: "She is a child and will forever remain so," she snapped.

"M'lady, she is fourteen and hardly a child anymore, considering all that she's gang through. Besides, I think ye could show a wee bit more respect towards her. Is she no' the heir to the throne?" His question, though put so innocently, countered like another knife thrown in the dark.

A period of silence followed his words, cutting deeper than the previous one, as if the breath had been knocked out of all of them. Fiona stared at both the harper and the lady in turn, too surprised at Rhiada's boldness to say anything. She half-expected Lady Nuith to order his execution immediately.

But the lady only fabricated a smile upon her face and spoke through clenched teeth, the words somehow more terrifying with the hateful grin she wore. "She is a child and no longer the heir to the throne, nor will she ever be." Spinning on her heel, she left, the echo of her footsteps booming in the quiet remaining in her wake.

Fiona's heart jumped into her throat at those words. What did Nuith mean by that? Did she finally mean to end her life? Was this a warning? She turned to speak to Rhiada, but he silenced her with a wave of his hand.

When he spoke, there was an undertone of warning in his soft, solemn voice. "I said those things fer a reason, Fiona. We'll meet after breakfast in yer room, if there is nothing else fer ye to do." He rose to his feet and exited the chilly Great Hall, his harp bag slung over his shoulder, his staff reverberating much like Lady Nuith's step had done.

Fiona hesitated to follow him. He had dared to challenge Lady

Nuith and defend her honour, aye, but what were his true motives? Did he want Nuith to kill them all before their attempt at freedom had a chance to become more than an idea? Had he lost his mind?

She swallowed, her heart slowly resuming its normal course, but her thoughts were still in turmoil.

Angus had been shocked to discover she was still alive. Rhiada... Rhiada seemed to know much about her, but from all events it seemed he couldn't decide whether to risk everything in the name of bravado or not do more than whisper about the future.

She did not have much of a choice. Expose him to Lady Nuith and face imminent murder from her greatest enemy, or trust someone from her past and hope to survive. In spite of everything, she would rather take her chances with him—what few they were.

Fiona opened the door to her quarters to see Rhiada sitting in the corner again, his hood drawn over his scarred face and his harp resting beside him, no longer in its covering. The cold hearth and the grey light looming through the rain-stained windows were not very cheering.

Without a word, she stepped up to the harper and stood still, waiting.

"Och, Fiona," he murmured without changing his position. "We donnae hae much time."

"Wha' do ye mean?" she questioned, drawing up a stool in front of him, the small flower of hope wilting away under the burning sun of fear. Surely there had never been much time left for her, and even less now after what Rhiada had said, but all the same, she had wished the harper to carry good news. Why else had he said those things?

Rhiada sat up straight, leaning against the back of the chair. His voice was quiet. Worried. "I thought we would hae more time than this, but 'twould seem we only hae until next month."

"More time than wha'? I donnae understand wha' ye're saying." It was hard to keep the panic out of her voice.

Rhiada sighed. "We need to get ye to the Lowlands," he whispered. "And we must do it soon, much sooner than we anticipated."

"Why so much sooner?" Fiona whispered back in surprise. What had changed from last night? Was it his words to Lady Nuith? Had she threatened him?

"Because we need to establish ye upon the throne and bring Scotland back together. Ye remember what I said yesterday, do ye no'?"

"Aye, I do." Her words belied the despondency in her voice. She hesitated before continuing, a pause broken only by the soft rain hitting the window glass. "Rhiada, I donnae mean to be disrespectful to ye, but are ye very certain tha' this is wha' the chieftains want? Ye and I both ken about the War."

"Aye, Fiona, I ken. Sad business, to be sure, about the Danes. But the chieftains indeed wish to undo the evils done so long ago, to finish what yer father should hae done."

She did not answer right away, bitter memories coming unbidden to mind. The War had been six years ago, but she still remembered her brother leaving as keenly as if it had been yesterday. Memories of his goodbye often haunted her in her sleep, or whenever she thought of the War or the time before her captivity in the tower.

"Douglas never came back," Fiona whispered, the dull pain once more beginning to throb against the emptiness in her chest.

"Nae, he didnae," Rhiada answered sadly. "Almost none of the warriors who left to fight in that war returned at all."

"Why did the Lowlanders no' send their men to help us fight against our enemies?" Fiona demanded, not really expecting an answer, for it was more a rhetorical question than anything else.

"If ye really want to ken, ye can ask Angus McCladden himself."

She sighed in frustration. The chieftain's son from the other morning. That was not quite the answer she had been hoping for. She had hoped to escape further communication with the lad who was little more than a stranger, but it seemed unavoidable. Rhiada seemed to think their acquaintance important, and from a political standpoint, it made sense. He was the son of the High Chieftain, she the heir to the throne. But he had seemed so intense yesterday! Shifting from teasing to brooding seriousness, the changes unpredictable—for all those things, she did not trust him.

"Rhiada, why come here at all?" she asked, hoping to change the uncomfortable subject. "Ye speak often of yer own country and yet ye serve the lords of another."

He smiled sadly. "I hae few ties left to Cymru. My family was slaughtered during a Saxon raid. I survived, being elsewhere when they came, and joined King Brenin ap Brynnmor's *teulu*. I wed his daughter and hae a son by her, but that was before my sight was stolen. He is a wee bit older than ye, but I hae nae seen him in three years."

"Do ye nae miss them?" Fiona asked, knowing she would give almost anything to be reunited with her family again, were they still alive. And yet Rhiada chose this life? What compelled him so?

"Aye, I do. But my loyalty belongs to Scotland. I hae an oath to fulfil, and until I am freed from that oath, I cannae gae home. And my king kens this."

"Wha' oath?" Her father and her brother had never mentioned such to her before. What man would sacrifice all for something that was not even his?

"To protect yer throne. When I heard the news that yer father had passed beyond the sunset, I said farewell and journeyed to the Lowlands. And now, I am here."

Fiona was silent, listening to the rain as Rhiada took out his harp and tuned the strings. Humility swept over her like waves lapping against the shore, shame that she had doubted his integrity after he had sworn to protect her. Oath or no oath, this man from the past was willing to risk his life to save hers while Lady Nuith would risk her life only to end Fiona's. Surely this, if nothing else, was proof enough to trust him.

Rhiada cleared his throat, breaking into her thoughts. "Come, princess, I must teach ye the harp. We must no' give Lady Nuith reasons to think I am here fer any other purpose."

The wind blew cold through the open window, but Fiona hardly concerned herself with it. The fresh breeze was better than the stuffy air otherwise present in Caerloch.

She was alone in her room, for Rhiada had left some time ago. She knew she should be working on becoming better acquainted with the harp's different strings and their various pitches, but she had no desire to play the instrument at present. Her thoughts refused to be at rest.

Rhiada seemed to genuinely want to keep her alive at all costs and bring her safely to the Lowlands, without appearing to act from any evil motive of his own. She could not remember him very well from the past, having only seen him once when he entertained them all at a feast. Her father had spoken of him on a few occasions and his words had only been of the highest praise, a rarity with Daibhidh McCurragh. Daibhidh must have trusted him very much, enough to give him the task of protecting the throne. Though exactly why he trusted him, she did not know. It wasn't common for mere messengers to be assigned such responsibility, unless Rhiada had been more than just a messenger.

Another chilling gust interrupted her thoughts and she closed the window, the latch falling to with a sharp *click*. Turning, she went to the harp with a sigh and sat down, plucking the individual strings at different intervals just as Rhiada had taught her. It required much patience, a virtue that Fiona had not been born with. Yet the three years spent in captivity, hidden away from the rest of the world, had begun to teach her the meaning of perseverance, even if it was a hard lesson to learn.

She could afford to wait a little longer, but not for too long.

Lady Nuith wanted her dead.

~ 4 ~

STRINGS OF FATE

A chorus of male voices echoed through the corridor, hovering in the early morning air. Pale dawnslight glinted off the company's fine chainmail as they stood in the courtyard entrance. Though they spoke the Scots' Gàidhlig, their strange, heavy accent marked them as Danes.

Fiona ducked her head down, hoping to pass by them unnoticed. Perhaps they were some special guests of Lady Nuith's newly arrived—they often came at unreasonable hours, and surely this time was no different.

She had almost succeeded in slipping by them when a hand shot out and grabbed her wrist, preventing her escape.

Fiona glanced at the strong hand gripping her, catching the flash of a blood-red jewel in the sunlight. She looked up in terror at the wearer's unfamiliar face, taking in his dark eyes, mud-brown hair, and simpering grin.

"Och, wench, where do ye think ye're gang this fine hour?" His voice was smooth. Too smooth.

"Let me gae!" Fiona cried, panic rising in her throat, threatening to choke her. Where was Rhiada? Not that he could do much to help, but his presence would be better than nothing!

"Why? We hae only jist arrived. There's nae sense in wasting the morning hours!"

A wave of heat washed across Fiona's face as she tried to wrest out of the young man's grip. She failed utterly, and his other arm encircled her waist, pulling her against him. He reeked of sweat and heather beer; the stench was nearly suffocating. Her breath came in choking, short gasps. This could not be happening, it could—

"Lachlan, wha' hae I said about staying off the lassies?" another voice broke in. Fiona did not care who it was, for this Lachlan had loosened his hold on her waist at the sound, even if he still kept her wrist tightly locked in his hand. Relief washed over her, even as she continued to struggle for freedom.

"Och, Drummond! She's jist a wee mite. Nae one would miss her," Lachlan protested.

Fiona looked up into the face of her rescuer, noting his dark eyes and curling beard; his facial structure resembled Lady Nuith's and she shuddered at the very idea.

"This lassie is nae yers," Drummond shot back, his voice firm. "She jist happens to be the royal prisoner of my sister, which means any harm upon her person would cost ye greatly. I suggest ye let her gae."

Fiona's stomach flipped. Despite Drummond's intentions to free her, she was terrified to learn Lady Nuith had a brother. One such vengeful person in her life was enough.

Lachlan's mouth tightened in a firm line, but he said no more, releasing Fiona.

She did not wait another moment. She set off again down the corridor, nearly at a run, her heart still thumping hard in her throat as she rubbed her sore wrist.

Danger could not be escaped, even in this impenetrable prison.

Entering the Great Hall, Fiona stepped down its empty length, lost in the horrid memories of what had just transpired in the corridor. She sat down in silence beside Rhiada and took the harp from him without a word, settling it in the hollow of her left shoulder as was the tradition of Cymreig harpers.

"Is everything all right?" he asked softly, his eyeless face laced with worry. Strange, how a face lacking the mirrors to the soul could still show so much.

"Aye, I am fine," Fiona replied, trying her utmost to keep her voice from trembling.

Rhiada did not answer, for which she was glad. She was not ready to speak of it, not yet. Not until she had at least calmed her racing heart and the mixture of fear and disgust coursing through her veins. So instead, she sat erect, hesitantly plucking the strings one by one and telling their musical name to the harper who sat beside her. The sounds reverberated in the high-roofed hall, their harshness seeming to taunt her rough skills and shaking hands.

"Gentler, Fiona, gentler. The strings are no' bowstrings. Ye must be gentle wi' them if ye wish to make any music at all."

The lass sighed, closing her eyes for a moment, the thoughts of before slowly dissipating in the broken music. "Aye," she answered softly before trying again.

She must forget what happened. She did not want to have nightmares of Lachlan and Drummond added to those of Lady Nuith, her worries materialised in her dreams. Life was too short for her to remain in fear.

She delicately plucked the strings as if afraid of hurting the instrument. But such anxiety could not be so easily banished by focusing on the simple notes. It lurked beneath the surface, merely waiting for a chance to break free. And with this Lachlan staying at Caerloch for who knew how long, it would only be a matter of time before his predatory manner tormented her beyond endurance.

"Sa ha, sister," Drummond drawled, swirling the remaining contents of the cup in his hand. "What is this ye're worried about?"

His strong brogue accented his Danish tongue, much to Lady Nuith's disgust. He was only her half-brother, after all, but the fact he constantly revealed his Scottish mother's blood even when speaking had never made things better between them.

"I am worried about nothing save that brat and her tutor," she snapped, looking out the window down at the courtyard below. The stable hands mucked the stalls and a guard chatted with one of the maids by the well, drawing water for her and flirting all the while. The servant girl's squeals of delight floated up to the window, doing nothing to lighten the tension in the room.

Drummond snorted mockingly before draining the last of the mead down his throat. "Ye are afraid of a mere child and a man whose eyes I gouged out because ye asked me to do it. They are both absolutely harmless!"

Nuith wheeled about, her round, soft face distorted in anger. Sarcasm dripped from her words. "Aye, no one would suspect him of treachery against the Danes, would they? Certainly not after he had been rightfully punished for it before! And no one would ever suspect that princess to be eager to escape and end our lives and the hopes of our people!" The sarcasm vanished from her next words. "Even if he hasn't done anything treasonous in years, I do not trust him. Nonetheless, Drummond, that child is still a threat! As soon as our celebration is over, I wish to see her dead. Quickly and quietly. I do not care as to the manner in which you do it, but it must be done."

The flippant smile fled from Drummond's face. Lost in thought, he stared at the cup in his hands. Setting it down on the table after a moment, he walked away from the cold hearth and stood by his sister in the empty quiet of the Great Hall. "Ye hae a claim to the throne then? Ye cannae murder her unless ye are certain ye can claim it, else the clans will rise up against ye when they find out."

Lady Nuith met her brother's brown eyes, the same as her own, the same as the Danish father they both shared. "Aye, I can claim it." She rested her hand for a moment on her abdomen, which was beginning to show signs of the child growing within.

Drummond hesitated, debating asking if she knew the child would live. This was not the first time in the last two years since her marriage to Lord Erland that she had become pregnant, but the child had never survived the pregnancy. If Nuith was willing to acknowledge she expected an heir now, then she either had confidence or could no longer wait. Princess Fiona would not remain forgotten forever.

But he only nodded. "As soon as yer party is over and the guests have drunk themselves into a stupor, I will do it." He turned away from the window, striding towards the doors of the hall. "It will be done."

Rain fell cold and hard against the window panes, running down in mournful streaks. Perhaps the song Fiona practised was indeed so sorrowful that even the heavens could not help but weep.

Fire crackled in accompaniment while Rhiada listened quietly in Fiona's room. Elsewhere in the castle, they were subjected to constant interruptions.

Fiona finished the song and stilled the strings. When the last hum of melody silenced, she placed her hands in her lap, quietly awaiting remarks from her teacher.

"Ye are getting better, Fiona, much better," he said simply. "Yer voice fits the song well.... But I would remind ye that ye need to ride out now to meet wi' Angus, as if ye would hae ridden out any other time. 'Twas agreed by the chieftains that he—or another Lowlander, if nae him—would meet wi' ye if they could. Ye can practise this evening when ye return."

Fiona reluctantly set the harp down beside her, not wishing to speak to that quiet and solemn lad, nor some other Lowlander. They had not come to Scotland's aid when the Danes first came; why should she trust them now? Besides, even if communicating with them would help her cause, she did not desire to talk to the son of High Chieftain McCladden. Especially not when the world cried in bitter farewell to the long lost summer. "Rhiada! 'Tis raining. He willnae come."

"Och, ye'd be surprised. Angus gave his word that he would meet ye again. Ye need to keep yers. Now gae."

"Why?" Her tone was not meant to be disrespectful, but it came across as insulting nonetheless.

He sighed. "Because ye must, Fiona. It has been nearly a week. Ye cannae keep him waiting forever."

"Wha' if Lady Nuith doesnae agree to let me ride out this time?" she persisted.

"And why should she no'? Has she nae done so before?"

"Nae, she hasnae, but perhaps wi' ye here, she might suspect something."

"Perhaps, but we'll ne'er ken unless we find out, will we?"

Helpless and frustrated, Fiona pinched her lips together and left the room, grabbing her cloak. She ran down the corridor and stairs beyond, coming to a pause outside the Great Hall. She raised her fist up to knock, hearing murmuring voices on the other side of the door, but hesitated first to catch back her breath. She wondered for a moment what Rhiada would say if Lady Nuith truly denied her request. But there was no time to wonder.

She knocked, gulping down the sudden rush of anxiety that threatened to choke her. Someone called entry, a man's voice.

Fiona pushed open the door, seeing Lady Nuith, Drummond, and a few of his men gathered around one of the tables. Lord Erland stood a few feet behind Nuith, gazing dully around the room, his eyes glancing over Fiona in boredom.

Drummond—or whoever had been speaking—fell silent.

"What is it?" Nuith asked, her voice as cold as ice.

Fiona swallowed again, her knees suddenly feeling weak. "Do I hae permission to ride the moors?" She asked this every few days; it shouldn't be any different than any other time. But with Rhiada....

Lady Nuith hesitated, staring at her as if she could see Fiona's innermost thoughts.

The princess fought the urge to squirm under her scrutiny.

"Aye, be back before sundown. If you so much as ride through in the dusk, I will punish that harper companion of yours." Nuith did not speak of the threat Fiona recognized. No, Nuith would try to imprison her, too.

"Understood." Fiona bowed her head for good measure before leaving the room, closing the door and exhaling deeply. Sundown was not far off. She had just enough time to get there, speak with Angus, and ride back if she were careful.

Gathering her courage, she continued on her way, walking quickly into the courtyard towards the stables.

The rain had lessened slightly, but it was still drenching and cold. She entered the stables and inhaled deeply the scent of sweet hay as she walked to the stall where Sgàil was waiting. Swiftly, she saddled her horse and rode at a breakneck speed out of the castle gates and into the countryside, heading south, pausing only to withdraw her sword from its hiding place.

The wind blew harshly into her face, tossing her flaming hair wildly behind her, and the rain pelted her skin like little needles as she and her horse rode as one to the burn in the Lowlands.

About an hour or so of hard riding later, she finally pulled up short at the burn, feeling breathlessly exhilarated from the ride. Sgàil stood still, panting heavily, white foam visible on her chest and neck. Dismounting, Fiona freed Sgàil's mouth of her bit and pushed the wet strands of hair out of her face as she surveyed her surroundings. Tor-na-Cruithne, the old landmark from a battle long ago, was nearly hidden by the mist. The leafless trees mourned, their branches drooping in the wind, and the rainy burn gurgled in the silence, but that was all. She saw no one.

I thought as much, Rhiada.

She gazed around her once more before turning to remount Sgàil when something cold and solid suddenly rested against her neck. She froze where she stood, her chest tightening in panic.

"Ye should always keep up yer guard." A male voice behind her spoke into the rainswept silence before the blade left her neck.

Fiona exhaled sharply and whirled around to see Angus McCladden, naked sword in hand, watching her with an uncertain attempt at a smile on his face.

"Ye came!" she exclaimed, her mouth hanging open in surprise.

"Of course I came!" he replied indignantly, the smile vanishing like the sun behind clouds. He sheathed his blade and stood with his arms clasped behind his back, still watching her every move as she did his. "We Scots always keep our word, regardless of circumstances."

"Nae always," Fiona retorted. "Where were the Lowlanders when the Danes attacked?"

"The Lowlanders did come," he spat back just as vehemently.

"Och, really?" she snapped, her cheeks flushing crimson. "If the Lowlanders had come, my brother wouldnae hae died, the clans would still be united, and I wouldnae be in danger fer my life because my father would still be reigning o'er Scotland!"

The rain fell harder in the silence.

"Ye're nae the only one who's lost their family fighting the Danes." His voice was soft, so horribly soft, the fire in his blue eyes vanishing into mist. "We sent our men. Few of them returned alive."

"Maybe if ye had sent more men, we might hae driven the Danes far from our shores," Fiona returned, trying in vain to find some way to win this argument.

Angus shook his head. "Very few of the chieftains could send their men as they were dealing wi' the Saxon menace in the south."

Fiona opened her mouth, but, discovering that she could say nothing more to prove her point, closed it again.

"Considering tha' ye were surprised to see me here," he continued, "I'm supposing tha' Rhiada made ye keep yer promise, which proves tha' Highlanders arenae the ones very good at keeping their own word."

"How do ye ken Rhiada is at the castle?" she demanded, ignoring the rest of what Angus said.

"Och, he told us before he left fer Caerloch wi' Cameron Mac-Claerthun. The Lowlands hae been talking about scarcely anything else since."

"So ye ken about the plans fer my escape to the Lowlands?" Fiona went on cautiously.

"Aye, I ken most of it. Which is why I promised to meet ye here again once I kent who ye were."

"Then why did ye nae tell me this at the beginning?" she sputtered.

Angus shrugged, glancing down at the rain-soaked ground by his foot. "Ye hadnae met Rhiada yet. Besides, I was only supposed to ken if ye were the lost princess; others had seen ye riding out here, and I was sent to find out if ye were Fiona McCurragh. Ye seemed shocked, so I kent ye didnae ken about the plans; I left that fer Rhiada to tell ye."

Fiona looked at him in silence, uncertain as to what to make of it all. "How did ye ken I would come today?"

"I didnae, which is why I hae come every day since we met. Now," Angus went on, fiddling impatiently with the hilt of his sword, "are the Highlanders as fierce wi' their weapons as they are wi' their words?"

Fiona answered by drawing her blade.

Then they were locked in fierce combat, all other grievances laid aside while the sharp whistling and shrill clangs of steel upon steel shattered the mournful silence of autumn winds. Equally matched, Fiona found it impossible to disarm her opponent, though she was not always on the defensive. But there was no time to think, only to act—or else admit defeat, which was something Fiona was loath to do.

Several minutes later, they stepped back, breathing heavily. Fiona's hair clung to her sweaty face and neck, tickling something awful.

Angus was in a similar condition, and he wiped his forehead with the back of his hand. He slid his weapon into its scabbard and questioned, "Where did ye learn yer knowledge of the sword?"

"From my brother," Fiona answered, sheathing her blade also. "He taught me everything I ken, most of it here by this burn."

"Do ye ken anything of any other weapons?" Angus asked next, leaning against one of the trees by the burn. The rain slowed to a fine mist, but both of them were soaked by now, though not only because of the rain.

"I ken something of the bow, but nae much else."

"And yer brother taught ye that as well?" Angus continued, his dark brows drawn together in the way that he seemed to have when he was thinking. Douglas had done that too, once....

"Aye, he did. But tha' was a long time ago," she finished quietly, gazing at the faded green of the wet autumn grass and the moist earth showing beneath it.

"What do ye think of Rhiada?" He spoke again after a pause.

"I am nae very sure. I want to trust him, and yet I donnae ken him as well as I would like." She gestured helplessly. How did one put vague feelings of unease that had no apparent, logical ground into words? "My father trusted him; tha' alone should be reason enough since my father trusted very few.... But still, I am wary of him."

Angus' pensive gaze flickered up and met hers, a question lurking unasked in the depths of his blue eyes. "Ye trusted me readily enough."

She ignored the warmth of embarrassment that swept over her. "Aye, mayhaps I did." It was not entirely true. He might not turn her over to the Danes, but she did not trust him to save her life instead of his own if it came to that.

He attempted an encouraging smile, though failing because of the seriousness that still shone in his eyes. "I think ye can trust Rhiada. He genuinely cares about ye and the crown. There's nothing ye need to fear from him. Lady Nuith, on the other hand—"

"Ye ken nothing about Lady Nuith," Fiona interrupted through clenched teeth.

He raised his eyebrows, but said nothing for several moments. "I suppose I'll hae to take yer word fer it, nae kenning her myself."

Fiona did not reply, only squishing down the soft earth beneath her boot as if to avoid the topic entirely by doing so.

"Why do ye hate her so much?" Angus prompted.

Fiona sighed heavily and looked up towards Tor-na-Cruithne shimmering in the grey distance. "She is the symbol of my three years' captivity, my brother and father's deaths, and the destruction of the world I kent and loved. I hae nae love fer her in my heart. Besides, she wishes me dead."

"How do ye ken tha'?"

"Rhiada's hinted at it more than once. And I ken she loathes me as much as I do her. She sees me only as a threat tha' lies between her and the Scottish throne. Once she has a child of her own, she can claim it once I nae longer stand in the way."

Angus did not reply, leaving a silence broken only by the sighing wind.

Fiona watched him, trying to somehow read through the invisible barrier the lad seemed to keep between them. For all Rhiada's attempts to get them to speak and understand each other, they were failing miserably. "How did ye get here?" she asked, hoping to talk of something other than Lady Nuith.

Angus looked up. "I ride up to *The Raven's Wing* inn not far from here and walk until I reach this place. Rhiada asked my father to spare one of his clan to do so."

"Why?"

He shrugged, his glance darting off into the distance. "I think because Rhiada wished ye to become more acquainted wi' us Lowlanders? I donnae ken. 'Tis nae so dangerous as long as ye donnae speak too much or—" He suddenly stopped, the blood draining from his face.

Fiona followed his gaze, seeing only the mist-enshrouded hills. "Wha' is it?" she asked, worry stabbing her chest.

He continued to stare into the distance before turning abruptly to her. "Nothing of importance." Then he added, "But I think it best if ye went on yer way back to the castle."

"Why?" Fiona questioned as she walked with him, the words choking in her throat. What was he hiding from her? "Why the sudden urgency?"

Angus sighed impatiently. "I need to get back."

"Was it something ye saw on the hills?"

"Aye and nae."

"I donnae understand."

Angus turned to face her. "Please, Fiona, jist get yerself gang. Danes are hunting about the hills there and if ye're seen here, things may nae gae well. I promised Rhiada tha' I would keep ye safe out here until we managed fer yer escape. Please donnae make it hard for me to keep tha' promise."

Fiona was stunned into worried silence, holding his gaze for a moment. She did not understand what had changed between them, but she did not want to risk either of them getting caught. "Aye, I will gae," she said at last, turning and whistling for her horse, who had been cropping what grass remained from summer.

After placing the bit in Sgàil's mouth again, she swung her leg up over the saddle and took the reins from Angus, who had held them while she mounted.

"Keep yerself safe, Fiona," he said softly by way of farewell.

Fiona's lips parted in surprise at his concern; she had been shown so little of it from anyone the last three years. What did it mean? These Lowlanders made no sense at all. But she only replied, "I will." Then she wheeled around and rode swiftly away, leaving Angus standing in the autumn mists alone.

~ 5 ~

ESCAPE

HOOVES thundered across the moorlands as Fiona and Sgàil raced back to Caerloch, the sound matching Fiona's racing heart. Her eyes continually strayed from the ground before her to the crests of the hills where she could see figures through the mist. They seemed indeed to be hunting—perhaps a stag—and she was glad that she was not the prey as she sped homeward to a place that was more a prison than a home. Nor did anyone speak to or stop her when she arrived at the castle; perhaps she was only imagining the fear, the reason they would suspect something. After all, she was allowed to ride out sometimes.

But the thought brought only short relief. She had learned years ago that Lady Nuith was not so easily deceived and that she would strike without warning. One slight move might destroy everything they had all been working towards—as well as her life.

Fiona sighed heavily once she was safely in her room, catching the attention of Rhiada, the dying daylight spilling around him as he sat still in the corner by the window.

"Did all gae well?" he murmured softly, turning his head in her direction.

She untied the strings of her cloak and shook her curls, damp from the rain. "I suppose so. I jist donnae understand the waiting. 'Tis been a week since ye first came. If I am to escape, why are we still here?" She hung her cloak by the door and sat down before the harper, her arms crossed over her knees.

"Fiona, I ken wha' ye're thinking. But come, the servants say that Lady Nuith is wi' child—though I cannae see the evidence fer myself. The fact that she desires ye to play at that celebration is proof that ye will be allowed to live until then. I donnae ken fer certain, but I do ken that 'twill be easiest fer ye to be done away wi' during the celebrations. Nae one will notice yer absence, and nae one will hear yer screams."

She shivered involuntarily, tears springing unbidden to her eyes. Would she ever be able to live without the constant fear of murder?

As if he could read her thoughts and see the tear that trickled down her face, Rhiada continued in a softer tone, "But donnae be afraid. I will nae let harm come to ye if I can help it. Aye, we will smuggle ye down to the Lowlands the day ye must play the harp before Lady Nuith. If they can jist as easily murder ye during the feast, then we can likewise use the noise and distraction to aid in yer escape. And then ye will be staying wi' Angus' family."

Fiona blinked, searching for a smile on her teacher's face, thinking he was jesting. "Wha'?" she exclaimed. Angus' vehement words as he passionately defended the Lowlanders' actions during the War echoed in her ears.

"Aye? Anything wrong wi' that?"

"Nae, only tha' I ken none of tha' family except Angus, and we are nae on good terms."

"Och, Fiona! If ye donnae get along, that is merely because of yer pride; such goings-on were what started the War in the first place. Ye need to put aside yer misgivings and trust him. Angus is fiercely loyal to ye as the heir to the throne, even if ye two cannae agree on anything else. If it came down to it, he would gladly give his life fer the crown. His family is one of the finest in the Lowlands, and I ken ye will be safe there until I can join ye, which I hope will be soon."

"Ye mean ye willnae be gang wi' me?" Fiona looked up at him, the cold, invisible hands of panic snaking themselves around her neck. "I donnae ken the way there; how will I be safe if I am alone?"

Rhiada shifted his position, the chair beneath him creaking in the silence of the room, a silence broken only by the rain beating against the window glass. "Fiona, when ye finish playing at the celebration, I will take the harp from ye and entertain them. Then gae to yer own room, grab yer things which ye will hae previously gathered together, and leave while the celebration is at its height. Ride south by way of the old trackway until ye come to *The Raven's Wing* tavern and send Sgàil back to Caerloch. She kens the way well enough."

Fiona swallowed, remembering Angus mentioning the tavern's name before.

"Donnae tell anyone who ye are," Rhiada continued. "The innkeeper is loyal to Lady Nuith. It would do nae harm to say ye are waiting fer yer lover"—Fiona blushed in horror at the thought—"to avoid suspicion until the messenger comes for ye. Ye will ken him by the symbol he will be wearing, a thistle with heather and pine sprigs. I wish I could gae wi' ye, but we cannae all disappear at once. 'Tis of the utmost importance that ye gae as quickly as ye can to *The Raven's Wing* and wait there until the messenger comes."

"And if they donnae come?"

Rhiada was quiet. "Fiona, donnae think about the possibilities until the problem arises. Worrying about what might happen doesnae prepare ye more fer when the bad things do happen—if they do. When the time comes that something gaes wrong, then ye can fret if ye feel like it."

Fiona looked down at her lap, chagrined. His plans were all perfectly reasonable. But she knew all too well how plans could often go awry. What would she do if she was discovered? Or if the messenger never arrived, being caught by the Danes? Yet arguing would do nothing. Inhaling deeply to calm her frantic thoughts, she merely said, "Aye, Rhiada. I will do as ye say."

He smiled tentatively, a concerned look on his face. "Good. Now, take my harp, tune it, and practise. Jist because yer escaping right after ye play gives ye nae excuse to nae practise," he replied, leaning back and closing his eyes as if to concentrate better on her playing.

She obeyed in humble silence, wondering how learning an instrument could somehow be the key to her survival.

Time passed swiftly, days of rain and broken sunlight mingling together into a blur as the time of Lady Nuith's celebration drew ever nearer—and with it, Fiona's escape. She learned the harp well enough to please Rhiada, hoping it would be enough to convince Lady Nuith that she did indeed spend her hours learning the instrument instead of discussing plans for Fiona's restoration to the throne.

She met twice more with Angus McCladden, though they never spoke of the plans for her escape. They spent almost all of their time duelling or, sometimes, arguing heatedly about events that had shaken Scotland in the recent past—events that were not entirely their own fault, but of which they felt they were still to blame. Fiona could never shake off the feeling that perhaps Angus held her responsible for the Danish yoke that Scotland was under and perhaps that was why he constantly tested her weaponry skills. After all, it was her father who had married a Danish woman to make peace with the enemy after so much Scottish blood had been shed in an attempt to drive them out. Angus never mentioned it, but she still felt as though that might be why he was so closed off to her, so distant, even though Rhiada claimed that Angus was willing to give his life to protect her.

As she looked out the window of her tower, watching the courtyard below, Fiona wondered if Angus truly would, if it ever came down to that.

"Wha' do ye see?" Rhiada asked from where he sat beside her, the empty holes in his face horridly shadowed in the bright sunlight that poured through the window.

Fiona swallowed, pushing away the memory of Angus and his unsettling, intense silences. "Lady Nuith and Laird Erland greeting their guests. I see her brother and his companions, standing by the stair above the kitchens." She continued to relate brief descriptions of each person to Rhiada, who listened intently. Then, "Rhiada, wha' did ye say about Lady Nuith being wi' child?"

"I merely heard the servants speaking of it; why?"

She paused, looking out the window again and gazing at the woman who hated and feared her so much. "Her stomach is swollen—the child growing within her..." Her voice trailed off, realisation dawning on her. "Tha' is why they are celebrating tonight, is it no'? Why they hae waited this long to murder me—because they had to provide a claim to the throne through her child." She struggled to keep her voice from panicking.

Rhiada laid his hand on her arm gently. "Fiona, 'twill be all right. Ye are escaping tonight as soon as ye finish playing. Donnae fret about it. 'Twill all gae according to plan."

Fiona bit back the response that was forcing its way out. She had no choice but to trust him and believe it would all be right in the end.

"Would it help if ye played through yer songs one more time?" he offered kindly.

She turned away from the window in reluctance, swallowing down the lump continually rising in her throat.

The sun was already nearing the western horizon. Only a few more hours of waiting. Then she would know whether she would have a chance to live or would succumb to the Danish axe like her brother before her.

The Great Hall resounded with laughter and ceaseless chatter that night. Rhiada stood waiting with Fiona in the entrance and, though the doors were closed, they could hear the joyous din as clearly as if they were in the hall itself.

Fiona clenched the pine-green folds of her woollen dress in her fists, trying to drive away the tingle of nerves sparking in her fingertips. Her stomach twisted within her and she closed her eyes for a moment, resisting the urge to reach up and touch the crown of ivy resting on her head. It had been a long time since anything had adorned her wild locks, and the light weight felt strange, even if it was not the crown she should be wearing. If they succeeded tonight, she might reclaim that stolen crown yet. Nonetheless, the ivy circlet was a good distraction from the sickening panic and the whirlwind of thoughts in her mind.

She must not think of what could happen, of what could go wrong; she must only think of performing and then leaving the room when finished. Only that, and nothing else.

Then Rhiada laid his hand on her shoulder and placed the harp in her hands. "'Tis time."

Fiona stepped through the doors, her head pounding, nearly dimming her vision. The conversations in the hall gradually quieted down as the occupants noticed her presence. They stared as the red-headed princess walked through their midst, the silence broken only by intense whispering. A surge of sound arose as a pair of dogs snarled beneath one of the tables, fighting over the piece of meat a noble had tossed them. But even that died away when she reached the dais.

Fiona McCurragh lifted her head high, looking straight ahead and unintentionally meeting Lady Nuith's brown eyes. Fiona held her gaze as it hardened—but for the barest flicker. Uncertainty? Worry? The lady's mouth tightened in a firm line, but she only bowed her head as a sign for the lass to begin.

Fiona turned and sat on the dais's steps, settling the harp into her shoulder as she glanced around the room. Most of the faces were unfamiliar, but she recognized one figure sitting at a table nearby, his dark eyes glazed over by drink, the torchlight glinting off the blood-red jewel in his ring.

She watched him for a half-breath of a moment, fear strangling her movements. If Rhiada's plan failed, who knew what Lachlan and others might do to her before she was murdered?

She tore her gaze away from him and ran her fingers lightly over the strings, the sweet sound calming the racing of her heart. The expectant silence weighed heavily on her ears, and she was reluctant to break it. She looked up from the harp and saw Rhiada standing by the door. He motioned with his head for her to start.

Breathing deeply to steady her hands, she placed her fingers on the strings again, plucking them in rhythm as the gentle yet mournful melody echoed throughout the quiet hall.

Then, despite the blood pounding her ears, she opened her mouth and began to sing.

Over the hills
The wind is sighing
The Highlands are calling me home
Over the waves
The sea is singing
The Highlands are calling me home

The raven cries
Over the moorlands
The Highlands are calling me home
Rivers murmur
Rippling lullabies
The Highlands are calling me home

The mountains weep
For wanderers lost

The Highlands are calling me home
The heavens mourn
Forgotten years
The Highlands are calling me home

I will go home
I'll return again
The Highlands are calling me home
Soon I'll return
To my land of birth
The Highlands are calling me home

Songs of freedom
Cries of liberty
The Highlands are calling me home
The sun will rise
Our foes slain and gone
The Highlands are calling me home

I will go home
Home to the mountains
The Highlands are calling me home
I will go home
Scotland beckons me
The Highlands are calling me home

When she finished, silence hung in the air for a moment before it broke into scattered applause. It was over. Fiona rose to her feet, cheeks flushed, and walked to Rhiada, placing the harp in his hands.

"Well done, lassie. Now get yerself gang," he whispered hoarsely to her while stepping forward with the help of his wooden staff.

Fiona left the Great Hall and walked to her room as quickly as she could without seeming suspicious. Everything depended on speed and secrecy now. She only wished she could move as hurriedly as her pulse raced.

Grabbing her weapons and a bundle containing a few spare changes of clothing, she tied the strings of her cloak around her neck and flew down the stairs to the bottom of the tower.

She glanced around the empty and windswept courtyard before

walking swiftly to the stables. Cameron MacClaerthun—whom she had seen once or twice guiding Rhiada around the castle—was waiting for her, having saddled Sgàil while Fiona performed for Lady Nuith in the Great Hall.

"Ye ken wha' to do?" he asked softly while the other horses nickered to one another.

"Aye. Thank ye," Fiona replied, swinging up into the saddle.

Cameron bowed his head. "Keep yerself safe, princess." Then he stepped back.

Fiona dug her heels into Sgàil's flanks and took off. She hugged her mane tight as they raced across the courtyard and out the open gate, following the old Roman road south to the Lowlands while the rain darkened the twilight skies of her escape.

"Sa, your step-daughter sings and plays well. Ye had no' told me that."

Lady Nuith looked to her left, meeting her half-brother's brown-eyed gaze. "What makes you say so?" she asked coldly.

He shrugged. "I was merely complimenting her. Or do ye despise her so much ye cannae stand the mere mention of her?" he replied with a teasing smile on his face. He raised his drinking horn in a toast to his lips as if to make light of the whole thing.

"I loathe that child. As long as she is alive, the throne is not safe for my child to inherit. I suspect that blind harper is hatching a plan for her escape, though none of the servants have reported anything suspicious, nor have I seen anything to give proof of such. I do hope you will dispose of her tonight as you promised..."

Lord Erland, sitting on the other side of Nuith, met his wife's gaze briefly but said nothing. He was her husband, yes, but every Dane knew who truly ruled from Caerloch. In this thing as in others, Nuith's commands were what mattered. So he did not question what any Scot would consider utter base treachery.

Rhiada's playing finally ended, and Lady Nuith watched him with shrewd eyes as he bowed and departed the room, a few Danish musicians taking his place.

"Drummond," she said softly, turning to him, "I wish I knew which side you are on."

"I wish I did as well. Fer now, I am just waiting," Drummond MacDougall replied, his crooked smile as usual looking like a sneer. "But yes, I will do what ye hae asked." He finished emptying his horn and set it down with an ominous *click* on the trestle table. "Blind harper or no', Fiona McCurragh will not see the next sunrise."

~ 6 ~
NIGHT ON THE MOORS

*T*HE *Raven's Wing* tavern bustled as various persons—mostly men—ate their suppers and drank their mead, discussing the latest news, of which there was little. Occasionally the gentle, murmuring conversations were interrupted by a sudden, raucous laugh. The air was thick and hazy from the smoking fires in the kitchen and the sputtering of dripping tallow candles. The overwhelming smells of roasted mutton, fresh bread, burning peat, and stale sweat created a compelling aroma that had been new and exciting the first hour. But Fiona McCurragh was sick of it now.

She slipped farther into the shadows where she would not be so easily noticed and leaned her head against the wall, her shoulders drooping.

She had been there for nearly a day, having arrived early that morning. She had spent the night hidden in the heather and slept little after setting Sgàil free, hoping the mare would indeed find her own way back. Fiona was exhausted and terribly frightened, especially as there was still no sign of the man who was to take her to the McCladden croft. Her pretence of being a young woman waiting for her lover would not last for long, even if she did appear older than her fourteen years. Taking her mother's name, Fionnuala, as part of her disguise, would not save her. Once a search party from Lady Nuith arrived—which surely would not be long now—she would be recognized instantly.

The relief she had felt upon safely reaching *The Raven's Wing* was gone, replaced with the familiar dread of waiting for something to go wrong. When might soldiers from Caerloch come to this inn, looking for the runaway princess? Or when might the tavern keeper, Gavin McFrae, hear of it and suspect something? He was fiercely loyal to Lady Nuith, having Nuith's family emblem of crimson ravens displayed on the wall, and he would stop at nothing to turn Fiona in for a rich reward if he knew who she truly was.

The door swung open, startling her out of her thoughts. She turned her head to see a newcomer step inside the tavern, lingering a moment in the doorway as if surveying the place before entering. Perhaps this was his first time visiting; most patrons did not seem so uncertain. His face was hidden by his hood, the rest of his muddied cloak concealing his clothing and clan identity save when the folds parted as he stepped across the room. She could see that this man did not wear the McCladden tartan; she did not know the clans well enough to recognize this one, some weave of white, blue, and violet. Nonetheless, she searched him with her eyes, looking for the symbol Rhiada had told her to watch for. His actions clearly marked him different from everyone else she had seen that day; could he be the one she had been waiting for?

He hesitated halfway across the room, turning around as if looking for someone, his face still shadowed by his hood.

Fiona felt hope rise within her and she inched closer to him. Had the messenger come at last?

Then he took a few steps towards her, glancing towards the counter where the innkeeper stood. The man's presence, aside from opening the door, had gone unnoticed, most continuing their conversations in peace.

Fiona backed up against the corner, swallowing hard, her hope vanishing. If this was not the messenger, then what would she do? Would anyone else pay heed to this apparent local girl if she cried for help? Memories of Lachlan flashed before her eyes, and she bit her tongue against whimpering. She was a McCurragh; she must not cower, not like this.

But the stranger only spoke in a soft voice. "Fiona?"

She stared at him, the voice oddly familiar. Surely it could not be—

He pulled back his cloak over one shoulder, her eyes following the subtle motion. There, pinned to his plaid, lay the thistle with pine and heather sprigs. Relief flooded her veins even as he thrust back his hood, his cloak covering the pin once more.

Fiona stifled a gasp, recognizing Angus McCladden despite the blue woad swirls tattooed across his face in the style of the ancient Pictish tribes. The colour brought out the brilliance of his eyes, which sparkled in the dim light. Her chest fluttered against her will and she forced herself to look away, her thoughts racing. No one wore those patterns anymore except for special ceremonies such as funerals or youths' coming of age or the rise of a new chieftain or—weddings...

Her face grew hot. What had Rhiada put her up to?

"They ken me as Fionnuala," she forced in a whisper. She glanced back at his face, searching for a reaction. Did Rhiada tell him this part as well?

His jaw clenched as if he was as nervous as she felt. "Well, then, Fionnuala," he said in a much louder voice that trembled at the edges, "are ye ready to gae? We mustnae keep them waiting." He grinned broadly, but it did not reach his eyes.

In her peripheral vision, she could see the other patrons of the tavern suddenly looking at them with interest, some of them jesting with one another about it.

Her cheeks burned. If she ever saw Rhiada again, she was going to give him a piece of her mind.

She swallowed, holding her head high. If this was how her life was to be saved, then she too could play this ridiculous game. She wasn't some peasant lass; she was the princess, and while she had no crown, she still had her dignity. "Aye, if ye can wait jist a moment." Her voice squeaked out of nervousness. She plastered a smile to her face, hoping to cover it.

Turning on her heel, she rushed upstairs, her breath catching in her throat. She grabbed her things, looked around the small room to make sure she'd not forgotten anything, and ran back down the stairs. Despite her attempts to sound carefree, her boots thumped like a fleeing fugitive. But perhaps no one noticed—they were not as well-attuned to potential danger as she certainly was.

Once she reached the main floor, she searched frantically for Angus, who was exchanging what seemed quite an ordinary conversation with the tavern keeper. His light tone surprised her in every way. If she had not known him as he was on the moors, she might have never thought otherwise. He was almost convincing...

"Aye, yer lass waited quite awhile," Gavin McFrae answered, stroking his dark beard.

Angus shrugged, a smile across his face. "Och, I couldnae help it. My horse cast a shoe and I had to gae to the nearest forge to fix it. Took far longer than I expected, which is usually my luck. My lassie is the only thing in life that has gang right fer me so far. But I am sorry if she was a burden fer ye."

"Nae, nae, nae burden at all," Gavin replied. "I was only a-worrying we would hae to put a bed up fer her fer the night if ye didnae come." He turned to another newly arrived patron, the conversation ended.

Fiona stepped towards Angus, biting her tongue against speaking. If he was going to make up lies, he could at least thank them for caring for her instead of apologising to them for the burden. Too many people had thought of her as such. She wondered then whether Angus considered this whole adventure a burden as well....

At seeing her, he only smiled again, the same cheerless smile as before, and slipped his arm around her waist, gently pulling her to himself.

Fiona shrank back from him, the sneering face of Lachlan springing to mind. She was glad he did not hold her tightly, his hand resting so lightly around her as if he was as uncomfortable with the whole thing as she was. She closed her eyes a moment, forcing herself to lean more against him. Make it look natural; give no one any reason to expect otherwise. But she hated it all the same.

She wondered what Douglas would have thought if he could see her now. Certainly he would understand her role, but she had a feeling Angus would be dealing with a bloody nose if he had attempted such a thing around her brother—even if it was all an act. A pity Douglas wasn't there now to guide her instead.

"Come, my sweet lass, 'tis time we gae. Mother is waiting fer us!" The soft, yet eager voice of a young lover reached her ears. Angus' ardent facial expression was so unlike anything she had ever seen from him that she struggled to keep from laughing in disbelief. Even as her ears burned, she was glad everyone else in the tavern thought it the best thing to happen yet that evening. Their laughs and ill-humoured jokes raised a blush to both their faces, hiding any other sort of reaction from the strangeness of the whole thing.

Angus called out one last joyous farewell to all and sundry before they stepped outside the tavern. As soon as the door was shut behind them, Angus slipped away from her and splashed water from the drinking trough onto his face. She stood beside him, inhaling deeply the cool, crisp night air, a welcome relief after the stuffiness of the tavern.

A full moon shone brightly from a cloudless sky. The silence of the night rested heavy on her ears after the perpetual noise of the tavern, disturbed only by a soft, moaning wind singing a whispered song of loneliness.

At last, Angus straightened, running his wet hand across his face one last time, wiping away the remaining marks of the blue woad that had only been painted on all along. The look of a seasoned warrior was washed away, revealing a lad only a couple years older than herself. The gentle breeze ruffled his hair, which was midnight black in the twilight. Then he spoke, his voice his normal, solemn self. "So, who's Fionnuala?"

"That was my mother's name, if ye must ken—Rhiada said I had best nae use my own." She stared at him, disbelief still beating a warning in her chest. "Wha' kept ye?" she asked softly, wondering if they must still keep up the act even out here, where someone might see them as they travelled home.

"I wasnae even supposed to come," he replied, his voice low. "My elder brother, Duncan, was gang to, but he injured his leg falling from the loft in our *sabhal*. My father isnae at home, being elsewhere in the Lowlands at present, so 'twas decided I would take the journey. Sorry fer the delay," he finished in an apologetic tone.

Fiona shook her head. "Never mind that now. Jist..." She paused, wondering whether it was impolite to even mention it or not. "Please donnae treat me like yer bride if ye donnae hae to."

He made a strange sound in his throat; she couldn't tell if it was a strangled laugh or a sigh of disgust. "Aye, donnae worry about tha'," he said swiftly, as if eager to reassure her he had felt the same way about it as she did. "Rhiada said it would look most inconspicuous fer any spies, but I loathed every minute of it."

"How did ye ken how to act like tha' then?" she asked, suddenly, painfully curious if he had a lass of his own, the poor girl.

Angus hitched his shoulder in a shrug. "My brother Duncan has a lass of his own. I merely mimicked them. I am rather glad ye played along." He stretched his arms out behind him, glancing around them to see if anyone was near. "We must get gang from here before someone comes out."

With that, he gestured for her to follow him as they took off across the old Roman road and into the braes beyond. His quick, even stride was noticeable in the moonlight, and she struggled at first to keep up in her long skirt.

Fiona wished, as they scrambled up and down hillsides, that Rhiada had let her keep Sgàil instead of sending her back to Caerloch. She was none too thrilled at having to walk the whole way, even if Angus had done so in coming. Yet despite the weariness of both mind and body, she was glad to be free of that tavern. The threat of constant discovery had vanished away like sunrise after a long night. For the first time in three years, she would soon be in a place devoid of Danes, a place where Rhiada said only people loyal to her throne were. She would no longer be hated. She would no longer be alone.

It almost seemed impossible to believe.

The moon hovered high in the peaceful sky when a wisp of cloud fell across its face, darkness descending upon the land.

Angus halted, glancing up at the heavens as he paused to catch his breath.

Fiona stopped as well, glad for a chance to rest her weary legs, even if she did not understand his reason for pausing so suddenly. "Angus—"

He motioned for her to be silent, turning to look at the foggy valley behind them.

She saw no one, but she could not mistake the sudden whinny of a horse that broke the nighttime stillness. She inhaled sharply, all the terror she had thought finally laid to rest now rushing back like an angry wave. Were they being followed? What else would explain a horse on the moors at this time of night? Unless it was Rhiada... But why would he and Cameron be riding at this hour? It was near midnight!

She glanced at Angus, whose face was turned too far to really guess what he saw. "Angus, wha'—" she attempted once more, but Angus turned and grabbed her hand, sprinting across the moors as if a ghaist were after him.

Fiona clutched her skirts and the edge of her cloak with her free hand and ran with him, trying her best to keep up with his swift, loping stride.

The moon broke free of its thin shroud and shone its eerie brightness once more on the land. Fiona turned to look behind her as they ran and saw men on horses standing far off, each one several spans from the next, scouring the countryside.

Danes—no true Scot would be seen without a kilt and plaid—and they were looking for her.

Fiona tripped and fell to her knees, yanking down Angus' arm, but he only pulled her up and continued running. She struggled to keep pace with him, even as she knew they would not be able to keep up this speed for long, especially if the Danes began to chase them on horseback.

"How much farther?" she gasped, breathless from exertion.

"Nae much," he panted. "Jist a wee bit longer. I ken a place—we'll be safe."

She glimpsed their shadows as they ran, darker figures elongated across the ground. She fancied in terror to see the forms of horses running towards them, only to realize it was merely the ominous shapes of gorse and heather, harshened by the light of the moon. The ground danced before her eyes, rising and falling in rhythm with their steps, matching the pounding in her ears.

Then Angus yanked her to a halt, falling to his knees and parting the heather grown over a small hollow in the ground. Her lungs burning, she threw herself into it, hitting the ground hard. He followed her, closing the heather over them once they were lying on the bottom.

The dip in the ground was rather large with plenty of room for them to lie there without touching, and she edged to the far side as the hollow became silent, filled only with their heavy breathing.

"Are we—?"

Angus clamped his hand over her mouth before she could finish, pulling her body across the hollow until she lay right beside him, his arms tightly locked around her.

A moment later, horse hooves plunged right where she had been lying. If Angus had not pulled her out of the way, she would have been trampled.

Her courage crushed, Fiona buried her face in Angus' neck, feeling like she was going to be sick. She clung to him, silent sobs wracking her frame in gasping breaths, a scream threatening to escape her. So close to death, always so terribly close! Would she ever be free? Would she ever be safe? Was it always to be like this, constantly on the run?

Angus only held her closer, his arms about her as if to keep her from shattering completely. "Shh," he whispered with such tenderness that her breath caught in her throat in surprise. "'Tis gang to be all right, but we must be quiet until they hae gone." His fingers brushed her shoulder gently, warmth spreading throughout her shivering body, and she released the breath she had not been conscious of holding.

Fiona closed her eyes, the tension slowly slipping away with every beating moment. She let go of his shirt that she had been clutching so tightly and wrapped her arms around his neck instead, breathing in the pungent aroma of sweet pine and heather, the smell of safety. So unlike the stench and the fear of when Lachlan had tried to take her for his own. She was safe, safe with the person she had not known she trusted until this very moment.

Rhiada was right. Angus would risk his life fer mine, and I had nae believed him.

Voices passed in front of their hiding place, voices speaking in the Danish tongue of which Fiona was largely unfamiliar, even after living among them for three years. She stiffened, daring to open her eyes and gaze towards the skies, seeing the gleaming moon and twinkling stars filter through the heather bushes.

Shadows fell over them as the voices faded away into silence. Fiona glanced at the lad who was holding her, seeing the moonlight reflected in his eyes.

Angus looked up as well, his dark brows wrinkled in concentration, and then he whispered, "We are safe as long as we donnae make a sound. Gae to sleep, if ye can, Fiona. Who kens how long we'll hae to remain here before 'tis safe to continue on our way." He loosened his embrace, though he did not let go of her entirely.

She closed her eyes, still holding onto him as the only sure thing in a world of faceless voices and uncertain shadows.

Peaceful silence reigned over the quiet braes, but it seemed a long while before the welcome oblivion of rest opened its arms to her and she fell into a deep sleep.

~ 7 ~

The Lowlands

PRESSURE built on Fiona's chest, as if the weight of the world had fallen upon her and would not let her breathe, suffocating her minute by agonising minute.

Gavin McFrae, the tavern keeper of The Raven's Wing, had his knee pressed against her, pinning her to the ground. An evil smile spread across his face, the light of golden coins shining in his eyes as he spoke. "Finally I've got ye, rebel lass. Ye'll pay fer this sure enough. Aye, yer capture will bring me many a pretty gold piece." His foul breath made her want to gag, if she could somehow gather enough air to do so.

Fiona struggled to get away, but she could not move. She was helplessly trapped under the portly man's leg. Panic rose in her throat. Was this how it was supposed to end? Had Rhiada's grand escape plan failed after all? Had Angus failed in keeping her safe? Where was Angus anyway? Had Gavin already killed him?

She tried to turn her head to see, but found that she could not. Her neck was frozen in place, as was the rest of her. Had Gavin poisoned her, so that whatever he would do to her next would leave her without the ability to struggle or scream?

A surge of sound arose, voices coming from a distance, a voice that was familiar to her ears—

"Angus!" She tried to call out as Gavin raised a dagger above her head, but her voice refused to obey, the sound dying in her throat.

So hard to breathe.

The smoky torchlight glittered on Gavin's weapon. Fiona shut her eyes, afraid to watch as it plunged into her chest.
But the blade never pierced her.

Fiona's eyes flew open and she sat up with a jerk, gasping for air as if she were drowning. Her heart still raced, but the pressure was gone, having fled with the remnants of sleep. Sickening relief washed over her and she sighed heavily, pushing away the awful memories of the nightmare and gazing instead at her unfamiliar surroundings.

She was no longer at Caerloch, that was for certain, but neither were these white-washed and tapestry-covered walls the same as those at *The Raven's Wing*.

All at once, like a wave crashing onto a beach, scenes from yester-night came flooding back to her: Angus playing the part of a youthful lover, running together on the moonlit moors, lying in the heather and falling asleep beside him as the night slowly waned away.

But those recollections did not explain where she was now.

Rising from the straw mattress she had slept on, Fiona made her way to the edge of the tiny loft and peered down.

A woman clothed in the McCladden plaid sat in the corner of the room below, spinning wool into thread. A loom stood to the woman's right, and to her left a fire burned brightly in the raised hearth, though it must be mid-morning. Grey daylight streamed through the two windows opposite the hearth, shining dully on the rough wooden floor.

Fiona climbed down the small ladder and quickly ran her fingers through her tangled locks. She glanced outside and saw thatch-roofed buildings, not the ground nor the doors and windows of other living places. An exhilarating breeze blew in, carrying with it the heavy scent of woodsmoke. Rhythmic clanging came from somewhere in the distance; she supposed it was a blacksmith at work.

Turning away from the window, she noticed that the room was similar to a castle's in some ways, but not exactly, though it was cornered with stone architecture. Skillfully woven tapestries covered many of the white-washed walls just as in the loft above, but that was where the similarities to Caerloch ended.

Gazing around the room, Fiona's eyes came once again to rest on the woman who sat in the corner, her spindle and distaff now lying still in her hands.

"Welcome to the Lowlands," the woman said, a dimpled smile on her face. Her voice was like warm honey, even and soothing, and something within Fiona longed to trust her, even though she did not know who she was. The lady's reddish-brown hair was plaited into a crown around her head, traces of silver amidst the lush dark strands woven through with a thin fillet of gold. She was not young, but certainly not ancient, for the only wrinkles in her face were those from smiling. She was beautiful in a sweet and innocent way despite her age, like a dewy flower beneath the morning sun. There seemed to be nothing insincere about her, unlike Lady Nuith, who wore a syrupy smile before her guests like an ill-fitting mask.

"I thank ye," Fiona responded at last, still undecided whether this woman was trustworthy or simply excelled at deceiving her. "If ye donnae mind my asking, who are ye?"

"I am Annag McCladden, Angus' mother. And ye are Fiona Mc-Curragh, I presume?" she questioned, kindness shining in her deep, amber eyes.

"Aye, I am," Fiona answered, twirling the folds of her skirt in her fingers. So she was free then, after all. Rhiada's plan had succeeded. The thought only brought a small amount of relief, however. What was she supposed to do now? And when would Rhiada join her?

"How did I end up here?" she asked. "The last thing I remember is falling asleep on the moors."

"Angus carried ye back, of course," Annag replied.

A hot wave of embarrassment passed over Fiona and she looked at the floor, too ashamed to meet Annag's gaze. Why did she have no memory of it beyond falling asleep in his arms beneath the uncertain moonlight? And why did she blush at the thought?

From the window came the shrill clashing of steel and quick shouts. Bewildered, the princess glanced at Annag before making her way to the window. Angus' mother picked up her spindle and distaff again, a faint smile still playing on her lips.

Fiona looked out into a broad courtyard of sorts whose open gates revealed the town beyond. Directly opposite was a *sabhal* with a forge nearby, great billows of smoke rising from the chimney. In the centre of the courtyard, two lads were sword fighting—fighting in dead earnest, she realised as she watched them more closely.

The taller one with dark hair side-stepped swiftly, his sword raised high above his head, his face revealing him to be Angus. The other one, though, had an unfamiliar face and a head of red hair like her own.

Angus suddenly thrust forward, and the sword flew out of the hands of his opponent, landing several feet away.

"Tha' isnae fair! Ye've won the last seven rounds," the red-haired lad cried out in exasperation.

Angus' expression was grimly impassive. "Ye're the one who needs to be paying better attention, Malcolm. Ready to gae again?"

Malcolm shrugged, his face awash in a wave of embarrassment visible from where Fiona stood above them both. He ambled over and grabbed his sword, not appearing eager to continue the match.

They began again, a fury of steel crashing together. The flying blades caught the light from the watery sun that peeped between the clouds, flashing many times over.

"Who is Malcolm?" Fiona asked, looking over her shoulder at Annag.

Annag glanced up, her spindle pausing its spinning for a moment. "Malcolm is my youngest son, Angus' younger brother by three years."

"I didnae ken ye had other sons," Fiona replied, wondering how much else Angus had not told her. "It wasnae until Angus met me outside *The Raven's Wing* tavern and said that his brother Duncan was supposed to come fer me that I kent he had other siblings."

"Aye, well, Angus isnae exactly one fer talking now." The spindle spun again.

"What do ye mean by now?" Fiona inquired curiously. Was it true that Angus, so pensive, so quiet, once chattered as freely as her own brother, Douglas, had? The thought was nearly beyond imagining.

Annag looked up again from her spinning. "I once had four sons: Sioned, Duncan, Angus, and Malcolm. Angus was ne'er given to words around others, but wi' Sioned, Angus could talk the wings off an eagle. They were very close, and very rarely would ye find one without t'other.

"But then the War came and Sioned perished beneath the Danish axe, as did many of Scotland's pride. When my husband came home without my son, Angus was never the same. Ever since, he's nae talked fer the sound of it, as Malcolm does. He was forever changed by the War, even as we all were."

The room fell silent when Annag finished speaking. Neither of them made an effort to break the solemn stillness.

Angus' bitter words echoed in Fiona's mind. *"Ye're nae the only one who's lost their family fighting the Danes."* So that was why he was always silent and brooding, the mere mention of the War and its losses causing him as much pain as it did herself. And, it seemed, he also locked away his grief just as she did, afraid to break and show it to anyone who might cause the old wounds to hurt. Scotland's broken clans were as deeply scarred from the War as she was. Even if she was restored to her throne, would it heal and unify all that had been destroyed?

Feet pounded on the stairs to the second story, and the door to the room burst open. In its wake came a panting Malcolm and a scowling Angus. Both of them pulled up short when they caught sight of her, Angus hurriedly looking away and his brother simply gawking at her.

Malcolm reached shoulder-height to his older brother, with freckles sprinkled evenly about his face, accenting his soft, grey eyes and fiery-red hair. His expression was at first one of confusion and then he seemed to understand something, for he asked, "Ye are Fiona, then? I was asleep when ye both came home last night so I didnae see ye until now," he explained, his words tripping over themselves in an attempt to rush out of his mouth.

"Aye, I am Fiona," she answered, perplexed at the strange question and still trying to understand the words that followed it.

"Ye're nothing like what Angus told us," he replied with the swift energy of a chipmunk.

Fiona glanced at Angus, whose pale complexion coloured in embarrassment. He continued to stare out the window instead of meeting her gaze.

"Wha' do ye mean by tha'?" she asked, both curious and flustered at the idea that Angus had mentioned her to his family, especially considering how little he spoke at all.

"Well, he described ye as a lass wi' flaming hair like a wild Celt and a personality more stubborn than the rocks on the Giant's Seat."

"Fairly accurate," Fiona stated, rather disappointed at Angus' opinion of her and wondering if there was anything else, or if that was all he thought of her. Then again, would he have acted in the way he had the night before if he thought as little of her as that? Or were those actions done only out of loyalty and nothing else?

Malcolm's words snapped her back to reality. "Nae, he left out something very important."

"And wha' would tha' be?" Her heart leapt into her throat out of nervousness for what the lad would say next—or was it something else and not nervousness at all?

"He failed to mention," Malcolm continued, his grey eyes dancing in merriment and looking sideways at his brother who pretended to be very occupied adjusting his sword's sheath, "tha' ye are the bonniest lass in all of Scotland."

Fiona's face burned, and Angus glanced at his brother as if he would knock him down right then and there, his blue eyes storming in silent rage.

A tense and awkward silence followed, remaining unbroken until Annag rose to her feet, looking at both of her sons, stern even while a smile of amusement tugged at her mouth. "Angus, Malcolm," she said firmly, "I want ye to take Fiona and show her the way about An Dùn. Now get yerselves gang."

~ 8 ~

AN DÙN

ANNAG had not quite finished speaking when Malcolm bounded out of the room, disappearing down the stairs. Angus turned away, glancing briefly over his shoulder at his mother and the princess before descending himself in silence.

Fiona hesitated before following them, uncertain whether she was ready for this new change of pace. She had not been around others her age since Douglas had left for the War, and knowing only one of the two McCladden brothers—and not very well—she was not eager to rush into this new life, whatever Rhiada might say. But she went, regardless of that fact, reaching the bottom of the stairs a few moments after the lads to see Angus whispering heatedly to his brother. She did not hear what he said, as he finished speaking whatever it was when she drew near.

"Are we gang to show her the inside of An Dùn, or the outside?" Malcolm asked eagerly, as if his brother's fierce words had never been spoken.

"The inside first, then the outside. Ye still hae nae practised yer archery fer today," Angus snapped, turning towards the door. Then he halted and commanded over his shoulder, "Come ye."

Fiona obeyed without question, astonished at this sudden change in the Angus she thought she knew. He had been closed off before, aye, when they were first becoming acquainted. Yet she had also seen a gentler side to him when he had safeguarded her the night before.... It was almost as if, no longer in the role of protector, he had slipped back into the pensive Angus she had met at the first. But still, why so angered? Had Malcolm's teasing offended him in some way?

Her stomach growled in hunger, disrupting her thoughts—she had not had breakfast, nor even a proper supper at *The Raven's Wing* last night—but she did not wish to disappoint either of the McCladden brothers, or Annag, who had told them to go. So she ignored it and said nothing.

The chilly air bit her face as they stepped outside, a thin wind doing nothing to dissipate the fog lying in small drifts strewn about the town of An Dùn. The fort itself was fairly quiet, much to Fiona's surprise. She had anticipated a louder bustle than the general calm that greeted her ears, the sort of which she was used to at Caerloch and the village beyond the castle gates. There were sounds of life, to be sure—the clanging of hammer upon steel from the forge, echoes of a brawl from farther up the street, and a faint bairn's cry from within a nearby croft. But not the clamour she expected of such a large communal living place as this. Then again, she had never been beyond Caerloch's walls aside from the few times she rode out on the moors. Her time at *The Raven's Wing* had been the most adventurous experience of her short life.

Fiona had no trouble matching the fast pace Angus set as he marched determinedly down the street. Malcolm, however, struggled to keep up, following them at a lop-legged trot. It did not help that he occasionally tripped over loose stones on the path, as if the offending pebbles were trying to cause his fall.

She struggled to remember all the names of places that Angus muttered as he proceeded to show her more of the fortress town. Unlike Caerloch and the accompanying village beyond its gates, An Dún was not its own thriving society. It was a fortress town, meant only for defence and survival. Beyond the familial crofts and occasional tavern, there were few places worthy of note besides the armoury and stables by the gates. The Council Hall, where the elders and chieftain would gather at meeting times, was near the McCladden croft, but it was nothing like the feast hall at Caerloch from what she could see of it.

She wondered whether she would ever be summoned there to meet with the chieftains—of whom she had dim memories from before the War—and how she would speak with them, she who knew so little of such things. Her brother had learned all that, being the prince. She had been taught nothing besides what little Rhiada had tried to instruct her in.

Through it all, Malcolm stumbled along behind them, trying and failing to win their undivided attention as his brother ignored the lad's commentary completely.

After a few minutes in the cold air, Fiona wished she had brought her cloak in which to wrap her numb fingers. Perhaps the McCladden brothers, still heated from their sparring, did not notice the chill, but she felt it deeply. The sun showed no promise of shining his warm face. The skies were grey above them, their blank billows foreboding.

At last, they neared the tall wooden palisade winding around the entire village as a protective defence. It was as tall as three men standing on one another's shoulders and made of sturdy pine logs buried in the earth and bound to one another with ropes, their tops sharpened into points that might draw blood from the sky. Fiona shuddered to think what it must feel like to be impaled upon them.

Angus slowed to an easy walk, following the wall for a few paces. Turning, he ran up a flight of stairs leading to a ledge jutting out from the wall on the interior side. Fiona followed him with Malcolm bringing up the rear. Once on top of the crude battlements, she looked out over the land beyond the gates of An Dùn.

Heather-covered braes and glens with desultory mounds of various shrubs and the occasional tree lay as far as the eye could see. The rolling but lonely hills stretched to kiss a horizon that had the dullness of an empty grey sky. Far off in the distance came the raucous call of ravens living amidst the wild beauty of the Scottish moors. Even this was different from Caerloch, whose view was marred by the sprawling village to the south and the dark rise to the far north that marked the Pass of Carbinenth.

Fiona turned and gazed behind her, seeing a muddy chariotway leading southwards from one gate to the next, though both remained shut. A couple men were positioned at either entrance, girded in fine chainmail rather than the black, plated armour the guards at Caerloch wore.

The village streets were mostly deserted, though a handful of stray dogs scurried about. A blanket of thick quiet lay over the whole fortress, as if An Dùn was waiting for something to happen, an eerie silence broken only by the wind and the clanging of the forge. Thin tendrils of smoke spilled from the chimneys of crofts here and there, but that was all.

She looked to Angus, who continued to gaze at the barren landscape. "Where is everyone?" she asked softly, her voice sounding strange in the expectant stillness.

He glanced at her and she was struck again by the intense blue of his eyes. "Some are at the meeting of chieftains in the south. The rest are inside because of the cold. The harvest is in; they hae little reason to be outside in the wind." He turned his gaze again towards the hills.

"Should we nae gae back fer breakfast?" Malcolm piped up. "I'm hungry."

Looking over her shoulder, she saw the lad's arms wrapped around himself as he shivered with cold. An unfamiliar warm wave of sympathy rose up within her as her eyes met his. "Aye, can we gae back?" she asked, directing her question to his brother. "I'm also hungry; I hae nae eaten since I was at *The Raven's Wing*." Fiona clenched her teeth to keep them from chattering. The moaning wind was becoming unbearable.

Angus gave the faintest of shrugs and headed back down the stairs without another word.

Malcolm looked at her gratefully and followed his brother in silence.

The warmth from inside the McCladden croft hit them like a welcoming embrace. Within moments, the cold began to leave Fiona's numb fingers and wind-torn face.

Angus and Malcolm flung themselves down on benches beside a large wooden table, leaving her to follow suit in her own time. Annag was bent over the raised hearth, stirring something that smelled delicious in a large black cauldron. She straightened and smiled when they entered, but did not speak to them.

Fiona watched as she generously ladled porridge into the bowls. Stepping forward, the lass took them one by one from Annag and set them at the table, eventually sitting down with her own breakfast, which she devoured hungrily.

The porridge was warm and sweet, sliding down her throat

smoother than water. It had been a long time since she had eaten the dish, as Lady Nuith simply loathed it.

Fiona froze, her spoon halfway to her mouth. No, she had not tasted of it since she had heard the news that Douglas would not return home. So embittered was she by her loss, that she had refused to eat his favourite food since. The taste, though long forgotten, brought back fond but heart-breaking memories of her dead brother.

She forced another bite into her mouth and gulped it down, and then another and another. It did not slide down so easily now, instead lumping in her throat against the tears that threatened to spill. But she blinked them back and swallowed hard; this was no place to cry, not here in front of Angus, in front of Malcolm, in front of their mother. She glanced at them, but neither of the brothers paid her any attention, for which she was grateful. Only Annag, meeting her gaze, furrowed her brows as if wondering why Fiona had suddenly paused.

The rest of the oatmeal disappeared rather quickly into the mouths of the hungry brothers, Fiona finishing hers more slowly. She had to keep up her strength, even if her appetite was gone.

Having eaten her fill, she ran up to the loft and grabbed her cloak from the small bundle of belongings she had brought with her from Caerloch. Returning downstairs, she joined the lads as they stepped outside into the chill of the autumn day, bringing with them their bows and quivers.

The sun peeped its golden face on the world and made everything look brighter, even if it failed to warm the chilly day. The wind stopped its mournful cries, and the moorlands were still as the trio left An Dùn and turned westward in silence. They followed a tiny path along a small wood, birds twittering unseen in the yellow-leafed branches, until at last they entered the forest itself.

Presently they reached a clearing where the ground fell away to a trickling burn, banks of trees rising on either side. But Fiona hardly noticed. Her eyes were drawn to a large piece of wood painted in bright colours, sphere disappearing into sphere until it reached a golden circle.

"Is tha' the target?" she asked as the brothers undid their cloaks and left them lying on a fallen log.

"Aye, it is," Malcolm replied with a grin, belting his quiver around his waist as he waited for Angus to string his bow.

Angus' face was twisted in intense concentration, his arms quavering in exertion as he slipped the string over the notch for their bows. He handed one to his brother and the other to Fiona before stringing his own, never giving them so much as a glance in return for their thanks.

Fiona bit back the argument that she was capable of stringing it herself and merely stood back as he nocked an arrow to the string. Malcolm plunked down on the log by their cloaks and stared at the faint sunlight filtering through the trees, his chin resting in his hands. Fiona soon joined him, watching in silent amazement as Angus landed arrow after arrow in the centre circle with an almost careless rapidity. The continual *thwunk* of arrows hitting the target slowly became as much a part of the forest as the birds singing in the treetops, and Fiona stared off into the wood. Her mind wandered, images from the past day and night passing before her eyes without focusing on any particular memory.

Suddenly Angus was standing in front of them, his arrows in his hands, beads of sweat on his brow. He nodded to his brother and proceeded to replace the shafts in his quiver, sitting beside Fiona without a word spoken.

Malcolm jumped to his feet and fitted an arrow to his own string. He emptied his quiver into the target, but with more care and deliberation than his brother had shown. Fewer arrows hit the target's centre, but none of them missed it completely.

Fiona watched him more closely than she had Angus, if only to ignore the silent and capricious presence sitting beside her. Angus made no effort at conversation and therefore neither did she. It was almost a relief when Malcolm finished, though a chord of nervousness resounded in her, for she knew that the McCladden brothers would be watching her every move.

She knew she should be used to scrutiny and judgement, having lived under Lady Nuith's shadow for six years. All the same, Nuith had never seen her practise. Only Douglas had, and he never hurt her in his critiques.

But Douglas was not here now.

She rose to her feet, sore from sitting on the uncomfortable log, and tested her bowstring, plucking it softly with her finger. Hearing it resonate with its vibrations in her hands, she nodded in satisfaction and went on to draw an arrow, fitting it to the string. Lifting her bow, Fiona drew the string back, peering down the shaft at the golden circle and mentally calculating the distance and arc her arrow would speed upon release. She locked her arm away from the string and exhaled softly, holding the bow steady.

Then she let fly.

The arrow hit the target dead centre with a satisfying *thwack*. Followed by another and another landing more or less by the first, until her quiver was empty.

Fiona felt nothing but sickening relief when it was over. Whatever low opinion Malcolm and Angus might have of her, at least it could not be attributed to her lack of aim. Douglas had taught her well. But then, he had always striven to prepare her for a day when she might have to defend herself, as if he had somehow known he might not always be there for her. In any case, it had paid off in the end, had it not? Had she not done as well as Angus and Malcolm? Whatever prejudice Angus might have against her for her father's actions, or whatever it might be, surely it would be lessened by her ability to shoot as well as he did.

She searched their faces as she walked back towards them. Malcolm grinned encouragingly, while Angus did little more than dip his head in a quick nod of approval. She did not quite feel satisfied—perhaps she could have done better, after all—but at least she did not feel ashamed.

They continued to practise as the sun rose to noon and continued on its quest towards the west, each of them taking turns according to the order in which they had begun.

While Angus shot again, Malcolm found his tongue once more and chattered away to Fiona, who listened eagerly as she had naught else to occupy her time. Through him, she learned many comical stories from the past and then some that weren't so pleasant, such as the boy's memories of the War. Those were confused and sad remembrances, ones of fear and uncertainty, giving Fiona yet another glimpse of the Lowlanders' view on what had happened six years ago.

"...Aye, then Sioned and Angus ran off wi' the yearlings and Father punished them both soundly when he found out! Angus did it again, though, but Sioned brought him and the runaway colt back before anyone kent wha' had happened....

"One time, Angus was out on the moors and didnae come home by nightfall. Mother was so distressed, she was weeping—Father and Sioned and Duncan all had to gae find him in the dark. 'Twas Sioned who found him, curled up in a hollow hidden by the heather, sobbing because he was frightened by the dark and thought he had seen a ghaist. Of course, he was only three, it was soon after I was born so I donnae remember it, and Angus never cries now. But whenever he did, Duncan says Sioned told him funny stories until he was laughing instead of crying."

"Were Angus and Sioned really tha' close, then?" Fiona asked suddenly, interrupting Malcolm mid-story. It was hard to imagine Angus as a sensitive and emotional child in contrast with the stoic lad she knew. Could Angus really have loved someone so deeply, cared so much? Annag had said so that morning, but Fiona had not thought about what that really meant.

Malcolm blinked, perhaps in surprise at someone finally listening to him. "Och, aye. I donnae really remember it as I was only seven years old, but aye, he was changed when Sioned died. When Father came back alone and told us Sioned had taken the Warrior's Road, Angus turned so white I thought he would swoon. And then he ran off and didnae come back until twilight." He paused, watching his brother land another arrow in the target, oblivious to their conversation. "His face was so red and swollen and he ne'er talked much after that. 'Tis been wha', six years? And I hae ne'er heard him laugh since, if he even smiles because he is happy and no' because he is teasing—ne'er a genuine smile, at any rate. Mother wonders if he'll ever truly smile again."

There was a painful pause after that, a stretch of silence in which Fiona became acutely aware that the shooting had stopped.

As if Malcolm had also noticed, they glanced up to see Angus looking down at them, his gaze completely blank, though Fiona was certain he had heard the last part of what his brother had said.

The blood rushed hot to her face and she looked away hurriedly in shame, her thoughts too confused by Malcolm's words to feign otherwise.

But Angus only remarked in a dead-level voice, "Yer turn, Malcolm."

The sun was setting, golden fingers of light spreading across the crimson sky as they returned to An Dùn. Angus continued to lead them as they walked back, but he remained silent, staring at the ground as if lost in his own thoughts. Malcolm had ceased speaking at last, as if he too was worn out with the long archery practise. It was just as well, for even the robins trilling their evening song sounded distant, though they sang right above Fiona. Her mind was elsewhere.

She contemplated both what Malcolm had said and Annag's words to her that morning. Truly the War had had an equal—if not greater—effect on these people as it had on her. Because of it they had lost family dear to them, even as Fiona had lost her only brother. Likewise, they felt grief at the separation of their country and shame in failing to drive the Danes out years ago. The free-spirited Scots truly groaned under the burdensome yoke of Danish rule.

Angus and Rhiada were right, she mused bitterly, ashamed at her insensitivity to their pain. *I am nae the only one who has lost those dear to me because of the War....* And Rhiada said the Lowlander chieftains wanted to restore her to her throne, which would almost certainly lead to another bloody war. Lady Nuith would not relinquish her stolen crown without a fight. How many more lives would Scotland's princess be required to sacrifice before the Scots' freedom and country were finally regained?

On the wings of the wind came the thundering of hooves, shattering her thoughts. Angus' head whipped up as all three of them glimpsed in the distance a pair on horseback riding swiftly to the fort as if their lives depended on it.

"Who is tha'?" Malcolm inquired, straining his neck to try to catch sight of them again, though the riders had passed out of view.

"Rhiada and Cameron," Angus shot back, a sense of urgency in his voice. "We need to hurry." He gripped his bow and broke into a run.

Malcolm sprinted after his brother, leaving Fiona to hitch up her skirts and follow despite her heart suddenly pounding in her throat.

If Rhiada, a blind man, was riding that swiftly, it could only mean one thing.

Something was unquestionably wrong.

~ 9 ~
HARDINGER

FIONA and Malcolm struggled to keep up with Angus' brisk pace as they raced back to An Dùn. They were all panting with exertion when they arrived at the walls, and Fiona and Malcolm nearly bent over double in an effort to catch their breath. Angus, undeterred as usual, walked up to the gates, which were shut against them, and demanded entry.

A youth with flaxen hair and a stubborn mouth appeared at the top of the gate, gazing down disdainfully at the dishevelled trio. He looked to be Malcolm's age, or a few years younger.

"Please open up the gates!" Angus cried out for the second time. The other two stood behind him, having regained their composure.

The youth replied saucily, "Me father said to wait fer him and no' to open the gate fer anyone else—and tha' includes ye, Angus McCladden."

"Why is yer father no' here, Cadwal MacNain?" Malcolm retorted before his brother had a chance to respond.

"He had to open the gate fer a very savage-looking blind man and his companion jist now, and Father's gang wi' both to the Council Hall. Besides, t'others from the south hae returned at t'other gate and are there as well, I think. At any rate, he said no' to let anyone in and I intend to see to it tha' his orders are obeyed." He smirked at them. Fiona was surprised he didn't stick out his tongue at them for good measure.

Angus had, by this time, had quite enough. "Cadwal, if ye donnae open the gate right now, I'm gang to knock it down myself and bash some sense into yer daft head."

Cadwal blanched white for a few moments and then eyed Fiona. "Who's the lass wi' ye? I had thought ye werenae fancying any lassies, but now I see one wi' ye."

Fiona's face burned in embarrassment and she stared at the ground, a knot of shame twisting within her, and not just for herself. Angus, for all his faults, did not deserve to be teased like this. Not by a mere child.

She glanced up again in time to see Angus' cheeks also burning red.

"I donnae," he snapped.

"Then why is she wi' ye?" Cadwal returned, his tone as careless as if asking how many squirrels Malcolm had frightened away with his chatter.

"Because our family has been entrusted wi' care of her."

"Who is she to demand such importance?" the lad scoffed from atop the gate.

Angus swallowed hard, his nostrils flaring. His next words were spoken through clenched teeth, frustration giving way to anger at Cadwal's lack of respect. "She's the future queen of Scotland, ye daft sheep, and ye better be a-letting us in or ye'll be regretting it."

Fiona stared at Angus. She had not expected him to defend her this far, even if he had already begun to prove true Rhiada's words of his loyalty.

"Queen? Bah!" Cadwal spat back with the impetuous wrath of youth. "There is nae queen of Scotland, the Lowlands or the Highlands. And even if there was, why should it bother me? She's nae my queen!"

Fiona heard Malcolm gasp beside her. She glanced at Angus, her heart beginning to race, wondering how he would respond now.

Angus glared up at the boy, his eyes darkening in silent fury, and stepped up to the gate, his mouth drawn into a firm line. Unsheathing his dirk, he ran it into the crack between the gates and levered up the wooden bar that held it in place. Fiona heard it clatter to the ground on the other side before Angus pushed open the doors and rushed in.

Malcolm and Fiona followed through the gates as Angus dashed up the stairs to the lookout tower into which Cadwal had ducked to hide the moment the gate was open. Angus' bow and quiver, useless for whatever he intended upon the lad, lay on the ground where he had dropped them. Fiona hitched up her skirts again and ran after him, Malcolm lingering for a moment to bolt the gates.

All thoughts of Rhiada were completely forgotten.

She reached the top of the stairs and entered the tower, pausing in the doorway to let her eyes adjust to the dim lighting. In a moment, she saw Angus and Cadwal locked in a fierce struggle. Though they made no verbal noise beyond grunting in exertion, the scuffling they created was fairly loud and she wondered why she had not heard it before. A blush spread over her face. They were fighting over her—she whom Lady Nuith would rather see dead—and all because Cadwal had not shown the respect Angus believed she deserved. Her heart stung in humility; she did not deserve his defence by any means.

Footsteps sounded behind her, and Malcolm pushed into the room, trying in vain to separate the two. He was accidentally jerked aside as the pair rolled over on the floor, Cadwal struggling to hold dominance over his larger—and nimbler—opponent.

Pushing her thoughts away, Fiona saw an opening and thrust her leg in between the two grappling each other and, grabbing the one nearest, who happened to be Angus, pulled hard. Malcolm caught on to her plan and tugged on the other until they were separated, catching Cadwal's wrists and jerking them behind him despite the lad's struggles to break free.

Fiona released Angus a moment later, her heart still racing, and he glowered at his opponent before saying, "She is yer queen whether ye like it or no'. And if ye dispute about it one more time, I willnae hae mercy." He rubbed a hand across his face, wiping away a trickle of blood from his nose. Both he and Cadwal were in sorry shape, their chests heaving in an attempt to regain the breath knocked out of them.

But Fiona only continued to gaze at Angus in astonishment, reminded now more than ever of the sharp contrast between the way he constantly defended her and her honour, and the manner in which Lady Nuith had always belittled and shamed her. She wondered if perhaps the other Scots would also be so loyal, or whether they would share the same sentiments as Cadwal. She hoped it was the former, but was afraid to know for certain and be disappointed if not.

"Shall I let him gae?" Malcolm piped up, breaking into Fiona's thoughts.

"Only if he agrees to treat her wi' respect," his brother replied, sniffing hard against the blood that continued to flow from his nose. His hand was now red with it.

Cadwal nodded sullenly, yanking his wrist loose as he gingerly touched his swelling eye. "Aye," he agreed hoarsely.

Angus turned and left without another word, his brother and the princess following him in silence.

Fiona glanced at Cadwal before she left, feeling guilty for being the reason for his suffering, though she doubted Angus or Malcolm would see it that way. She would much rather Lady Nuith have a black eye than a mere lad who was also a Scot. She was not queen yet, nor did she feel like the princess—such honour did not feel hers at any rate, regardless of what the McCladden brothers and Rhiada might say.

She only hoped she would one day be worthy of such loyalty. She certainly did not feel deserving of it at present.

It was a dismal threesome that made their way back to the Mc-Cladden croft. Malcolm's hair flew every which way, and its fiery colour made it seem even more ridiculous. Loose strands of Fiona's darker locks stuck out of what had once been a simple plait. Even Angus looked as bad as the other two with his dark hair askew and his plaid pulled loose out of his belt. He attempted to wash the dried blood off his face at the water trough by the stables, but some of it still remained on his woollen shirt nonetheless. Disheartened by the encounter with Cadwal and exhausted by the long hours of archery practise, they stumbled wearily into the welcoming warmth of the croft.

Close behind on the heels of heat from the hearth came a wave of relief as Fiona saw Rhiada sitting at the table with two others, whom Fiona did not recognize; perhaps they were the rest of the McClad-dens. Were it not for their presence, she would have greeted him as openly as Malcolm did, but she was too shy to appear so forward before those who were strangers to her. He seemed in good health; she must content herself with that until a more fitting time to speak with him.

She glanced at Angus, who looked in agitation from Rhiada to the others as if searching their faces to learn what urgent news Rhiada had ridden so swiftly to carry. But the conversation—what she could hear of it—did not seem to be pressing or weighty. Angus seemed to think so too, for his hands, which had rested clenched at his sides, uncurled, even if the rest of him remained tense in expectation. Perhaps the news, whatever it was, had already been discussed. Or perhaps, she mused, as her shoulders eased from the release of tension, perhaps the news was not as bad as they thought. Perhaps they had only ridden so swiftly to be within shelter before dark.

Annag straightened from bending over the fire, stirring what Fiona assumed must be supper, and took their cloaks from them while they hurried to make themselves more presentable. When finished, they hastened to the table where the remaining members of the family were already eating.

Oaten bannocks sat on a platter, still hot from baking, and some sort of thick stew with various vegetables and mutton lay steaming in their bowls. It was warm and filling, very different from the meaty feasts Fiona had experienced with much distaste at Caerloch. She had greatly missed the simple—yet hearty—foods of her own native people since her father had died. Though Annag's cooking was delicious, the stew sometimes stuck in Fiona's throat with emotion as half-forgotten memories of her childhood resurfaced at tasting it again.

No one spoke during the meal, all eating in peaceful silence, aside from Malcolm, who occasionally slurped his broth loudly.

After one such noisy gulp, Fiona heard something between a thump and a smack and looked up to see Malcolm and Angus glaring at each other, Malcolm with some broth now adorning his face.

"Wheesht, ye two," said the young man sitting towards the end of the table. Fiona supposed him to be Duncan, the elder McCladden son. His voice was sharp in his reproval, but his hazel eyes twinkled with the same teasing laughter that Malcolm had, though his hair was much darker in colour than his youngest brother's, as was his youthful beard.

"Angus thwunked me!" Malcolm sputtered. "He made me spill my soup!"

Rhiada chuckled, a warm sound like sunlight upon golden fields, and Fiona smiled. She had rarely heard him laugh, let alone like that.

"Aye, maybe eat it a wee bit more quietly," Angus hissed, his cheeks flushed as if in embarrassment. "Ye're disgracing yerself in front of the princess."

Malcolm looked from his brother to Fiona, an eyebrow cocked in disbelief.

"Angus is right, Malcolm," Annag put in sternly, though Fiona could see her resisting a smile. "Do remember yer manners and donnae slurp yer stew quite so loudly. I am glad ye enjoy it, but all of An Dùn doesnae need to ken it." She shook her head as if to further emphasise her words. The thin fillet of gold woven into her plaited hair, the crown of a chieftain's daughter, gleamed in the dying light of day spilling from the windows as she did so.

"Malcolm, listen to yer mother. Angus, mind yerself. I donnae wish to hear another word from either of ye two until the meal is over." The words, though spoken firmly, echoed with laughter. Fiona glanced up the table to see an older man with greying hair and a beard that still had remnants of a vibrant scarlet. She assumed he was the High Chieftain, Donald McCladden, for he was the oldest one there besides Rhiada, and she could see in his face a resemblance to Malcolm and Angus. A twinkle of merriment danced in his deep blue eyes when he met her gaze, and Fiona decided in that instant that she liked him and his openness, so unlike a certain one of his sons.

No one else said a word until the end of the meal when Rhiada set down his wooden spoon with a slight clatter to arouse everyone's attention.

Malcolm glanced up, his spoon halfway to his open mouth, but seeing that Rhiada was not going to address him, resumed eating in peace.

"So, I heard ye arrived in the Lowlands without much incident?" the harper questioned, an uncertain look on his face. Perhaps Annag had spoken to him, since Fiona did not recall seeing Chieftain McCladden or Duncan at all that morning, unless her arrival was common knowledge in the village.

"Aye, I suppose ye could put it like tha'," Fiona replied after a moment, looking at Angus.

He did not meet her gaze, staring instead at the candlelight flickering on the surface of the table. She did not understand. He had seemed amiable enough last night. What had changed?

"And ye and Cameron?" she added nonetheless.

"We had a wee bit more difficulty." He sighed softly and pushed his empty bowl forward, leaning his clasped hands on the table. "The morn after ye disappeared, Lady Nuith had me thrown in the dungeons, accusing me of plotting against her and intending fer my execution in yer place."

"In the dungeons?" Malcolm squeaked. "How did ye ever escape there?" He licked the last of the stew off his spoon.

Rhiada smiled, though whether it was because of the way Malcolm said it or because he was glad to tell the story, Fiona did not know; she supposed it to be both. "Cameron found a way, smuggling me out under pretence of execution. If ye wish fer the full story, ye can ask him. All I ken is he rescued me out of there and we rode south as swiftly as we could. He is now safely wi' his family. And, Fiona, Sgàil is in the stables here."

The princess smiled, not having expected that piece of good news.

But she said nothing as the harper continued after a moment, the smile vanishing from his scarred face. "However, we need to act quickly."

Fiona's heart sank heavily to the pit of her stomach, a cold discomfort creeping over her. She had only arrived in the Lowlands last night. She had hoped for a reprieve from the constant threat of death. Was she not to find peace, even here? Must she always be on the run for her life?

"Wha' do ye mean?" Angus questioned, glancing up at the Cymreig bard. Fiona thought perhaps that she saw the same fear in her own heart reflected in his blue eyes, but she could not be certain in the dim light.

"Lady Nuith kens Fiona's gang, and she also kens where, though no' the exact location. She is already making plans to find her, gathering forces among the Danes to battle against us if need be and bring her back dead or alive. Dead, she will bury the body herself. Alive, and she'll hae her executed publicly as a warning. 'Tis only a matter of time until she wages the first battle, and we need to be ready if we are to survive at all."

A tense silence followed his words.

Angus looked from Rhiada to Fiona, studying her for several moments. She felt her face grow hot, but did not look away, forcing him to return to staring at the candle flame reflection, a wave of red embarrassment rushing over his features.

Though she had known Malcolm for scarcely more than a few hours, she supposed that no matter the situation, she was fairly certain she could guess how the lad would respond. Angus, on the other hand...warm loyalty sometimes peeked through his typical, cold quietness. He was unpredictable, and that made her uneasy around him.

"What is the plan?" Duncan inquired. His voice was much deeper than Angus' but still had the lively lilt of the Lowland peoples.

"We need to meet wi' the other Lowland chieftains and decide what to do. Donald, wha' are yer plans wi' that? Do we ken where they stand?"

Fiona looked nervously from her teacher to the High Chieftain, wondering how he would reply.

Donald McCladden pushed away his empty bowl and cleared his throat. "We're gang to hae a council meeting tonight wi' those from the Lowlands tha' arrived this afternoon. I wish fer Princess McCurragh and my sons to be present as this is a serious matter in which their futures, as well as ours and Scotland's, are at stake." He glanced at each of them in turn, his sober tone matched by a look of sympathy in his light eyes as if pitying their youth, thus shadowed by the threat of war. "We had all hoped to hae more time wi' ye, princess," he continued in a gentler voice, addressing her directly, "but tha' is yet to be seen. Nonetheless, let us hope tha' things are nae so dark as they seem." He smiled encouragingly, but his words fell hollow on Fiona's ears, lost as she was in a resurgence of despair.

She had come all this way, and still, it seemed, she was not free.

"Donnae fret, sweet lass," Annag said softly to her as they rose from the table. "We must nae give up hope so easily. Nae all is lost." She touched Fiona's shoulder briefly, warm against the sudden chill in the lass's bones that had followed Donald's words.

Fiona forced a smile to her face.

Aye, she must hold to hope.

~ 10 ~

Flamelit Council

SHADOWS rose as the sun sank beneath the darkening horizon. Fiona stepped into the chill of the autumn twilight and walked to the Council Hall, Chieftain McCladden and his elder sons guiding Rhiada a few paces ahead of her. Malcolm's tripping footsteps sounded behind her as he kicked the occasional pebble out of the road and breathily whistled snatches of a jig tune. The village was otherwise still, the smoke from the croft chimneys trailing softly into the star-pierced sky. Her breath came out in white puffs, and the cold air nipped at her cheeks and nose, no doubt colouring them rosy red. But despite the restful calm around her, her mind was not at peace.

Within her breast warred various emotions and thoughts of what lay ahead. She wondered with nervous apprehension whether the Lowland chieftains—like so many in the Highlands—held her accountable for the deeds of her father. Would they blame her for the state Scotland was in now?

Fiona sighed heavily, tasting bitterness in her mouth. It was not her fault, was it? She was not the one who married Lady Nuith, nor the one whose armies failed to conquer and drive back the Danes. As for the War—no one could truly be held accountable for that. The Scots had done their best; their best had simply not been enough.

Now the threat of the Danes had arisen again, and the Scots must rise again to meet it. To do any less would be nothing short of cowardice. Fiona hoped that she would not fail the chieftains' expectations of her, whatever those might be, and if the chieftains judged her for her father's deeds, so be it. It was beyond her control to dictate how they might think of her.

The thought was little comfort.

Breathing deeply to calm the fluttering of her anxious heart, Fiona McCurragh entered through the doors to the hall, held open by Chieftain McCladden, leaving the starlit twilight behind her.

The Council Hall was lit by torches stuck in brackets along the walls, though peat also burned brightly on a raised hearth in the centre. Around it was a long round table with benches on its outer rim. Intricately engraved wooden beams supported the roof above, firelight dancing upon the carvings, the uncertain light casting eerie shadows upon them. The earthy smell of peat smoke filled the air, and Fiona inhaled it with delight, the familiar scent putting her slightly at ease.

Malcolm slipped around her as Duncan and Angus helped Rhiada take a seat at the table. At that moment, Fiona noticed the others present in the hall with her and she clenched her hands, nerves tingling painfully in her fingers.

"Chieftains, gathered here from yer own clans and valleys," Donald McCladden began, still standing, "may I introduce Princess Fiona McCurragh, the last of her line and the heir to the Scottish throne?"

Fiona glanced around the room, trying to smile but feeling as though the effort failed miserably. The chieftains bowed their heads in acknowledgement of her, their faces in the firelight a distant memory from the days before the War. Malcolm grinned at her, the sight of it warming her more than the fire did. Angus' gaze flicked up and met hers for a moment before he looked away in silence, his expression unreadable.

"Princess Fiona," Donald McCladden continued, smiling kindly at her, "may I introduce the other High Chieftains of the Lowlands?"

She took a step forward into the firelight and nodded, wondering whether she was supposed to remain standing or if she was permitted to take a seat with the rest. She inhaled sharply to calm her nerves, her mind racing. She was terrified of doing the wrong thing by accident and then suffering the chieftains thinking ill of her because she was ignorant.

"As ye might have guessed," Donald began, "these High Chieftains are only figureheads of the many clans. They represent those who cannae be here this evening, and will lead their men should this come to war. But all of us, regardless of what we might otherwise disagree on, are loyal to the true crown of Scotland and thus are united against Danish oppression." He paused to clear his throat. "Jamie McBride, the youngest of us, is from the south where danger also lies at the hands of the Saxons."

Fiona met the soft brown eyes of a man not much older than Duncan McCladden, his curling hair falling to his shoulders. He bowed his head gently in recognition but did not speak.

"Bryce MacClydno governs the lands to the west of the Lowlands, where they face attack from Danes by sea, as well as by land," Donald continued, gesturing to the man closest to her. "He is also my *athair-cèile*," he added in a soft undertone, acknowledged by others around the table with knowing smiles.

Fiona's first impression of the man was of a wild boar, and from his looks, she had no doubt that Bryce was equally dangerous when provoked. Short but stocky, he emanated a fierceness she had scarce seen. Dark eyes glistened in his tanned face, and the very air around him seemed to tingle with suppressed energy. He clasped his fist over his chest and bowed respectfully, his thin lips tightened in grim silence. She could not believe he was Annag's father; Annag seemed so gentle in comparison. How had Donald ever won MacClydno's trust to wed his daughter? And yet she recognised his plaid as the one Angus had worn at *The Raven's Wing*. It made sense to wear another clan's tartan if that clan was not so distant from his own.

"Welcome to the Lowlands, my princess," said another chieftain before Donald could speak again, his soft voice ringing with musical tones much like Rhiada's did. He was wiry and lithe, hinting at the same power that Bryce possessed, but in a gentle, subdued way, like a forest bear. His brown eyes shone in the light as he smiled encouragingly at her. "I am Eachann MacDonald, High Chieftain of the lands to the southwest."

"By Cymru?" Fiona asked, attempting a timid smile in response. She was overwhelmed by their respect, something she had not experienced much of in all her years at Caerloch, even before her father married Lady Nuith.

"Aye, by Cymru." He sat down at the table, his smile seeming to grow brighter at her knowledge of his lands.

"And I am Alastair McThraedan, yer highness," said the last chieftain, his flaxen hair betraying his Saxon-Scot ancestry. His blue eyes matched Angus McCladden's, though his gaze twinkled with laughter more like Donald's. He dipped his head in a quick bow before sitting down beside Eachann.

Donald smiled at Fiona, gesturing to the empty seat beside Malcolm, the others taking their places in silence.

"Now tha' the danger of the Saxons has been repealed, we must turn our attention to the north," Donald McCladden began. "The Danes are growing stronger under their new leaders, Laird Erland and Lady Nuith of Caerloch. Soon they will muster enough forces to push through our guard, and we will be utterly defeated." There was an unmistakable tone of urgency in his usually passive voice.

Hopelessness once again washed over Fiona at his words. She stared into the fire, exhausted and despairing, the chieftains' voices rising and falling like the ocean tide. She had thought—had hoped— that escaping into the Lowlands would bring her freedom from the threat of death and the importance of Scotland's political state. Of course, as princess and the last heir to the throne, the latter thing would be inescapable, but it seemed death intermingled with anything pertaining to Scotland's future, a cost none of them wished to pay unless absolutely necessary.

"We mustnae forget the Saxons," Alastair warned, clasping his hands on the table before him. "They can still overrun us if they gather all their forces."

"Some believe 'tis a hopeless case nae matter wha' front we fight on," Bryce broke in, his deep voice firm and unquestionable. "We cannae hope to e'er regain the forces we once had. Many believe we will ne'er defeat the Danes and that 'tis useless to even try."

Silence fell.

"'Tis true the Lowlanders lost many in the War against the Danes, but so did those in the Highlands," Rhiada answered softly.

Fiona glanced up quickly at Angus, but he did not meet her gaze, his fingers fiddling with the edge of the table, chipping away at some minuscule splinter in the aged wood. But as she looked closer, she could see his knuckles showing white through his skin, as if gripping the wood helped him hold his composure. Was he thinking about Sioned?

"Are there any in the Highlands tha' are wi' us, or are they all fer Lady Nuith?" Bryce inquired, looking at Fiona.

Fiona met his gaze, realising he was speaking to her, and her cheeks flushed hot. She squirmed under his penetrating gaze and glanced nervously at Donald and then Rhiada, her mouth suddenly very dry. "I donnae ken," she said hesitantly. "I believe there are some, but I think Rhiada would ken better of tha' than I."

"Ye must remember that Fiona has been locked away fer at least three years," the harper replied, "and kens almost nothing of what has taken place outside the walls of Caerloch Castle. But aye, there are some loyal to our cause."

"How many?" Jamie questioned, speaking for the first time, his voice gentle like a summer breeze.

"Perhaps four High Chieftains; I donnae ken fer sure."

"Is tha' all?" Malcolm broke in, forgetting he was not an active voice in the assembly, even if he was a present witness. "I'd hae thought there'd be more."

Fiona saw him wince and then scowl at Angus; perhaps Angus had kicked his younger brother beneath the table.

Rhiada turned his scarred face in Malcolm's direction. "Nae, but they hae many clans underneath their rule who are answerable to them, same as in the Lowlands. There may be more, but we donnae ken where all their loyalties lie. 'Tis hard to measure reluctance to bow to Lady Nuith's wishes and answer her invitations to Caerloch as loyalty to the Scottish crown. I could be mistaken entirely in this," he admitted. "Besides, even if they are loyal, they may no' be willing to take up arms against the Danes. If we fail, they will be punished first, being nearest Caerloch."

Malcolm nodded in understanding. "Aye, I see now."

"Wha' are we to do then?" Eachann asked, looking from one man to another. "We cannae jist sit here while the Saxons and the Danes overrun us, and we become nae more than a memory in the history of this nation."

"Nae, we willnae jist sit here," Rhiada responded gently, soothing the anxieties that had risen to a palpable state in the hall. "Lady Nuith is gathering forces now that she kens that Fiona has successfully escaped—and, she presumes—to the Lowlands. She will overrun us soon if we donnae prepare fer war now."

"So soon?" Angus McCladden gasped, looking up suddenly. The

blood drained from his face, and something flickered in the depths of his eyes.

Fiona gazed at him, wondering if perhaps he shared the same fear she did. Then again, perhaps it was only the light from the fire dancing across his face, eerily shadowing his high cheekbones, that gave the appearance of fear. He had seemed courageous enough at *The Raven's Wing*; why would he suddenly be afraid now?

"Aye, war, and soon," Rhiada returned solemnly.

If any hope of peace and security remained in Fiona's heart, it vanished at those words like sun behind storm clouds. She stared into the fire again, wondering whether there had been any point in fleeing from Caerloch to begin with. Her troubles were not over at all, it seemed; if anything, they had only just begun.

"War is inevitable," Donald declared, rising to his feet. "There is nowhere left to flee. If we fled from the Danes, there would still be the Saxons. We must fight if we are to survive. Either we will stand together and fight fer our families and our belov'd country, or we will die fighting each other. We mustnae fall to tha' as we hae in the past. We mustnae dishonour the name of our belov'd Scotland. I donnae ken the standings of everyone here, but I do ken where I stand.

"This is nae longer a matter between clans. This is nae longer a matter between chiefs. And this is nae longer a matter of the High-lands and the Lowlands. This"—his finger jabbed at the table before them—"is about Scotland, our Scotland. Wha' we decide here and now will affect the future of the nation tha' we and our ancestors hae struggled so hard to build." Donald paused and looked at each of them in turn, his eyes afire with passion that likewise inflamed his words. "I willnae leave and abandon my country when her future is at stake. I willnae dishonour the charge tha' was given to me by my father. I willnae dishonour my late king, and I will nae dishonour my princess.

"I will die before I let the fate of our fathers come upon us." His voice climbed in volume until it seemed to break through the very rafters above them. "We must not die fighting in petty squabbles while the future of our nation hangs in the balance. Death before surrender! Death before dishonour! Death before disloyalty!"

His fervent words hung suspended in the air, as if one had only to reach out and touch them. There was silence save for the crackling flames on the hearth as a chunk of peat crumbled, the firelight rising and falling back down again.

Strong emotion welled up inside Fiona and she blinked back the tears, not understanding Donald's fierce passion to her family's throne, to her father's crown, to her! For so long she had been treated as a nuisance, as something to be gotten rid of as soon as convenient. To suddenly be worth dying for was almost beyond comprehension, and she looked down, too overwhelmed to do anything else. A passionate ache throbbed in her chest, and she did not trust her voice to reply; it was hard enough to keep the tears from spilling over.

Rhiada stood, leaning on the table for support. "Are we all agreed then?" His voice, though soft and gentle, shattered the quiet that had fallen upon them.

Murmurs rippled through the room, but they seemed to be in agreement rather than dissension.

"Death before dishonour," Eachann repeated solemnly.

Fiona rolled over and opened her eyes, her brow beaded with sweat. She could see nothing except a darkness deeper than her dreams.

She sat up and pushed away the tartan blanket, creeping towards the window in silence, careful not to wake the others sleeping in the room. She pushed the shuttered window ajar and gasped at the chill air that pierced through her like icy arrows.

The skies were black, the stars having vanished behind clouds, and there was no lighter band near the horizon.

Must be still many hours till morn, she mused regretfully. No matter how exhausted she was, she dreaded lying down and closing her eyes again. Nightmares of Lady Nuith plagued her, stealing what rest she might otherwise have found.

She had scarcely been in the Lowlands for more than a day and already there was talk of war. The peace she had hoped she would find did not exist. She had practised beyond what she had ever done before with the McCladden brothers, and gone to a council with the Lowlander chieftains, with whom she had never previously spoken to in her life. The relief she had felt at arriving safely and seeing Rhiada again had faded away, the old, familiar shadow of fear and despair darkening what hope she had left. Not even Donald's passionate words of courage and loyalty could spark it back to life.

Fiona closed the shutters and snuck back to her bed, looking at the dim forms of the sleeping individuals and seeing an empty place in the corner beyond where the McCladden brothers slumbered. She rested her hand for a moment on the hearth wall beside her, embers still glowing faintly. Perhaps the fire yet burned downstairs.

Glancing once more at the occupants on the other side of the room, she crawled to the door and opened it, flinching at the slight creaking noise it made, before tiptoeing downstairs.

Fiona blinked in the reddish light of smouldering peat. Rhiada sat before the hearth on a chair, his cloak bunched up around him, his eyelids closed over empty sockets. He turned his head towards her as she reached the bottom of the stairs and asked softly, "What is it, Fiona?" His voice was soft and tender, like Douglas' had been whenever Fiona was frightened or sad and he had wished to comfort her.

She came closer to the harper and sat down, leaning her head against one side of the hearth. "How did ye ken it was me?" she said in a low, dull voice.

"Ye are the only one who goes down those stairs like that, gingerly as a cat does. Annag walks down gracefully, her footsteps light as a feather. Donald goes down firm and determined, as he is wi' everything else. Duncan charges like a horse in battle, while Malcolm skips 'bout half of them and jumps t'other seven steps, usually managing to trip o'er at least one on the way. Angus runs down them in a strange, peculiar pattern. I heard none of that, so it had to be ye. But come now, what is bothering ye, Fiona?"

She pulled her knees up under her nightgown and clasped her arms over them. "I donnae ken." She stared into the flames, letting her vision blur against the dancing shadows.

"Ye donnae ken?" he repeated, leaning forwards a little.

"Well, I donnae ken how to say it," she admitted. "At least, nae in a manner which ye'd understand."

"Gae on. I'll understand ye well enough." He leaned back, his eyelids remaining closed as if to better concentrate on what she would say.

But there was only silence for some time.

"I'm afraid, Rhiada," she finally said in a small voice, tears welling up in her eyes and the painful lump rising in her throat as it always did when she thought about the War and the uncertain future.

"Afraid of wha'? Ye didnae seem to be so afraid earlier during the council."

"Och, but I am!" It was a quiet cry, barely more than a whisper. She sighed softly before continuing, a shuddering breath that caused the embers to glow brighter for a moment. "I suppose I am afraid of wha's coming. Of another war. Of wha's expected of me. Of failing. Of appearing in their eyes as a little child unable to lead an army—let alone a country.... I'm afraid of losing, of being held captive again, of facing imminent execution and nae kenning if I will live to see the next sunrise.... So much is expected of me and—and I donnae ken what to do."

The embers ever so slowly diminished into a faint, uncertain light.

"Fiona, ye shouldnae be afraid," Rhiada said at last.

"Why no'?" She turned to look at him, no longer cringing at the staring scars on his face that ensnared shadows where his eyes had once been.

"Because ye're a human being jist like the rest of us. Ye fail, and so do we.... War is coming and there's nothing we can do about it except face it head-on. I will guide ye in leading the forces and so will Donald. Nae king or queen is ever without their councillors; and ye hae been locked up fer three years. We ken ye will need advice, and we donnae think the less of ye because of that. The chieftains donnae see ye as a little child and neither do I; ye are our princess—and hopefully one day our queen."

She did not answer, returning to staring at the dying flames. Rhiada's words were none too convincing.

"Fiona," he continued, his voice soft like the whisper of a wind. "Life is full of battles. Ye cannae escape them. Ye can only prepare to stand yer ground and fight them. Else ye can only flee; if ye flee, the battle will only be postponed fer another day.... Life is full of defeats, even as it is full of victories. Defeats may be devastating, but if ye survive them, they will make ye stronger in the end."

She looked up at him again, his words echoing in her head, and answered his question with another. "Rhiada, wha' happens if I am captured again?"

"Ye neednae be afraid. Ye will be rescued."

"How can I ken that?" she asked, her fears anything but at rest.

"Fiona," Rhiada bespoke with a sigh, "loyal people still exist. Wha' hae I been telling ye about the McCladdens all this time?"

Fiona hung her head. It was true. Yet she still felt uneasy, for a reason she could not exactly explain. Perhaps it was because of the late hour and the exhaustion of the day before. Perhaps it was something else entirely, but she was too tired to try to think it through.

Bidding Rhiada good night, she climbed back up the stairs, lying down and staring into the darkness, the harper's words echoing in her mind.

Loyal people still exist. Life is full of battles; ye can only prepare to fight them.

If what Rhiada said was true, then would she ever be at rest? Or would she be fighting for her life until the end of her days? If that was the case, then life would not be worth living. Surely there was something else in the world that was worth fighting for: beauty and love and peace and security...

Or had the Danes destroyed that, too?

~ 11 ~

A NARROW ESCAPE

YOU promised me she would be dead!"

Drummond MacDougall heaved a sigh and wheeled around. "Sister, this is but a temporary setback—"

"I do not wish to hear of temporary setbacks!" Lady Nuith snapped, looking up at him, masked terror in her eyes. "If they succeed in raising a rebellion, they might strike before we have gathered enough forces to counterattack, and then all we have worked for will be lost!" Her voice rose to fever pitch throughout her speech until it collapsed into silence, her chest heaving as she struggled to catch her breath. Her crimson skirt billowed around her as she halted her pacing, coming to a standstill before him.

"Raising a rebellion requires time. If we strike before they are ready, we will still win." He held out his hand as if to calm her, but then decided against it, his arm falling slack at his side. "I will yet keep my promise to ye."

"How can I trust that you will do so? You promised she would not see the dawn, but the dawn has come and yet she lives. Do you even know her whereabouts?" Her voice was more controlled now, but a note of fear still hovered in her tone.

"Lachlan jist came back wi' word that she swas at *The Raven's Wing* tavern last night." He turned and gestured to the young man standing behind him who had remained silent all this while. "Nae other place within a day's ride has seen her."

"But she is not there now?" Lady Nuith prompted when he did not continue, terrified anger darkening her eyes.

A heavy silence lay between them for a moment, the pale glimmer of early morning beginning to shine in the torchlit hall.

Drummond shattered the silence with a cough as he cleared his throat. "Nae, she isnae there now." He flashed his gaze towards his half-sister. "I hae sworn to ye that I will end her life. But now I must do it in my own way and in my own time. If she resists capture, be certain that I will do unto her and all that hae sworn loyalty to her the same as I did unto that harper she dares to call her protector." He spat the words out as if they disgusted him.

Lady Nuith pursed her lips. "Fine words indeed," she scoffed, "but I still do not know where your true loyalties lie, brother." She drew out the last word, usually a term of endearment, twisting it until it seemed to be as distasteful as mentioning the princess herself.

He hesitated before replying, Lachlan scuffling behind him. "I had thought—I believed my motives were clear enough by my actions against our enemies, but if ye cannae believe that, I donnae ken how else to persuade ye. Whatever it takes, I will see Fiona McCurragh dead, and nae jist herself, but also those who support her; ye hae my word." He turned his back on Lady Nuith and addressed Lachlan. "Get a troop ready to leave within the hour. Search all the towns, villages, and crofts within a day's ride and farther, if need be. I will join ye presently."

Lachlan bowed his head and left, leaving Lady Nuith to follow him out.

Drummond turned and placed his palms on the table, heaving a sigh. This was quickly becoming far more difficult than he had anticipated. But nonetheless, a promise was a promise.

And he intended to keep it.

Fiona opened her eyes, blinking as the world around her came into focus. A faint, bluish light lingered around the cracks of the shutters, hinting at the coming dawn. She sat up cautiously, not wishing to wake anyone, and glanced over at the sleeping figures through the dim darkness. No one else stirred at this early hour. Their even breaths disturbed the chilly, silent morning, and someone snored softly—perhaps it was Malcolm. A smile spread across her face at the idea of Malcolm snoring.

After listening a moment longer, she seized the small bundle of her clothes that lay beside her, which she had brought from Caerloch, and crept down the stairs as softly as she could.

The room below was dark, a reddish glow burning on the hearth, remnants of the peat embers. Rhiada had fallen asleep in the chair where she had left him hours ago, his head drooping over his chest.

She hesitated, uncertain whether to wake him or not—his position appeared very uncomfortable—but he must have been exhausted from the day before. So she let him be, slipping outside the croft without a sound.

The air was bitterly cold and, for a moment, Fiona regretted leaving her warm bed. But she soon walked on, clenching her teeth to keep them from chattering. It would be worth the chill to finally scrub off the dirt of her journeying, and she did not wish to bother Annag or the rest of the McCladdens by asking for heated water and privacy to do so.

Fog lay in eerie swaths about the buildings, nearly hiding them from view, but running back and forth the day before gave her a general understanding of her surroundings, and she felt fairly confident as to where she was headed. Making her way to the north entrance, Fiona glanced upwards at the towers, glad the fog was thick enough to hide her from the guards' gazes. She did not wish to answer questions of where she was going. She unlatched the small door inside one of the double gates and stepped outside An Dùn, heading towards the wooded burn where they had practised archery.

Low, hazy clouds obscured the late autumn sun, wrapping the golden horizon in silver. Birds sang, hidden amid the leafless boughs of the forest, their sweet song piercing the cold morning air. All was still, a peaceful stillness, and for a moment, Fiona forgot her fears of the future, sighing in delight at being free and able to go where she liked with no one to stop her.

At Caerloch, she always had to obey Lady Nuith's wishes, hoping the lady would be in a pleasant humour to let her ride out on the moors. But that was seldom, her freedom dependent on the whims of her captor. Yet now she was no longer the captive.

Fiona reached the burn at last, the distant target where they had practised only yesterday covered in sparkling frost. She scarcely noticed the frost or the chilling breeze, feeling as light and free as the clouds suspended above her in the dawning sky. Glancing around to make certain she was alone, she slipped out of her clothing and entered the burn, flowing still this late in the year.

She gasped in shock as the freezing water met her bare skin. Fiona grimaced at the cold and did not linger in the frigid burn longer than necessary, washing herself with more haste than she had in years.

Shivering, she dressed quickly in the clean clothes that she had brought with her from Caerloch, her numb fingers trembling as she tied the back of her dress. She ran her fingers through her wet hair, pulling back some of the crimson strands into a plait, a shaky hum of a tune escaping her lips as she did so. It was a wonderful feeling to be able to scrub off the dust from the last several days, even if it meant diving into an icy burn.

Placing her old, begrimed clothes into the bundle she had brought with her, Fiona made her way back out of the forest to the path running towards An Dùn. The hum had turned into song, a lilting jig that matched the rhythm of her steps. The birds twittered merrily with her as the sun rose higher and higher in the sky, scattering the drifts of fog. She glanced up occasionally from the dirt path, gazing at the moorland stretching as far as the eye could see and musing on what it would be like to be lost in such vast, untamed beauty.

Thundering hoofbeats choked the melody in her throat as she neared the main road.

Fiona lunged into the heather bushes closest to the path, grateful that the spiny gorse lay opposite. Her heart hammered in her throat and she felt sick with fear, much as she had when the Danes had nearly discovered her and Angus on the moors. Only this time, Angus was not here to protect her.

She squeezed her eyes shut, wondering why she had been such a fool as to leave An Dùn in the first place. Of course she was not free! Danger still lurked even here, in the Lowlands, and always would until Lady Nuith was no more.

Her eyes flew open as the horsemen passed right before her, riding out from the fortress town. A chill ran down her spine as she recognized the crimson raven on their tunics. There was no reason for men from Caerloch to be here, unless they were looking for her— she and Rhiada, and possibly Cameron if they also suspected him guilty of treason.

Her breath hitched, and it was several tense moments before she deemed it safe to rise from her hiding place. Grabbing her long skirts with her free hand, she began to run the remainder of the way to An Dùn, hoping that Rhiada was still alive. She had not seen him among the horsemen, but they had been some distance away.

The gates came into sight within a few moments, and she slowed her pace to a brisk walk, staring in horror at the two Scottish guardsmen lying before them, unmoving. She looked down as she approached, her face burning, noticing the heavy silence; the birds had stopped their singing. One of the guardsmen was clearly dead, the other one—it was hard to tell. She swallowed, her throat suddenly dry. If the Danes had found her...would they have killed her too? Or just taken her to Caerloch for Lady Nuith to do so?

At that moment, others came running out of An Dùn, speaking hurriedly to one another and shouting commands to those now standing in the guard towers. None of them noticed her.

She stood still, watching them check the two men for signs of life and carry them into the village, their words imperceptible. But it didn't matter whether they yet lived. It was all her fault, was it not? If it were not for her, the Danes would not have come to this fortress town, the home of the Lowlanders' High Chieftain, and taken the lives of his guardsmen. Any treaty between the Lowlanders and Lady Nuith would not hold now. The thought sickened her.

"Fiona?"

She raised her head at the familiar voice, her cheeks still inflamed. "Aye, Angus?" Her voice was barely a whisper.

He reached her side a moment later, his dark brows drawn together, his cheeks and nose rosied in the cold wind. "Fiona, where hae ye been? I—we were so worried fer ye!" His voice was soft but urgent, the weight of guilt growing only heavier on her shoulders.

Biting her lip to keep back the tears, she answered, "I went to the burn to wash, tha's all. I thought it would be safe, but...it seems I was wrong after all." Her gaze flickered upwards to meet his, something of sympathy or understanding shining in his deep blue eyes.

"Nae, 'tis fer the best. Danes came here jist some time ago and only now left. They were looking fer ye. Of course, they couldnae find ye because ye were gang, so I suppose it was a good thing ye werenae here." He hitched his shoulder awkwardly in some sort of shrug, peering off into the distance where the Danes had gone. "I jist hope they donnae come back." This last part was said in a whisper, as if he did not mean for her to hear.

"Is Rhiada safe?" she ventured, shivering in the morning chill, her damp hair sticking to the back of her dress. The image of the wounded guardsmen being carried inside flashed before her eyes and she shuddered.

"Aye, he is well. We hid him up in the loft and they didnae search hard enough to find him." Angus paused, looking at her in silence. "Ye shouldnae be out in the wind, no' wi' yer hair all wet. Come ye." He took her gently by the hand, a comforting warmth spreading from his fingers to hers, driving away the cold. Without another word, he led her to the croft, slowing his steady stride so she could keep up in her long skirt.

Fiona said nothing, wondering at the quick change in him. This was more of the Angus she had known on the moors, not the quiet and brooding lad of yesterday. What had happened to soften him so? And what caused him to clam himself up against the world at times? She received no answers by merely thinking and she was too timid to ask. All she knew was that the sense of danger had vanished, safety taking its place as it always did when she was with him. Though she found his manner towards her confusing, Angus was nonetheless an asylum against the threat of the Danes and the fear they had wrought in her heart. She only wished she could understand him and his moods.

Thin trails of smoke rose from several of the chimneys as people began to prepare themselves for the new day. The air was crisp and cool, carrying with it the rich scent of peat smoke. Here and there, a few men walked about, changing the guard at the gate, and others on various errands. It all seemed as if the Danes charging into An Dùn that morning had never happened.

They reached the McCladden croft at last and Angus let go of her hand, opening the door for her instead. Fiona released the breath she had been holding as she entered, feeling the warmth emanating from the hearth.

Annag stood before the flames, stirring up the embers and feeding the fiery blaze for making porridge. She stood and turned around as Angus shut the door behind them, staring at Fiona curiously and then chuckling. "Ye're a brave one and nae mistake," Annag said, shaking her head and smiling.

"Wha' do ye mean?" Fiona asked, confused by her words. She had expected Annag to show the same worry that Angus had, not smile at her in wonder.

"Fer going out there and bathing at this time of year. No' even my own sons do that. Most of the time during late autumn and winter we bathe inside, each taking turns upstairs. I could hae heated the water fer ye if ye had told me 'bout it."

She was about to say more when Angus whispered something in her ear, the smile on her face fading into something like shock. Fiona supposed it to be the fate of the guardsmen, at least what little they knew of it. Then Angus, giving Fiona one last glance, slipped out the door again.

As soon as he was gone, Annag continued, "I suppose it was fer the best, wi' ye nae being here. We were all so worried fer ye when they came."

"I am sorry fer that, truly, I jist didnae wish to make a fuss about it." Fiona's voice trembled against her will. "I forgot tha' I was still in danger and I—"

"Hush, sweet child." Annag came to her and laid her hand on the lass's shoulder. "Nae one's laying the fault at yer feet. We cannae change wha' happened, but 'twas safest this time that ye were gang. But next time, if ye wish to bathe, tell me. And if ye are gang out, even if 'tis jist fer a walk, take Angus or Malcolm wi' ye. Ye are Scotland's only hope of regaining the throne, and none of us wish to lose ye," she said tenderly. "Donnae worry about it more."

Annag turned away to the fire, leaving Fiona to make her way to the room above and place her bundle beside her bed, folding up the tartan blankets and stacking them neatly against the wall. The room was empty of anyone else, so she made her way downstairs again to help Annag prepare for breakfast.

She smiled kindly as Fiona laid places at the table and took steaming bowls of porridge from her hands. Fiona wondered if, perhaps, her own mother would have treated her with the same kindness that Annag did. Would her mother have been so kind to her if she knew that her daughter had come so close to capture? Or would she have treated her as Lady Nuith would have? Then again, Annag was the first woman of Fiona's acquaintance to treat her with any kindness at all. Lady Nuith scorned her and plotted her death. Annag treated her as if she were her own daughter. Fiona was not quite certain what to make of it.

She was, however, certain of one thing as the other McCladdens came in for breakfast, bringing Rhiada with them. Though none of them mentioned what had transpired that morning, the feeling of danger and broken peace still hung in the air, a discordant sound against the usual hum of life. After years of an uneasy truce between the Danes and the Lowlander Scots, the Danes had entered An Dùn without warning and without a justified reason except that they wanted her. They had left without her or Rhiada—but had taken the lives of two innocent men.

Whatever plans or expectations the Scots once had for the future, the peace between them and the Danes was broken. No other course remained for them now except a declaration of war.

~ 12 ~

WAITING

THWACK.

Fiona jumped as another arrow sped from Malcolm's bow and landed in one of the outer rings on the target. The fallen log she sat on was uncomfortable, and she shifted her position. Her thoughts disrupted, she glanced at the burn beside them where she had washed only a few hours ago. It was a slightly embarrassing memory to think of, with both of the McCladden brothers here now.

She was glad no one had mentioned the incident at breakfast, either her disappearance or the Danes arriving in An Dùn, let alone the attack on the guardsmen. All seemed to act as if none of it had happened, as if they did not wish for the shadow of the Danish threat to darken what little safety they had as a family. Only Donald had spoken of another meeting with Rhiada, Duncan, and the chieftains, that the three of them did not need to attend, of which she was grateful. She knew little of such councils, and constantly worrying about saying the wrong thing or appearing inadequate as the heir to the throne made it more unpleasant than anything else.

Seeing Cadwal on their way to the archery range had been unpleasant enough.

Malcolm had bid him a cheery "hail and well met!" but was returned with stony silence. Cadwal's face was still bruised and swollen, his eye a dismal black. His scowl towards Angus was more an ugly grimace with the colours on his face. Angus had only sniffed in response, as if he remembered the bloody nose the lad had given him in return. Fiona felt sorry for Cadwal, for it was indeed partly—if not entirely—her fault that he was in such a pitiful state. She also hoped his father was not one of those attacked that morning; Malcolm, she was sure, would not have greeted him so genially otherwise. But Cadwal did not look at her at all; only bowed his head slightly as he passed, his eyes warily fixed all the while on Angus' face.

Fiona turned and looked at Angus now, where he sat on the other end of the mossy log. He rubbed a piece of rabbit skin up and down his unstrung bow, polishing the ash wood until it gleamed in the grey light.

She had relished the sunlight pouring through the windows when she, Rhiada, and the McCladdens had broken their fast. But, an hour or so later, the sun hid its golden face; Fiona disliked the dreary darkness, chilled by the early November winds. Winter was on its bitter way, and she did not know what would become of her—of any of them—before spring came again to the world.

She wondered whether the Scots would go to war this winter. The Danes' arrival that morning was enough of a threat to incite such, but only a fool would march out with the threat of snow. She averted her gaze to the ground. Wondering would not bring her answers. So she said to nobody in particular, "I wonder wha' they are meeting fer this morning."

"Wha' do ye mean?" Malcolm inquired over his shoulder as he fitted another shaft to his string.

"I thought we had said everything tha' needed to be said last night. We are all in accord wi' the matter of fighting against the Danes, are we no'? Wha' else needs be said?"

"They are making plans," Angus put in quietly, running his hand up and down the smooth wood of his bow. Seeming satisfied, he tucked the rabbit skin in his belt and laid the weapon aside.

"Wha' sort of plans?" Fiona questioned, turning to him.

"Plans fer the war." He did not meet her gaze, staring at something in the grass by the burn instead.

"War?" Malcolm exclaimed, turning around. "I mean, I ken we hae to fight battles, but an actual war?"

"Aye, of course, daft limmer. Ye cannae fight battles without there being a war."

Fiona laughed, a hollow sound that stuck in her throat. It was not truly something to laugh about, not when she just might be fighting in it herself. True, she was the princess and one of the reasons it would be fought—if not the main reason—but Scotland needed every warrior she could muster; the last war had cost so many....

"They hae to ken how many men there are, wha' place would be best fer the first battle, the amount of weapons we need, where the women and children need to gae to be safe, and wha' place would be best fer a meeting place of all the men who will fight against the Danes—among other things," Angus put in, as if the interruption had never happened.

"Tha' is a muckle amount to discuss," Malcolm mused, turning his attention back to the target.

"Aye. Tha' is why the chieftains are meeting," Angus responded in a low voice. His face was paler than usual, his blue eyes dark and fearful. But of what? What was he afraid of? Sioned was long dead, even as Douglas was. Unless it was the preparations that reminded him of that time before, and he was reliving those days all over again. But she did not think Angus to be that sort. He was young, not an old man like her father had been.

Fiona turned away from him in silence. Despite Rhiada's words from the night before, she was still frightened. She had hoped to at last be free and spend a few weeks at least in this place before war needed to be spoken of. It appeared as if that was not to be, especially after the Danes' intrusion only that morning.

"How soon do ye think until they are ready?" Malcolm asked, breaking the quiet that had fallen upon them. He had finished his round, gathered his arrows, and was now walking towards his brother.

"Och, I donnae ken," Angus said lightly, as if he was merely observing the weather. He held up his bow and peered at it in the fickle sunlight. "Could be a few days, a few weeks, or even months. Maybe there willnae be a war trail, nae until spring." The note of fervent hope in his voice caused Fiona to look at him suddenly. Memories of the last few weeks flashed before her eyes: his challenging words when they first met, questioning her on her weaponry skill; the council, Rhiada speaking of coming conflict; sharpening his weapons, sparring for hours. The mere mention of war always resulted in the same reaction from him—fear. She swallowed hard, understanding dawning upon her.

Neither of them were made for war, were they? Whatever his reasons, perhaps something to do with Sioned, Angus was terrified of it. Fiona herself abhorred the thought of killing, of destruction and the taking of human life.

But war there must be, while the Scots remained hunted outcasts and the Danes ruled the land.

"I hope it's sooner than spring," Malcolm answered excitedly, bringing Fiona back to reality. He plopped down on the log beside her as his brother rose for his round of archery.

"Ye willnae be gang wi' us," Angus warned over his shoulder. "Ye're far too young."

Fiona did not hear Malcolm's retort. She heard only what Angus had said prior, "a few days, a few weeks, or even months." Would it really be that soon? She hoped not. Was war truly the only answer? It had already claimed the life of her brother and, in a way, her father—as well as the lives of many Scots, not to mention severed Scotland in two.

And so she wondered, with dread in her heart, what this war might bring.

The growing wind's hostile gusts prevented any more practice at archery, much to Fiona's momentary relief. She was exhausted by the happenings of that morning, and her arms were sore from the constant practice. Even at Caerloch, she had never practised this much nor so often. But her relief was short-lived when Angus and Malcolm pulled out their swords and began to fight sham fights. Malcolm used a wooden blade as he had not yet acquired one made of steel, which perhaps made the match uneven on his part, but Fiona noticed that he was skilled enough to not need one.

Angus and his brother fought several rounds first, the elder winning most of them, his size and skill being greater than Malcolm's. Fiona watched them with interest, her arms locked around her knees and her long skirt tucked in around her ankles. The sounds of metal hitting wood and the shouts of the two as they exchanged blows disturbed the otherwise peaceful quiet near the burn.

When Malcolm tired after ten minutes had passed, he threw himself to the ground beside Fiona and clasped his hands over his eyes, his chest heaving from the effort of his swordplay. Sweat streamed down his face, though the wind was frigid as it whispered through the leafless trees.

A shadow fell over the princess, and she glanced up to see Angus glancing blankly at her. Sweat beaded his face, his nostrils flaring in an effort to regain his breath and yet slow his breathing to normal. "Ye ready?" he questioned flatly, squinting against the bright sunlight that shone for a moment through the dense cloud cover.

"Aye," she responded, rising to her feet. Picking up the sword lying beside her, she pulled it out of its sheath with a ringing sound.

They began slowly at first, and then faster and faster until they were striking and dodging blows too fast for Malcolm to follow, as he announced by exclaiming, "Och, slow down a wee bit before one of ye gets hurt!" Neither of them paid him much attention, not when the duel was so much in earnest.

Angus' face was stern and fierce, his dark brows drawn together as he parried one blow after another from the young princess. His intense concentration was intimidating, as if he was focused solely on defeating her, as if..she was the Danish enemy and not the princess to whom he had previously shown passionate loyalty.

If she had not been so concerned with blocking his blows—she wondered how much of this was really a sham fight—she would have been terrified by his cool-headedness. It was eerie enough just glancing at him in between parries. She struggled enough keeping up with him and blinking against the sweat that rolled into her eyes and burned her vision.

At last, they pulled back in a draw, neither of them winning against the other.

Malcolm clapped his hands together, grinning. "Now tha' was a fine sight fer sore eyes!" He feigned a groan as he stood up. "I but wish these old bones were young again. Aiee! A fine fight indeed!"

Fiona smiled, unable to laugh as she tried to catch her breath, and wiped the sweat off her forehead. She slid her sword back into its sheath and peered up at the sky, the sun vanishing again behind the clouds.

"Shall we go back then fer luncheon? I'm starving," Malcolm continued, picking up his wooden sword.

"Aye," Angus gasped, his chest still heaving from exertion. "Let's gae."

Rain poured from the skies after the midday meal. Torrents of icy water pooled on the earth, turning the dirt paths and courtyards of An Dùn into muddy puddles and streams. Thunder rumbled in the distance, ominous and frightening.

Fiona watched it all from the only glass window in the croft, the raindrops racing down the panes. She was glad, if only because it was quiet and peaceful in the McCladden home, and because the rain meant practice time was over. Her arms were sore, and her head ached from the constant activity of the last few days.

Annag sat in the corner where her loom was, her shuttle passing in between the threads with a rhythm that suggested a tune, except the melody was lacking. Rhiada sat before the fire, his hands resting in his lap, his eyelids closed. Donald and Duncan had returned before the rains came, but they were elsewhere in the village now, perhaps meeting with the families of the lost guardsmen.

As for Malcolm and Angus, they were lying on the floor, engaged in a game of nine men's morris. Or, at least, Angus was actually playing while Malcolm squeaked at odd moments when his brother succeeded in removing one of his pieces.

After one such loud exclamation, Rhiada stirred in his seat, turning his head in their direction. Fiona watched him, beginning to feel the chill of sitting so close to the window but unwilling to sit by the fire for the time being.

"Hush ye both," Annag warned, her shuttle never hesitating in its horizontal dance.

"I donnae mind," Rhiada said gently. "'Tis good to hear their young voices after so long. Caerloch is lacking in that regard."

"Aye, but I donnae wish fer them to bring down the roof," Annag replied, glancing over her shoulder at her sons.

"Yer move," Angus mumbled, resting his chin in his hands as he lay on his stomach, facing his brother.

Malcolm hunched over the board, scowling. "Why doesnae Fiona play? She's the only one yet who doesnae lose against ye. 'Tis nae fair tha' I always hae to play this daft game."

"'Tis nae daft. Now make yer move," came the swift reply.

Fiona rose from her seat by the window and crossed the floor, sitting beside Rhiada's chair. She stared into the dancing flames, glad of the warmth but struggling to keep from falling asleep. Her eyelids felt so heavy, ready to close at any moment.

"Is everything all right, princess?" The harper's voice was gentle and soft, intended only for her ears.

She shrugged, blinking sleepily. "I am jist tired, tha's all."

"I suppose the sudden scare this morning hasnae helped matters, has it?" he continued in the same whisper.

"Nae," she replied after a moment. "It has no'. I suppose I shouldnae be surprised by it, but...I still wish it hadnae happened all the same."

He shifted in his position, withdrawing his arms from where they were buried in the folds of his cloak that he wore even indoors. Perhaps it kept him warmer in the cold, damp weather. "Well, if ye donnae mind, ye could always practise the harp. Jist because ye donnae hae to play it fer Lady Nuith nae more doesnae mean ye need give it up. Besides," he added with a slight smile, "it always made me feel more at peace in hard times. There is something healing about music that brings comfort that words cannae."

Fiona rose to her feet and stepped to the corner to fetch Rhiada's harp. At that moment, Malcolm threw his game pieces across the room, narrowly missing his brother's head.

"Why, why, why do ye always win? I swear, I am ne'er gang to play wi' ye again!" He jumped to his feet and collapsed in front of the fire, his chin in his hands, glaring at the flames as if they laughed at his plight.

Angus merely gathered the pieces together and put the game away, settling on the other side of Rhiada's chair in silence.

Fiona hesitated, holding Rhiada's beloved harp in her hands, wondering where she was supposed to sit now and wishing the brothers were still playing their game. She did not wish for an audience, especially not them—especially not Angus. She was terrified of him hearing her rough skills. He probably knew how to play the instrument himself and therefore would gauge her playing against his as he did with her knowledge of weaponry and everything else.

As if he could read her thoughts, Angus moved to sit on the stones beside the hearth, leaning his head against the wall and closing his eyes for a moment. Malcolm edged away from him, still scowling.

Fiona settled by her teacher's side once more, tentatively plucking the strings one by one, acutely aware of Malcolm's and Angus' eyes on her. She wondered if Rhiada expected her to simply run through the dance tunes he had taught her in the beginning, or whether he also wished for her to sing. She hoped it was not the latter.

The firelight danced on the harp strings as she began, but the strathspey was far too slow. The strings did not obey her fingers and buzzed unpleasantly on the wrong notes. She finally stopped midway, her hands falling into her lap. Her face burned, and not from the heat of the fire. She had never played so terribly in her life. What must Angus and Malcolm think of her now, a princess who knew little of her country, knew little of harp music, and only had skills in weaponry? She should never have bothered to practise it in the first place.

"Why'd ye stop?" The scowl on Malcolm's face was gone, his clear grey eyes glistening with interest in the light.

Fiona's gaze flickered up to meet his, her cheeks still hot with embarrassment. "I messed it up." Her voice was barely more than a whisper.

"Everyone messes up. There's nae shame in tha'," Rhiada put in softly. "Try the song ye practised fer Lady Nuith, nae the pieces ye hae barely played before."

Fiona was not much comforted by his words, for even if it was the song she knew best, she was none too keen to sing for Angus and Malcolm, even if they did not mind.

She began again, more hesitantly this time, a mere echo of the song she had once triumphantly played before the woman who wanted her dead. Perhaps it was the rain and thunder outside, perhaps it was the blue eyes gazing at her so intently while she played, perhaps it was the taste of freedom and broken peace—perhaps it was all those things that made it so different this time. Only the nervousness was the same as before, her heart fluttering in her throat, choking the words that must be sung.

She did not quite know how she was able to sing it through without making any more mistakes. Fiona was only aware of how melancholy the song seemed now, the last line of *The Highlands Are Calling Me Home* lingering as a sad echo in the air. It had never caused her chest to tighten as it did now. Perhaps having left the Highlands which had been her home made the song all the more dear to her, but perhaps it was also because it was a lament; in light of the inevitable war, the words seemed all the more meaningful. A lament, and yet a song of hope. She had left her home, but now was among those who respected her and treated her as the princess she was supposed to be. They might all yet come home.

"Tha' was beautiful," Malcolm said with a wistful sigh. He was about to say more when the door opened below, Donald and Duncan's voices flying up the stairs to greet them. The lad jumped to his feet and ran down the steps in the same flighty manner Rhiada had described last night.

Fiona set the harp down beside her, glancing at Angus.

He met her gaze briefly and returned to staring at the fire, but she thought she saw tears in his eyes before he blinked them back. He clenched his jaw and swallowed, refusing to look at her again.

Fiona bit her lip. Why did he always bury his feelings inside of him? Why did he refuse to let anyone in? Fear, she understood, but this was something more than fear. This was pain, deep pain, but she did not understand it. What had happened to make him feel this way? Was it Sioned? Or something else? She could see it was breaking him, killing him from the inside out—and he would never see it, not even if she told him. He had protected her from her greatest fears, aye, but could she protect him from himself?

She rose to her feet, looking at him once more before going down the stairs with Annag, who lent her arm to Rhiada to guide his way. They would be eating supper soon—the smell of simmering stew had teased her senses the past hour—and there was no reason for any of them to remain there any longer.

As soon as Rhiada was safely seated at the table, she returned up the stairs, hoping that she could speak to Angus, even if it was only to tell him that she understood perhaps why he hurt so much—did she not at times feel the same about Douglas?

But he was no longer seated beside the peat fire. He stood by the harp, his dark, curling hair falling in shadows over his face. He reached out one finger and plucked a string, the sweet sound reverberating in the empty room. A look of twisted pain crossed his face and he turned away, the same tears as before shining in his eyes, threatening to spill over.

He caught sight of her, standing on the steps watching him, and the pain vanished, replaced by the stiff, pale mask of nonchalance.

Fiona felt as if someone had stabbed her in the heart, even if she had only meant to tell him that she understood now why the

War was so painful to him. Why did he not trust anyone? "They're waiting fer us downstairs." It was partly true, though she said it more out of a need to distract from the fact she had seen him exposed in the firelight.

He only nodded. "We'd best be gang down, then." He passed her on the stair without so much as a glance.

Fiona swallowed, her chest aching with helplessness. He was not only hurting himself, but her as well—and certainly his family, for surely they saw his wounds too, did they not? They must see it, but perhaps they did not know what to do about it. Unless she was the only one to truly notice, having struggled much the same with Douglas' death. She looked at the harp sitting before the fire, a silent witness to all that had happened.

Would any of them ever heal from what the War had done? Or would the coming war only make it worse?

She returned to where the rest were gathered around the table as Annag began to ladle out stew for the evening meal. If Angus could fool everyone, then certainly she could feign that what had just transpired never took place. So she smiled and she laughed at the things Malcolm said as everyone else did.

Everyone except a blue-eyed lad who buried his pain deep within and never let anyone understand why he hurt.

~ 13 ~

NO TIME

WIND gusted across the sweeping moorland, bending the heather in waves like the rolling ocean. Fitful sunlight peeped through the clouds, the golden rays devoid of warmth.

Fiona reined Sgàil to a halt as she crested a rise, laughing in breathless exhilaration while she waited for Malcolm to catch up. Her cheeks were ruddy from the icy mistral and her hair was blown every which way, but she did not mind. It was a glorious morning, and she was glad to run free, escaping the rumours and plans of war for a time.

Malcolm rode his brother's horse, a soft brown mare with a gentle temper. Fiona was not quite certain whether it was better that the mare did not share Angus' high-strung tendencies or not; she was easier to control, but too subdued for warfare if indeed it came to that.

The smile vanished from Fiona's face at the thought even as Malcolm drew alongside her, panting heavily, his curly hair all askew from the wind.

A wide grin broke across the lad's face once he caught his breath, and he threw his head back and laughed. "Aiee, tha' was a fine ride, was it no', Branwen?" He patted his horse's neck, and she neighed softly in reply, tossing her fine mane. Malcolm turned to Fiona, his grin fading into a look of concern. "Everything all right, princess?"

She forced a smile on her face, thrusting aside the thought of the Danes and of the coming war. "Aye. I was only thinking."

He scowled, squinting into the brightness of day. "Angus must think a lot then. If thinking turns people so solemn, I want none of it." He glanced at Fiona, and she laughed at the expression of disgust on his freckled face.

"Thinking isnae bad in and of itself," she protested with a smile. "But I agree, 'tis a waste to spoil a day by thinking instead of riding." She dug her heels into Sgàil's flanks, leaving Malcolm to shout in remonstrance and attempt to match her pace again.

The wind beat against her as she rode into it, leaving her too breathless to say anything in reply to his outburst. Not that anything needed to be said; the world was wide and free and theirs for the taking. Together, they raced over the braes, laughing for the sheer joy of simply being alive. They did not return to An Dùn until the rains began to pour from the skies, soaking through their clothes and leaving them shivering with cold.

Fiona and Malcolm walked their horses into An Dùn, their merry spirits broken by the rain. Malcolm wrapped himself in his cloak, his teeth chattering as he handed the reins of Branwen to one of the stable hands. Fiona did the same for her mount, pausing to kiss Sgàil's nose in farewell before following her companion and bodyguard to the McCladden croft.

It was odd to think of Malcolm as such. Angus seemed more a bodyguard than his brother, with his seriousness and passion for Scotland's crown, but Fiona disliked riding with him at the best of times. Malcolm talked more than enough for both of them, but Angus' silence often unnerved her when they rode together. All the same, she was glad at times when he guarded her instead of Malcolm, for his silence or quiet words could be a comfort when she wished to avoid conversation.

"I hae to say," Malcolm piped up, startling her thoughts. "Ye're a much better companion than either of my brothers."

Fiona chuckled nervously. What was that supposed to mean? "How so?" she asked aloud.

"Well"—he drew the edges of his cloak tighter around him—"ye laugh a lot more than Angus does. Riding wi' him brings about as much fun as riding wi' a ghaist. And when we're no' riding, he must always practise swordsmanship or archery or some other nonsense." The lad sighed heavily. "And Duncan's most always teaching the young lads weaponry at the practice ring and when he's nae there, he's wi' his lassie, Elsie McDrumnoll." Malcolm cast a woeful glance down an alley as they passed it.

"Wha's wrong wi' Elsie?" she asked when he did not continue.

Malcolm shrugged, biting his lip. "Och, nothing." But his voice betrayed that it was everything.

Fiona placed her hand gently on his shoulder and was glad that he did not push it away. She did not think Angus would let her do such a thing to him.

"There's nothing wrong wi' her, only that Duncan spends more time wi' her than he does wi' anyone else. He used to teach me how to use the sword—he's a much kinder teacher than Angus—before he met her and before Father began taking him to all the chieftain gatherings.... I jist miss the times we used to spend together, tha's all."

The melancholy tone in his voice tore at her heart. Fiona slid her arm across his shoulders as they walked through An Dùn, wishing there was something more she could do besides speak meaningless words.

Malcolm inhaled sharply and plastered a grin on his face. "But I can understand why he likes her."

Fiona smiled, uncertain of where this was leading. "And tha' is?"

"She makes delicious meat pies." He skipped on ahead and laughed over his shoulder at her expression of confusion. "Come on, princess, Mother's waiting fer us! 'Tis almost time fer the midday meal!"

Only Rhiada and Annag were in the McCladden croft, but Malcolm and Fiona did not mind. Angus and Duncan were usually at the practice ring training the other lads in the village anyway, and Donald was in more councils with the other chieftains. All in all, the midday meal was a quiet affair, and when they retired upstairs for the afternoon, the rain made a peaceful sound as it drummed on the roof.

Malcolm dozed as he lay before the fire, his head resting on his arms. Annag sat in the corner, working on the tapestry that formed beneath her fingers on the loom. As for Rhiada, he sat in his chair, listening intently as Fiona played her slow airs, the songs coming as readily to her fingers as she wished they would have when Angus had been there before.

She finished and laid her hands against the strings to silence them, listening to the rain falling softly upon thatch above them.

It was a pleasant sound, and she just might have fallen asleep like Malcolm if Rhiada had not asked her to practise her strathspeys next.

Fiona sucked in a breath, the familiar tingling of nervousness shooting through her fingers. The music came hesitantly at first, the notes laughing at her as she tried to catch the tune and wield it to her own advantage. But it grew nonetheless, becoming confident and strong, like her and Sgàil rushing across the moors beneath a wind-torn sky.

Malcolm rolled over onto his back and blinked. He hoisted himself up with a grunt as she continued to play, resting his hands on his waist, his feet gently tapping the floor to the rhythm of the dance.

Fiona met his gaze briefly, a smile playing on her lips as she guessed what he was about to do. With a stream of running notes, she began the strathspey from the beginning, counting eight bars before repeating the melody again.

Flashing a lopsided grin, Malcolm danced, arms held high above his head like the antlers of a stag, his feet pointing and kicking in heart-pulsing rhythm to the music. His plaid, hanging loose from when he had fallen asleep, started to slide off his shoulder when his arm rested at his waist for a few bars. With one deft motion, he pushed it back up without missing a beat, turning until he faced Fiona again.

Fiona's hands fell into her lap in helpless laughter at the comical sight. Malcolm continued nonetheless, his face beaming. He finished the dance and kicked his heels together, managing to lose his balance as he landed, promptly collapsing on the ground in front of her and Rhiada.

Annag turned around to see what the commotion was but merely shook her head and returned to her weaving.

As for the victim himself, Malcolm merely rolled over, facing Fiona upside down, and winked. He laughed breathlessly for several minutes before sitting up and heaving a great sigh. "Aye, tha' was fun."

Fiona giggled, the corners of her eyes wet from such amusement. She could not recall the last time she had laughed so hard. Had it really been six years or more?

The door below them opened and closed, and before Fiona could give the harp back to her teacher, who had listened to them both with a smile on his face, Malcolm was already bounding down the stairs.

Fiona followed in enough time to catch the latter half of the story Malcolm was eagerly relating to his father and brothers. When he came to the part of him falling on the floor, both Duncan and his father chortled merrily, but it was Angus who surprised her the most. A slight smile spread across his face, brightening his features in a way nothing else could.

Her breath caught in her throat at the sight, and she felt almost intruding to have seen it. He smiled so rarely, and almost never because of joy. Had he ever smiled for that reason since Sioned had died?

He glanced up, meeting her gaze, and the smile faded as swiftly as it had come. Though it might also have been because Donald mentioned the boredom of war councils to Malcolm, for the same haunted look she had seen before replaced the smile. His eyes darkened in fear, and Angus turned away as if ashamed. But of what?

Fiona returned upstairs, not certain what to make of him. She did not understand why he held himself so distant. Was it because of Sioned, or because he was afraid of believing in beauty and hope, in good things that would last? She did not know how she could help him, only that she understood and she wanted to ease the burden if she could.

But would he ever let her?

A week later, Donald McCladden summoned his sons and the princess to the Council Hall. It was a grey day, the clouds without form or shadow but dark against the hidden sunlight. The air was still and biting, making Fiona's face numb by the time they stepped into the firelit hall. Even during the day at this time of year, peat burned on the hearth, providing warmth and light to the room. Malcolm blew loudly on his hands to warm them and stamped his feet as they entered, ignoring the dark look Angus shot towards him as he did so.

The High Chieftains were already seated around the table, Rhiada and the others soon joining them. Cheerless daylight streamed in through the windows, and Fiona could see the dim carvings on the rafters, looming dark in the shadows.

She sat down between Malcolm and Rhiada as they waited for Donald McCladden to speak. It was silent in the hall, peacefully so, but a tense energy filled the place, a spirit of expectancy. The future of Scotland hung in the balance, and her fate would be determined by what Donald would say.

At last he rose to his feet, his fingertips resting on the table, almost as if to support himself. Then he addressed them all, saying, "War is coming upon us, and we must be ready. We had hoped, once the princess was safe, to wait until spring before assembling our hosts. But the Danes' intrusion of An Dùn, and their meaningless wounding and killing of our guards, destroyed tha' hope. Our few spies reported yesterday evening tha' Lady Nuith is assembling a small army against us. She means fer war, and we hae nae choice but to attack before we are overrun. We hae had nae word from the chieftains in the Highlands and methinks we cannae wait fer them. We must strike first and we must strike hard before the Danes hae a chance to destroy us." He sighed heavily, one hand reaching up to stroke his scarlet beard in thought, and Fiona noticed the dark circles under his eyes. "I had hoped we could wait to fight at any other time than winter, but we hae nae choice. Therefore, this is the plan of action the other Lowland chieftains and I hae agreed upon."

He paused, glancing at Bryce MacClydno and the others before continuing. "The women and children will stay here wi' a small guard, enough to protect this place should it be attacked. If Rhiada does no' object, I would like Fiona to ride wi' us as she is the heir to the throne and may provide hope fer those who are despairing of our cause. All men and youths of fighting age will assemble here within two weeks' time before we ride out, including my sons, Duncan and Angus."

"I donnae object, but I prefer to keep the princess out of the fighting unless absolutely necessary. In the event that we need every warrior on the battlefield—which may well happen, considering the odds against us—I willnae stop her from fighting wi' us, since she has been trained. Nonetheless, her life must be protected, as much as we can do so," Rhiada replied, the other chieftains nodding in agreement.

Fiona glanced at Malcolm beside her, his face crestfallen at being considered one of the "children" that his father mentioned. As for her, she was glad not to be left behind but still more terrified to be going with them. What if the Scots failed? What if she was captured by the Danes? Was it wise to ride into danger after having so narrowly escaped it? Her stomach twisted at the thought of being disloyal to the cause, but her fear often got the better of her.

"Then it is settled." Donald's voice broke into her thoughts, bringing her back to attention. "I want every able-bodied and fighting man in yer provinces to equip fer battle and to meet us at An Dùn in two weeks. We shall encamp southeast of Drumdae Forest, and there await news from our scouts regarding the Danes' movements. Any questions?"

The chieftains shook their heads, murmuring in agreement to what Donald had said. It was clear that they had already discussed it at length, perhaps during the times when Fiona and the McCladden brothers had practised weaponry together.

Only Rhiada raised an objection, his voice soft and yet carrying throughout the entire hall. "It will still no' be enough men."

"Wha' do ye mean?" Fiona questioned. The combined forces of the Lowland clansmen seemed a mighty enough war host to her.

"The Danes are many, and they surely hae sent fer reinforcements from their own countries. We will be outnumbered. We still donnae ken how many from the north are wi' us. Nae word has been heard from the Highlands, even as Donald said. Who kens, perhaps they will even fight against us."

Fiona gazed at her mentor in shock, not recognizing the words of despair that came from his mouth. He had always been the one to speak hope to her, but now his speech was hopeless.

"But wha' other choice do we hae?" Bryce asked.

"Aye," Alastair McThraedan agreed. "We cannae jist do nothing."

"We can ask fer help from my own country, Cymru. They are also beset by the Saxons and by Danish pirates along the coast," Rhiada stated. "They understand our struggle and may be willing to ally themselves wi' us, unless things hae changed since I was there last, some seasons ago."

"Perhaps 'tis best to wait," Eachann said softly. "'Tis an ill thing, this winter's warring."

Donald sighed. "We donnae hae the time to send men to Cymru and wait fer a response. If we cannae turn the tide in our favour, I will consider it then. Unnecessary lives may be lost without enough men, but we hae nae choice. 'Twould indeed be best to wait, but if

we donnae attack now, despite the coming winter, Scotland may no'
see spring again."

There was a pause. No one dared to argue, for his words were
true. Fiona closed her eyes for a moment, wondering if they could
even succeed. What small hope they had was only a little light against
the great darkness against them. She could not bear for more lives to
be lost for her sake and for freedom's. Was it truly worth it?

"Anything else?" Donald inquired, but no one said anything
more. They all rose and bid one another farewell, the other Lowland chieftains departing to their own provinces. They would return
within two weeks to bind themselves for one purpose.

War.

~ 14 ~

RIDE OUT

FIONA walked among the picket lines outside An Dùn, pausing to check that Sgàil's saddle girth was not too tight. She ran her hands through the pack containing her weapons and extra clothes, making certain she was not forgetting anything. There would be no turning back once they rode out.

That was not an especially comforting thought.

Fiona patted Sgàil's flank, leaning her head against her mare's warm neck. She closed her eyes, breathing in the sweet scent of horse. In the last two weeks of preparation, she had not had much time to simply exist, to not be constantly rushing from practice to practice, the knowledge of what it was for haunting her steps. She almost wished she could stay in An Dùn, stay with Annag and Malcolm during this winter's warring. Then she could be safe, even if Angus and Rhiada, her protectors, were going with the war host and would leave her behind.

War. The very word sent a chill up and down her spine, her hands clenching Sgàil's mane, her fingers tingling in nervous anticipation. War had cost her so much already; she was afraid of what it might cost her now. She was afraid of what was coming, of the inevitable storm. Yet she let no one know of the turmoil that was inside her. She would rather die than admit to anyone she was afraid—except maybe Rhiada. But even then, Rhiada's words of courage had not consoled her. Maybe someday they might, but not now. Perhaps Angus was right to hide his pain. It almost seemed as if it would be easier, that way.

"Ready to ride?" Malcolm's voice rang out from above, interrupting her thoughts.

Fiona glanced up to see Malcolm perched bareback atop Branwen, his brother's horse. "Wha' do ye mean?" she asked, giving Sgàil a gentle pat on the mare's neck before stepping away.

Angus came up to them with a scowl on his face. "Get off there, Malcolm. Ye're nae gang wi' us. Stop fooling around."

Malcolm slipped off with a thud and snapped back, "But ye and Fiona are gang!"

Fiona followed them in silent curiosity as Malcolm went after Angus, who was busy inspecting the horse lines, making certain all was ready for departure.

"Fiona needs to be wi' Rhiada, who's also riding, and I'm already of age. Ye're still too young to fight in a war, so ye're staying home. I doubt we'll destroy all the Danes this once, so I'm certain ye'll get yer chance soon enough." He moved on, leaving them behind.

Malcolm huffed, his shoulders drooping. "Och, right? 'Tis nae fair!"

A memory of Douglas, eager and excited for the war trail, flashed before Fiona's eyes. She swallowed the bile that rose at the thought of Malcolm likewise riding out and not coming back home, such a young soul crushed forever in death.

Before Malcolm could wander off, Fiona grabbed his arm and turned him around, her words harsh. "Malcolm, stop being such a daft limmer. Ye cannae gae wi' us because ye're simply too young, so stop trying to change tha' as 'tis nae gang to do anything." She sighed softly. "Why do ye even want to gae to war?"

Malcolm's face flushed in embarrassment. "I am strong enough and skilled enough! And Father says they need all the men they can get."

"Aye, but war is a dangerous affair. If Donald didnae wish fer me to come, I would stay wi' ye and Annag."

He bit his lip, holding back words that in any other circumstance he would have had no trouble saying.

"Malcolm, wha' is it?"

But he only muttered some sort of reply she did not catch and then trudged off, leaving her alone.

Fiona stood still, wondering where she was supposed to be. She inhaled deeply as a sudden, icy gust of wind blew through the picket lines, carrying with it the damp smell of horse and cooking fires. She looked up at the grey sky and shivered, noticing how the darkening clouds hailed coming rain.

She returned to the McCladden croft and stepped inside, glancing at the diminishing stack of Rhiada's and the elder McCladdens' necessary belongings remaining by the door. Some of these effects could be worn, such as their weapons, but the rest would need to be carried in some way. Hers were already secured to Sgàil's saddle.

Annag swept the hardened dirt floor; Fiona had noted early on that she was not one to sit around doing nothing. She looked up as Fiona stood on the threshold but did not say a word until she finished sweeping and put the broom in the corner.

"Wha' is it?" Annag asked tenderly, coming towards her and placing her hands gently on the princess's shoulders.

Fiona sighed softly, glancing at anything but Annag's face for fear of losing her composure. An uncomfortable lump lodged in her throat that she could not swallow, and a bitter taste remained in her mouth. "I wish I didnae hae to gae—or at least, tha' ye could come wi' us." Her voice sounded odd in her ears.

Annag wrapped her arms around Fiona, holding her tightly.

The young princess buried her face into Annag's shoulder and tried not to cry. But the tears came nonetheless, and muffled sobs broke the silence between them. She clung to Annag as though she was the only certain thing left in the world.

Annag stroked the lass's hair, running her fingers through the crimson locks. "Shush now," she whispered soothingly. "There's nae reason to be afraid. Ye are strong. Ye can face this coming war."

"But I cannae!" Fiona cried out in frustration, tears streaming down her face. "I donnae hae the strength. Ye and Rhiada say tha' I am strong, but I'm no'. I hate it—I hate this fear. I hate feeling vulnerable, but I cannae do anything about it."

"Och, but aye, ye can." Annag held Fiona in front of her and looked into her eyes, wiping away the tears. "Ye can because ye must. Ye represent something more now. Ye are our princess and our hope fer freedom. Our lives are bound up in yers. Our fates are wound up in yers. Ye are our only hope to survive against the Danes and bring Scotland back together. Ye must try to be strong because of who ye are and who ye stand fer. Yer courage will come when ye need it. But I ken, it doesnae feel like tha' now, does it?"

Fiona shook her head. "Nae," she choked. "It doesnae."

"It always feels like tha' in life. Ye cannae find a way to end fear without hope. Ye must believe ye will win or die trying. Everyone has fear in different ways. I fear I will lose my sons and my husband. Ye fear about losing the war and being seen as a failure, or even being captured and killed. Donald fears losing the war, let alone too many men and his sons. Rhiada fears losing ye and Scotland to the Danes. And every warrior fears before battle tha' they might die."

Fiona looked at Annag incredulously. "Truly?"

Annag stroked Fiona's face tenderly. "Aye, Fiona. They ken tha' they cannae fight and survive wi' tha' fear, so they tell themselves tha' they will win—tha' they must win. They hae to win or die trying in the attempt. 'Tis called courage, Fiona."

"I thought courage was the absence of fear." Annag's words puzzled her. She had never been told this before. But then, Douglas had died before he could tell her that true courage was more than riding off into the golden sunrise with a smile on one's face.

"Och, nae. They are afraid, Fiona. They are frightened of the coming ordeal, but they push on in spite of it. Tha' is wha' makes a warrior; being able to press on in spite of the barriers. Tha' is courage, and I ken ye hae it within ye. Ye will find yer courage when ye need it most."

Fiona was silent, letting Annag's words sink in. What Rhiada had told her some nights ago made more sense now. *Life is full of battles, Fiona. Ye can only fight them.* "I see," she answered at last. "Thank ye, Annag."

Annag smiled. "Aye, Fiona McCurragh. I ken tha' ye will face this storm and tha' ye will face it bravely. But fer now, I suggest ye dry yer tears and gae join the rest. They're gang to ride out now."

Fiona smiled and rubbed her face, hoping neither Angus nor Malcolm would be able to tell she had been crying. Bidding Annag farewell, she turned and left the croft, heading for the picket lines.

Once there, she located her place beside Rhiada and Donald and pulled her weapons out of her pack. She buckled on her sword and slung her quiver over her shoulder, adjusting her plaid underneath it. Her unstrung bow was tied onto her saddle, within reach in case it was needed. Climbing onto her horse, she nodded to Donald that she was ready.

He grinned reassuringly in response, despite the trepidation glimmering in his blue eyes, and waited as the rest of the company prepared to ride. There were about fifty men gathered outside An Dùn, but according to Rhiada, there would be about a thousand more waiting a few leagues north.

Fiona craned her neck and tried to find familiar faces upon the many men and lads behind her. Duncan was riding on the other side of Donald, exchanging jests with another young man in the saddle beside him. Angus was next to Rhiada, staring straight ahead as the wind blew his dark hair about. His face was expressionless, but his deep blue eyes had a guarded look in them. Fiona thought she could see Malcolm standing with Cadwal upon the gate wall, watching them, but she was not certain. There was more than one youth with scarlet locks upon the battlements.

Donald McCladden called out, "Are ye ready to ride?"

The others responded in unison, "Aye. Ride out!"

"Ride out!" Donald cried, turning back around and starting off.

The horsemen led those on foot, five abreast, past the north gate of An Dùn. They rode by the open gate and Fiona saw Annag in the entrance, waving farewell.

She smiled when she caught Fiona's gaze, and suddenly a surge of warm courage filled Fiona's heart, bright like the sun breaking out of stormclouds. The danger of what they faced remained, but she did not feel as incapable as before. Perhaps, after all, they stood a chance against Lady Nuith. Fiona raised her hand in farewell, grinning back as they continued north, leaving An Dùn and safety behind.

The grin faded into grim determination as Fiona turned and faced the distant horizon—and the unknown future—with the rest.

~ 15 ~

Sound of War

THE horses' manes flew in the frigid gusts of wild wind. Fiona had long ago given up attempting to keep her hair out of her face. Her curling locks stung when the wind whipped them again and again into her eyes, hindering her vision at times, but, like many other annoyances on this long march, it was something she had gradually grown accustomed to.

The war host had joined the warriors from the other Lowland clans some hours before, and now the company, some thousand strong, hurried to arrive at Drumdae Forest before sunset. If sunset it could be called, for the sun had not shone its cheery face all that day, the second day since they left An Dùn. Grey skies warned of coming snow should the air become much colder. Fiona wondered how fighting would be possible if it did snow, since the frost sometimes made the sword blades stick to their sheaths and the bow strings stiff.

A cry resounded on the braes as Donald McCladden called for a halt.

Fiona reined in her horse, having crested the last rise. Before them lay a vast plain and—beyond, a dark, distant blot on the horizon. But she saw nothing that would cause alarm. Baffled, she turned to Angus, who had drawn up beside her, and asked, "Why are we stopping?"

"I donnae ken," he answered softly with a shrug. Squinting as he looked about them, he continued, "Actually, I'm a-thinking tha' dark line o'er there is where we are headed."

"Already? I didnae ken Drumdae was only a few days' ride from An Dùn."

"Aye. We hae been riding fast, but we might yet no' get there before dark." He loosened the reins, and Branwen tossed her mane, still holding her head high.

Fiona looked at him, her brows creased together in a frown. Sgàil nickered to the mare beside her, tossing her head in the fierce wind. "Then should we ride faster?" Fiona continued, wishing for him to speak more than just the few words he usually did. She missed Malcolm's eager chatter and quick laugh, even if it had sometimes made her weary and long for silence.

Angus nodded, inhaling deeply as he peered again at the distant horizon. "Aye, and tha' is why, I think, tha' Father has probably stopped. He wants to ken tha' we are all together. 'Tis a wee bit of a distance to Drumdae yet, and 'twill be easy fer swift riding. But we cannae leave the foot soldiers behind." He glanced over his shoulder. "Father may let some of us ride on ahead to scout out the forest, though. A pity Malcolm will miss tha' riding." He flashed a sudden grin, and Fiona's breath caught in her throat.

He had her brother's smile, Douglas' smile, the sort that lit up his whole face and made others want to smile in response.

"'Tis perhaps a good thing he isnae wi' us. We'd ne'er hear the end of him lamenting his sore feet and empty stomach," he continued, cocking his head to the foot soldiers slowly coming over the hill. A laugh escaped her at the image of Malcolm deploring his hunger and aching body from the long march.

Duncan McCladden glanced at them both as he rode by, those on horse fringing out across the plain. He said nothing as he passed, but the look of curiosity in his face was unmistakable.

The light moment between them vanished, and Angus was once more his silent, withdrawn self. He picked up the reins and urged Branwen forward with the rest, jerking his head for her to follow.

She sighed inwardly and watched him ride on, feeling again the frustration at trying to figure him out. Two months, and he was still as inscrutable as ever. Why had he stopped smiling? Was it because Duncan had seen him? But why would his brother seeing him smile cause Angus to cease?

Her thoughts were interrupted as Donald called out a command among the host for Alastair and himself to lead the cavalry across the plain to Drumdae. The remainder of horsemen would stay with those on foot to protect them should the Danes suddenly attack.

Fiona glanced behind her, seeing Rhiada riding beside Cameron, trusting his horse where his eyes failed him. He would not be going ahead with her for now.

Cameron, catching her gaze, merely nodded, as if to say he would look after the harper until she could rejoin her mentor.

A faint smile of thanks crossed her face in response and then she turned around again, digging her heels into Sgàil's flanks and swiftly rejoining those riding ahead into the cold wind and the gathering night.

The sky darkened unto twilight when the Scots finally reached the southern eaves of Drumdae. The wind died away to an icy whisper as they dismounted to rest for the night.

The encampment spread out along the edge of the forest, tents set up on the outskirts of the wood. Horses were picketed on the plain and tended to for the night while watches were set, guards beginning to walk around the perimeter of the camp. Small fires gleamed in the darkness, bright flares of cheery warmth against the black, chilly night. As nothing was known of the Danes' movements, it was a fragile hope that they would not be drawn to the light. It was too cold to forgo the warmth the fires provided, but all of the Scots knew it might become a danger in the future.

Fiona was grateful for the chance to stretch her cramped legs after many hours spent in the saddle. She had not stood upon solid ground since early that morning when they had set off after their last camp. She was exhausted with so much riding and longed to fall to the ground where she was and sleep. Were it not for her empty stomach and fear of losing her dignity before the chieftains and clansmen she might someday rule, she just might have done so.

Angus came up behind her, resting his hand briefly on her shoulder before taking Sgàil's reins. With a nod in recognition of Fiona's thanks, he led Sgàil and Branwen to the picket lines, leaving her standing alone amidst all the warriors preparing for the evening meal and a night's much needed rest.

Donald McCladden strode up to her and smiled kindly. "Jist a wee bit longer, princess. We must see tha' all the chieftains hae arrived here safely, and then ye will be free of us fer the night." His eyes twinkled merrily in the dim twilight, and she could not help but smile back.

"I think I am nae the only one exhausted by the long march," she replied with a laugh. "But I thank ye fer yer concern," she added softly, still overwhelmed by the thought of other people caring for her.

"Of course, yer highness." He bowed his head respectfully as Bryce MacClydno walked towards them, his face darkened in a scowl.

"Chieftain McCladden," he said grimly as he drew near, looking up at the High Chieftain. "yer highness," he added with a nod to Fiona, acknowledging her presence. His mouth remained tightened in fear...and perhaps anger, though at what she didn't know.

She hesitated, uncertain whether she was to remain with Donald or not. What had made Bryce so worried?

"Aye, Bryce, wha' seems to be the problem?" Donald questioned, his voice betraying both his curiosity and his fear.

"Drummond MacDougall jist arrived wi' four hundred, mostly on foot."

Fiona's heart stopped beating for a moment. What did Drummond mean by joining up with the Scots? Was it a trap to capture her? Or did Drummond truly wish to fight against his father's people? She wished Rhiada was with her at that moment. Her thoughts in turmoil, the old fear came rushing back, threatening to suffocate her. The ground seemed to swim beneath her feet.

Donald laid his hand on her shoulder to steady her, glancing at her with concern. "Danes or Scots?" he replied to the other chieftain.

Bryce shrugged, his eyes glinting in wrath. His hand tightened on his sword hilt, his knuckles showing pale in the dimness. "'Tis hard to tell in the uncertain light. They speak the Scots' tongue readily enough, but tha' may be learned from living here so long. None of our men recognize them, yet our clans hae long been separated because of the War. I donnae ken whether Drummond's words speak true, and I fear if we should choose wrongly by letting him remain wi' us." He jerked his head towards Fiona to further emphasise what remained unsaid.

Fiona closed her eyes, concentrating on the warmth and security radiating from Donald's large hand, on the sounds of men's voices in the distance, the nickering of horses—anything but the imminent danger that had suddenly befallen them all.

"Aye, but any men to help our cause are welcome," she heard Donald continue.

"Unless they slaughter us all in our sleep," Bryce retorted.

There was a sigh, perhaps from Donald. "True enough. This is best discussed wi' the others when we hae a chance. Allow Drummond and his company to rest wi' us, but tell our guards to watch them closely and alert us if there be any sign of danger."

Fiona opened her eyes in time to see Bryce clasp his fist over his heart and walk away. Donald let go of her shoulder and pursed his lips, glancing around the camp. "I am sorry, princess," he murmured, his eyes usually light with laughter now sober and dark. "But we swore to protect ye whate'er the cost and we will do all tha' is necessary to keep ye safe."

She merely nodded, not trusting her voice to reply.

"Angus!" Donald called, and she turned to see the lad come towards them, his hair all askew from the dying wind. "Angus, see to Fiona. Make certain she gets something to eat tonight, and find Rhiada if ye can. I need to speak wi' him."

Angus bowed his head and gestured for Fiona to follow him. As soon as they were a few paces away, he placed his arm across her shoulders and kept her close to him as they walked through the camp.

She did not understand why he did so, but she was grateful all the same. After riding all day and then the news from Bryce, she had no strength left to remain steady on her own feet. She was utterly weary and glad to have him beside her, even if he kept silent.

Someone brushed by them in passing, dark eyes glinting from underneath a hood. Fiona met the hardened gaze as the person hesitated, searching her face. Then the wind picked up, thrusting back the stranger's hood, and she recognized him in an instant.

"Fancy seeing you here, *princess*." Lachlan drew out the last word in disgust.

Fiona shuddered, his voice bringing back the awful memory of being caught in his grasp, unable to escape. She drew away from him even as Angus turned, placing himself as a shield between her and Lachlan. She saw the lad's hand tighten around the handle of his dirk, his back stiff and tense, waiting for any further sign of a threat.

"Who are ye and wha' do ye want?" Angus demanded, his voice harshened in anger. He held onto Fiona's hand behind him, refusing to let go of her.

Fiona clung to him, watching both him and Lachlan in terror. While she did not doubt Angus' skill, she feared what would happen if it came to blows. If anything happened to Angus, she would never forgive herself.

"I want nothing," Lachlan hissed at last. "I was only trying to find my way about. Good e'en to you." He pulled his hood over his face and stalked off into the darkness, vanishing behind a nearby tent.

Angus relaxed his grip on his knife and turned around, his lips parting to speak when he caught sight of her face. "Fiona, wha's wrong?" he asked softly, a look of concern shadowing his face in the warm glow of the nearby fire.

She could not stop trembling. From the moment Bryce had spoken of Drummond's presence here in the camp to catching sight of Lachlan as he passed, fear had choked her. She had escaped death only to run right back into its arms. Gasping sobs of panic escaped her as she sank to her knees, muffling her cries in her hands. She hated Angus seeing her cry, seeing her at her most vulnerable, but she could not hold it back any longer. She felt like she was going to be sick; had her stomach not been empty, she just might have.

"Fiona, 'tis all right. He's gang. I willnae let him hurt ye." She heard Angus' voice, but it seemed to come from a great distance.

There was nothing between her and the great black void of terror.

Strong arms encircled her, pulling her to her feet and gently wrapping themselves around her. Fiona clung to him, tears falling down her face, tears of fear and tears of shame. She was so weary of it all, weary of her life always hanging by a thread but meaning so much in the power struggle between the Scots and the Danes. Would there never be a reprieve?

"Hush now, 'twill be all right, Fiona," he whispered, awkwardly stroking her hair. "I willnae let him harm ye, I promise." He released her and hesitantly wiped the tears from her face. "Rest easy," he murmured, as if calming a nervous horse. "None of us will let him touch ye. Father said we must protect ye at all costs, and I willnae break tha' trust."

She nodded, rubbing the back of her hand across her face and sniffling. "I ken," she choked with a heaving sigh. "'Tis jist...at Caerloch, Lachlan—he tried to..." She glanced off towards the nearest fire, biting her lip.

"But he didnae, did he?" Angus prompted.

Fiona met his gaze and shook her head, one last tear slipping slowly down her face. "Nae, he didnae. Lady Nuith's brother, Drummond, stopped him...but wha' if he tries again?" Panic rose again in her throat.

Angus laid a finger against her lips. "Nae, Fiona. Donnae think about it. 'Tis nae sense to fear wha' may ne'er happen. Come, we must find Rhiada, and then ye must eat and rest to keep up yer strength."

"But wha' about Lachlan?" she said as Angus began to walk off.

"Jist stay close to me or Father or whoever is able to protect ye and kens about this." He sighed and rubbed his temples, evidently as exhausted as she was. "I promised ye, Fiona, and I am nae about to break tha' promise." He held out his hand to her and she took it, the only warmth and protection she had against the cold wind and the tightness within her chest.

They found Rhiada by one of the fires near the centre of camp, wrapped up in his heavy cloak. Cameron was beside him, finishing the last of his porridge. He noticed their approach and nudged Rhiada.

"Fiona?" the harper asked, his eyeless face eerily shadowed by the fire.

"Aye, Rhiada, 'tis Angus and I," she replied, sitting next to him and taking his outstretched hand.

Angus rested beside her, having taken two bowls of porridge from Cameron and giving one to Fiona. He blew softly on his, steam rising in the cold air.

"Ye hae been crying?" Rhiada questioned gently. "Yer voice betrays it," he explained a moment later.

"Rhiada, Drummond is in the camp," she said, her voice trembling at the end. Inhaling a shuddering breath, she warmed her hands on the warm porridge bowl, gingerly setting a spoonful in her mouth.

The harper stiffened, his dark brows furrowing in concern. "Does Donald ken this?"

"Aye, Chieftain MacClydno told us both." Fiona swallowed the tasteless porridge, which lacked the sweet, homey comfort of Annag's but nonetheless heated her up from the inside. "And we passed one of Drummond's men on our way to find ye."

Angus glanced at her, his spoon halfway to his mouth, his eyes asking a wordless question.

She merely shook her head before taking another bite, struggling to force it down. Were it not for necessity, she would not eat at all, not after what had happened.

"Father wishes to speak to ye when possible, Rhiada," Angus said, entering the conversation for the first time. "I assume, to discuss this."

"Did Donald say anything about Drummond?" he asked further.

"Only tha' he welcomes more men to our cause, but he doesnae ken if 'tis safe to trust him," Fiona said.

Rhiada nodded slowly. "Aye, 'tis so." He sighed heavily. "There are things I ken from years ago...." He rose to his feet, leaning on Cameron, who came to his aid. "Unless I see ye again this evening, good night, Fiona. I hope ye rest well." He started off and then paused, turning towards them. "Angus, donnae ye leave her. Dangerous men sleep in our camp tonight, and who kens wha' they might attempt."

"I willnae leave her," came the grim but ready response.

"Good night then to ye both." He shuffled off with Cameron to lead the way.

"Ye done?"

Fiona looked up, seeing Angus standing over her, holding his empty bowl. She glanced down at what remained of her porridge and nodded. "I cannae eat anymore. I am sorry; I donnae mean to waste it."

He shrugged. "I can eat it if ye donnae mind. I think we may be the last to eat."

A grin spread across her face. "I donnae mind. If Malcolm were here, I'm certain he wouldnae hae even asked before it was gang."

He smiled, his blue eyes sparkling in the firelight. "Aye, I suppose 'tis a good thing he isnae. Else yer porridge might hae been gang before ye had a chance to e'en take a bite."

A strangled exclamation pierced the air.

Fiona's laughter died in her throat. "Wha' was tha'?" she asked, jumping to her feet.

The smile vanished from Angus' face, the familiar scowl taking its place. His eyes glinted as his hand slid to his dirk. He set the bowl of porridge down on the ground and stealthily crept to where the sound had come from behind a hastily-erected tent, Fiona following behind him.

A horrid thought crossed her mind: what if Drummond and his men were single-handedly murdering the Scots in the dark?

But before she could voice her worries, Angus stumbled into a shadow and yanked whoever it was into the firelight, thrusting back the green hood.

"Malcolm? It cannae be!" Fiona exclaimed.

Angus merely stared at his brother in horror, the blood draining from his face.

As for the culprit himself, he stared at the ground, his freckled face flushed in embarrassment.

"Malcolm, why? Ye were safe wi' Annag! Why did ye risk yer life to sneak wi' us? Wha' will yer father say?" Fiona threw her hands into the air, completely frustrated and glad to see him at the same time.

"I didnae wish to be left behind," the lad mumbled, the tips of his ears the colour of the flames near them. "Ye and Angus are gang; 'tis no' fair I couldnae come."

"So ye came anyway?" His brother's voice was colder than the air around them. "Did ye think of how grieved Mother would be when she discovers yet another of her sons may die?" He paused, inhaling sharply. "Did ye think of how angered and concerned Father will be when he realises he will hae to worry fer yet another of his sons on the battlefield? Wha' if something happens to ye? Did ye care to think about tha'? Or did ye care only to no' be left behind?"

"Peace, Angus," Fiona broke in, laying her hand on his shoulder. He was bristling in...anger? Or was it more? Was the panic in his eyes fear for his brother? "Malcolm, does anyone else ken ye're here?"

He met her gaze and shook his head.

"Hae ye had anything to eat, then?"

Malcolm shrugged, scuffling at the ground with his foot.

"Here, eat the rest of my porridge." She picked up the bowl and placed it in Malcolm's hands. "I suppose ye'll hae to sleep wi' Angus then tonight." She glanced at Angus, his blue-eyed gaze refusing to meet hers. "We'll tell yer father in the morning once we all hae had some sleep."

Angus sat on the ground, scowling at the flames and refusing to speak to either of them.

Malcolm finished the porridge within moments, setting the empty bowl in front of him, likewise saying nothing.

Fiona watched the firelight sink and rise, the flames providing warmth in the cold darkness.

This would be a long night indeed.

~ 16 ~

SWORD DANCE

LADY Nuith gazed out the window, watching the fine mist fall from the sky and water the earth. Dark grey skies stretched as far as the eye could see, a gloomy light cast over the rolling moorland.

She laid her hand on the stone sill, the dampness sinking into her skin. She was the only one in the room, and for some, the quiet might have been oppressive. But silence was what she needed, a silence in which to sort her racing, tangled thoughts.

"I promise ye I will dispose of her. But I will do it my own way, no' yers, and I will no' hae ye meddling."

Such were Drummond's last words to her when his search for the missing princess had proved futile. And yet she was all the more discouraged by it. Would he truly keep his promise and dispose of that threat to her and her unborn child? Or would he switch his loyalties to his mother's people and destroy her—his half-sister—in aid of the Scottish cause?

Her grip on the windowsill tightened, her knuckles showing white. Would he really fall that far? Could he really fool her so much that she would put him in leadership over the Danish hosts and then take all his men to the Scots to fight against his father's people? Her people?

She heard the door to the room open behind her, but did not turn to see who entered. The footsteps were familiar enough to her.

"Dearest, what are you thinking of now?" her husband, Erland, whispered into her ear as he wrapped his arms around her.

She did not answer, leaning her head back on her husband's shoulder. She closed her eyes, listening to the raindrops patter against the window pane and feeling the warmth of Erland's embrace.

"Is it about the princess again?" he prompted.

Nuith bristled as if poked with a hot iron. "I have told you this before, Erland: I cannot rest until I know she is forever done away with. Our child will not be safe until she is gone."

The silence following her words was as cold as the early winter winds driving the rain against the window.

Lord Erland released his wife and only said, "I will let you know when word from Drummond arrives."

Lady Nuith heard the door click shut, and nothing else disturbed the quiet except the rain. She felt a sharp pain in her abdomen and placed her hand on her swollen belly. "I know, child," she crooned. "I will do my best to ensure your protection in this world." She looked out the window, her pretty mouth hardening into a firm line. "No matter what it may cost."

Fiona walked through the camp, her arms wrapped around herself for warmth. It was a pleasant change to escape endless hours in the saddle, which left a stiffness in her limbs that even sleep could not remove. She paused at the edge of the camp and gazed at Drumdae's dark depths beyond the row of tents and cooking fires. What might lie on the northeastern side? The Danes? The Highlanders? A decisive battle? But the forest's secrets remained as elusive and hidden as the future.

After breakfasting on dull porridge, Rhiada and Cameron had gone off to yet another discussion among the chieftains regarding their next move; it seemed the scouts had returned. Malcolm was helping his brother Duncan to see to the horses' breakfast, leaving her alone. He seemed eager to escape everyone's company after his father had spoken to him that morning. Fiona guessed it was along the lines of what Angus had said to him last night. Malcolm was too young—not that she was much older—and he would be yet another responsibility that no one needed nor wanted. His desire to not be left behind wouldn't be worth the pain and grief if the McCladdens lost yet another son.

The rasping sound of a whetstone broke the morning quiet. She came round a tent to see Angus sitting at the edge of the forest, leaning against a pine with his sword across his knees.

She walked forward until she stood next to him. "Do ye mind if I sit wi' ye?"

He looked up, searching her face, and then shook his head. "I donnae mind."

Silence lay between them as Fiona gazed out over the camp, broken only by the whetstone running over Angus' blade. She watched some of the men practise weaponry in open spaces between tents, others conversing beside fires, some grooming the horses. Watery sunlight spilled over the plain, giving light but no warmth. The distant horizon was veiled in cloud, shadowing the rolling braes beyond.

"I donnae think tha' sword is gang to get any sharper," she said at last with a grin.

Angus glanced up and shrugged before running the whetstone over the blade again. "Probably no', but at least it passes the time," he answered. He hesitated before continuing, his voice dead-level. "Besides, it doesnae hurt to be prepared, does it? Who kens wha' the war will claim from us this time?" He said no more, but Fiona knew what he was thinking of.

"What was Sioned like?" she questioned suddenly, not wishing the conversation to be at an end.

Angus jerked his head up and stared at her, his face tight and strained, surprise giving way to a hurting look in his gaze that she had seen before. His blue eyes welled up in tears and he looked away quickly, clenching his jaw.

Fiona swallowed the lump that rose in her throat, feeling as though she had done something very wrong. She had not meant to hurt him! She only wanted to help, but he never let her, never let her understand the pain he always buried in his heart.

She laid her hand on his shoulder, wishing to tell him that she understood—she had lost Douglas, the person she loved most in the world, had she not? And to the same war?

But the words never left her lips.

"Come ye both!" Fiona jumped at Malcolm's shout as he ran up to them. "Father wants us." He did not wait for a reply before bounding off again.

Fiona withdrew her hand and rose to her feet, knowing anything she said now would be useless. The moment had been broken, and any words would only seem superfluous. "Are ye coming?" she managed at last, her chest tight at his suppressed, silent grief.

"Aye," he replied with a voice as cold as ice. He stood, sheathing his sword. "After ye," he said, gesturing with his arm for her to walk ahead.

She sighed, biting her lip. The war had not even begun, and she had already lost the battle most important to her.

Fiona followed the way Malcolm had gone, Angus shadowing her in silence. No longer in the protection of the forest, the wind bit through her woollen clothing. A lack of warmth within made her shiver, and not only because of the icy breeze and scarcity of sun.

Within moments, she came in sight of the High Chieftains standing together, Rhiada sitting with them before the fire. Both he and Malcolm beside him were wrapped up in their cloaks, staring into the flames. All of them had faces chapped by the cold, noses and cheeks ruddy, eyes bright and piercing in the faint daylight.

Angus left her to stand next to Duncan, who gazed at his impassive face in concern. He glanced at Fiona, his eyebrows raised, but she only hitched her shoulder in response.

If Duncan did not know why his brother withdrew into his silent, passionate moods, then she certainly did not.

"Princess," Chieftain McCladden greeted, a twinkle in his blue eyes even if the smile did not reach his mouth. Dark shadows beneath his eyes betrayed a loss of sleep; Fiona wondered if any of the High Chieftains had rested that night. With the news of Drummond, she imagined much had been discussed into the wee hours of the morning.

She bowed her head in acknowledgement before walking over to Rhiada. Without a word, she stood behind him and Malcolm.

"Right, we're all here then, are we no'?" Bryce MacClydno grumbled, holding out his hands to the fire to warm them before wrapping them up in his cloak again.

"Peace, Bryce," Alastair McThraedan warned. "Donald will speak in his own time."

Silence fell upon them, broken only by Jamie McBride coughing. It was a wonder more of them weren't sick from being constantly exposed to the rough wind of early winter. If it weren't so necessary to the preservation of Scotland's future, none of them would have ridden out on the war trail this late in the year.

Donald cleared his throat, straightening as he looked at all of them, much as a father would at his beloved children, even though many of the chieftains were older than him. "Some events hae transpired since we departed on the war trail. Most of ye ken that Drummond MacDougall—half-brother to Lady Nuith, who is plotting against us—has joined our warband in the night. Fer good or fer ill, we hae decided to let him stay wi' us as his men are an asset against the enemy forces marching against us." He paused and met Fiona's gaze, his face grave and concerned.

She inhaled sharply but said nothing. There was sense in it, for Drummond's men strengthened the whole host, and if turned away, what was to prevent Drummond from attacking them right then and there? But still, why had he come at all?

She glanced at Angus, wondering if he was also thinking of the night before, but he only stared into the fire, his hands clasped in front of him. His face was as white as marble, no warmth or light showing at all.

Fiona looked away as Donald continued, knowing she would never be able to see beyond the mask of apathy unless Angus shattered it himself.

"Therefore, there is only one thing left fer us to hae done." Donald hesitated once more, looking at Rhiada, who remained silent. "We will head fer the northeast side of Drumdae, keeping the forest between us and the Lowlands. The Danes hae been seen heading fer the hills beyond, and 'tis best we claim the high ground before they do. Meanwhile, we will watch Drummond's men and do our best to protect our princess from any fell plans they might hae fer her."

"Are they nae to be sworn to an oath of honour?" Eachann asked, his brown-eyed gaze steady and fearless.

Donald shook his head in reply, but it was Bryce who answered for him.

"Those Danish dogs hae nae sense of honour," Bryce growled, spitting into the fire. The spittle hissed among the flames as he added, "Such an oath will only be broken. 'Twill provide nae more security than if we did without."

"Bryce is right," Rhiada spoke up, his voice soft but commanding nonetheless. "Drummond cannae be trusted. I hae had dealings wi' him before, years ago, when he followed his sister's cause. 'Tis in my heart that we may yet face more treachery from him, though his men are welcome as fellow blades against the Danes. But donnae trust them. We must always protect Princess McCurragh here, nae matter how the war goes."

"I am wi' Rhiada on this," Alastair murmured, the others nodding in agreement.

"Aye, I ken Drummond's past," Donald replied grimly. "Tha' is why I willnae hae his men swear an oath they willnae keep. Nonetheless, all our warriors must dance the sword dance before we move camp. If none of ye hae further concerns, ye are dismissed to tell yer men to prepare fer the testing."

The chieftains dispersed in silence, only the fitful wind speaking in wordless whispers. Duncan and his brothers also scattered, perhaps to prepare for the coming dance. Within moments, the wailing notes of bagpipes droned over the camp, summoning all to the outskirts where the tents were few and the ground even. Horses neighed in the distance, perhaps wondering what the sound meant.

As for Fiona, she remained beside Rhiada, nervousness shooting through her veins, tingling in her fingers. Sword dance? Testing? The last time she had danced the sword dance was six years ago, before Douglas had gone away to the War...

"Rhiada?" she began, her voice trembling. "Did Donald mean *the* sword dance?"

"'Tis the ancient custom, as ye ken. Before a battle, or in this case, the first encounter wi' the enemy in war, all warriors dance the sword dance. If they even brush the sword blades no harder than a gentle breeze brushing a blade of grass, his enemy will dance o'er his sword in death—or so they say. 'Tis more a test of a warrior's strength and control than anything else. Jist as in battle, one must be quick and light on one's feet, and yet in complete discipline of one's movements, in order to survive. So also in the sword dance."

"Must I dance it as well, seeing as I am no' a warrior? Or must I because I am the princess?" His words had done nothing to allay her fears. What if she touched the blade? It had been so long since she had danced it. If she failed, what then? Would she doom the entire host by her actions?

"Fiona," he replied simply, rising to his feet. "Come wi' me."

Baffled, she followed him into the tent nearest the fire as he knelt and fumbled in opening a large satchel of sorts. Then he pulled out a kilt with the McCurragh tartan of green and brown, as well as a pair of woollen breeks, and handed them to her.

"Here," he said, "ye'll be a-needing this. Ye cannae dance in tha' dress, and ye cannae fight in it either. I hae another too, if ye need it. They belonged to yer brother, Douglas."

Fiona's breath caught in her throat. And here she had thought all his belongings she had not salvaged were burned or repurposed by Lady Nuith. "Where did ye get these?" she asked, her voice no louder than a whisper.

"I found them before I left Caerloch," he explained. Then he added with a slight smile, "I wish ye the best of luck wi' it, Fiona. I ken ye will do well. Donnae listen to yer fears."

She smiled nervously, only a little comforted. "Thank ye, Rhiada. I only hope ye are right."

"Ye credit yerself too little, princess. Ye are more capable than ye think." Rhiada rose to his feet and turned to leave. Then he paused, saying, "There are a couple shirts of his in there, too. They should fit ye well enough." He nodded once, as if affirming what he had said, and closed the tent flap, standing in front of the opening to prevent anyone's going in.

Fiona swiftly changed her clothes, trying to think of anything but the testing. She rolled up her dress and placed it in the satchel with the other kilt and shirt from her brother. She would put it on again at a later time. As she tucked the shirt—which was a bit too large—into her belt, the collar brushed against her nose and her breath caught in her throat.

Six years, and it still smelled like Douglas. Still smelled of grass and rain and horse mingled with the sweeter scent of heather.

Tears sprang to her eyes that she pushed back with a struggle, not wishing for anyone to see her crying. Not until after the sword dancing was over with, at least. All the same, it was comforting to know a part of her brother was still with her even if he was gone.

She adjusted her plaid over her shoulder before stepping outside the tent, shivering in the wind. Already she longed for the warmth the long skirt of her dress had provided. It felt strange to be bare-legged from the knee down, even if her woollen socks nearly came to her knees. Feeling awkward and exposed, she stumbled along until she reached the growing group of men and lads waiting to dance.

Fiona soon found Malcolm fidgeting to one side and stood next to him, glad to see a familiar face in the crowd. Cameron's piping drowned out most of the conversation happening and some were practising their steps as they waited for the chieftains to arrive.

"I like ye better in a dress," Malcolm observed with a smirk.

She rolled her eyes heavenward, stifling a laugh, and jabbed him with her elbow.

"Aiee!" he protested. "I didnae say ye look terrible in a kilt, but it jist looks awkward, especially the way ye keep yer knees locked in front of each other like tha."

Fiona glanced down and saw she had placed one foot in front of the other. It did indeed look odd and uncomfortable, even if it kept her legs somewhat warmer. She shifted her position as Angus came up to them, sheathed sword in his hand.

"Ready, Malcolm?" he asked, a teasing tone in his voice, though his face wore no smile.

"Thanks to ye, I should hae nae problem," Malcolm shot back. "We did it so many times I could do it in my sleep. All the same, 'tis hard enough as it is without ye making jests 'bout it."

"Angus, leave them alone," Duncan interjected, walking up to them, his hands resting on his waist as if preparing to dance right there and then. "We all hae to dance it, even ye."

Fiona heard Malcolm giggle beside her, but Angus only looked crestfallen, hurt by his brother's blunt rebuke.

"I didnae mean to cause offence," he said softly, no spirit left in his words. He kept his gaze on the ground, fidgeting with the sword hilt in his hands.

It pained Fiona to see him so, but she did not know how to help him, not when he pushed her away all the time.

"Aye, well, nae harm done," Duncan replied matter-of-factly and walked on, offering encouragement to his friends and laughing with them.

Fiona watched Malcolm giving his elder brother a longing look, seeming to hesitate about whether to tag along. He took one step forward to join him when the piping suddenly stopped, a wheezing sigh ending the music, and Cameron walked up to the place that had been cleared for the dancing. The windy silence felt empty without the piping, and all heads turned to see what would happen next, their conversations silenced.

Donald McCladden and the other High Chieftains entered the open space, Drummond included, and took off their cloaks, leaving them by the side of the clearing. As one, they raised their swords to their faces, the blades glinting in the grey sunlight. They laid their claymores and their respective sheaths in a cross pattern on the dead grass and stood at one of the hilts, waiting for the piper to play, their hands resting in fists at their waists.

His face contorting from the effort of blowing so hard, Cameron began a skirling strathspey, his fingers flying along the chanter as his right foot tapped the rhythm.

After silently waiting eight bars of music, they began to dance.

Fiona watched as the chieftains pointed and leaped above the blades. Their hands were held high above their head, imitating the graceful antlers of a deer, as they danced in and out of each crossing of the swords. Their steps were light, concise and controlled, a level of mastery that Douglas had never quite achieved before he left for the War. She had never seen her father dance this, but she doubted even he had the finesse that these chieftains did. No wonder they were such skilled warriors.

The piping ceased and they finished flawlessly, bowed, and took up their claymores and sheaths. Without a word, they walked to the edge of the cleared area, vacating the space for the others to dance. Another set of warriors took their places while the chieftains judged them, observant of their every movement.

Fiona glanced at Malcolm, who bounced up and down on his feet in excitement—or was he also nervous? She knew she was. Every breath trembled, and her fingers ached with the constant tingling of anxiety.

What if her feet touched the blades? Would they consider it an ill omen of the inevitable battle? What if they lost the battle and then laid the blame on her for dishonouring the dance?

She felt fingers brush against hers, and a familiar voice whispered, "Ye'll do jist fine, Fiona."

She looked up to see Angus pass her by with his brother Duncan and a few other lads their age on their way to dance.

In a moment, their swords and respective sheaths lay on the ground as the piper continued to play the lilting melody. Angus met her gaze, his blue eyes emotionless and dark, and then looked away, his eyes fastened on the crossed blades in front of him. After eight bars, the lads placed their fists on their hips and began the dance, their faces serious in concentration.

Angus pinched his lips together so tightly his mouth almost disappeared from off his face, his eyes always focused on the swords. His brother, Duncan, who was dancing in front and a bit to the side of him, looked almost as if he was enjoying the whole thing. Fiona noted with a small knot of quiet pride that none of them—especially Angus—came close to touching the blades.

They finished all too soon, and then it was Fiona and Malcolm's turn with five other persons.

The seven of them walked forward as Fiona unbuckled her sheath, struggling to keep her shaking and sweating hands steady. With a flourish, she drew out her sword and held it in front of her perpendicular to the ground. She inhaled deeply, hoping to calm her nerves, but it did little good. Her knees still quivered as she laid down the blade over the sheath, every action seeming distant, as if someone else commanded her movements.

She stood at the sword's hilt, her feet turned out to either side, and her hands resting on her hips as the music began again. Silently, she counted the eight bars in her mind, her heart thundering in her ears, beating almost louder than the music.

Aon, dhà, trì, ceithir, còig, sia, seachd, ochd...

Her cheeks flaming and eyes straight ahead, she rose up on her toes, pointing out to one side and hopping over. Holding her arms high above her head, she focused solely on the music and the blades glistening in the afternoon winter sun.

In. Out. Point. Jump. Turn—

Fiona's heart jumped in her throat as her leather shoe brushed against the blade. Had anyone seen that?

She landed too hard on one foot, something in her ankle snapping. Gritting her teeth against the pain, she continued nonetheless, feeling terribly light-headed. No one had said anything yet, so perhaps they had not noticed, even if she was the only lass dancing.

She landed on her right foot again, this time correctly, but her ankle throbbed, begging for relief. Her breath came out in ragged gasps as she tried to focus on not touching the blades again.

Step-two-three. Switch-two-three. Point. In. Out. Hop over.

A sudden ringing in her ears drowned out the music, matching the aching in her foot. Gritting her teeth, she threw what energy she had left into keeping her arms held high and steady, her feet controlled as she jumped in and out of the crossed blades.

In. Out. Point. Out.

And then she stood at the sword hilt, bowing with the rest as relief washed over her, leaving her giddy. The dance was finished.

Fiona picked up her sword and sheathed it, buckling it again around her waist, her shaking hands slipping on the leather. Cheeks flushed and blood pounding in her ears, she limped her way wordlessly to where Duncan and Angus stood, Malcolm following her. Any moment, she anticipated someone to shout her name and tell her to dance it again.

But it never came.

"Ye did well," Angus murmured to them both as they came to stand beside him. The piping pierced the air again, but none of them noticed.

Malcolm nodded his thanks while panting with exertion, sweat trickling down his face. "Do ye think I'll pass?" he asked no one in particular.

"Och, ye will. Ye didnae touch the sword or the sheath," Duncan replied, his arms crossed as he watched the remaining individuals dancing.

"Wha' about Fiona? Did she pass? I couldnae see," Malcolm said, wiping his forehead with his sleeve.

Fiona's heart sank to her toes.

"I donnae see why she wouldnae either. She danced better than ye did," Angus teased, but his face was not smiling. He caught Fiona's gaze and held it for a moment, his blue eyes softening.

He knew, then. But no one else seemed to have seen her mistake. She was not certain whether to sigh with relief or fear someone else had caught it. Angus would not betray her, but someone still might have seen it.

Malcolm snorted. "Ha! I highly doubt tha', Angus. Ye were the worst dancer I hae seen yet!"

"Tha's enough," Duncan broke in, nearly stepping between them. "Malcolm, Angus, I donnae want to hear another word between ye until we eat this evening. Understood?"

They both nodded silently and held their peace, watching the other dancers as the sky began to darken towards twilight. Fiona flexed and pointed her foot, trying to loosen her ankle, which was stiff from landing wrong. She needed to walk tomorrow, whatever the dawn would bring. All the while, she attempted to forget about her mistake, but it haunted her all the same. If no one else had seen it, then did it matter? Or had she doomed them all?

She turned her attention back towards the remaining dancers, shoving her thoughts out of her mind. Drummond's host danced well enough, though they lacked the grace and strength that the Scots had. Lachlan especially—though she loathed to watch him, even if curiosity dictated otherwise—was stiff in his movements, the dance seeming more like the jerkiness of a young colt than the smooth precision of a deer. Fiona wondered how many of Drummond's men were truly Danish or if any of them had intermarried with the Scots— such dancing was taught from a young age and was not easily learned.

At last, the dancing was all finished and everyone had managed more or less to stay in the ranks. One by one, they dispersed in silence to eat the evening meal. Fiona could not help but hope Cameron was all right after blowing the pipes for a few hours' time.

Rhiada joined Fiona's side, placing his hand on her shoulder for a moment. "Donald says ye did well," he said with a smile. "Now try to eat something before we rest or move camp, whatever Donald agrees to fer tonight. I assume ye and yer companions will receive some sort of protection. We donnae hae enough chainmail, but something will be provided."

Fiona was about to reply when a horseman rode through their midst, pulling up in the clearing where they had danced. The man leapt from his horse, who stood still with sweat flecking its flanks, and made his way to Donald McCladden. He was panting, as if the ride had cost him as much exertion as it had the horse.

"Aidan," Donald called out, urgency in his voice. "What news hae ye?"

Aidan clasped his hand over his heart and bowed slightly before replying. "We hae seen the Danes, Chieftain McCladden."

"Where are they?" Rhiada broke in, his hand tightening on Fiona's shoulder for a moment even though his voice remained calm.

"There's an army of about two thousand men heading this way. They will be by the hills when the dawn breaks."

A heavy silence followed, a silence so sharp it could have drawn blood from the wind that murmured among the tents and cooking fires.

Fiona's stomach lurched. *Nae, nae, nae!* a voice screamed in her head. She looked in panic from one face to another and saw no comfort. All had the same look in their eyes, a look of fear; even Malcolm, who had spoken of war with such excitement. Angus looked as if he had seen a ghaist, his form wavering against the light of the fire behind him.

Donald made his answer at last, his voice grave. "Tell the men to prepare to march. We'll skirt the forest and encamp east of it where the hills begin. Guards will be posted to alert us of the Danes' arrival. Everything must be torn down and ready to leave within an hour. I'll leave ye to tell those under yer charge."

The chieftains and others dispersed to obey Donald's orders, commands being relayed across the camp. Cooking fires were doused, shrouding the land in winter gloom. Torches were brought out that had been saved for this purpose, tiny flares against the coming twilight as the sun descended towards the western horizon.

"We are marching, then?" Angus asked softly, the wind gently tossing about his raven locks of hair. His eyes were dark, but his mask of nonchalance remained in its place.

"Aye," his father replied, placing his hand on his son's shoulder. "We cannae fight on this ground, nor can we allow the Danes to claim the high hills first. 'Twill be hard enough when we hae but half their force to oppose them."

"We are going to fight tomorrow?" Malcolm asked, his voice sounding strange. Excited, no. Fearful, maybe.

Fiona remained silent, not trusting her voice to speak. So much depended on the dawn, and she found she did not have the strength to meet it. They had expected to have a few more days before they encountered the Danes. It was almost as if, by her touching her blade during the dance, she had somehow summoned their doom.

"Aye, tomorrow," Donald replied. "I wish we had more time, but we hae nae other choice. The Danes are coming, whether we are ready or no'...." He sighed. "I ken only one thing: whatever happens, we must stand our ground."

~ 17 ~

FIRST BLOOD

FIONA McCurragh watched in helpless fear as the Scots tore down tents, doused fires, and saddled up to move east of Drumdae Forest. All the while, Donald's words replayed themselves in her mind with horrific clarity. *"The Danes are coming, whether we are ready or no'... Whatever happens, we must stand our ground."*

She knew she was not ready for the coming battle. The thought that men would be dying for the sake of freedom in a matter of hours sickened her. What if Angus or Malcolm or any of them—herself included—perished beneath the Danish axe? How could she bear to lose them?

"Fiona, is everything all right?" Rhiada asked gently, his dark brows drawn together in concern.

"Aye, Rhiada." She laughed nervously, as if to make light of the whole thing. "I was only thinking."

He seemed unconvinced but said no more. Cameron came alongside them to guide Rhiada to his horse, glancing at Fiona.

She merely nodded and said, "I will see ye later then, Rhiada. Safe riding."

"And to ye, Fiona. Keep yerself safe."

Fiona left Rhiada and Cameron without another word and scrambled through the buzzing maze of the encampment, heading for the tent where she had left her things, ignoring her aching ankle. The tent had already been torn down, but the bundle remained. She slipped her dress on over her clothes, glad for the extra warmth it provided, and tied her cloak's strings over top, the heavy folds settling around her. The night was already freezing, and one could not be too warm in early winter.

Fiona grabbed the leather satchel containing her brother's clothes and slung the strap over her shoulder, making her way to Sgàil while dodging people running here and there on various errands. All around her could be heard the shouts of men fulfilling Donald Mc-Cladden's orders and bewildered whinnies from the horses at the sudden action in the camp.

The sun was setting in a darkening blue sky, tongues of red flame leaping across the clouds, burning away into early winter twilight. The chilling wind whipped through the trees of Drumdae Forest, tossing the last fragments of the brown, crumpled leaves in a flurry to the ground. To Fiona, those leaves, so light—and so easily crushed—were too akin to the lives soon to be spent on the distant hills. The thought was no comfort. She turned away from gazing at the sky and the forest, heading for the picket lines.

Fiona's hair flew wildly in the moaning gusts as she mounted her horse from the left side to spare her throbbing ankle, though the pain had lessened. Flinging her leg over Sgàil's back, she ignored the sore muscles that complained at finding themselves in a saddle again. It was far better than walking, even if she loathed the thought of getting down to her feet again in a few hours.

All around her, the other warriors cut loose the picket lines and climbed into their horses' saddles, preparing to move out. The shouts lessened as they waited for further orders from Chieftain McCladden. Only Sgàil, sensing Fiona's uncertainty, delicately played with the bit in her mouth much like a lassie would a flower, shaking her mane at times when the wind blew the mare's hair into her own eyes.

Angus mounted Branwen beside Fiona and stared into the sunset while they waited to ride, his face grim. After a moment, he turned to her and said, "Are ye ready?"

She glanced at him and nodded, stroking Sgàil's neck. "Aye, as ready as I'll e'er be."

Silence fell between them, broken only by the wind, the shouts of men, the whinnies of horses, and the creaking of leather.

"I'm a-thinking..." Her voice faltered as she struggled to put her warring emotions into words.

"Gae on," he encouraged, loosening the reins so that Branwen might lower her head with greater ease.

"'Tis in my heart tha' some of us may no' see the next sunset." Her voice felt thick, grief and fear rising in her throat and choking her.

Angus followed her gaze to the falling sphere of fire in the skies. "Aye, I suppose ye're right," he answered in a tone that was almost sad, nearly regretful. The same haunted look appeared in his eyes for a moment, shadowing his face. Was he thinking about Sioned? Or was he simply terrified of the coming battle, as they all were? No, it had to be something more, something more than the expected anxiety, something that went far deeper, that was perhaps buried in his past.

"Angus, can I ride wi' ye?" a familiar voice piped up from behind them, destroying the moment.

Both turned to see Malcolm standing beside Branwen, his short cloak billowed out by the wind. His sword was belted around his waist, his other things tied in a bundle behind his back in the same manner as the rest of them had done.

"Nae, ye cannae!" Angus protested. "I thought ye were a-going wi' the others on foot."

Malcolm sighed and rolled his eyes heavenward. "Father says I donnae hae to if I can ride wi' ye. And Duncan says his horse cannae carry us both—I already asked him," he added, as if expecting Angus to ask that question next.

"Well, ye're nae riding wi' me," his elder brother replied just as firmly and turned away, his face darkened in a scowl.

Fiona shook her head and scooted forward on her horse. "Come ye, Malcolm. Ye can ride wi' me."

Something akin to a squeal of delight escaped from Malcolm's lips and he clambered on, sitting triumphantly behind her and smirking at his brother. Angus merely shook his head, digging his heels into Branwen's flanks and urging his mare forward, leaving the two of them behind.

Before they could follow, Donald rode his horse before the lines of men and horses, calling out in question to the chieftains if they were ready. They answered more or less in unison, and then they were off, riding into the wildness of a December night.

The sun rose that morning bright and close, bloodshot gold piercing through the darkness of the dying night. The wind, which had keened all night, was silent and still. The air remained frigid, each breath coming out in white puffs as Fiona awakened and rose to her feet, wrapped up in her cloak for warmth.

Around her, many were stirring with the dawn, donning weapons and heading for the few cooking fires for one last breakfast of porridge before the battle. Fiona ate a few bites of the tasteless stuff to keep up her strength and then gave the rest to Malcolm, unable to swallow more because of nerves. She had slept ill that night after they had encamped northeast of Drumdae, and she felt far from refreshed. Her legs were stiff from sleeping on the hard ground, but at least her ankle did not hurt anymore. Nonetheless, her hands ached from clenching against the constant worry that flooded through her veins like blood, but the knowledge of the coming conflict could not be thrust away. It loomed over her like the rising sun, darkening the approaching day, filling her with hopelessness in light of lives soon to be violently spilled on the distant hills.

She was not the only one afraid of the ensuing battle.

Fiona heard many muttering about blood being spilled that day as she walked about the camp looking for Rhiada. Perhaps the sunrise in all its harshly potent beauty had also instilled in the Scots thoughts of fear, or at least fortified them. She wondered whether they were right, but she did not want to think much on it. The less she mused on death, perhaps the less it would happen—or so she hoped.

She found Rhiada soon enough, sitting among the chieftains. Malcolm and Angus, normally present with their brother Duncan, were not there, so she stood beside her teacher, resting her hand on his shoulder for a moment.

He turned to face her, the morning light shining in the hollows where his eyes had once been.

"Aye, Rhiada, 'tis Fiona," she whispered before giving heed to what the chieftains were saying.

Donald had scratched out a map of the hills in the earth with his dirk, giving tactical instructions for the coming battle. All the chieftains stood around him, dressed for war. Eachann held his strung bow in his hand, watching as Donald told him where to place his archers on the hills surrounding the plain where the scouts said the Danes were headed.

He nodded and then left, shouting orders to the archers beneath his charge.

"Bryce," Donald continued, "ye keep yer men on foot to the right behind this hill." He pointed to the crudely-drawn map. "Drummond and Jamie, ye take yer men here on the left side and wait until the archers have run out of arrows. Then gae out wi' all the men ye hae got. Alastair and I will wait as reserves until we're needed, and then we will come on horse. Understood?" He looked up at the men around him.

They nodded, murmuring in agreement, and left to relay the commands to their men before the Danes arrived.

Fiona watched them walk away, still confused as to what she was supposed to do. No one had given her any specific instructions, and she felt awkward simply standing there while others busied themselves for the battle ahead. She was anxious about the coming ordeal, never having fought in a real battle before, and longed for someone to tell her what to do, if only to escape her own thoughts. It all seemed a terrible nightmare, and she could only wish to wake up from it. For though she was glad enough to no longer be held captive by Lady Nuith, this freedom came with a price she was none too eager to pay.

Angus passed Fiona and paused, glancing up at her before heading off again, his face hard, his eyes dark and hidden. He wore a leather jerkin, reinforced with bits of horn plate in the most vulnerable places. Perhaps the chieftains were handing out what armour they could before the battle. Certainly Donald would want his sons to be protected, not wishing to lose another like he had Sioned, especially young Malcolm. Fiona remembered well the shining chain-mail Douglas had worn when he rode off; but for all that, he had not come back.

Nonetheless, she followed Angus without a word, hitching up her skirts to keep up with his swift, long-legged stride.

He wound his way around the groups of men gathering in battle formation as he headed for the picket lines. He came to a stop beside Branwen, stroking her neck for a moment before pulling his sword out of the saddle pack and belting it on. Then, turning, he pulled it out of its sheath, testing the sharpness of the blade before pulling out a whetstone and running it along the edge.

"Angus, ye jist sharpened it yesterday," Fiona protested, pulling up handfuls of dead grass and giving them to Branwen. The mare took them from her hand, her velvety lips brushing Fiona's palm ever so gently.

Angus ran the stone along the blade once more, a rasping sound filling the silence between them, and sheathed his weapon with a jerk. "Ne'er hurts to be prepared," he replied in a voice as cold and rough as the whetstone. He pulled out his bow and quiver, slinging the quiver over his shoulder and then stringing his bow, pulling back on the thin cord to test its strength.

Fiona laid her hand on his shoulder, ignoring the scowl on his face as she did so. "Ye're afraid, are ye no'?"

He flinched away as if struck and stared at her in mute terror, his hand clenched on the lead rein, knuckles showing white through his pale skin.

"Tha' is why ye're so bent on yer weapons being in best form, why ye're so concerned wi' always practising wi' Malcolm, is it no'?" she continued, throwing caution to the wind. It was as if the missing pieces to the puzzle that was Angus were finally falling into place. He was not merely in pain because of Sioned. His fear was another kind of pain, terror at the thought of facing loss yet again and being help-less in the face of it. She wanted to help him so badly, for friendship's sake since he had helped her face her fears before, even if it meant she might hurt him with her words. "Ye're afraid of death, afraid of pain and loss. Ye're afraid of losing those ye love ever since Sioned died, and ye work so hard to protect them, especially Malcolm, who is younger and weaker and more vulnerable—"

"Wheesht, Fiona! Jist—jist wheesht. Ye donnae ken of wha' ye're speaking." He took a step back, tears glimmering in his blue eyes that he visibly forced back. She could see how he was so terrified of break-ing, of being vulnerable and exposed. "I ken ye think ye mean well, but 'tis better this way." His voice was thick with repressed emotion, so close to shattering and yet never letting himself free.

Without another word, he mounted his horse and cut loose the rope to the picket lines. He did not even glance at her before making a kissing sound and urging Branwen forward, leaving Fiona standing alone.

She watched him leave, tears smarting in her eyes. Was he so blind to how this grief and fear was killing him from the inside out? Would he ever listen? If anything happened to him out on that field...

She rubbed her hand across her face. No, she must not think of it. She must not think of something that just might kill her too, if it happened. Then again, it might not come to pass at all, but did she not also feel the same when Douglas left her all those years ago?

Someone grabbed her arm as she began to walk away and she whirled around, seeing Rhiada standing there, also holding Malcolm captive. "Ye're staying wi' me this time," the harper explained grimly.

"I'm wha'?"

"We are gang to tha' hill there." He pointed in the general direction of the hills nearest them where many of the archers waited, nearly hidden in the leafless shrubbery.

"Ye want me to stay safe out of this battle, then?" Relief crept over her, only to be destroyed in the next instant.

"Nae, Fiona. Those are nae my reasons. I want ye to see how a battle must go so tha' next time ye'll be more prepared fer fighting. These chieftains ken war from years past; so do their men or at least most of them. Ye hae had nae taste of war and I wish fer ye to see the grander picture of a battle than to experience at once the chaos tha' comes from fighting hand-to-hand. Ye may hae to join the Scots later, but we shall see."

"And me?" Malcolm squeaked, still squirming in Rhiada's grip on the neck of his tunic.

"Ye are staying wi' me until this is over," the harper declared firmly. "I promised yer father I would keep ye safe and if ye prevent me keeping that promise, I will find ye where'er ye are and show ye tha' even a blind man is to be feared."

Malcolm shut his mouth and nodded meekly, no longer struggling.

"Aye, tha's more like it. Now come, the battle is soon to begin, and best we be safe on the high ground."

Glancing at the subdued lad, Fiona followed both him and Rhiada as they made their way to the hill, eventually finding a well-hidden spot from which to view the coming conflict. Once concealed, Rhiada loosened a bundle he bore on his back, handing them both leather jerkins and a pair of bracers to Fiona. Should they be forced to fight, it wouldn't be much protection, but it was better than nothing at all.

The ground was cold and hard beneath her, but from their perch on the hilltop, she could view the dappled valley, shadowed by distant mountains, stretching across the horizon. Archers shifted in the bushes near them, waiting for the enemy to come. Fiona could see the foot soldiers and horsemen hiding behind the hills until the time came for them to ride out.

Fiona clenched and unclenched her hands, fear tingling her nerves. She searched the nearest group of horsemen, trying to espy Angus and Branwen, but she could not see them. He could be with an entirely different company. Nonetheless, she still wondered where he was and what he was thinking. No doubt focusing on the coming conflict, staying alive, and protecting his brother, Duncan, and his father.

She glanced at Malcolm, who stood beside her, his eyes wide and eager as he peered into the distance to catch sight of the enemy. He did not seem afraid at all, and for that she envied him.

She would do anything to be free of her fear.

Duncan McCladden stood with the rest of Bryce MacClydno's men, shifting from foot to foot in nervous anticipation, his palms sweating. He wiped them again and again on his plaid, not wishing to have a loose grip on his sword when the time came to wield it. Positioned towards the back of the company, he peered over the other heads before him, his heart hammering in his chest while they waited for any sign of the Danish hosts.

The Danes were not visible yet upon the battlefield and until they were, the Scots anxiously strained their ears for the coming enemy, listening in a painful silence through which every breath pierced the air like a knife.

Duncan glanced behind him, wondering where his father was. His father had bade him fight with his grandfather's company as he was a better fighter on foot than on horse. But still, he longed to be beside his father or at least be near him, especially in this battle. His father had fought many, but this was Duncan's first taste of war. Though, truth be told, it was not only his first, but also his brother's.

Angus was somewhere among the horsemen, or so he thought; he had lost him in the general organisation of things. He hoped he was all right. Always so silent, he carried himself with cocky dismissiveness towards everything, but sometimes Duncan caught glimpses of what he believed was more truly his brother—more the Angus he had known before the War. Ever since Sioned's death, Angus had thrown himself into endless practice of weaponry, as if a shield against his grief. He wondered whether all his brother's frenetic training would pay off in the battle to come, Angus' first true encounter with war.

He heard a shout in the distance, shattering his thoughts, and he stood up tall, clenching his hands against the nervousness that bled over him.

The Danes had been seen.

Bryce MacClydno gave hurried orders, and his words were passed down the line from one man to the next: "They're coming. Stay close. Wait fer my command."

Duncan inhaled sharply, tightening his grip around his claymore's hilt. He saw one of the men to his right glance up at the sky and say, half under his breath, "There is the sound of battle."

Duncan strained his ears, but only heard the soft whisper of winter's wind and the crows squawking from above in the trees, eager for the kill.

The man continued nevertheless, hands clenching and unclenching around his spear in anxious repetition. "I can hear it, aye, and I smell the blood." His voice, though only a whisper, trembled at the edges. "We will be dead before this day's ending...."

The first line of Danes marched across the plain, their armour shining in the grey sun. Their weapons shone cold and menacing in the morning light, and a shudder crept up Fiona's spine as column after column came into view, spreading across the valley. Not only were their numbers far greater than the Scots', their weapons and protective plate were superior to the few suits of chainmail and horn and leather armour the Scots had.

"Tell me wha' ye see," Rhiada said gently, his voice low as he placed his hand on her shoulder to steady her.

"Men, thousands of men, walking in even lines across the plain..." Her voice quavered in spite of herself. "The light shines on their weapons and their armour, and their faces are hidden." How were the Scots ever to defeat such a great host?

The harper sighed. "'Tis as I feared. However, we still hae one advantage."

Fiona turned to him, glancing at Malcolm, who watched it all with youthful, innocent eagerness. "The hills?" she asked.

"Aye." Rhiada nodded gravely. "Let us hope everything goes as planned."

"Aye," she repeated, looking again at the plain. "Let us hope."

The rows of marching men came ever closer, their feet thundering across the wide field. There were lower hills at the end of the plain, not as high as those where the Scots were hiding, but Fiona hoped all the same that the Danes would not remain there and force the Lowlanders to fight them on that ground. If so, that would put their plan to ruin and result in the Lowlanders having to fight uphill, which was precisely what Chieftain McCladden intended for the Danes to suffer.

As company after company passed by, heading closer to where the Scots were waiting, she knew with a sigh of relief that the Danes were not going to fight on the low hills. But still, she felt her heart sink, awash in a deep ocean of hopelessness.

There are so many. How shall we ever defeat them?

Then a great shout echoed off of the braes, a challenging roar to the approaching army. It rang in the chill air, a song of defiance.

"Scotland!"

At the cry, bowstrings twanged and arrows whistled through the air. Several Danes fell to the ground, groping to pull the barbs out in vain. Volley after volley followed, crimson raven emblems embracing the earth, never to fly on armour again.

About a hundred of the Danes lay dead before the Danish host counter-attacked. Shouting a reply in their own language, they charged, breaking from an orderly march into a mad run, their swords and axes raised in anger.

Echoing the cry first uttered, the Scots dashed out from their hiding places on either side of the hill, their claymores raised in triumph and shining in the winter sun.

The enemy halted, stunned momentarily by this new turn of events before breaking out in a run once more. They were scattered across the field, some remaining behind as reserves. But the greater part of the Danish host charged at the hills, attempting to gain the high ground.

The arrows still flew, but they were fewer than before. Fiona watched, aghast, as many a fine shaft hit a Scot as well as a Dane, and soon men from both sides lay dead, some killed by their companions. She wondered whether the Scots knew the cause of their death and what they thought of it—if they could think of it at all. Surely in the chaos that was battle, there was no time for thinking, not if one wished to survive.

Petrified, Fiona watched as the line of men rallied and pushed the Danes back before they too were forced backward in this deadly game of war. The line rippled back and forth like a ribbon in the wind, giving and gaining in turn. The clash of steel upon steel and the cries of the men came up to the three of them watching the battle, a distant cacophony of death. The peaceful silence of early morning had long since been slaughtered as men slew one another in the name of freedom.

She relayed the events as they happened to Rhiada, who listened with an anxious look on his face. Malcolm asked questions from time to time, but mostly he remained silent, just watching. The look of eagerness remained on his face at first, but as the Scots were pushed back more often than they thrust forward, pale fear crept over his features. The sparkle in his grey eyes dissipated into shadow like the darkness that haunted his brother's gaze. Fiona worried, if the battle did not go well, whether he would become like Angus, full of pain and terror at the thought of loss. But she could not think on it for long; the events happening below them denied her that.

The cry of *Scotland!* echoed again as the Scots on horseback thundered out from their hiding place.

The Danes were once more caught by surprise and forced back as the Scots charged, their swords raised above their heads. They rode swiftly across the body-strewn plain like arrows loosed from a bow, driving a wedge into the Danish line.

But yet again the Danes rallied, and the Scots were hard-pressed to fight.

Fiona saw one Scotsman's sword fly out of his hand during the fight, but he was not deterred. He raised his strung bow that had been slung over his shoulder and nocked an arrow while riding full-tilt across the plain, firing again and again. He was not the only one. Many of the Scots on horseback did the same, sheathing their swords until the time came when they could better use them. For now, speed was on their side.

Yet it did not remain so.

The Danes knew well how to use their axes to their advantage, attacking the horses that bore their riders and bringing them down. Fewer and fewer riders remained on the field, most having resorted to the sword again, their bows useless in close combat.

Fiona told Rhiada all these things and he replied grimly, "It will-nae be enough. The archers must gae down there if we hope to take back the field now."

As if they had heard his observation on the hills across from them, the archers charged down the hill, drawing their swords and shouting at the top of their voices, their kilts rippling behind them.

"Gae wi' them, Fiona," Rhiada said emphatically, his mouth set in a firm line.

She whipped her head around, fear choking her. "Wha'?"

"Gae down there! They need ye. If all ye say is true, those archers may no' be enough. We need everyone we can get, and ye hae trained fer this as much as any other man. Malcolm can be my eyes," he continued before she could object further.

Without further questioning, Fiona tugged loose the leather jerkin and then the ties of her dress, glad she had kept her brother's clothes on underneath. Malcolm helped her slip back into the jerkin, yanking his head down in a nod as a form of farewell.

Then she ran down the hill after the archers, the blood pounding in her ears. Once she reached the bottom of the hill, she drew her sword and joined the others in combat with the enemy, becoming yet another part in the chaos of battle.

Nothing in her life had prepared her for this. All her fears melted away in the cool calm of battle frenzy. There was no need to think, every action practised so often coming to her aid, despite the jerkin that was stiffer than her woollen clothes. She parried and thrust against men twice her age, staining her sword red, drawing first blood. This was her first battle, and it sickened her, the bodies whose life she stole so nauseatingly soft against her blade.

Was this what Douglas thought before he died?

She pushed away the memory of him. She had to survive, had to thrust back her fears even as Rhiada had said, and focus on the immediate danger before her. Douglas had died to protect her, and she could not let his sacrifice become void.

The battle shifted west, a shieldring of men rising around a chieftain—she could not see who—and she was left behind in the lull. A moment's reprieve in battle, a rare thing, but she was grateful to catch her breath.

"Fiona!"

She turned to see Duncan headed towards her, his sword bloodied to the hilt. A gash dripped red on his forehead, but it did not seem to be serious.

"Keep yerself safe, princess," he panted. "We hae yer back." And then he was gone, swiftly engaged in another conflict.

Fiona side-stepped as a riderless horse charged by, its eyes wide in terror. She brushed a loose strand of hair out of her face, painfully reminded how precarious life was out on the field. Duncan's words were of great comfort, but she did not wish to test them.

With one last glance at the high hills behind her, she returned to the fray, hoping against hope they would live to see the next dawn.

The sun was setting by the time it was over.

They had neither won the battle nor lost. The Danes had lost, that much was clear, but the Scots had barely survived. Less than half of their men were left; nine hundred warriors were hardly enough to continue this hopeless war.

Fiona McCurragh walked about the quieting battlefield, her sword hand clumsily bandaged against a slash across her knuckles. It was nothing serious, but it still hurt and made grasping things a painful business. Her shield arm throbbed from blocking a blow when there had been no time to evade it otherwise; perhaps it was dislocated—she would have to have it looked at once she returned to camp. She had also twisted her ankle tripping over a dying man at some point, and she limped as she crossed the body-strewn field, her foot still not recovered from the sword dancing of yesterday.

But it could be much worse. She was fortunate to be alive at all.

She stared in exhausted dullness at the bloodied and mangled corpses that were left. She felt as if a large weight had been tied on her heart and was pulling her down, as if she was responsible for this day's death, as if the mangled bodies of the dead Scots around her were her fault. And was it not? Had they not all danced the sword dance without mistake? Except for her. She had brushed the sword. By her actions, she had condemned the war host that fought in her name. That was the work of a traitor, one disloyal to the crown, not one who was supposed to inherit it.

Glancing up, she saw a figure standing on one of the low hills near the end of the plain. He was staring into the sunset, his feet planted firmly on the ground beneath him.

Fiona stepped closer and squinted against the beautiful and dying sun, trying to see if she knew who it was. Thus far she had encountered few familiar faces, and she worried. So many had perished beneath the Danish axe that day; had those she loved also been slain? Yet there was something familiar about that stance—she had seen it before...

Then, with a rush of chilling clarity, she knew.

~ 18 ~
MY BROTHER

FIONA limped up the small hill, not stopping for breath until she reached the top. Panting, she walked through the dead grasses until she reached Angus McCladden. He did not turn to her, nor did he acknowledge she was even there at all.

He faced the fading sunset, his arms hanging loose at his sides, the wind ruffling his dark hair. A crimson gash tore across his temple, blood matting his soft curls. His linen shirt was stained with dirt, sweat, and the all too-familiar scarlet, but the blood did not seem to be his—or so she hoped.

"Angus?" she asked, both confused and worried at his dazed composure.

He turned to her, his face tired and strained, his eyes blank and expressionless, as she had seen before when he tried to hide his pain. But he said not a word in reply.

"Angus McCladden, is something wrong?" She ran her tongue over her lips, her mouth suddenly dry.

He turned to face the sun again as he finally answered, his voice little more than a whisper. "My brother..."

Her heart stopped for a moment. "Yer brother?"

"My brother is dead." He said it in the same cold voice as he had to her that morning, except this time, there was no anger. Only an empty stillness that sent chills down her spine.

She felt as though the breath had been knocked out of her. "Which brother?" she gasped in horror. Had something happened to Duncan since the last time she'd seen him? Or had Malcolm joined in spite of Rhiada? Had that spark of joy and exuberance been snuffed out forever? Had he—

"Duncan." Angus closed his eyes, his lips tightening in the struggle to control the trembling emotion that wracked his face. He clenched his hands into fists at his side, nothing else betraying the turmoil within but his nostrils flaring in harsh, laboured breaths.

"Duncan's dead?" Her voice was barely audible. She had not expected that answer at all.

He nodded. "Aye," he choked, opening his eyes.

Fiona did not reply. What could she say? She remembered how hollow-sounding the words of consolement had been when her own dear brother, Douglas, had died; how she had hated people's words of sentiment or physical touch in the name of comfort, even though she knew they were only trying to help.

She turned away and walked back the way she had come, aimless, overcome with guilt. It was her fault, was it not? She should never have ridden out so far on the moors that day. She should never have agreed to escape. All this loss would not have happened if she hadn't missed her execution day, if she were dead as Lady Nuith wished. Perhaps the Scots would still have fought for freedom, but not so soon in the birth of winter, against such hopeless odds. Were it not for her, Duncan would still be alive and Angus would not have lost yet another brother to the war against the Danes.

Truth it was, the old War and this one were really one and the same.

Tears smarted in her eyes at her last memory of him. *"Keep yerself safe, princess. We hae yer back."* She had known him the least out of all the McCladden brothers, but he had always been as loyal as his younger siblings. Annag had said that Angus was not as close to him as he had been with Sioned, but surely this loss only aggravated the old wound. Did it not rip open the scars that had never healed, causing more pain than before?

Her hand strayed up beneath the plaid that hung over her hurting shoulder, brushing the cold clan pin that had once been her brother's. She rarely touched it, the remembrance too painful to dwell on often. He had given it to her before he had left for the War, saying she should safeguard it against his return—only he had never come back. She had kept it ever since, the one tangible memory she had from the last time she had seen him.

That had been all he had left her with.

Fiona raised her head slowly, numbly, vision blurred. Then, she began to walk. It was nearly a hopeless cause, even though she had last seen him in this part of the battlefield. She walked precariously among the bodies, nearly losing her balance at times, bile rising in her throat at touching the cold corpses. It was even worse when they were still warm, their eyes lifelessly staring at the embered horizon. Were it not for her empty stomach, she might very well have been sick. It was only for the thought to give Angus something to remember his brother by that she did this—else she would have given up long before.

At last, she found him lying against another fallen Scot, his face turned towards the sky. Duncan wore no jerkin—perhaps he had given it to Malcolm; after all, it had been far too large on him. A great blot of crimson stained his torn linen shirt, revealing the gruesome wound beneath. His hazel eyes were open, forever frozen in a look of terror that was now glazed over. A trickle of blood had escaped his open mouth, drying into his young, curling beard. But he was cold; his life had already been lost, perhaps not so long after the moment he had called out to her on the field some hours ago.

Fiona sank to her knees beside Duncan, the sense of helplessness washing over her, drowning her in its dark, despairing depths. She swallowed against the aching in her chest as she looked out over the battlefield, shadowed in the fading light.

So much death—and fer what? What hae we accomplished?

Heaving a shuddering sigh, she forced herself to ignore the dried blood that crusted Duncan's shirt and took out her dirk. Though it was not the best thing to use for this, she cut out the section of the plaid with the McCladden crested pin stuck through the wool. She winced as her strained left arm protested, holding the plaid still in her hand as her knife jaggedly tore through the cloth. She slid her dirk back into its leather sheath and pulled a faded sprig of heather from her own brother's pin, sliding it between the delicately crafted metal and Duncan's plaid. Gazing at Duncan one last time, she brushed her hand over his cold, still face, closing his eyelids in the quiet sleep of death. Then she rose to her feet, intending to return to Angus.

As she made her way back, she saw Donald McCladden moving toward her, a grave look on his face. His shield arm was wrapped in a sling, but otherwise he seemed unhurt. "Jamie McBride has fallen," he said simply, his forehead creased in grief.

"Are any of the other High Chieftains dead?" she answered in a dull voice, what hope she had of making peace between her and Angus dashed at the news. She was not certain she could handle any more such tidings before she broke under the strain of keeping back the tears.

"Nae, but most are wounded." There was a pause. "I was wi' Jamie when he died. He made me promise to tell ye tha' at the last, he still held his faith wi' ye, 'the true heir of Scotland.' He did no' regret dying fer such a worthy cause." His voice softened at the end to a gentle, fatherly whisper, a ghost of a smile shining in his blue eyes.

Fiona looked at the ground, ashamed of the tears threatening to spill over. "Thank ye, Donald. I only wish—I hope I can honour his sacrifice." She could barely make her voice heard. Her throat constricted with suppressed emotion. She longed to let the tears fall, but now was not the time, if ever it could come.

He smiled grimly. "I am certain ye shall, princess." Then his smile faded. "Hae ye seen Angus?"

She pointed in the direction she had been heading towards, where the sun was setting fast. "He's on tha' hill. I was jist gang to him."

Relief relaxed the creases on his forehead. "Thank ye. Do ye also ken where Duncan is? I ken Malcolm's wi' Rhiada, but I hae yet to find my other son." The relief vanished into a look of anxious doubt at the expression on her face. "What's wrong?"

"Duncan's dead." She choked on the words even as she said them.

Donald McCladden's eyes fluttered shut for a moment, his features twisted in heart-wrenching grief as she heard him groan, "No' him too..."

"I'm sorry," she whispered, not knowing what else to say. She hated to be the one to tell him that his son and heir had perished, lying cold on the fields around them, but she had little choice. What was she to do in the face of such loss that was, in a sense, all her fault?

He opened his eyes, tears flickering in their blue depths, and asked in a louder, though quavering voice, "Where is my son?"

Fiona turned and pointed from where she had come. "Back there.

I am so sorry," she murmured, her eyes stinging against repressed grief.

He nodded and turned away from her, walking to the place where Duncan lay. His hands clenched at his sides, but he held his head high despite the grief that surely warred within him. In that moment, he seemed far older, a mere wreck of a man, like her father was before he died.

She pushed that thought away from her mind. There was enough loss that day without her having to revisit her own. Turning away, she continued, limping her way back up the hill to Angus.

He stood much as she had left him, staring into the remnants of the sunset. He did not turn to her this time either, but all the same, she gently pressed the cloth with Duncan's pin into his hand.

Angus started, glancing at her before raising his hand to see what she had placed there. He recognized it immediately, and the tears that he had been holding back for so long began to flow. His right hand, clenched into a fist, rose to his mouth as he tried his utmost to hold back the cries of anguish and sorrow that threatened to escape.

Fiona watched helplessly as silent sobs shook his frame. As if someone else was commanding her movements, she stepped forward and embraced him as she had used to do to her brother so many years ago, ignoring the pain it caused her injured arm.

Angus flung his arms around her and buried his face in her shoulder, clinging to her as if she was the only sure thing left in his fragile world. He trembled in her arms, each broken cry fracturing the walls he had built up between himself and the world since Sioned's death, the floodgates pouring free. She tightened her arms around him, trying to hold together the damaged pieces and keep him from shattering entirely.

Tears slipped down her own face as the weariness and sorrow of the day overcame her, and she no longer struggled to hold back the tide of her own grief. She clung to him, as the sun faded from the heavens, afraid to let go and be lost and alone in her anguish.

The sky darkened towards winter twilight when the sobs at last subsided. Angus let go of her slowly, as if reluctant to pull back, his eyes red and swollen, and traces of tears on his face. "I'm sorry," he said, his voice breaking.

"Angus, ye donnae need to apologise," she replied gently, rubbing her hand across her face that must look as bad as his. "I was the same when the news came tha' my own brother, Douglas, was dead. There is nae shame in weeping fer those we hae lost."

He looked away towards the faint golden light that still lingered in the sky. "I thought—" His voice shuddered, and he took a deep breath to try to steady it. "I thought tha' I could bear it if another of my brothers would fall after what happened to Sioned." He bit his trembling lip and gazed at her, his blue eyes glistening in broken sorrow. "I was wrong. This is even worse." A tear slipped down his face, but he did not brush it away.

Fiona sat down on the cold, hard earth, gesturing for him to do the same. If a story was coming, she wanted to be able to hear it without standing on weary legs.

"Sioned was more than a brother," Angus began haltingly, as if reaching deep within to the memories he had kept hidden in his heart for the last six years. "He was a friend to me, and we did everything together. He was the one who taught me the use of weapons and took me hunting many times. Unlike Duncan and Malcolm, he was more serious and earnest, but he did jest at times, and when he did, it was so whimsical!" His voice broke off for a moment, a tearful smile crossing his face before fading away. "Then when Father came home without him..." What he could not say struck her far more than words ever could. It was several moments before he could speak again. "Ever since tha' day, I hae been so afraid of tha' fate happening to the rest of my family and those I love."

Fiona brushed his fingers with her own and he did not thrust her away, gently wrapping his hand around hers and holding it, the only warmth against the rising, chill wind.

"I saw Duncan fall, the Danish sword piercing his chest, and there was nothing I could do to prevent it..." His voice trailed off again, but this time he did not go on, only gazing at the swiftly darkening horizon.

"'Tis all my fault," she murmured, not quite intending for him to hear. Angus might be free of the pain he had kept locked away for so long, but she still drowned in guilt.

He stared at her, his dark brows drawn together. "Fiona, wha' are ye saying? How is all this"—he gestured behind them—"yer fault?"

She rubbed her face again as a tear escaped her eye. "If it were no' fer me, this battle would nae hae taken place. There would be nae rush to fight in winter and against a far greater host." She heaved a shuddering sigh. "I touched my sword in the dancing." Her gaze flickered up to meet his, and she saw understanding cross his face.

"Fiona, the sword dance is no' tha' important. 'Tis only tradition now and means nothing more than tha'. I saw yer mistake because I was watching ye, but I doubt anyone else did." He reached up and gently brushed away the tears falling down her face. When he spoke again, his voice deepened in soft tenderness, in a way she had never heard him speak before. "Donnae think yerself too unworthy fer men to risk their lives fer ye, Fiona. But ne'er imagine yerself so highly that the War is entirely because of ye. Ye are no' the sole reason it is fought. Ye are, instead, our greatest hope in fighting it."

Fiona bit her lip, too shocked by his kind words to know how to reply.

Angus looked down and fingered the scrap of plaid she had given him before glancing up at her, a sad smile on his face. "Thank ye—fer this."

She smiled back through her tears and nodded. "Douglas gave me his before he left fer the War. I still hae it." She reached underneath her plaid and pulled it out into the fading light of evening. The pin was larger than her own and the metal tarnished, but the sprig of dried heather was still there, the ancient symbol of Scotland. She replaced it after a moment and then Angus also pinned Duncan's underneath his plaid before rising to his feet.

With one last glance at the fleeting remnants of the sunset, he extended his hand to Fiona. "I suppose we should be a-going back before they start looking fer us." His voice was light, almost wistful, as it is sometimes after a hard cry.

"Aye, we should," she replied. She took his hand, grateful for the warmth against the winter wind. Together they returned to the camp, leaving the grassy hillside to the coming night.

~ 19 ~

AFTERMATH

FIONA and Angus returned to the hastily erected camp as the sun finally sank below the horizon and chilling darkness drenched the world. The swirling storm of guilt and grief had melted away into a fine mist of exhausted peace. Angus had placed his arm across her shoulders to give her more support while she limped alongside him, her ankle and left arm still throbbing painfully, yet she was also grateful for the warmth and companionship he gave so willingly without question. She was glad to have him beside her against the despair that awaited them at the encampment.

The camp was a ghost of what it had been south of Drumdae. The tents that had once been in many places were few and far between, hastily erected for the wounded. Most of the Scots were too fatigued to care about a layer of canvas between them and the open sky. As long as no rain or snow fell, they would be just as well without it, for the wind was still for the first time in days. Fires were scattered in odd places, essential to ward off the freezing cold of early winter, especially for the wounded who would need the warmth the most during the crucial hours of the night. It could mean the difference between life and death. The Danes would not dare attack that evening, for they had fled the field before the sun had set.

Fiona and Angus found Rhiada first, sitting among the chieftains as they gave an account of how many remained of their men. The flames burning before him thrust light into the shadows from his hood. It was grim news that the chieftains gave, and Rhiada's scarred face betrayed his tearless grief.

~ 175 ~

"From Bryce's company, five and seventy alive. From Drummond, twoscore and three hundred remaining. From Jamie, thirty. From Donald, fourscore. From Eachann, six and ninety. Alastair has left to him three and a hundred." The list went on and on, the numbers devastatingly lower than they had been early that morning. More than half their numbers had been lost that day.

Fiona bit her lip as she listened, the guilt rushing back like a swollen tide, and she wavered with weariness.

Angus' hand on her shoulder tightened its grip and she glanced towards him, seeing in his steady blue eyes a firm determination. He shook his head, as if to say, *"Donnae hold yerself responsible. 'Tis nae yer guilt."*

She attempted a smile, but she did not feel it was successful. She was utterly spent, her shoulder, ankle, and cut hand aching with pain—and with the cold. She knew she was fortunate not to be more severely wounded, but the agony, such as it was, seemed nigh unbearable.

"Who shall finish off the rest of the Danes before they return to Lady Nuith?" Donald McCladden asked, his voice strained. The fire cast odd shadows in his face, making him appear far older than his years.

Drummond, who had remained silent so long, cleared his throat. "I am willing, I and my fastest riders. We hae travelled less than ye and are fresher because of it. We should soon be able to catch up to them. They cannae hae gang far."

Donald glanced at the other chieftains, who nodded slowly in agreement.

"I will send ye some of my men to aid yer cause," Bryce said stiffly, his dark eyes glimmering in challenge, despite his arm wrapped in a sling.

"Then it is settled. May the wind be at yer back and bring ye good hunting," Donald concluded, his shoulders heaving with a silent sigh.

Drummond bowed his head in acknowledgment and left, the folds of his black cloak billowing out behind him as he turned.

In his absence, Fiona espied Malcolm coming to sit beside Rhiada, drawing his cloak about him for warmth; he no longer wore his leather shirt. When he caught sight of her and his brother, he jumped to his feet again and joined their company. "Where's Duncan?" he asked in a soft voice as the chieftains continued to speak among themselves. He looked from Angus' tear-stained face to Fiona's, awaiting their answer in nervous apprehension.

"He has taken the Warrior's Road," Angus replied, his voice cracking a little at the end.

The expression on Malcolm's face changed from one of fear to shock, and then to broken grief, his grey eyes shadowed by more than the winter darkness around them.

Fiona watched as a tear spilled down his face, and he turned and ran. She made to follow him, but Angus caught her wrist and said quietly, "Let him be. I ken how I was when Sioned fell. Malcolm and Duncan were once like Sioned and I. Let him grieve alone. He will return in his own time."

"Angus; princess," Donald said, addressing them for the first time as the other High Chieftains dispersed.

"Aye, Father, we hae returned," Angus replied to his father, inhaling sharply and rubbing any remaining signs of tears from his cheeks.

"Ye need tha' head wound looked to, my son," his father said with sorrowful tenderness, unable to show more affection in the presence of his men about them, even if none of them would have cared.

"I can see to it," Fiona replied before she realised what she had said, shivering with cold and desperately wanting her cloak. "I can see to it," she repeated more firmly despite the wave of hot embarrassment that swept across her face.

"Ye donnae hae—" Angus began.

"Please," she whispered pleadingly. "'Tis the least I can do in return for wha's been sacrificed this day."

"There is nae debt, princess," Donald said for them both. "But I willnae stop ye from helping as ye will. 'Tis the mark of a leader to serve others. Jist remember that ye both also need some food and rest. Who kens wha' the morrow will bring." Donald laid his hand for a moment on his son's shoulder, wordless communication passing between them.

Angus placed his hand on top of his father's and bent his head. Then he turned and, with one glance at Fiona, took her hand again, leading her to sit beside Rhiada. "I will be back wi' bandages and whatever else ye need," he explained softly before vanishing into the darkness.

The smell of woodsmoke and the faint waft of cooking porridge drifted over the camp. Fiona barely felt the hunger pains. All the blood, gore, and death she had seen that day had taken away her appetite for now.

"Fiona?"

"Aye, Rhiada, 'tis me," she murmured, brushing his shoulder gently.

"Are ye wounded?"

"Nothing serious. Jist...twisted my ankle and did something to my shoulder. I hae a cut across my hand, but it could be worse."

"See that Angus tends to it before ye rest fer the night." He held his cloak tighter around him, and Fiona clenched her teeth to keep them from chattering.

"I will," she said, her fingers wrapped around themselves for warmth as the biting air seemed to penetrate through her skin and scrape away at her bones. She had no idea where her cloak was by now, if it was even still in Sgàil's saddle pack from yesterday.

Angus returned at that moment, a flask of water in one hand, something dark and large underneath his arm, and shredded fabric in his other hand that looked like it had once been a good, sturdy shirt. "They had nae more bandages, only this," he replied timidly. "Will it work?"

Fiona shrugged. "'Twill do, I think. I hae ne'er done this before." She laughed nervously.

A smile flashed across his face, lighting the depths of his eyes where the fire before them failed to reach. "Neither hae I." He sat down beside her, holding the flask between his knees and handing her the makeshift bandages. "I hae also this." He pulled out the bundle beneath his arm and Fiona saw that it was her cloak.

She took it gratefully and tied the strings around her shoulders, the warm folds settling around her. "Thank ye, I sorely needed that."

"I had mine already, but ye looked nigh to freezing," he explained.

"Aye," she replied. "I donnae suppose ye'd ken where my dress is? I took it off before joining the battle earlier."

Angus shrugged. "Nae, but I can look afterwards if ye'd like."

"I would indeed," she said, taking the bandages from him. One of them was a short piece and raggedly torn, hardly worthy of binding the slightest wound and certainly useless for the purpose it might have been intended for.

Cameron came up at that moment, giving a bowl of steaming porridge to Rhiada, who took it gratefully and began to eat in silence.

Angus shook his head when Cameron offered them the same tasteless supper. Neither of them could eat yet, so the piper simply placed the single bowl and spoon down on the ground, leaving them with only a nod to the princess.

Fiona pressed the torn cloth against the mouth of the flask of water, dampening it. It was a pity she lacked the herbs Annag might have used. She did not know yet how serious the wound was; Angus behaved as if it were nothing, but he was skilled at hiding his pain.

Pinching her lips together, she placed the wet cloth on his temple, her hand against the other side of his face as she attempted to wipe away the blood, that had dried hours ago on his skin and clumped in his hair, without causing him hurt.

He sucked in his breath sharply, his dark lashes fluttering shut a moment, but he made no other sign of the pain.

It was slow work, and difficult to clean it properly, especially when going slowly so as not to hurt him. She glanced at him from time to time as more and more of it came away, revealing the nasty gash across his temple and cheekbone that started bleeding afresh a little, watching to see whether he was grimacing or not. She was so afraid of hurting him. And yet the look that shone in his deep blue eyes shocked her.

He gazed at her steadfastly, but it was neither fear nor grief nor hurt in his glance. It was something that blazed against the darkness and despair of that day, like the warm light and beauty of a golden sunrise; a look of pure adoration.

Fiona turned away, her face burning, and not because of the heat of the fire. She hurriedly finished wiping away the rest of the blood and began to dress the wound, avoiding meeting his eyes again until it was finished. She tied it in a clumsy bandage, hoping it would hold.

"Will it do?" she asked softly as other men and youths sat down around the fire, warming their hands before its shadowing flames.

She glanced up to see a smile playing on his lips. He reached up and gingerly touched the bandage, wincing as he pressed too hard. "Aye, it'll do, princess." And there was no mockery in his tone.

"That is good." She sighed with relief.

"Now take yers off and I'll see to it."

A loud cry burst across the field and fires, one of many already heard that evening. She heard Angus suck in his breath sharply, perhaps sympathising with the pain of those in far worse states than them both. But when she looked up to meet his gaze, he shook his head. They could do little to help the wounded until their own hurts were seen to.

Fiona unwound the clumsy wrapping from her hand, the movements slow as her shield arm was nearly useless by this point. Beneath the bloody, makeshift bandage, the skin was raw and angry where she had been cut hours ago. It hurt more to take the cloth away than it had when the sword had slid across her knuckles, and she gritted her teeth against the pain.

Angus took her hand and bandaged the wound as tenderly as she had done his, every movement as delicate and purposeful as a harper's. He had hands like Rhiada's, long and slender, more suited for creating beauty in music than wielding death and destruction through the means of sword and bow.

It was a pity, she thought then, that she had never heard him play the harp, if he could play it. Or sing. She imagined he would have a lovely voice; it was beautiful enough to simply listen to him speak.

She blinked as he tied the cloth around her injury, realising she had nearly fallen asleep watching the way the firelight shadowed his face and flickered in the depths of his eyes.

"There, I think tha' should do." He cocked his head to one side and examined his work. "Nae other injuries?"

She shook her head. "Only twisted my ankle and did something to my shoulder. But tha' cannae be fixed wi' cloth and water and wha' else."

His brows furrowed. "Wha's wrong wi' yer shoulder?"

She shrugged, crossing her right arm over herself for warmth against the cold air. "Disjointed it or something when blocking a blow. I didnae hae a shield, but I couldnae swing my sword fast enough so I stopped his arm wi' mine."

"Let me see," he said, reaching out and feeling her shoulder gently but firmly. Then without warning, he suddenly gripped her right above the elbow with one hand and her shoulder with the other, snapping it back in.

"Aiee!" she exclaimed under her breath, not wanting to draw attention from the others conversing around the fire, nor from Rhiada, who seemed to be falling asleep beside them. "Ye could hae warned me first!" she sputtered.

He grinned. "Aye, and then ye would hae been expecting it and tensed up, and I might hae harmed ye instead of helping ye. But I think it should be fine now. 'Tis happened many times when my brothers and I hae been sparring. If we e'er get back, I will teach ye how to fight wi' a shield and nae jist use it as a defence."

Fiona smiled in return, unable to resist the open expression on his face. "Aye, I would like tha." She tugged loose the ties of her jerkin on the sides, not wanting to sleep in that thing.

"Here, let me. Yer shoulder needs to heal." He helped her pull it off before he took off his own, setting them both aside. They would not be wearing them again tonight. Then he rose to his feet, saying, "I'll be back."

She closed her eyes in the silence, the horrors of the day fading away into the edges of her consciousness. She might have fallen asleep altogether except that Angus returned after several minutes had passed, carrying yet another bundle in his hands.

"I found yer dress," he murmured simply, holding it out to her.

Her arm still stiff, he helped her into it much like his younger brother had done the opposite earlier that day, drawing it over the shirt and kilt she already wore. In any other situation, it might have been quite awkward, but she appreciated the help, the ties being difficult to reach with her hurting arm.

At that moment, Malcolm walked up to them, his eyes red and swollen and the remains of tears on his cheeks. He sat down without a word beside Angus and leaned forward, his head propped up in his hands, staring into the flames.

"Malcolm," Fiona whispered, "are ye hungry? There's enough porridge fer us to share."

He glanced up but did not answer verbally.

"Malcolm, are ye all right?"

He nodded and looked away, swallowing hard.

"Fiona, let him be." Angus spoke gently.

She gazed at the young lad, his face turned from the fire, and then at Angus, nodding in answer.

Angus picked up the bowl of porridge before them and murmured, "Ye gang to eat?"

"I should, but I hae little appetite," Fiona replied soberly. The air around them when not broken with conversation was rent with the cries of men in agony, and it sickened her to guess at the pain they must be experiencing to break composure like that.

"Jist a few bites. I will eat whatever ye donnae, but ye must eat." His face was darkened with worried concern. "If ye donnae keep up yer strength, 'twill be as bad as if the Danes killed ye anyway."

"Nae quite as bad as tha'," Rhiada suddenly broke in, the firelight flickering across his closed eyelids. "But Angus is right, princess. Ye must eat a wee bit at least."

Fiona took the bowl from Angus. "Aye, then, I will." She managed to swallow at least three bites of it before handing it to Angus. "I cannae eat anymore."

He merely shrugged and finished it off in silence.

He rose to give the empty bowl to the camp cook when a piercing scream cut through the air like a sword blade. It chilled Fiona to the bone and she shuddered, wrapping her cloak closer around her as if to drown out the moans of the wounded and dying, the horror of that night following the battle.

"Fiona, ye should help tend to the wounded," Rhiada said as Angus left them. "'Twould do yer men good to see ye serving them. As their princess and their future queen, to serve yer people is the greatest honour ye can give them."

She bit back the retort that she was exhausted and inexperienced in proper healing. He was right, and she knew it. These men had risked their lives for freedom's sake and also for hers; she owed them this much, if only to help ease their suffering for a few hours.

She stood up, her body aching with weariness, and set off in search of one of the tents housing the wounded. She ducked beneath the tent flap, meeting the worn face of a Scot evidently more knowledgeable about treating wounds than most. He was bandaging a bloodied stump that had once been an arm, his own hands stained crimson. The other clenched his remaining hand in pain, silent tears streaming down his cheeks.

The sight sickened her.

Kneeling beside the man, she hesitated before asking in a shaky voice, "Is there anything I can do to help?"

He cleared his throat and finished dressing the wound. Then, sitting back, he said, "Aye, if ye're nae afraid of the sight of blood."

He had a rough voice, and his simple, woollen clothing and hunched frame seemed to be more the appearance of a sheep herder than a warrior—or a healer.

She shook her head and swallowed hard. "Nae, 'tis only the pain tha' they must be going through tha' hurts me." She sounded so much weaker than she wanted to; she only hoped that this man, whoever he was, mistook it for weariness and not for cowardice.

He murmured a few words to the warrior he had just attended to and rose to his feet. "This way, princess." He led the way to another tent, the icy air biting their exposed skin as they crossed the way beneath a starlit sky. Fires gleamed around them and torches shone beneath the tent coverings, but that was the only light. It was dismal and dreary even with the warm torchlight flaring against the dark.

The man knelt beside a youth who could not have been much older than Angus, but it was hard to tell in the dim light. The healer took off the blanket covering the shivering, thin body, and Fiona clenched her jaw against the sight beneath.

The shirt was torn into rags and drenched with dried blood. An ugly mass of torn flesh and broken bone lay beneath. Perhaps he had met a Danish axe—what else could cause such a thing? It was a wonder he was still alive; perhaps the wound was not so serious if he was. Oftentimes the wounds looked worse before being properly cleaned. Or so she hoped.

"Do ye ken where to find water?"

Fiona blinked, realising the man was addressing her. "Nae, but I can fetch it easily enough."

"Gae find it. Those by the fires should hae some. And be quick," he added as she disappeared out into the air.

She ran to the nearest fire, catching her breath before exclaiming to the surprised group of men and youths, "Do any of ye hae water?"

One wordlessly held up a leather skin and handed it to her.

She shouted her thanks over her shoulder as she rushed back, dropping beside the mangled youth and giving it to the healer. "Will this do?"

He nodded, easing away the lad's bloodied shirt and pouring water gently over the wound.

Some of the blood washed away and the boy gasped, moaning in pain. His sandy brows twisted in a grimace, his eyelids fluttering but never opening.

"Sa, sa, 'tis all right then," the man murmured as gently as if speaking to his own bairn. "I need ye to fetch bandages," he added to Fiona. "I hae none left wi' me."

"I'll get them," she said, rising to her feet and nearly colliding with Angus who came into the tent at that moment. "Och, I am sorry," she gasped.

"Nae matter," he replied, reaching out to steady her.

"Do ye ken where to find bandages? We need some, and..."

He shook his head. "I came in search of them myself."

"We'll hae to use something else then," said the man behind them. "I donnae suppose any of ye hae any shirts to spare."

Fiona paused. She had some from Douglas, but who knew where that saddle pack was now. By the time she found them, it might already be too late. Bending, she reached beneath her dress and tore at her underskirt. It came away easily, having been worn until it was almost threadbare. "Will this—?"

"Aye," he interrupted, reaching for it. Tearing it in half, he drenched it in water and cleaned the wound as best as he could, the torn flesh more apparent now than before.

Fiona and Angus both knelt down and aided him, wrapping the lad's legs with the blanket to stop his shivering.

"He's burning," Fiona gasped when her hands brushed against his skin.

"Aye, wound fever. And I hae nothing to help him fight it." It was not a complaint. Only a grim declaration of the truth.

Fiona glanced at Angus, but he did not meet her gaze, his mouth set in determination.

She stood and tore the rest of her underskirt away, knowing the flimsy piece she had given at the first would not be enough to properly bandage the wound.

The man took it gratefully and began to wind it around the lad's tremoring body, but it was already too late.

With a shuddering sigh, the youth relaxed and moved no longer, his shivering gradually subsiding into a deathly stillness.

Fiona stared at him in shock even as the man placed the blanket over the lad's body and left them, laying a hand on her shoulder in passing. All she saw was a body already losing its warmth, a life snuffed out, a life that might have been saved if they had come sooner, a life that was destroyed because of the Danes, because her father failed years ago to drive them out, because she had failed....

"Fiona, let's gae." It was Angus, his voice soft and tender like his mother's had been when she had comforted Fiona before she left An Dùn. "'Tis nae use to be here now, and ye need yer rest." He wrapped his arms around her and lifted her to her feet.

She wept into his shoulder, wearied cries escaping her lips, muffled in his shirt. "Is—freedom—really worth this?"

"'Tis a dishonour to this lad and those tha' hae died today to think otherwise," he whispered into her ear, holding her closer.

She pulled back and brushed the tears off her face. "I'm sorry—I didnae..."

"Nae harm done. But come, we all need sleep to face tomorrow and whate'er comes next."

Taking her by the hand, he led her gently like a little bairn back to the fire where Rhiada and others already lay asleep. Malcolm sat up at their approach, blinking sleepily before lying down again and yawning.

Fiona nestled in between him and his brother, their cloaks and plaids piled upon them for warmth against the cold winter night. Malcolm sniffled from time to time, traces of tears still on his cheeks, but no other sound disturbed the silence. The horses were quiet, and the cries of the dying had ceased. Only the whispering wind, the crackling fires, and the spoken watchwords of the guards at the outskirts of the camp disturbed the silent night.

Fiona's eyes closed at last in utter weariness as all of them slept uneasily, waiting for a dawn that might never come again.

~ 20 ~

UNREST ANÒ ÒOUBT

ÒRUMMOND MacDougall inhaled sharply the sweet, chill air of early winter as the small warband rode down into a little dell. It was slow going, all that night into early morning, but it was hard to ride far in darkness when pursuing panicked men fleeing for their lives.

His concentration was broken as a scout, one of Bryce's men, came riding into view.

"The Danes are jist around the hill! Shall we get them, sir?" the young man panted, reining in his horse. The fine creature tossed its head in fierce agreement, pawing eagerly at the ground with its hoof.

Drummond gazed into the grey-misted distance, coolly calculating in his mind. His plan depended on fooling them all, even if it meant sacrificing the lives of those who had once been his sworn blood-brothers. "How many of them are there?"

"Och, 'bout our number and a half more."

"Aye," Drummond replied briskly, his mind made up. Then he called out behind him, "Argyll! Take half our number and go around by the east side. We shall surround both flanks so they hae nae choice but to surrender."

Argyll, a thick-set and broad-shouldered man with golden hair that curled like a ram's fleece on his head, nodded and gave quick orders to the men in his command.

Drummond beckoned the others to follow him.

Without another word spoken, they charged, their horses' hooves thundering across the misty plain. Drummond pulled out his broadsword and held it straight in front of him like a spear parting the wind, pointing it in the Danes' direction.

As he had hoped, he and Argyll's band came together, outflanking the Danes and driving them against the hillside. Forced to higher ground, they scattered over the barren moorland, any semblance of a fight having fled with the windswept rain.

One by one, the Danes were cut down. Several Scots and their fine horses fell also, but not as many as the Danes who, exhausted from running, and many with wounds and lacking weapons, were slain without a fight.

At last, only a few remained, and one, seemingly their leader, stood defending himself with a bloody sword, the rain and crimson running down in rivulets upon the blade. The wind blew into his face, his dark hair sticking in strands to his skin. His men gathered their courage, what little was left of it, and gave a hoarse cry of defiance.

In wordless agreement, the Scots without horses ran towards them, their claymores raised in an attempt to finish the small band off for good. Drummond neither joined them nor stopped them.

It was an odd thing, remaining in the middle ground. And yet it was a struggle, attempting to convince the Scots that he was on their side while hoping to not lose the Danes' trust in him. And sooner or later, the deed he had promised must be done. That in itself would be difficult enough, especially if Lachlan continued to grumble about it instead of having the patience to wait for the right time.

Aye, time; that was never on anyone's side...

Drummond shifted in his saddle and suddenly recognized the leader remaining among the few Danes left. Urging his horse forward, he cried out, "Stop!"

The Scots halted in their last attack, surprised at this strange command and looking to him in confusion. Nonetheless, one of them still kicked the Dane behind his knees, forcing him down. The Scot yanked the man up again by his hair and held up his head, his blade pressing against the man's neck. The Danish leader began to make a feeble attempt to ask for mercy, but his words faded away into silence when Drummond drew near.

Drummond MacDougall dismounted, giving the reins to one of his men standing by, and signalled the Scot to let go of the Dane. The man did so and sheathed his sword, but he still gripped the weapon's handle, waiting for further orders.

The Dane rose to his feet and stared defiantly at the man who had spared his life.

"Sa ha. I did not think to find you here, Bëorn," Drummond said, speaking in his own tongue so that the Scots around him would not understand.

"I did not think to find you fighting with the Scots, Drummond MacDougall, and not against them." He spat at the ground. "Lady Nuith will not be pleased."

"She already knows."

Bëorn stared at him in shocked silence.

Drummond glanced hastily around at the group of Scots who were gathered around him, listening for a word of command and, perhaps also, an explanation for what was transpiring before their eyes. "She wishes for the death of Princess Fiona. And I have promised my sister that I will do so, albeit in my own way. I intend not only for her death but the simultaneous surrender of the Lowlander Scots."

Bëorn started, a light illuminating his otherwise jet-black eyes. "And just how do you plan to do that?"

"Tell my sister to send as many men as she can muster to the Pass. There are spies at Caerloch, and they must also know the news so that Chieftain McCladden will send his men there. 'Tis a tricky business, but I think we can easily overwhelm them and force their submission. I will give you more details once your men arrive as I have scouts of my own."

Bëorn nodded grimly. "I shall tell her, provided you give me my life and the lives of my men yet living."

"I shall try." Drummond turned on his heel and mounted his horse, beckoning the other Scots to do the same. "Let him and his men gae free," he said in the Scots' Gàidhlig.

"But sir," Argyll protested, "he will return to Lady Nuith!"

"Aye, to tell her that the Danes hae lost," Drummond said, forcing a smile on his face. "Wha' is the use of their defeat if she cannae hear of it from the few survivors?"

His own men laughed at the jest, but those who belonged to Bryce MacClydno only stared at him and turned away, a couple of them muttering to themselves. Then Drummond's company rode off, leaving Bëorn and his few remaining men to return alone.

Fiona McCurragh watched absentmindedly as the Scots went to and fro about the camp, some still attending to the needs of the wounded and others repairing—or practising with—their weapons. Those who remained alive would stay alive until the next battle, but those who had died during the night were being buried with the rest to protect their bodies from the wolves, which surely still lived in Drumdae Forest.

Angus and Malcolm had gone with their father to see to the burying of their brother. In better times, the death of a chieftain's son would be accompanied by the solemn music of bagpipes and the recounting of the warrior's deeds. But Donald had wished for it to be a private grieving, since the Scots had enough losses of their own. The McCladdens had left some time ago, and Fiona expected them to return at any moment. Meanwhile, she waited huddled in her cloak, occasionally blowing on her numb fingers.

The air was cold and bitter. Winter was coming; that much was certain even if the snow had not yet fallen this far south. Would they have to fight in such severe weather? It was already difficult, even with fires, to sleep in such frigid temperatures, unprotected from the wind. She had heard much sniffling and coughing.

Of course, it would seem pointless to stop fighting after just one battle, but it would also be foolish to continue attacking in the middle of winter when they could so easily be cut off from supplies. They were already short on food. Not to mention they did not have enough men to persist in resisting Danish rule.

Glancing up at the black, naked tree branches silhouetted against the murky grey sky, she saw a small band of men returning from the battlefield, one of them heading toward her.

A moment later, Angus came and sat down next to her in silence, peering out thoughtfully across the plain covered with mounds of upturned earth, the last resting place of those who had perished in freedom's name.

"How was it, the burying?" she asked simply, glancing up at the strangeness of the white bandage across his temples.

He shrugged. "I suppose it went well as far as those things gae." He sighed softly. "'Tis hard, still, to believe he's really gang." His voice was scarcely louder than a whisper. He looked at Fiona, tears glistening in his blue eyes.

She reached over and placed her hand over his, squeezing gently. His fingers wrapped themselves around hers tenderly so as not to hurt her bandaged knuckles, providing warmth against the unforgiving wind.

He smiled through his tears and spoke, his voice cracking at the edges. "I donnae ken if I shall ever realise tha' he's really gang until years later as I did wi' Sioned." He paused once more, staring into the distance. Then he inhaled sharply and turned to her, saying, "Fiona, I want to thank ye fer yer friendship. I ken tha' I hae no' been the kindest of people to ye, but I am truly sorry. I appreciate ye being there w-when Duncan died.... Thank ye," he ended in a whisper before reaching up with one hand to brush the tears out of his eyes. "I'm sorry," he said, almost laughing.

"'Tis nothing, Angus," she answered, but she was smiling too. "I am also glad of yer friendship and yer loyalty, and I donnae deserve it, regardless of wha' ye say."

"I'm beginning to think tha' Cadwal is right," a voice said from behind them, interrupting before Angus could reply.

Fiona and Angus turned to see Malcolm coming towards them, his hands on his hips as if he were about to dance the sword dance.

Cadwal? She had not thought of the lad since she'd seen him, his face swollen from his and Angus' tussle. "Wha' do ye mean?" Fiona questioned.

Malcolm walked forward and plopped down next to her. "Ah well, what he said 'bout being surprised tha' Angus is fancying a lass."

"I donnae, so wha' are ye gang on about?" Angus retorted, his pale face reddening in embarrassment.

"Ye're holding hands!" his younger brother exclaimed.

Fiona snatched back her hand and hid it in her lap, her cheeks burning.

Angus glared daggers at his brother, his lips pinched together. A swirling storm flashed in his eyes, but he said nothing.

"Anyway," Malcolm continued, rising to his feet, "Father wants both of ye."

Fiona and Angus both stood and made their way to Donald Mc-Cladden's tent, Malcolm walking with them a ways before disappearing in another direction. Fiona supposed he was in search of food. He seemed more himself than last night, but his lightheartedness felt shallow, as if the wind had been knocked out of it.

Angus held open the tent flap for her as they entered. The light through the sheepskin tent was dim, but the cloth was still a barrier against the thin, piercing wind. Rhiada and Donald were the only ones within, in addition to Drummond, his hand resting on his sword hilt and looking as though he had just returned from chasing the last of the Danes. His dark hair was every which way, and his face was strained from little sleep.

"So, wha' news have ye?" Donald McCladden asked while glancing at Rhiada, who was listening intently for the reply.

Drummond was about to answer when he caught sight of Fiona and stopped, closing his mouth. A strange look was in his eyes, a fierce yet guarded look, and she suddenly felt uneasy.

Donald looked from Drummond to Fiona, his brows furrowing.

She stepped closer to Angus, a chill shuddering down her spine. His fingers brushed against hers for a moment, as if to remind her that he would not let her come to harm.

"We ran down the remaining Danes and cut them off, slaughtering most of them," Drummond finally replied.

Donald's blue eyes darkened. "I thought I said nae survivors," he said quietly through clenched teeth. The soft harshness of his tone unnerved Fiona, and she was glad she was not the recipient of his wrath.

"I thought it best if we let some gae to tell the Lady Nuith we had won." Drummond appeared unfazed.

"I had hoped tha' if she had been kept in the dark as to wha' had happened to her army, we might hae been granted a breathing space so our wounded could heal and we could decide what our next course of action might be."

"And is that so changed?" Drummond asked with the slightest hint of mockery in his voice. A dangerous light danced in his brown eyes.

"Maybe. Ye can leave," Donald replied, fire burning in his glance.

Drummond bowed his head and left, the mockery showing even in the energy of his step. He did not bow to Fiona as he passed her. Not that she minded, for she never knew how to respond to such respect, but the sudden absence of it struck her.

Donald straightened and sighed. He attempted a smile, but the creases on his face betrayed his worry. "I suppose ye wonder why we called ye."

Fiona tried to smile back, if only for the sake of appearing at ease. "I supposed ye and Rhiada had good reasoning."

Rhiada moved to stand beside Donald. "We should hae done this long since, but there was no' time before as the threat of Danish attack was too near. But we hae a reprieve, at least fer a moment, and 'tis time to properly introduce ye to the warband who fights in yer name."

She nodded solemnly. "Aye, tha' makes sense. But why was Angus also summoned?"

Angus stared at the ground in silence, his eyes misted over, and his father paused before answering. "Perhaps, before, it would hae been enough to say tha' ye must always be guarded by one of my sons, especially wi' men like Drummond in the camp. But there is a greater reason. Now tha' Duncan is dead, Angus is the heir and will be High Chieftain if I die. He must therefore take on the responsibilities tha' were Duncan's, and tha' includes coming wi' me when we inspect the warriors beneath our charge and make certain tha' they and their weapons are in fighting condition."

"Aye, I understand."

"Well then, shall we gae?" Donald asked, taking Rhiada gently by the elbow and leading him out of the tent.

Fiona glanced at Angus and he gestured for her to walk ahead of him. Once outside, she saw Donald signal to Cameron, their piper, who had been waiting nearby.

Cameron acknowledged the command and placed the blowstick in his mouth, filling the bag with air. A few moments later, his fingers flew along the chanter as he played a fast jig on his pipes, calling the attention of all the soldiers in the camp.

Those who were able came running to gather in their respective companies, creating a path between the clans. The ranks were ten men deep and stretched onwards, winding out of sight between the tents set up for the wounded. The chieftains stood in front of their divisions, looking to High Chieftain McCladden for further orders.

The piping finished with a broken wheeze and Cameron joined the ranks, setting his pipes aside. All waited in wind-torn silence for what Donald would say.

At last, clearing his throat, Donald spoke. "Fiona McCurragh, as many of ye ken, is the only surviving heir to the throne and our sole hope in winning this war. Laird Erland and Lady Nuith wish her dead, but thanks to our piper, Cameron MacClaerthun, and our harper, Rhiada ap Derlyn, she was able to escape and has been wi' us since we left on the war trail. Though she hasnae officially ascended the throne, she is our princess and one day will be our queen. Therefore she should be treated wi' higher respect and honour than even yer battle leaders, regardless of the actions of her late father, King Daibhidh." He did not continue for a time and when he did speak again, his voice was grim and earnest. "But even here, among us, she is still in danger. If anything is to happen to her, our last hope is lost. I implore ye, as well as my own sons, to protect her wi' yer lives. I ken tha' most of ye are honourable men, and I hope and trust tha' ye will be loyal to her, even to the end."

Fiona wondered for a moment why he did not say that all of them were honourable, and then she realised he was speaking of Drummond and those beneath his command. She glanced at Angus beside her and saw him gazing straight ahead, but there was no fear in his eyes, only a soberness that, combined with the dignity with which he now carried himself, belonged more to a man and not a lad. For a moment, she caught a glimpse of what perhaps he would be as High Chieftain someday, if they survived. He would make a good leader, she mused, if he were given the chance.

Having finished speaking, Donald stepped forward and walked down the path, Fiona, Angus, and Rhiada following him. Malcolm gave her a little wave and a friendly grin from where he stood with the men of An Dùn. Fiona smiled back before continuing on.

She heard many of the Scots say to her in a general way that they had known her father, and some his father before him, because of their driving back the Danes in years past and other such great deeds. One day, mayhaps, they might also know her for her own.

In a sense, it was humbling to be so respected by the same men who had known her father, but at the same time overwhelming, for what if she lost their respect through some foolish act, like her father did by marrying Lady Nuith? What if they lost the war? Would they still care so much for defending her life with their own?

Angus nudged her gently, disturbing her thoughts, and she realised that they were finished. The men were dispersing, mostly to eat the midday meal and rest in hopes of allowing their wounds to heal.

Angus and Fiona found Malcolm sitting near one of the fires, which burned even in daylight to thwart the winter chill. He leaned against a tree, busy cramming half an oaten bannock into his mouth, his other arm entangled in his cloak and wrapped around himself for warmth. Two whole bannocks lay on the ground beside him, and Fiona felt warm water flood her mouth. She too was sick and tired of the tasteless gruel called porridge, and those oaten bannocks might as well have been honey cakes.

"Where did ye get those?" Angus asked in amazement, probably thinking the same thing she was.

"Och!" Malcolm sputtered, swallowing. "From him." He jerked his thumb in the general direction behind him.

They glanced where he was pointing and saw the man, whatever his name was, give out what appeared to be the last bannock to a soldier with his arm in a sling.

Fiona's heart sank to the pit of her empty stomach. *So, nae bannocks after all.* She heard Angus sigh beside her.

Malcolm stood and brushed the crumbs from his woollen kilt. He picked up the two bannocks and said, "Here—I hae already eaten me fill," and gave them to the other two.

Angus nearly ripped it from him, and Fiona watched in amusement as it quickly vanished.

She took hers and then nearly crushed Malcolm in an embrace—despite his squealed protest—before devouring her bannock just as rapidly as Angus, who was now licking the crumbs off his fingers.

"Well," Angus said, "I'm off."

"Where ye gang?" Malcolm asked, intrigued. "Thought ye couldnae stand tha' foul porridge stuff."

"I'm gang to see if they hae anything else," Angus replied over his shoulder before disappearing around a tent side.

Fiona sat down on the cold, hard earth and leaned against the rough bark of the tree behind her. Wrapping herself up in her cloak, she held out her hands to the flickering flames before her, the heat stinging her numb fingers.

Malcolm sat beside her in silence, rubbing a small whetstone over his sword's blade-edge.

She watched him, surprised. He had never been one to care so for his weapons like Angus did. "Malcolm, are ye all right?" she questioned softly, worry filling her. Would Malcolm become like his brother had when Sioned died? She was almost terrified to find out.

He looked up after testing his blade and swallowed. "Aye, I suppose so." He shrugged.

"Honestly?"

He was silent for a moment. "Nae, perhaps no'.... 'Tis jist so strange now. I think of something tha' would make Duncan laugh and I gae to find him, only later to realise he—he isnae here anymore." Malcolm heaved a shuddering sigh and put the whetstone away.

Fiona was silent, thinking of the days, weeks, and months after her brother had died. "I am sorry," she replied at last, then added softly, "I lost a brother too."

"Ye did?" He looked at her curiously, the pain for a moment gone from his grey eyes. "Wha' was his name?"

Fiona gazed into his open, freckled face for a moment, seeing another freckled boy but with soft hazel eyes and a winsome, dimpled smile that lit up the depths of his eyes in ways the sun never could. "Douglas," she heard herself mumble. "His name was Douglas." She looked away, the old, familiar lump rising in her throat. What would he think if he could see her now, fighting alongside men and lads to overthrow the same enemy that had stolen his life?

"Wha' was he like?"

Fiona bit her lip. She had not spoken of him, not like this. Not even to Angus, who would understand more than anyone else the pain of irreplaceable loss. But Malcolm had just lost someone dear to him, and the first loss was always the most memorable—at least, in her experience. Perhaps speaking of this might make him feel less alone. Was that not her calling as a princess, to bear her people's burdens and help them as best she could?

"He...he was..." She heaved a broken sigh and forced it out, the words trembling on her lips. "He was a brother, aye, but he was more than tha.'" She rubbed her hand across her face, as if daring the tears to fall. The words now came like a torrent, like the spring floods swelling down from the mountains. "My father ne'er cared much fer me, being the cause of his wife's death and because, as Douglas always said, I look like her. Douglas was both my brother and my father, and the best friend I could e'er hae asked fer." She inhaled sharply and looked through the hazy smoke of the fire before them, seeing in its wavering, sparking veil the distant forms of men finishing up their midday meal and walking to and fro in the camp.

Malcolm placed his hand on her shoulder as if he was afraid of breaking her. "I am sorry," he murmured. "He seems like the sort of person ye'd want beside ye all the time."

A slow smile spread across her face in spite of herself. "Aye, he was." A pang of sadness and fond memory, intermingled like rain and sunshine, washed over her. She closed her eyes a moment, listening to the sounds of the encampment in the silence that fell between them.

But the silence never lasted long, not with Malcolm. "Wha' of Rhiada? I mean"—he tripped over his words a bit—"ye donnae play harp anymore. Will ye ever take it up again? I miss the music."

She could not resist the playful longing in his eyes and nudged him gently with her elbow, grinning now. "I donnae miss practising. And maybe I will play it again, or better yet, perhaps Rhiada will play fer us sometime."

"Aye, but he's so quiet now. As if withdrawn and seeking a muse." The grin faded from the lad's face and there was no more laughter in his voice. "Perhaps he means to make a song of the War, to remember those tha' hae died."

"A worthy thing, then, to be so remembered in song."

"Aye, perhaps..." He shrugged off the cloud that had passed over his face and rose to his feet, offering her his hand. "But come, ye need to eat something more than a bannock fer supper. I cannae hae Angus stealing all the glory for looking after ye." He flashed a smile and winked.

Fiona laughed and took his hand, leaving the warmth of the fire to the cold wind and open skies.

~ 21 ~
THE HARPER'S SONG

THE night was bleak and frigid as the wind's moaning cry drove warmth away from even the strongest of hearts. The moon and stars were veiled, the sky an inky, endless black. And though Fiona lay in an immense field full of sleeping men, she felt alone. Ironic, that, for Donald had said just hours ago when he presented her to the war host that they were honour-bound to protect her. All the same, though she would have rather died than admit it to anyone, she felt vulnerable and scared, and a deep sense of abandonment filled her soul until she could stand it no longer.

Rising from the cold, hard earth, she wrapped her plaid around herself—though it offered as much warmth as the bitter winter's breath around her—and made her way to the nearest fire, one of many that bespeckled the otherwise dark field dotted with the forms of sleeping warriors.

She had fallen asleep out of exhaustion after eating some of that gruel they called porridge and no one, it seemed, had bothered to wake her. Now she was awake and alone, unable to find a familiar face in the darkness.

She stumbled in the black of night, unable to see where she was going.

A gasp escaped her lips as someone caught her, one hand snaking around her waist and the other moving swiftly upwards, locking over her mouth. The scream in her throat was stifled by the man's coarse palm and a touch of cold metal—a ring, by the feel of it—and she gazed with terror into eyes that glittered in the dim light.

"So, princess, we meet yet again," Lachlan sneered, holding her against him so tightly she could hardly breathe. It did not help that his hand was still clapped over her mouth, preventing her from crying out and letting someone know of her distress.

Oh, where were Angus or Rhiada when she needed them!

She writhed in his grasp as panic gave strength to her weary body, wriggling and kicking at turns until he cursed her under his breath. It had been cruel enough the first time; but even Drummond was not here to protect her now. If he would have even done so again—

"Be still, you vixen!" Lachlan hissed, taking his hand off her mouth for a moment to pin her arms at her sides. It was only for a moment, but it was enough.

Without bothering to fill her lungs with air, she screamed as loud as she could before Lachlan smothered her face against his tunic, bending her arms back as if to break them. Spasms of pain shot through her limbs and she choked on the thick reek of unwashed body and wool. Her shoulder, still healing, ached terribly and the scabbing on her hand was sore; her fingers having been crushed in his anger felt none the better for it.

Was it possible to be in this much pain and still know it was nothing compared to what was coming if no one stopped him? Had no one heard her cry?

Pain and panic rushed through her veins like blood. Her heart beat so fast she thought it would burst. How much longer until he—

A strong force crashed into them, the impact sending both her and Lachlan to the ground. It was fortunate that she fell on top of him and not the other way around, but it still jarred her, knocking the breath out of her lungs as her jaw slammed into his shoulder. At least his grip on her loosened, and she scrambled off of him as momentary relief flooded over her, ebbing away into acute nausea.

She crawled a short space away to be out of reach from both him and whoever it was that had knocked him down in the first place. She retched, the remains of her tasteless dinner now wasted completely. Heated arguing echoed beside her, but she cared little as long as Lachlan would not come near. Her stomach twisting, she wiped her mouth with the back of her hand and shuddered.

"Fiona!" A familiar voice called out from somewhere behind her, followed by footsteps drawing closer on the near-frozen ground. She felt someone lay a warm hand on her shoulder, bringing her back to reality. "Fiona, are ye all right? I am so sorry I didnae—"

"Nae, Angus, 'tis fine," she replied bitterly, her throat sore and everything burning inside of her. Though the icy wind bit through her woollen clothes and thick cloak, her skin felt like it was on fire.

"Fiona, I am so sorry." The words dripped with shame, rambling on as if they could somehow atone for what had just happened—for what had almost happened. "I thought ye were wi' Malcolm still and he thought ye were wi' Rhiada and Rhiada thought ye were wi' us, and there was a terrible misunderstanding, and I couldnae find ye, but Lachlan was also missing—"

"Please," she gasped. "Angus, please donnae speak of him. No' now." She rose to her feet and wavered, her knees weak. "I donnae hold it against ye. I fell asleep away from ye all and—"

"Fiona, 'tis my charge to protect ye, especially from the likes of him." His voice dropped to a hoarse whisper. "Whether ye hold it against me or no', 'tis still my responsibility and I failed ye. I...I am so sorry and I ken tha' nae apology will make up fer it, but...Fiona, will ye forgive me all the same?"

It was too dark to see his face, but she could hear the regret in his voice, lingering in the air like falling snow.

"Och!" she cried, a quiet gasp, as though someone had stabbed her with a cold knife.

She heard a rustling of clothing and saw, in the dim light, Angus extend his arms to her timidly. She collapsed into them, relief washing over her as strength and comfort enveloped her, everything Lachlan was not. The racing fear died away into the peace of security; she was safe.

"Angus, of course I forgive ye," she heard herself saying, her throat thick with a sudden surge of emotion. "And I donnae hold it against ye. Accidents happen sometimes."

"Aye," he said, releasing her and meeting her gaze, his face close to hers to see in the cold darkness of night. "But such accidents are no' worth the cost. One day, there may no' be a second chance. And I donnae want to risk tha'." He sighed softly, rubbing his face with his hand.

A surge of weariness swept over her and she wavered, her legs weak.

"Come ye," he said, turning away. "Ye need yer rest, and Rhiada and Father will be wondering wha' became of us."

"Wha' of Lachlan?" she asked, shivering as the wind blew into her face, stinging and bitter.

Angus placed his arm across her shoulders, holding out his cloak to better shield her from the cold. "He's senseless and will hae a bad headache when he awakens. I will let Father ken of wha' he did, donnae worry."

Fiona dared to glance at the form sprawled headlong on the ground as they passed, but turned away after a moment. The sooner the whole thing was forgotten, the better. She did not want to have nightmares about him like she occasionally did of Lady Nuith.

Angus led her to one of the fires, which flickered as bright, warm flares against the icy wind and bleak darkness. In the hazy light, she saw Donald and Rhiada speaking to one another, glancing up as she and Angus sat down. There were a few others, but they were sleeping, their plaids wrapped around them for warmth.

"Fiona, are ye all right?" Donald asked, his scarlet brows drawn together in concern.

"Aye, I will be," she murmured, too exhausted to say much else.

"Will be?" Rhiada asked, his voice soft, probing the air as if searching out what had occurred, what had not been spoken of. "Fiona, wha' happened?"

"Lachlan tried to kidnap her," Angus murmured so that only they could hear and not the ones who were sleeping, or others who may be walking by in the winter darkness. "And 'tis no' the first time he's attempted it either," he continued, breaking the shocked silence between them.

"Fiona, is this true?" Donald's voice had a raw edge to it, one of suppressed horror and fury.

"Why did ye no' tell us before?" Rhiada pleaded. "'Twill do nae good to keep such silence. If anything were to happen to ye—"

"I couldnae bear to think of it," she replied, fear and exhaustion welling up inside her, bringing her close to tears. "The first time was at Caerloch, but Drummond stopped him. This was when they first came. And then—and then the next time was when Drummond came to our camp. Angus was wi' me and nothing happened except Lachlan threatened me—" Her voice broke off in a suppressed sob, a sharp sound that hung in the air.

Angus slipped his arm across her shoulders, giving her the stability she so longed for.

Leaning her head against his shoulder, she closed her eyes, feeling his warmth thaw her frozen bones. She heaved a shuddering sigh, the fear fading yet still lurking in the dark shadows of her consciousness.

"Wha' shall we do, then?" Donald asked, but he was speaking to Rhiada, not to them.

"Warn Drummond. If Lachlan cannae control himself thus far, he willnae listen to us. Wi' his chieftain, there may be a chance. Should he threaten her again wi' more witnesses, he will face trial amongst us. We cannae risk it otherwise."

"More witnesses? Is my word and Angus' nae enough?" Fiona pleaded, her voice scarce louder than a cracked whisper.

"I believe ye, as does Donald, I am sure," Rhiada replied gently. "But Drummond and his company hae no' quite been accepted by the rest of us—fer good reason—and tensions are already high. If we were to press these charges, they might accuse us and attack our already weakened numbers. Until we hae more witnesses, we cannae do anything further. I wish it were nae so, princess, but it is. Nevertheless, all of us who are faithful to ye must be more on our guard to see that ye are safe."

"Aye," Donald agreed. "'Twas an accident this time, but we cannae take such chances. No' now." He rose to his feet and disappeared into the darkness, Fiona supposed to take care of Lachlan and see that he caused no more harm that night.

He returned some time later, sitting down heavily by the fire, rubbing his temples with his hands.

"Well," Rhiada said, his voice soft. "Wha' do we do fer the present?"

"Keep watch on Lachlan, see tha' he doesnae harm Fiona again. Meanwhile, send the severely wounded home. They cannae help us, and it makes nae sense to make them suffer. The rest of us must march on the morrow." Donald sighed. "I donnae ken wha' the Danes' plans are, but we cannae remain here. Our food stores are dangerously low, and we are nowhere near any villages or chiefdoms where we might find supplies. I am thinking 'tis best to continue on north, perhaps northeast and then swing around directly south."

"To the Pass, ye mean?"

"Aye, I doubt Lady Nuith will guess us to come down on Caerloch from the north instead of from the unprotected ground facing the Lowlands. Besides, it seems a defensible place and a good standing ground fer either side." He paused, stroking his beard as he sat lost in thought for a moment. "If we donnae get there soon, the Danes will guess our plans and reinforce the pass, and then we shall be in a worse place than here.... Aye, I think 'tis best. I only wish we had more certainty, more hope." Hopelessness pervaded Donald's voice, even though Fiona was listening with eyes closed and could not see his face.

"We are ever seeking more certainty, more hope," Rhiada replied at last, his voice humming, an echo of a song in it. "The less we hae, the more we wish for it. But were times none so dire as these, were life none so fragile, we would perhaps nae hold to it so, like a shining light in the midst of darkness. The greater the darkness, the more precious that hope becomes. Were our lives, our homes, our country, our freedoms, our princess—were these none so dear to us, we would nae risk it all to keep them. Men donnae die fer something they donnae believe in. Because we risk it, then it must be worth it in the end. Should that no' give us hope?"

Fiona opened her eyes, seeing Rhiada's scarred face shadowed by the fire, the same dancing flames holding Donald's gaze captive. But perhaps he, too, was thinking of what the harper had said, the beautiful truth that was, in his telling of it, almost enough to give her hope again. Angus' eyes glimmered with sapphire tears, but she did not think it was because he was saddened. Perhaps he loved the words as well; perhaps he was trying to grasp that thin tendril of hope that whispered in the air...

Suddenly she heard Donald McCladden say in a normal tone and volume of voice, "Who goes there?"

The exhaustion and faint hope vanished in a moment, and both Angus and she jolted wide awake only to see Malcolm totter sleepily towards them, shivering in his plaid as he plopped with a rather hard *thump* beside Fiona.

Angus chuckled softly, a breathy sound, and Fiona could not keep the smile off her own face as she lifted the edge of the tartan blanket and placed it around Malcolm's shoulders.

Without a word, the boy curled up into a tight ball next to her, leaning his head on her shoulder and falling asleep almost instantly. And though Rhiada and Donald continued to speak far into the night, Angus and Fiona soon followed Malcolm into the realm of slumber, leaving the wintery night far behind.

It was in the coldest, darkest hours of the night when the sleep of nearly all the wearied warriors was shattered by the howling of a distant wolf. It pierced the cold air, echoing its haunting cry up to the clouded moon.

Fiona and the two brothers on either side of her jerked awake into heart-racing reality, the dullness of sleep pounding away with every passing moment. Around them, some of the men arose to calm the horses who neighed in terror, a sound that only heightened when the howls came again.

Malcolm looked around them, his eyes wide in confused, sleepy dread. "Wha' was tha'?" he mumbled.

"A wolf; nothing more," his father replied after looking about them for a few moments. "Let us jist hope there are nae more of them."

Fiona laid her head on Angus' shoulder again, but sleep was far from her. It was far from all of them, as sometimes happens when one is awakened out of a deep sleep by something startling. Her breathing returned to its normal pace, but the fear, awakened only a few hours before, was still there.

She looked through the flames before her at the faces of the two men beyond who led this army. Donald and Rhiada were speaking again in soft voices as they had been before she had fallen asleep, as if they had never stopped to rest at all.

Malcolm exhaled, wrapping his cloak more tightly around him. "Harper dear, will ye play us a song? The night is cold, and 'tis long since ye played fer us."

Fiona looked in surprise from the lad beside her to her mentor beyond the fire, shocked by his audacity. Even as well as she knew Rhiada, she would never dare to ask.

Rhiada turned his eyeless face to Malcolm, a smile playing on his face. "Wha' would ye hae me play?" he asked gently, taking his beloved harp from its carrying bag beside him where he always kept it. He began to tune it, the strings singing sweetly in the air.

Malcolm shrugged. "Any song would be good."

"Then perhaps I may give ye the song of our warband."

"A song of victory?" the lad piped in surprise.

Fiona glanced at Malcolm, remembering him speaking of this song-making before. Perhaps Malcolm knew Rhiada better than she did—that surprised her, for she did not think Malcolm to think so often of her teacher.

"It may yet be a song of victory, but such as it is, is more of a lament fer the fallen." He ran his hand across the strings one last time, a silver shower of notes. And then he started to play into the hushed, almost reverent silence, each note hanging in the air before fading away in solemn song. The words were hesitant, half sung, half spoken, the beginnings of an epic that would one day be sung in chieftains' halls for centuries to come.

They rode off on a morning fair
When the skies were pale and grey
Though no rain or snow followed
Winter was on its way

Courage burned within them
Like a shining flame
And though the wind was cold
None of them turned away

They marched out fine
In lines of horses and men
Through the late autumn's dawning
The union of Lowland clans

And among them that set off that day
Was their brave, noble princess
A blossoming rose of Scottish pride
And their greatest hope

Fiona looked away as her ears burned. She had not expected it and certainly did not feel that she had a right to be made part of song and legend that would last years beyond her time. But both Angus and Malcolm brushed her cold, numb fingers with their own, and she looked up to see quiet smiles of pride in their eyes.

Swiftly through to Drumdae
They tasted first of blood
Some drank its fatal dregs
And now lie among the slain

Rhiada continued on, singing of the men who had fought so bravely that day a few morns past, their names and illustrious deeds forever memorialised in song. The chieftains, the clansmen, those who had died—like Duncan—and those who lived still. But then the song broke off abruptly, the harper's voice and the last note shivering in the winter air.

"Tha' is all I hae. The rest must await until it happens in its time." He put aside his harp and spoke no more. And neither did anyone else who remained awake speak on it. For there was nothing to be said. The song had done justice, but the song, like the war trail and struggle for freedom, was not yet finished.

Fiona leaned against Angus once more and closed her eyes, the three of them—including Malcolm, who was already snoring softly—huddled together before the fire to keep warm against the bitter wind.

But the haunting melody remained in her mind, the words whispering at the edges of her consciousness, and together they murmured ever in her sleep.

~ 22 ~

TREACHERY

LADY Nuith clenched her hands, biting her lip to keep the storm inside. Still facing the wall, she spoke through clenched teeth. "Are you speaking the truth?"

"Aye, m'lady. They completely routed and killed us all, save myself and the few of us who escaped," Bëorn answered, standing alone in the centre of the Council Hall at Caerloch. His words echoed strangely off of the high ceiling and stone walls, hovering in the air a few moments after speaking them. Clad only in his torn and ragged clothing, he shivered, perhaps also from exhaustion, as if he truly had run the entire distance from the battle as he claimed.

"How? How could they have done this? Their numbers were less than ours, yet they have won this first battle! But how?"

"I know not, m'lady. I know that we greatly weakened them; they barely won against us and should not survive another battle."

Still, they could not have won—they should not have won!

"Thank you, Bëorn. You may go," she managed in a controlled tone, despite the emotions warring within her.

"M'lady, I also have news from your brother, Drummond."

Nuith turned, looking at him curiously, the edge of her wrath fading away. "Speak."

"He says to gather a group of men and send them to the Pass. If they get there soon enough, they can completely route the Scottish rebels. Drummond says he will give more information once we arrive, but that in this manner we might destroy both the Lowlanders and their rebellion, and also capture and kill their princess, as you wish."

Lady Nuith remained silent, staring at the grey stones beneath her feet. Perhaps her brother was loyal, after all.... Aloud, she said, "Thank you, you may rest now. When you go, please tell Asbjørn that I wish to speak with him."

He bowed and strode from the room, leaving her in silence.

Lord Erland, who had said nothing all this time, rose to his feet and came to his wife, laying his hand on her shoulder. Before he could speak, Nuith gasped from sudden pain in her abdomen.

Resting her hand on her swollen stomach, she murmured, "Hush, my child. I will do all I can to ensure you a throne and a kingdom that rightfully belongs to you. It is all I want and all that I ask."

"Do you think Drummond is being honest this time?" Erland said, his mellow voice softened by a whisper. He caressed her back gently, knowing it was the only thing that gave her relief from the pain.

"I do not know. I can only hope," she replied bitterly. "He has always been one to keep his plans to himself. But this plan of his rings true and seems most like his scheming, devilish mind." She inhaled sharply. "Yet if he is wrong, what I do to that brat they call a princess will seem like nothing in comparison with what I will inflict on him."

"Even if he is your brother?" There was a note of fear in her husband's voice.

Nuith sent him a piercing glance. "He is only my half-brother. A traitor is still a traitor, no matter their blood."

Before Erland could reply, the captain of the guard entered the hall, an embarrassed look crossing his face when he caught sight of them standing so close to each other. He cleared his throat softly and gazed at the floor instead, his hands clasped behind him.

Lord Erland returned to his seat without a word, observing what transpired in silence.

Lady Nuith took a breath and spoke to the captain, her features unruffled. "Asbjørn, how many men do you command?"

"Here? About fourscore and thirteen." His dark eyebrows twitched uncomfortably, uncertain what she wanted with him.

"Is there any way you can gather more forces?"

"Depends how many men you need. If we sent out commands to the Highland chiefs as well as the immediate Danish strongholds, maybe we would have enough. But I do not know where the Highlanders' loyalties lie." His brown-eyed gaze flickered to Lord Erland's and then to Nuith's. He was treading dangerous ground, and he knew it.

"You mean they are not faithful to the crown?"

"I do not know," he answered. "Some are loyal. Others... 'Tis hard to say whether they are loyal to Fiona McCurragh or simply want nothing to do with this matter at all."

Lady Nuith was silent for a few moments, absorbed in thought. Then, "I need you to gather all those loyal to us—and as soon as may be. Our plan depends on speed and surprise, and we cannot delay, even for a day, regardless of whether it should mean a thousand men more to our cause."

"And those who are not so loyal?"

"They must be bought. Every man has his price."

"You mean using bribery?" Asbjørn questioned incredulously.

"Of course. We must use whatever means we can to stop this rebellion and make an end to that baseborn child who claims to be the heir."

The captain of the guard raised an eyebrow at her remark. Perhaps he was not used to hearing such language from a woman, especially Lady Nuith, for certainly he must hear worse from his own men. Yet he only replied, "Aye, m'lady. I will see to it."

"Good. When you have gathered them, make your way to the Carbinenth Pass. 'Tis where those rebellious Lowlanders will be, if my brother keeps his end of the bargain. He will give you further orders once you arrive."

Asbjørn bowed, clasping his right fist over his heart, and turned to leave.

"Oh, Asbjørn," Lady Nuith called. "One last word."

He halted in his stride and faced her. "Aye, m'lady?"

"If you can, bring Fiona to me alive. I want the pleasure of killing her myself."

"Aye, m'lady. Anything else?"

"If she escapes, you have my permission to kill her."

Asbjørn paused, as if thinking over her command. But he never objected and at last only replied, "Aye, m'lady," and left the room, his boots clicking on the stone floor.

I will see you dead, Fiona, even if it is the last thing I do. Lady

Nuith sighed heavily, sitting down beside her husband and letting him take her hand in his.

You will no longer elude me, and you will no longer pose a threat to my child.

Fiona awoke to the pale light of dawn, the sun shining brightly, tipping the distant clouds with rosy hues. The sky beyond was a hazy, wintery blue that seemed almost like a pane of glass between her and the rising sun. Though the brightness in the heavens provided little heat, the cheer it gave was enough to warm even the most despairing of hearts, especially after so many days of endless grey.

She sat up, the tartan plaid wrapped around her crackling as the crust of frost broke with her movements. Her breath came out in little white puffs that slowly evaporated in the dawn's frozen stillness.

All around her, the men were stirring and rising, some finding wood to rekindle the cooking fires. A thin fog lay still about the field, and she could only see dimly in any direction.

Fiona shivered and reached up to brush back the tangled mess of fiery red curls from her face. Pulling her legs up to her chest, she locked her arms around them and yawned, the sleepiness slowly fading away.

Looking to her left, she saw Malcolm still sleeping, curled up beneath the tartan blanket that covered him also. She lay back down and pulled the blanket up to her neck, glancing to her right and seeing Angus lying on his stomach, his face buried in his crossed arms. She had no idea how early it was, nor where Donald and Rhiada were, for she did not see them by the fire where they had slept during the night.

A few moments later, she began to feel hunger pains and was tired of waiting for her companions to awaken. She nudged Malcolm with her elbow, but he simply rolled over, his freckled face flushed from sleeping, his crimson curls a tangled mess.

Frustrated, she turned to Angus. Leaning on her elbow, she pressed gently below his ear with her finger.

Instantly he raised his head and looked around him, confused, blinking away the sleepiness. "Fiona?" he mumbled in bewilderment.

"Angus, where is everyone?" she answered softly, some part of her still willing to let Malcolm sleep.

Angus rolled over and sat up, thrusting back the dark hair out of his eyes and yawning. Then he turned to her. "I hae nae idea. All I ken is tha' Father laid us down and covered us wi' this other tartan—probably one of his—sometime last night. Tha's all I remember."

"Hmm," she murmured in response, shivering again. She pulled up the tartan folds and wrapped them around her neck.

Angus peered around her at his sleeping brother. "Is Malcolm still sleeping?"

"Aye. He wouldnae awaken."

"Ah. Pull his blanket off."

"Wha'?" Fiona sputtered in surprise.

"Jist do it."

Shaking her head, she did so, hoping Malcolm would not be too angry at her.

The lad sat up with a jerk, arms wrapped around himself as he opened his eyes and blinked. "Why is it so cold?" he asked, teeth chattering.

Fiona turned and gave Angus an annoyed look while returning Malcolm's third of the plaid to him.

He snatched it from her and wrapped himself up in it, leaning against Fiona and glaring at his brother.

"Nae, nae. Both of ye, get off," Angus said, standing.

A bit confused, the pair rose and watched as Angus picked up both plaids and sat down again, gesturing for them to do the same. Then he placed one of the plaids behind them, across their shoulders, and the other in front of them so that they were all wrapped up against the bitter winter air.

They remained like that for several minutes, leaning against one another and not speaking, while the warmthless sun melted away the silvery fog. The field, once hidden, was now visible in the light. Men were rising, cooking breakfast, and preparing for a march. Perhaps that was why Donald and Rhiada were gone; perhaps they had already told the men their orders.

"I'm so hungry." Malcolm broke the silence, his head shifting on Fiona's shoulder.

"I am as well," she answered.

"I wish we had Mother's oat cakes instead of tha' foul stuff they hae the nerve to call porridge," he spat out.

"Och, 'tis nae as bad as all tha'!" Donald McCladden said, coming up behind them. All three turned their heads in unison to see him. "How are my sons this fine morning?"

Malcolm snorted. "'Tis cold enough to freeze a heated sword blade! If I wasnae already angry at the Danes, I would be now."

"Och, what's gotten ye into such a foul mood this morning?" Fiona asked in wonder. "'Tis nae like ye to be so sharp. 'Tis more yer brother's manner," she added with a teasing smile at Angus.

His scowl softened into a smile, but he did not reply.

"Duncan, the cold, my hunger, and nae satisfying way to satisfy it," Malcolm listed off with his fingers. He was about to continue when his father interrupted him.

"We shall be on the march soon and then ye will be glad of this chance to rest," Donald grunted, stirring the nearly dead embers of the fire back into life.

"How soon until we reach the Pass of Carbinenth?" Angus asked suddenly, stiffening as though expecting to fly into an attack at any moment.

"About four days, if we hurry. 'Twill depend on how swiftly we march and how quickly we are able to find supplies."

"Wha' if.." Fiona began, halting. "Wha' if the Danes gain the high ground of the Pass before we arrive?"

Donald McCladden hesitated in answering and when he spoke, his voice was grave. "Then we will hae to fight in spite of it. We cannae leave fer the winter months without another attempt at victory, and they ken so. Either they will come down upon us and slaughter us all, or we shall lose and have to surrender until a chance comes again to drive them out. But in any case, let us hope tha' we come there first." He stood, little flames appearing where only glowing embers had been before. "Better find something to eat even if 'tis nae exactly what ye're wishing fer," he suggested, looking at Malcolm and winking. "We will be marching soon."

Malcolm grumbled something about food fit for pigs and rose to his feet, one of the blankets wrapped around his shoulders as he followed his father in search of breakfast.

"Beautiful morning, is it no'?" Angus said, gazing at Fiona with the softened look he often wore since the day Duncan had died.

"Aye." She sighed deeply, content with the beauty of the moment but wistful that it would be gone so soon. "It seems to me to almost mock wha' has happened these last few days."

"Indeed," he agreed, looking out at the frosted field full of men walking to and fro. "Yet mayhaps it serves as a reminder tha', while men may die fer a cause they believe in, the world still goes on. Even though we may die fighting this war, it willnae change the natural course of things. The sun will still rise in the morning and set in the evening, regardless of who wins." He turned to her with a slight smile on his face. "All the great destructive forces in this world cannae mar this, the beauty of the sunrise in winter, and such things like it."

"If we donnae win, wha' then?" She did not see things the same way he did. She saw only the darkness, not the light beyond. But Angus could, and she wished for him to show it to her, or mayhaps, by his pure belief, she could trust to hope as well.

"Then the sun will come and gae o'er a world belonging in slavery to the Danes." A shadow crossed his face, and she cursed herself inwardly.

"And if we win?" she asked, forcing a smile if only for his sake. She could not bear to see him lose himself in his past again. The last few days had given her a glimpse of what he should have been all these years, what perhaps he had been before Sioned had gone to War. She did not want him to return to dwelling in fear of the future, of losing more of those whom he loved.

"Then it will rise and set o'er a free land," he returned, a grin spreading across his face, the shadows fleeing away. "Come ye. Best we get something to break our fast before Malcolm eats it all and we hae to march hungry." He rose to his feet and wrapped his plaid over his shoulder.

Fiona stood, stretching her cold and sore limbs. Sleeping on frozen earth for nights on end was not really sleeping at all, and if she could scarce rest properly, how much more were the other warriors exhausted?

"Are ye coming?"

She glanced up into his blue eyes, their azure depths glistening in the sunlight. "Aye," she replied with a smile, thrusting thoughts of the grim future away. "I am coming."

Lachlan's jest was half out of his mouth when he caught sight of Drummond walking towards him and his fellow Danes, a scowl on their chieftain's face. A companion nudged Lachlan with his elbow, snickering softly as Drummond stopped right before him, the sun shining on his dark hair.

"Lachlan MacDinnall, what have I said about minding yer own affairs and waiting fer orders?" he hissed in the Danish tongue so that any passing Scots would not understand what was being said.

Lachlan shrugged and spoke coolly. "I do not know what you are speaking of." Much to his annoyance, the other Danes did not disperse out of respect but watched the proceedings with amusement. It was rare that Drummond's favourite found himself facing their leader's simmering wrath. As for Lachlan, he only raised a mocking eyebrow in the brief pause of silence between them.

Drummond seized Lachlan by the arm with a vice-like grip and jerked him to his feet, his face inches from his own. "How many times have I told ye to leave that Scottish princess alone? By yer unchecked stupidity we may hae lost all the ground we hae gained. How many times hae I said we needed to earn their trust if our plan was to succeed? I hae told you that when the time came you could do with her as you liked—why can ye no' wait?"

Lachlan did not reply, only meeting the other's gaze with the same unperturbed air that angered Drummond all the more.

"I hae persuaded Chieftain McCladden away from taking action against ye, but if this or anything similar happens again—if ye so much as gae near her—I will no' hesitate to let them do to ye what they will." He released his grip on Lachlan's arm and sighed. "Yer time will come. But ye must be willing to wait until then." Drummond glanced at the men around them, his men, and said in a louder tone of voice, "The same goes fer ye all. Stay away from Fiona McCurragh until I give the word. Now, we hae orders to move out to the Pass. Prepare to march." Then he left them.

"Will you actually listen this time?" Lachlan's companion jested, taking a swig from the waterskin at his side.

Lachlan did not answer, his lips pursed in a thin, tight line. Drummond was always keeping his plans to himself, never letting anyone know what they were, not even his own men. His sister, Lady Nuith, was repeatedly incensed at this, and she was not alone. Lachlan knew personally how frustrating it was to be kept in the dark until a sudden action was needed. While he knew his fellow soldiers agreed with him, his opinions would be nothing short of treason. So he kept his thoughts to himself, thinking furiously.

If Drummond would make such plans and keep them secret to the annoyance of all, then Lachlan could as well.

Besides, his plan for revenge was nearly complete.

The Scots' camp was a swarm of activity, orders flying on the icy wind as the men found their places and prepared to march. Donald and the chieftains under him rode horses, the rest following the companies on foot. Rhiada was among the horsemen, riding Sgàil since Fiona, with younger, stronger legs, would do better marching than he would. She had not had much time to spend with Sgàil at all the last few days, but she did not mind Rhiada riding her. He would be gentle with her, as he was with all things.

But there was little choice for the others, who had been relegated to the roles of foot soldiers. There were too few horses left after the battle of several days ago. And a couple had to be spared to carry the worst of the wounded back to their homes.

Fiona hoisted her belongings, which consisted of her brother's extra clothes, her weapons, and a tartan blanket, all tied together with rope, over her shoulder. The warm, thick folds of her cloak settled in around her, protecting her from the cold that still managed to seep through her leather jerkin and many layers of woollen clothes. She found a place to stand amidst Chieftain McCladden's men, even if she knew none of them by name. But she was not alone for long. Malcolm and Angus soon joined her, standing on either side as bodyguards.

A great shuffling disturbed the morning calm as the warriors found their places in the ranks with a few complaints from the less optimistic of them. Fiona ignored most of it, gazing about her at the hilly land they were leaving and the plain beyond that had become a tomb.

What must the McCladdens be feeling now, leaving their son and brother behind? she mused, an echo of their loss resounding in her heart.

Her thoughts were interrupted as she noticed several of Drummond's men joining the ranks before and behind them. She was not certain of it, but she thought she had seen Lachlan's face among the rest, though it had only been for one swift moment.

Fiona laid her hand on Angus' shoulder, stepping closer to him.

He turned to her, catching sight of her expression. "Wha' is it?" he said softly so that no one else would hear.

"Why are Drummond's men in our company? I thought tha' everyone would be marching in each chieftain's wing."

"Aye, but Father doesnae trust him. Neither do I, even if he says he had nae hand in Lachlan's attempts," he added, glancing around them. "Anyway, Father wanted half of his men to replace half of ours so tha' we donnae hae any danger of treachery. Perhaps this way we can better watch them and protect ye."

"I jist hope tha' yer father's plan works."

"Malcolm and I will protect ye regardless," he hastily reassured her.

"'Tis always good to ken." She smiled, shivering against the sudden gust of wind that whistled across the plain.

He grinned and turned away as if the whispered conversation between them had never taken place. She saw him reach up and slowly adjust the bandage on his head; perhaps the wound was beginning to heal and itch beneath the cloth. They should have changed it, changed all such bindings on wounds, but they did not have enough supplies. All they could do was hope for no infection.

At last, Donald McCladden gave the order and they began to march, the tattered ranks leaving the forest and plain that had claimed so many lives.

As they left, Fiona watched as both the McCladden brothers turned to see the place where their dead brother lay with the other buried men. She said nothing. Sometimes an understanding silence was worth more than words.

By midafternoon, the ranks had spread out loosely across the plateau, wandering warriors bent to the same purpose. In the distance, the dim shadows of mountains loomed against the ghostly spilled ink of the clouds. Soon they would have to journey up to the Highlands towards the Pass, leaving the bleak moors behind.

The wind was not kind on the hills as it blew bitingly through the clothes of the warriors with immense ease. Malcolm McCladden shivered endlessly as he stumbled across the frozen ground, and he was not the only one.

Fiona's hands were numb and red with cold. Blowing on them did not help much, either. She had long ago given up trying not to shiver and sympathised with Malcolm greatly. There was little any of them could do about it. It was indeed winter, after all.

Angus suddenly stepped in between them and pulled both of them to himself, holding out the edges of his cloak with his hands. He placed his arms around their shoulders as they walked, the dual-layered wool protecting all three of them from the icy wind. The garment was too large for Angus, as it had belonged to Duncan, who had broader shoulders. But as such, it served a better purpose since the material easily enveloped them while Malcolm and Fiona's shivering gradually subsided.

Malcolm piped up, his usual buoyant spirit having returned. "I wish tha' it was summer and no' winter."

"Och, Malcolm!" Angus said, looking straight ahead to see the path before them so that they might not trip on any unseen stones hidden by the dead grasses and heather. "Summer will come again," he continued. "'Tis the natural way of things. Summer always comes again after the winter jist as the winter comes after the summer; jist as the moon always comes after the sun; jist as things must grow after they die; jist as the warmth always comes after the cold. Nothing interrupts this perfect pattern, no' even the threat of the Danes. 'Tis how it has been all these years and will continue to be e'en after we're long gang."

"Will summer ever come again fer Scotland?" Fiona questioned softly after a pause, leaning against his shoulder as they walked.

"I donnae ken," Angus replied, his dark brows drawn together as they always were when he concentrated very hard on something. "I believe it will come again because it must, but I donnae ken if it will come in our time. It may be tha' this struggle will gae on until years after we're laid in the earth before Scotland is finally free. But aye, it will come again. Good always triumphs o'er evil in the end."

"Well, I hope it comes in my lifetime," Malcolm concluded, scrunching his face against the bracing wind.

"I do as well," Fiona added solemnly.

"As do I," Angus said and then spoke no more.

Oilseacho ~ A Stolen Crown

It was late afternoon, and the cold winter sun sent slanting shadows across the moorlands and cragged mountains.

The ranks had drawn together as they crossed an ancient, crumbling bridge that spanned the dark waters of a deep, flowing river, ice fringing its edges. The bridge had been built by the Redcrests of a fallen empire in days long before the Danes ever came, when they had attempted to conquer all of Scotland as well as the rest of the world.

The warriors drew so close together to cross the narrow bridge that those near the centre were hard-pressed to move their limbs freely. Angus jostled his elbow against someone beside him—he didn't look to see whether it was a Scot or a Dane—to keep his footing as he stepped upon the ancient stone. He tried his best to keep his eye on Fiona, but it was difficult when everyone pushed to keep moving and get to the other side where they could spread out again.

Donald's company was halfway across when Angus suddenly felt someone shove him aside. Something red flashed in the sunlight, followed by a splash in the river below them. Angus whirled to find the source, only to realise someone was missing from the crowd in front of him.

Fiona.

He had no time to think. Ripping his cloak off in thoughtless panic and dropping his bundle of belongings onto the bridge, Angus jumped into the river after her.

The icy water hit him like a wall of stone, nearly driving the breath out of his lungs. The waters were dark and murky, the bottom invisible. He flailed helplessly, unable to see. The cold slowly seeped the life out of him. He knew if he did not find her soon, it would be too late for them both.

Thrusting himself deeper into crepuscule, he hit something mid-stroke. He grabbed hold, his numbed fingers feeling the roughness of wet wool.

It was his princess.

Locking his arm around Fiona's body, he struggled to reach the surface. His lungs burned. His limbs ached as though something in the water was dragging him to the bottom. The thought crossed his mind—perhaps they would never reach the surface. Both of them would drown today. Scotland would lose her princess, and the McCladdens yet another son.

Then the inky depths grew lighter and he broke the surface, gasping for air. His limbs were nearly paralysed and tingling with the cold as he struggled to keep afloat. But Fiona's unmoving body weighed him down, and he was growing so tired, the sunlight fading away into the frigid darkness of oblivion...

Something flew towards him, and though he could see it but dimly, he seized hold. Clinging tightly with his free hand, he felt the rope suddenly yank both of them out of the river and onto dry land.

The chill air was no warmer than the water, but Angus lay on the cold, hard ground for several moments simply panting, filling his burning lungs with air. Around them, he could hear voices and shouting, but they came from a great distance.

He turned his head, seeing Fiona lying beside him, motionless and limp, and his heart stopped its beating for a moment.

Nae! Please let me nae hae been too late!

He leaned over and turned her onto her back, his movements far too slow from numbness. He brushed her hair out of her face with shaking fingers, his heart now racing. The voices around him grew louder, but he only knew of the darkness and the fear that threatened to engulf him. He had conquered the river. But if Fiona did not live, it would most certainly drown him all the same.

Fiona, please, donnae leave me!

A wave of colour washed over her face and she started choking, vomiting up part of the river. Shivering violently, she tried to wipe her mouth with the back of her hand.

He collapsed next to her even as those around them undid their jerkins and outer layers of clothes, wrapping them in woollen blankets. He felt her quivering next to him, still coughing, but he could do little to help her—he was shaking with cold.

Someone started a fire nearby, using what few bundles of wood they'd managed to bring with them in case of an emergency. Another man—Angus' vision was too blurred to see who it was—tossed what remained in a flask of mead onto the flames to raise them higher.

But it seemed an eternity before Angus could feel the heat at all. Fiona's coughing slowly subsided, though every inhale was harsh to his ears. The warmth did not come gently but seemed to sear through his skin like fire with edges of ice, slowly thawing out his bones.

"Angus?" Fiona finally spoke, her voice raw from coughing.

"I'm here," he replied, tears springing to his eyes, though perhaps that was from the smoke drifting towards them. He moved his arm across her, trying to hold her closer despite the stiffness in his muscles.

She nodded, still shivering, though it was not as severe as before.

"Angus, Fiona, are ye all right?" Donald McCladden's voice broke through the haze, and the world became clearer.

Angus tried to nod, but the effort cost him too much.

"Bryce and Cameron are setting up a tent behind us so ye both can change into dry clothes once ye're warmer. We'll nae gae farther today."

Angus only grunted in reply, relishing the warmth of the fire and fighting back the sudden wave of sleepiness. He looked instead at Fiona, who gazed at the flames near them, a tear slowly trickling down her face.

She glanced up at him and mouthed, *Thank ye.*

He smiled faintly, the effort feeling as though his face would crack. "Always, princess."

~ 23 ~

bloodied blade

THE fire burned Fiona's face, stinging her cheeks numb. But she did not mind. She sat as close to the flames as possible without risking singeing the only dry clothes she had left. And yet she still shivered, though not as severely as before.

She glanced at Angus sitting beside her, his dark hair clinging in damp curls around his face. He too was bundled up against the bitter wind, a tartan blanket as well as his cloak wrapped around him. The cut by his temples did not look so raw and angry as before, the wound beginning to heal and form a scab. The bandage must have slipped when he dove into the river, or else someone had taken it off, the cold wetness no help for their current situation; the bandage on her knuckles was gone as well, and no one had bothered to rebind their healing wounds. They had little enough cloths for that.

Angus caught her gaze but said nothing, his deep blue eyes speaking a world of words. Sympathy. Compassion. The same shining adoration she had seen before that she did not quite understand. And something else. An echo of the fear that once had always drowned in their depths like a swirling storm.

But what was he afraid of?

"Are ye getting warmer?" he asked, his voice soft and low.

Fiona shrugged, holding the blanket she was wrapped in closer. "Nae by much. I feel as though the water chilled my very bones—or perhaps because I came so close to death..." Sighing deeply, she tried to draw more of herself within the folds of the blanket. The only other dress she had was lost somewhere within the depths of the river, lost with her weapons, which her dear dead brother had given her years ago. Were it not for Rhiada having one of Douglas' shirts and kilts with him, she would have had to suffer in a wet dress. But still, even a dry kilt left her knees bare and exposed to the cold where her woollen socks failed to reach. She would give much to sleep beneath a roof and within four walls, away from the cold and this infernal wind.

"Wha' exactly happened?" Donald McCladden asked, grieved and worried. "I thought I had taken care to prevent such a thing from taking place." He sat down beside them around the fire, joining Rhiada and Cameron, who tended the flames.

"Aye, Father, but evil men will still find a way." Angus took a deep breath before continuing, "I saw Lachlan push Fiona o'er the side. I only kent it was him because of his ring, the one wi' the chipped ruby—I hae ne'er seen its like. And who else would wish such harm to our princess?"

"And ye, Fiona, do ye also agree to this, tha' it was Lachlan?" Chieftain McCladden inquired, turning to her.

"I felt someone push me. I ken I didnae trip o'er a stone. Whether it was him or no', I couldnae say. It all happened so fast, I—" She broke off and bit her lip, still shuddering at the memory.

"Donnae dwell on it, princess," Rhiada said gently. "We hae evidence enough without this added atrocity. We will see that justice is done."

Fiona nodded and huddled closer to the fire, staring into its flames.

"It would seem tha' treachery of the deepest sort lies everywhere in our own ranks," Donald said softly to Rhiada, not quite meaning for Fiona and Angus to hear.

Fiona pretended not to listen, though she heard them well enough.

"How can we trust the word of anyone?" Donald continued, his voice strained. He was exhausted as they all were, tired of the fear and uncertainty that always seemed to haunt their steps.

"Loyal people still exist, though few and far between," Rhiada replied, his voice calm and soothing, like sweet music. But the music faded into a note of warning. "Yet we cannae wait any longer. Lachlan has gone too far, if he had no' before, and we must set an example.

Justice must be done. We cannae suffer any more such threats to our princess."

"Nae." Donald cleared his throat and rose to his feet. "I will summon the chieftains in a moment. Fiona, Angus, I will hae someone get some food fer ye both. It will help warm ye until we can hae supper tonight." And then he was gone, leaving them to the growing cold of waning afternoon.

The sun was sinking towards the west, and soon the land would be clothed in twilight. Fiona glanced around them, seeing similar fires across the plain, tents set up as protection against the wind. Some of the Scots tended to the horses while others paced as guards, blowing on their hands to warm them. All of them were weary and longing for home and safety.

If they did not win the next battle, they might not have either.

All thoughts of the coming conflict fled away when Malcolm plopped down beside her, a few crumbling oat cakes in his hand. Keeping one for himself, he gave the others to Fiona and his brother.

They were dry and had little taste, falling to pieces in her hands, but she was too hungry to care. She hoped, as she licked the last few crumbs from her fingers, that they would have warm food later, even if it was only the tasteless porridge again.

"Angus, Fiona, Father wants us when ye're ready," Malcolm said as he hoisted himself back up to his feet. He ran his fingers through his unruly hair and yawned. "Jist make sure ye both are warm enough."

"Aye, we'll come," Angus replied. "I want to see to it tha' Lachlan doesnae threaten my princess again."

"Yer princess?" Malcolm squeaked. "She's my princess, too!"

Angus rolled his eyes heavenward. "Our princess—it doesnae matter as long as she's safe. Now come, ye said Father wants us. We'd best no' keep him waiting then." He offered his hand to Fiona, helping her to her feet and giving her his cloak as it was much longer than the blanket she had wrapped around her shoulders.

Malcolm saw his chance and, linking his arm with hers, led Fiona away like some grand prize fairly won, laughing over his shoulder at his brother's shocked expression.

Fiona grinned, not certain whether she should laugh or pity Angus for being left behind, but he did not remain so for long. Within a moment, he was beside her, the three of them arm in arm and sharing

Angus' cloak as they marched across the makeshift encampment. But the jovial mood vanished as they approached the chieftains' council.

Rhiada and Cameron were there among Donald and the other High Chieftains, including Drummond. They spoke to one another in soft voices, ceasing when Fiona and her companions approached, but it seemed that they had come to an accord of what was to be done instead of a disagreement they did not want known.

"Ah, princess, are ye dry enough now?" Donald McCladden asked kindly, as if to drive away the pressing concerns he was facing.

"Aye, I am," Fiona replied with a faint smile. Even if it was only partially true, she did not want to worry him further. There was enough on his mind.

"Good." He turned back to the circle and said, "Drummond, would ye please bring forth Lachlan? Cameron, if ye would, summon forth the men, those tha' can be spared. I wish fer all to witness and take heed."

Drummond, who had remained silent all the while, left without a word, his usual fire extinguished. Fiona wondered why; whether it was because he was truly shocked by his second-in-command's actions, or because he had another, more devious scheme up his sleeve. Rhiada had said Drummond could not be trusted, but he had never told her why. Drummond had protected her from Lachlan before, but what if that was because he had other plans?

Fiona jumped in surprise at the cry of lilting pipes that pierced the quiet, sharper and brighter than the wintery air. Around them, men were gathering, most of them exhausted by the constant exposure to harsh weather, marching, and little food. Only their eyes bespoke the glittering, fierce life within them, shining brightly in frostbitten, hollow faces.

The piping ceased with a squeak, and the silence after was an empty void. No one spoke, and even the horses in the picket lines held their peace.

Drummond brought up Lachlan, his hands bound behind him with a strip of leather, his face set and angry. His dark eyes burned with suppressed wrath and his mouth was unmoving as stone. He looked defiantly at all the chieftains in turn as he and Drummond came to a halt before them, Drummond stepping to his place beside Eachann and Alastair. Lachlan turned his gaze to Fiona at the last, brimming with a hatred matched only by Lady Nuith.

Fiona shrank away from him, as if he would kill her simply by his glance. Angus slipped his hand in hers, squeezing it gently, and Malcolm laid his arm across her shoulders, his other hand on his dirk, as if daring the Dane to even try to harm her.

It was Rhiada who spoke first, his voice soft but commanding. He would have made a good war leader if he had but eyes to see. "Lachlan MacDinnall, ye are charged wi' the offence of treason against Her Royal Highness Princess Fiona McCurragh, by threatening the good health of her person more than once and forcefully attempting to drown her by pushing her into the waters of the river. As she is still alive, ye are permitted a fair trial and are no' instantly put to death, but donnae try our patience. Our mercy fer such traitors extends only so far. Therefore, Lachlan MacDinnall, do ye hae any words fer yer defence?"

Lachlan glared at the blind harper, pure hatred blazing from his eyes, darker than when he had looked at Fiona. He snarled through clenched teeth, "I am already declared guilty by your false words, you—" He ended in a curse, spitting at Rhiada's feet.

"Ye are no' permitted to show disrespect to Rhiada," Donald put in, his tone cool and dead even. His face was stiff, hiding any emotion beneath, only the faint wind ruffling his hair showing any sign of movement.

Lachlan laughed mockingly, a harsh sound that made Fiona wince. "I do not fear him. I was there that day. I was one of those who stole his sight, scarred his forehead. I wish to this day we had taken more, taken even his life, if it would have prevented that base-born brat's continued existence." He turned his gaze now to Fiona, the eyes that once burned with lust replaced by incensed loathing. "You will never be heir to the throne while Lady Nuith lives. She is doing everything in her power to get rid of you and will not stop until you are dead."

Angus held Fiona closer to him, eyeing every movement of the raving man in their midst, tensed against any sudden action.

"You will never be queen," Lachlan continued, emphasising every word on his tongue. "You will never rule."

Fiona only watched the traitor in shock, too horrified and ashamed to say anything. Had Lachlan truly blinded her beloved teacher and mentor? She felt light-headed and fought to remain steady. The Lowland chieftains and even Angus himself claimed that she was their hope against Danish tyranny. Still...what if Lachlan was right?

"She has every right to rule!" Malcolm shrieked, forgetting for a moment that he was not meant to take part in such counsels and assembly meetings because of his youth.

Lachlan snorted in contempt. "You know, *Fiona*, you are known at the Danish court as a baseborn child, an illegitimate heir to the throne, not fit to rule. You were never your father's daughter. Fionnuala died of grief and guilt from her betrayal, not from giving you life. Oh, aye, the truth is well known among my people," he sneered, suddenly snapping the cord binding his wrists and starting towards her, a wicked snarl on his face.

Angus' hand slipped out of Fiona's with lightning speed. A half-breath later, something silver whistled through the air.

Lachlan's next words died in his throat as the dirk embedded itself in his neck. He fell headlong onto the ground, his eyes rolling up into his head, a reddening stain where the knife had struck home.

Fiona glanced in horror from the dead traitor up to Angus, whose face betrayed no emotion. The sheath at his side was empty, the blade in Lachlan's neck. She felt sick at the sight of so much blood, at the sight of death, even though she had seen it before in her first battle. She turned away, swallowing down the bile that rose in her throat. And in her mind rang Donald's voice from what seemed like years ago: *"Death before dishonour; death before disloyalty."*

Angus gripped her hand hard, whispering in her ear, "Forget ye ever saw it. 'Twas necessary, but ye hae nae need to remember it."

She nodded, shutting her eyes tight for a moment.

"Take him away and bury him," she heard Donald command before he added, "Let this be a warning: nae traitors will be tolerated."

Angus released her hand and continued, "Gae wi' Malcolm and find some place to sit down and rest. Ye're still damp. And both of ye need to eat." He smiled comfortingly, an echo of his usual grin.

"We'll be waiting fer ye." Fiona tried to smile back, but it felt unsuccessful. How could she truly smile when Lachlan had dragged her name in the dirt, hers and Rhiada's? But now he was dead and would not harm her anymore. She only hoped no one else shared his sentiments. She had heard the rumours, yes, but had never believed them. Douglas had explained the matter to her well enough, that her father liked her little because she had been the cause of Fionnuala's death, not because of any unfaithfulness. Enough songs had been sung in years long gone to prove that the love of the former king and queen was not one to fade like that. But rumours, no matter how wild, often held a shred of truth. And if even some of the Scots believed them—though surely not Rhiada and the McCladdens—it could yet be her undoing.

Dusk was falling as the sun vanished behind thick grey clouds, darkening the bleak moorland. The cliffs of the distant Pass of Carbinenth were blacker than ever, and the icy wind, whispering its tragic secrets all that day, was rising in force. Perhaps it would truly storm upon them, and Fiona feared—as they all did—what that would mean. Several hundred men without shelter in early winter; it would be nothing short of disaster, destroying their fighting force before the reassembled Danes even approached the battlefield.

Fiona watched the flames flicker and die as the gusts of winter's fierce breath attempted to destroy it. She drew the edges of her blanket tighter around her, the shirt and kilt she wore not enough to keep out the wind. Her dress and cloak were still not dry enough to wear, and Rhiada refused to let her wear damp clothing, especially in this weather.

"Och, I hate the cold, especially this time of year," Malcolm sighed, disgusted. He shifted beside her and leaned closer to the fire. "Especially when I'm hungry."

"Ye jist ate!" Fiona sputtered, almost laughing at him.

"Aye, but tha' watery stuff doesnae keep one full fer long. I wish Mother were here," he added in the same breath, drawing on the frozen earth with a charred stick.

"Why?" Angus asked, sitting on the other side of the princess.

"Because then she could make the porridge," Malcolm replied. "Or oaten bannocks."

"She couldnae make it here," his brother stated before squinting at the edge of his dirk in the dancing flamelight. He was sharpening the blade, the rhythmic *whet-whet* sound disturbing the murmur of conversations around the fire as men spoke softly before retiring for the night. He had not done it since before the battle at Drumdae, and Fiona wondered for a moment why he did it now, unless perhaps it was a way to deal with the uncertainty that Lachlan's recent actions had brought upon them all.

"Och, why can she no' make it here? Mother can do anything." Malcolm dropped the stick into the fire.

"Because she puts things in it tha' the men here donnae or cannae because we donnae hae them."

"Like wha'?" Malcolm demanded.

"I donnae ken. I ne'er asked her."

"Then how do ye ken she puts things in it tha' *they* donnae?"

Angus snorted. "Because I jist ken. Get off wi' ye if all ye're gang to do is talk about food we donnae hae."

"Why?" Fiona smiled mischievously, having watched the banter in amused silence until now.

"Because I'm hungry, too," Angus replied, irritated, though perhaps the irritation was from something besides hunger, perhaps the same thing that drove him to once again drive the whetstone across his weapon's edges.

Malcolm sighed heavily and said no more, lying down before the fire and wrapping himself up in his blanket and cloak, the only protection he had against the cold and the wind.

Angus continued to run the whetstone across his dirk, the edge catching the firelight, an echo of the flickering warmth. Dark circles lay beneath his eyes, a sign of the lack of sleep they all suffered from, and his pale cheeks were hollowed, further evidence of the scant rations. And yet there was something harshly fair about the way the fire danced in the depths of his eyes, how it shadowed his high cheekbones and determined jaw.

"I think..." Fiona said in a soft, teasing tone, "tha' yer knife is sharp enough."

"It doesnae hurt to be sure," he replied, attempting to laugh, but the sound died in his throat.

He was about to run the stone along the blade's edge one more time when she laid her hand on his, looking into his face and asking, "Wha' are ye afraid of?"

Angus froze, the fear suddenly burning unmasked in his eyes. He hesitated before answering, the words seeming to rest on his tongue before he said them. "There's gang to be another battle—at least one, perhaps more—before we can gae home." His voice was a whisper, trembling at the edges. "We already lost Duncan—and I almost lost ye. Who shall fall now?"

"Ye must no' think of tha'!" she protested softly so that no one else would hear. "We must no' think of who might fall. Else we willnae be able to enjoy wha' beauty there is in life. We cannae always live in fear, whether fear of death or of loss." She exhaled sharply and took her hand away. "I ken tha' I am fearful enough of the future, but we must no' succumb to it. Rhiada told me so before we left An Dùn, and yer mother told me tha' pressing on in spite of our fears is the very essence of courage. And if I can find my courage, then so can ye. Ye willnae let me live in fear, I ken, but I refuse to let ye live in pain. Neither one of us will survive otherwise."

Tears glistened in his eyes, but there was a slight smile on his face. "Aye, princess." He sighed in willing surrender, sheathing his dirk and putting away his whetstone.

She gazed at her hands lying idle in her lap, her face burning in embarrassment. "I am no' really a princess."

"Aye, ye are!" Angus protested. "Or has Lachlan changed yer mind?" His words dropped to a whisper, as if he did not want anyone else to hear.

"Nae, 'tis nae him alone. I jist donnae feel like one wi' all tha' is going on—wi' the war and all."

"Fer tha' matter, I donnae feel like my father's heir." He laughed bitterly, shifting his position on the frozen ground. "But still, Lachlan's words were no' true. Ye must no' believe wha' he said. He was angry, and he was a Dane besides. They are no' kent fer their honesty."

Fiona looked into his blue eyes, so earnest and concerned, and forced a smile onto her face, even if she was only partially convinced. For what if the Scots, desperate for something to thrust back against despair, were blinded against the fact she truly would never make a good queen? Angus, she was sure, would not have chosen to fight for her unless he believed in her with all his heart. His loyalty was not the same as crazed devotion to a lost cause—it couldn't be! "True," she said aloud. "But sometimes I wonder whether anyone else, especially the Scots among us, think the same thing. Especially the farther we go on this war trail, the deeper into winter, how many of them might change where their loyalties lie?"

Angus shook his head. "They willnae desert ye, Fiona. They wouldnae endure the cold and privation wi' the rest of us if they thought such things.... But now, both of us need rest. Who kens wha' the dawn will bring?"

Fiona smiled and then buried herself beneath her blanket, glad for the fire and the shared warmth of her companions beside her. But it was long before she, or anyone else that night, fell asleep.

Drummond stared into the flames of the watchfire before him, his fellow officers sleeping around him. But rest was far from him, his mind in turmoil. He played with the twig in his hand, twirling the pine around his fingers, straining it almost to the breaking point and then releasing it before it could snap.

Since when had Lachlan's impatience driven him to direct disobedience of his orders? Why did his faithful second-in-command completely rebel against him? And was he the only one? Or were the rest of his men angry with his constant waiting, with his leashing them back, preparing for the one blow that would utterly destroy the Scottish rebellion.... He was too afraid to ask. And his men must not see his fear. That would certainly undo everything.

The twig snapped in his fingers, remnants of pine sap sticking to his palm. He cast the offending wood into the fire and wiped his hand on his woollen trousers.

Soon, the waiting would all be over. Provided his sister received the message and was sending a Danish force to the Pass of Carbinenth...Donald would be walking right into his trap. How he would enjoy the look on the Scots' faces then. Perhaps that princess's face would forever freeze into a fearful, freckled expression of horror.

He smiled to himself. Aye, it would all be worth it then.

A few more days.

But he had always been good at waiting.

Breakfast was a poor fare, only more crumbling bannock. There was no time to cook porridge, even had there been enough. Donald had hoped to come across villages at which to replenish the army's dwindling stores, but there was nothing to be found and therefore no use to continue searching. Better to spend every moment marching southeast to the Pass of Carbinenth and hope that the Danes did not reach it first.

Though snow had still to come, chilling rain poured unrelentingly down upon them.

Fiona, Angus, and Malcolm marched silently with the rest, nothing to be heard but the rain, the occasional cough or sneeze from the sickening warriors, and the squelch of men and horses walking across the soggy ground. The muddy, half-frozen earth quickly turned into miry sludge, and Fiona pitied those at the end of the columns who had to step in it. The trio had scarcely spoken since they had left that morning. Not that there was anything to say, except maybe to discuss when the rain would let up. But the dark clouds promised no such thing except more of the cold deluge, so the entire company trudged on in miserable silence.

Fiona had long ago given up trying to keep the soaking strands of hair out of her face. She had changed back into her dress sometime before the company had left camp, but that did not matter much now. Her cloak was not a large one and barely stretched over the new bow, quiver, and sword she wore, replacements for the weapons lost in the river. Though made of sturdy wool, her cloak was very worn and could not keep the damp out forever. The droplets of water that incessantly poured down from the heavens upon her face and hands felt like liquid ice.

"Will it ever stop?" she found herself saying without realising it. The two on either side of her did not answer for some time.

"It doesnae seem like it," Malcolm finally answered, his arms crossed over his chest for warmth, his scarlet locks dripping with water.

Angus remained silent. The rain had brought them all into a black mood.

"Och!" Malcolm exclaimed a moment or two later.

"Wha' is it?" Fiona asked, glad for a chance to take her mind off of the rain.

"'Tis so cold, so wet, I swear I'd be more than delighted to eat tha' tasteless porridge."

Fiona laughed and Angus answered, a slight smile appearing on his lips, "Donnae speak too loud. Ye might jist get yer wish."

Malcolm muttered something inaudible and then added in a louder tone of voice, "I wish we had Mother's haggis."

"Keep wishing. Ye're nae gang to get it anytime soon," his brother replied.

"I ken, I ken, but I still want it."

"Ye seem to want a lot of things lately," Fiona remarked dryly.

"Och, *lately*?" Angus mocked, his dark brows raised in astonishment. "Ye should see him at home during weapon practice! Or when he is supposed to be working in the horse-runs." He shook his head in disgust. "Nae, he is usually like this. Either tha', or acting so happy ye'd think he'd drunk too much mead."

"I hae ne'er drank half as much as ye hae," Malcolm retorted.

Fiona laughed, trying in vain to imagine the serious Angus she thought she knew participating in a foolish drinking competition. Surely he was above such things.

"Och, really?" Angus questioned in defiance.

"Aye, ye and yer stupid wager with Cadwal," Malcolm shot back. "I was counting, ye drank five!"

"Angus and Cadwal had a wager about how much mead they could drink?" Fiona squeaked in disbelief. Was that why Cadwal had barred them from entering An Dùn?

Angus rolled his eyes heavenward. "Aye, we did. It was after we'd had another wager about which of us could run the length of An Dùn the swiftest. He couldnae accept defeat, so he attempted another challenge."

"But five mugfuls, Angus?" Fiona asked, not sure whether to laugh at how ridiculous it was or shake some sense into him.

"Aye, he dared four, but I had to beat him somehow. Besides, it was mixed wi' water. Duncan would never hae allowed us to do it otherwise."

"Duncan was in favour of it?" Fiona turned to him, her mouth hanging open. "And here I thought ye were all wise, seasoned warriors."

"Och, aye," Malcolm added enthusiastically. "He said it was a good experience fer Angus, a chance to show his manhood."

"I think 'tis stupid," Fiona stated, shaking her head.

"I agree. And it has addled their brains e'er since. Too much of tha' honey-heather stuff can ruin yer pate." Malcolm gestured dramatically to his own head.

"Can ye three nae keep quiet?" one of Donald's older warriors asked in annoyance, ending their conversation.

The rain and the cold seemed more wet and chilling than ever, but none of them dared to say another word, trudging on in miserable silence, only the distant thunder disturbing their thoughts.

Three days later, the Scots arrived at the Pass in the early evening as the light began to fade. The hilly landscape flattened out into a rising plain, and before them cliff-like mountains reared up to the sky, their black rock shimmering dark with rainwater. The only break in the sheer, iron-like wall was the narrow pass ahead of them, the Pass of Carbinenth.

"So tha's wha' it is," Fiona murmured, awestruck as they came within view of it.

Beside her, Malcolm whistled shrilly in amazement.

"Such a fine sight, and yet it may be a place of death fer some before long," she continued, the wonder fading away like the fine rain falling from the sky.

"Aye," Donald McCladden replied from atop his horse, walking beside them in the ranks.

"Do ye think the Danes are here yet?" Angus asked, his voice soft. He looked at Fiona before gazing ahead of them again, his eyes dark.

His father shrugged, but the creases in his brow revealed his worry. "I will send our scouts out now before we come closer." He spurred his horse forward to the front of the column, leaving the trio behind.

They continued marching with the rest, the familiar *squelch—squelch—squelch* of tramping through the icy mud the only thing to be heard besides the heavy breathing of all the warriors, which formed white clouds in the chill air. Even the horses were quiet, as if all waited in silent dread to see whether the Danes held the higher ground or not.

Fiona glanced at the two on either side of her and saw Malcolm staring at the muddy ground as he walked, his cloak wrapped tightly around himself, perhaps watching so he would not trip on any stones that might lie in their way.

As for Angus, his hand rested on his sword hilt as he continued to watch the dark cliffs ahead of them, his deep blue eyes wide.

Fiona inhaled deeply and strode forward with the rest to whatever lay ahead, hoping that the Danes were not awaiting them; hoping that, despite all odds, they still had a chance.

∾ 24 ∾
Battle of the Pass

THE Scots waited in silence, horses and men huddled together for warmth against the cold, misting rain, waiting and hoping for good news from Donald, who spoke with their scouts some distance away. A fine fog advanced upon the plain, hiding the shadowy mountains behind a thin silver veil. Some of the horses snorted in impatience, longing no doubt for the safety of byres and fodder aplenty. The lack of food had affected them as well as their riders, and the once-fine beasts had been reduced to little more than skin and bones.

Fiona glanced at Sgàil beside her, the mare's soft, dark eyes sad and empty. She stroked Sgàil's velvety nose, wishing both of them safe and far away from danger. But that was not to be in this moment.

Rhiada, who still sat in the saddle and huddled in his cloak, suddenly stiffened, hearing the soft footfalls that approached in the rain-filled quiet.

All heads turned to see Donald McCladden walking towards them, his face expressionless. Coming to a halt, he spoke. "The Danes are nowhere to be seen. Gather up yer things. We are marching to the Pass."

It was only a few moments' time before the Scots were ready. Staying close to Angus and Malcolm, Fiona marched forward with the rest, wordlessly obedient, grateful for another chance to hold the high ground. They tramped steadily onward until they were in the Pass itself, relief giving strength to the weary.

The jagged cliff walls stretched up to the sky on either side of them, sloping back away from the path that ran through the Pass, which was as wide as ten men abreast. The light had dimmed in the coming evening, and Fiona squinted to see the caves that Angus pointed out to her. They appeared as little more than dark shadows on the cliff walls, nearly invisible to the eye.

About midway through the Pass, the entire company that was on foot split up into two groups. They clambered up the stone walls using rough-hewn stairs carved into the rock itself long ago by chieftains in their wars with one another. Narrow ledges ran out from the stairs to the caves, allowing a precarious entrance.

Fiona and the two McCladden brothers located one such rock shelter and climbed inside. They were unable to stand up inside without their heads touching the ceiling, but, as they looked out across the Pass, they could see many others who were unable to even sit in theirs without slouching to fit two or three men inside. But at least it was dry and out of the way of the wind, providing the first shelter they had experienced in the weeks since leaving An Dùn.

Depositing most of their weapons inside, with the exception of their dirks, the trio clambered back down to await further orders from Donald and the other chieftains.

Once below, the chieftains instructed the foot soldiers to find as many stones as possible and hoist them up to their caves, stacking them inside to throw down upon the Danish host whenever they came. It was wise to have other means of weaponry besides swords and bows.

Afterward, when the light vanished into chilling darkness, Donald McCladden called them all, save the scouts, to the plain on the northern side of the Pass. There was no firelight, no torches—nothing that might give away the Scots' position to their enemies who were soon to come. It was bitterly cold, and the moon, though providing the light they needed, was unfamiliar and strange, as if she too frowned upon the winter's warring.

"Tomorrow, the Danes will be here," Donald said once everyone was quiet. His voice was not loud, but somehow he managed to project it across the assembled men and reach those farthest from him. "Perhaps they will arrive at dawn, perhaps later, but the scouts were clear on one thing: they are coming and they are great in number. But we still hae the element of surprise, and I intend we use it as best we can.

"Those in the caves must wait until the Danes hae nearly marched to the northern end. Then they must rain down their stones, spears, arrows, anything upon our enemy tha' might be fatal. After yer arrows are gone, and please donnae waste them"—scattered ripples of laughter broke out at this statement—"ye must come down and fight wi' yer swords. Those who're nae in the caves will then ride in and wreak havoc among the enemy. We may be fewer than them, but we still hae a chance. This may be our last battle before winter truly sets in. Let us, therefore, make it worthwhile."

"A red harvest!" someone cried out, their voice ringing out harsh in the frigid air.

Another added, "Death to them all!"

Fiona was near the back of the company with Angus and strained her neck to see Donald in the centre. Malcolm, being smaller and bolder, had elbowed his way in closer, and the two of them did not know where he was.

"Do ye all understand?" Donald asked, as always ensuring that the warriors knew the plans. Best to prevent confusion in the heat of battle that would surely come in the foggy morning.

"Aye!" they all shouted in unison, many raising their fists above their heads, some unsheathing their swords, the blades glittering eerily in the moonlight.

"Nae matter wha' happens tomorrow, even if our plans gae awry, we must hold our ground! We cannae run away from the fight. We must hold our own."

Many cried out in agreement, their shouts vanishing in small white clouds that dissipated in the still air.

Donald raised his hands for quiet, and eventually they were hushed. "I ken ye're tired, I ken ye're hungry—we all are. But we mustnae let tha' hold us back. We are nae jist fighting to overthrow the Danes. We are nae jist fighting to be rejoined as a nation and restore the rightful heir to the throne. We are nae jist fighting to defend our homes and our families. We are fighting fer all these things and more. Fer we are the Scots! We will stand our ground. We will fight as long as we can! We fight wi' our last breath! We fight until we die! We fight until we win!" His next words were lost in the cheers and cries of the warriors.

Fiona felt tempted to put her hands over her ears, but decided against it. They needed to be brave. They needed to be told they would win. With the circumstances being as grim as they were, any encouragement was welcomed, even if the sound was deafening. Courage and hope—however small—were worth that.

Watches were assigned for those sleeping on the plain. The evening meal consisted of what little oaten bannocks they had aside from rations saved for the next day, as no fires could be lit to eat the last of the porridge. The bannocks were dry, sticking in Fiona's throat, but it was better than going to sleep hungry. If they survived the battle tomorrow, they would need to find food before they starved to death. But that was the least of their worries at present.

Those who would fight from the caves slept in them so as to be ready for the enemy in the morning. Sleeping on cold stone was little better than on frozen earth, but at least they were out of the wind.

Neither Angus nor Malcolm spoke, and Fiona did not wish to break the silence. Donald's words, as full of hope as they had been, were a defiance against the overwhelming despair they all faced—and he knew it. It was like throwing dirt against the wind and hoping it would not be blown into one's eyes. But winds shifted, not always blowing the same way.

Fiona only hoped, as she drifted into unconscious sleep, that with the Danish storm soon to break upon them, the winds would blow in the Scots' favour.

The moonlight was cold and quiet.

Drummond paced through the camp, his footsteps furtive but purposeful. His arms were crossed against the icy air, against the dampness that hinted at coming snow. A fog was rising, wrapping around the distant sentries like a ghostly shroud.

"Who goes there?" came a voice, close and thick, distorted by glowing murk.

"Drummond MacDougall."

"Oh, Chieftain, it is you." There was a sigh of relief and then, in a softer voice speaking the Danish tongue, "Do you wish me to go now?"

"Aye. Do ye think ye can make yer way through the Pass in this hopeless gloom without being seen or heard? If these Scots discover ye, they will not hesitate to kill ye. Lachlan went too far, I agree, but now they are even more suspicious. And if the Danes shoot ye in the dark, all will be for naught."

"Aye, I think I can. Shall I go now, then?"

"Aye, I will stand in yer place. Sleep is far from me." Drummond stood closer and whispered in the man's ear, "Tell them, or whoever is leading them, to send their men, but only half through the Pass. Keep the rest behind. Those in the Pass may die, but once the Scots are in, send the rest down through and I and my men will push them from behind, driving them into surrender. Now go, and be swift. I will await yer return."

The man bowed his head, adjusted his cloak over his shoulders, and slipped silently through the moonlit mist.

Drummond watched him vanish. He would be standing there awhile, perhaps until morning, even if the man ran all the way. But, as he looked up into the star-pierced sky, he knew it would be worth it. A few hours of standing in the chill, foggy air would be worth capturing the Scottish princess and crushing the hopeless rebellion: a triumph he could not wait to see.

"Wake up!" someone hissed into Fiona's ear. She opened her eyes, bewildered with sleep. Her heart racing, she dimly saw Angus crouching above her in the cave.

"Wha'—"

"Shh!" he whispered hoarsely. "The Danes are coming; a scout came by wi' the word jist a bit ago. We need to get ready to attack whenever they come." He moved over to his brother and began the process of waking him up.

With senses still muddled from sleep, Fiona got up from where she had lain against the cave wall. Her joints were stiff from lying on the stone floor. She loosened the ties of her dress, slipping out of it, still wearing her brother's clothes beneath. Then she pulled on her leather jerkin and buckled her sword belt around her waist, fingers numb with cold, before pulling back her hair in a rough plait.

Crawling towards the back of the cave and knocking against several piles of stones as she did so, she managed to locate her quiver and bow given to her a few days ago. Slinging the quiver over her shoulder, she struggled to string the bow while sitting down in the cave, as the ceiling was too low to stand. She heard rustling and whispered conversation from the two brothers as they prepared for the coming battle, interrupted by a yawn or two—probably from Malcolm.

Fiona clenched her teeth together in concentration, trying in vain to bend her yew bow to string it. It was not the bow she had trained with for years, and the unfamiliarity already proved a hindrance. No matter how much she strained to bring the string over the notch, she was unable to make the thin rope even touch the tip—let alone slide it into place.

She felt someone take her bow and string out of her hands, and she turned to see Angus slip it over the notch and pull the string back, checking the tension. He handed it back to her without a word and grabbed his own bow and quiver while Malcolm waited behind him to get his.

In a few moments, they were ready, waiting well within the entrance so they would not be seen. Out in the Pass, the ground was nearly invisible, thick fog swirling at the bottom. The world was dark and silent, the horizon paling towards a chilling dawn.

Except dawn did not break.

A gradual lightness appeared, growing brighter but dimmed by the dense fog that lay over the world. Things were invisible a few feet away on the ground, and on the opposite side of the Pass, only the openings of the caves showing as dark clefts in the rock were visible.

Breakfast was a poor fare of the remaining oat bannocks; they had not even water to soften it, and the three of them choked it down in miserable silence. Then they began to wait in nervous quiet, ears straining to hear the sounds of the inevitably coming host.

Below them, the fog began to thin, though it still lay close to the ground in thick swaths like ghaists. Fiona perched on the edge of the cave, peering down in vain to see any movement below. Angus sat behind her, leaning against the cave's walls and sharpening his dirk. Malcolm had fallen asleep while they waited, soft snores disrupting the silence along with the muffled whet-whet of the stone in Angus' hand.

At last, he stopped, running his fingers along the blade, and tossed the stone onto the pile in the back of the cave. The sound echoed, a light, hollow thud. Fiona, tense from waiting, jumped at the sound.

Behind her, she heard Malcolm sigh, the sound having woken him. She turned to see him sit up and rub his eyes. He blinked several times before pulling himself to the edge of the cave and watching the ground below, his lips pinched together in frustration.

She, too, was tired of the waiting. She hoped, as surely did everyone else, that this waiting would not wear off the fighting frenzy that Donald had built up within them last night. Or else the Danes might win after all. Not that the Scots had much of a chance to begin with, but they could lose even that.

Malcolm ducked back in and began munching on the remains of a bannock, licking the crumbs off his fingers. It was the only midday meal they had and, regardless of the hour, he was already eating.

A few minutes later, Angus peered out, the breeze blowing cold in his face and tossing about his soft, dark curls. He reached out to a pine sapling in the crack of the cliff wall and broke a sprig off of it before ducking back into the cave.

Fiona and Malcolm watched with interest as he twirled it in between his fingers and tied it, almost like a knot, twisting the thin branch and the pine needles so that it stayed in a rough circle. Then he took out the pin on the underside of his plaid, the pin that had been Duncan's. He stuck the pin through the pine knot and stabbed it back through his plaid, smoothing out the tartan folds.

"Wha'd ye do tha' fer?" Malcolm whispered, his mouth half-full of bannock.

His brother shrugged. "Fer luck, I suppose."

Then upon the faint, whispering wind was borne the sound of marching, echoing down the walls of the Pass, and the three fell silent. Fiona picked up two cold stones in her hands and squeezed them hard, the nervous tingling in her fingers paining her.

"Are ye all right?" Angus whispered, his face ghastly pale.

She shook her head, her knuckles white through the skin. "When.... Sometimes...I get very scared and...my hands and fingers ache—and it hurts, hurts more than the fear..."

Angus pried her fingers off of the stones and held her hands in his, gently caressing her wrists and knuckles, easing away the aching and the terror while silent tears slipped down her face, tears of shame, tears of dread.

The sound of marching men was closer, but it might have only been a trick of the wind among the rocks.

Malcolm crawled to them, embracing Fiona tightly and wiping away her tears. His grey eyes were wide in sympathy, but his cold hand trembled against her face.

They were, all of them, terrified.

The sun was shining now, though its light was dimmed by the grey clouds. The trio dared not look out to see if the fog had melted, or whether the host was visible within the black walls of the Pass. If they were seen, all would be for naught. They could only wait in agonising silence as the sounds of marching grew ever louder, deafening within the echoing confines of the Pass of Carbinenth.

Fiona glanced at her companions, seeing their pale faces and wide eyes, the same silent, scarcely-masked fear that beat within her own breast. When would the Danes reach the other side of the Pass? How would they know? She supposed they would know because those in the caves at the northern end would rain down their stones first.

Och, but when will tha' be?

Angus let go of her hands, his fingers clenched around his dirk, his eyes shut tight, awaiting the sound of the coming battle. His brother merely watched the opening, small stones in his hands. All of them waited for the command, dreading each passing moment that brought them closer and yet wishing for it to be over now.

Then chaos erupted.

Clangings and clashings resounded throughout the Pass where once the sound of tramping feet had reigned. All at once, the Danes were being rained on with stones and pebbles of various sizes, a grey, deafening storm. The rocks did not do as much damage as blades, but many Danes fell beneath the larger rocks. The rest spooked the Danes' horses, who ran wild, only to be impaled on the cruelly hooked spears of those following on foot.

There was no time to think. Fiona could only grab for stones around her and aim vaguely at the screaming, churning mess below. But such defences did not last long; the piles of stones were soon nonexistent, and the Scots in the caves resorted to spears and arrows, which did more injury than the stony rain.

Fiona soon gave up trying to hit the weak points in the Danes' chainmail and simply fired arrow after arrow in the general direction of the enemy, being unused to this new bow and unable to hit a constantly moving target. More Danes ran down the Pass, and some in a panic ran back the other way. All of them became stuck in the middle, cut down with no means of escape.

The bright *tran-tara* of a horn call rang out in the bitter, sunlit air. The cries of fresh soldiers and horsemen thundered through the Pass, the Scots trampling upon the Danes who put up a mock fight. It all seemed too easy.

Finally out of arrows, Fiona flung her bow and quiver aside. They would be of no more use to her now. Crawling out of the cave, she clambered down the stairs with many of the other Scots. Angus soon joined her, Malcolm close behind him. Drawing their swords, they descended upon the enemy, entering the maddening press of the living and dying, and fought in sword-to-sword combat. A deadly dance of death, a thoughtless killing of one's opponent before one was killed first.

Fiona soon became separated from her companions in the chaotic mêlée. Gradually, she became aware that the sun had vanished behind the looming, grey clouds that had shadowed them for days. The faint light reflected oddly off the bloodied blades. Her hilt slipped in her hand, though not because of her own blood. She elbowed her way out to the side of the Pass and was nearly crushed to death in a sudden surge that pushed against the rocky cliffs. Still, there was a moment's reprieve, and she gasped for air, trying to catch back her breath.

She saw in that moment small flakes of white drifting lazily down from the darkened skies, peacefully still against the anarchic red and damaged steel. Then the sounds of the battle rushed back, nearly deafening her in its discordant roar.

"Fiona!" someone cried above the tumult.

Glancing up, she saw Angus on the stairs above her, pointing at something behind her as he rushed down from his vantage point.

Whirling around, she glimpsed someone heading her way. She raised her sword in defence against the Dane, but he was too fast. It was inhuman to think she could possibly deflect such a blow.

But it never came.

Someone pushed her down from behind and she fell to her knees, her sword plunging point-first into the ground beneath her. She got up, tugging her sword out of the rocky soil, and turned to see Angus withdraw his sword from the Dane before them, the blade dripping red with fresh blood.

Angus caught her gaze and grabbed her hand, pulling her up the stairs and into the first cave they found.

"Wha' is it?" she asked in panicked confusion at this strange behaviour, her pulse still racing from the close brush with death.

"The plan isnae working," he panted, wiping his sweaty brow with the back of his hand.

Her breath caught in her throat. "W-wha' are ye talking about?"

"The Danes hae tricked us."

Her eyes widened. She opened her mouth to speak but no words came.

"Only half of their company was through the Pass," he persisted. "The other half was some distance back, as if to trick us if we tried to deceive them—as if they knew our plan all along. But tha's nae the worst of it. Drummond's company has turned against us."

"Wha'..." she gasped, her heart thudding to a halt. Her sword fell slack in her hand.

"Aye. He came up wi' the cavalry, but his men are fighting ours. I saw it wi' my own eyes!" Angus broke off and inhaled sharply, leaning his head against the cave wall. "I am gang to find my father. Someone needs to tell him wha' is happening before we are completely destroyed."

"Wha' do I do?" she murmured, feeling weak, the world beginning to spin around her.

"Find Malcolm and stay wi' him. We donnae need to lose more men than necessary. Keep fighting. Try to get back to camp if possible. Who kens wha' Drummond might do if he finds ye." Then he was gone, slipping out of the cave and plunging down the stairs, drawing his sword and fighting his way down the Pass. He was soon lost in the sea of men and horses, beyond her sight.

What is gang to happen now?

Fiona pushed the dark, frightening thoughts away and rejoined the fight below, hoping they would survive this day. They had given too much to be destroyed now.

But the battle was as good as lost. The Scots were exhausted and every minute were pushed farther back. More tartan-clad warriors lay among the fallen than stood amid the living.

Fiona easily found Malcolm, pinned against the cliffs as he tried to defend himself. She fought her way to him, the Danes being cut down or running to find easier targets. They clearly did not recognize her—dressed in a kilt and with her hair plaited back—as the wanted princess, else they would not have left her so quickly.

Without a word, Fiona motioned for Malcolm to follow her, and he stuck to her side like a shadow as they tried, with the rest of the Scots, to hold their ground even in retreat.

The snow was falling faster now, coming down in thick white flakes that melted as soon as they touched the heated bodies struggling for victory. The growing wind dried the blood on Fiona's exposed skin, but there was no time to think about it, of how sickening it had seemed to her at her last battle. For with every Dane the Scots cut down, two more came to take his place. And all the while, they were pushed ever back, ever back to the north, from where there was no escape.

Fiona thrust her sword through the body of yet another snarling Dane, her sword arm weary and nearly failing her as she drew back her blade. "This isnae working," she murmured to no one in particular, gasping in exertion. Turning around, Fiona began to push her way back to the Scots' camp, dragging Malcolm along with her.

"Och! Where do ye think ye're gang?" Malcolm sputtered in surprise as he ducked a sword whirling near his head.

"I am gang back to camp."

"Why?"

"I need to find Rhiada. Or yer father. Someone needs to find out wha' we are supposed to do now. We cannae continue on our own, nae like this. And ye need to come—Angus said ye must stick wi' me." Without waiting for a reply, she released his arm and took off, pressing through the ranks to get to the end of the Pass and trusting him to follow.

Fiona hurried through the camp, twisting and turning her path to avoid the many soldiers who were hurrying past her to join the battle. Others were going the same direction as she, bringing in the wounded to be taken care of—if they would even have that chance. With the Danes so bent on the Scots' destruction, there might not be any wounded left to see the next dawn.

Rhiada. I must find Rhiada.

The thought burned in her mind, matching her hurried step.

She searched the faces of all who passed her, hoping to see the one she was looking for. The skies were darkening towards evening, and soon there would be no light to see the battle. As it was, she squinted hard against the dying light, trying to find her way.

Someone suddenly caught her wrist, and she whirled around to see Angus.

"Fiona, ye must come wi' me," he said, his voice oddly strained. His face was ghastly in the fading light.

"I cannae. I must find Rhiada." Her voice rose nearly to a panic, the suppressed fear of the entire day now threatening to drown her.

"Fiona, I need ye to come wi' me," he repeated pleadingly.

Soldiers pushed their way past them, the last of the reserves going out to join the battle. None of the chieftains were among them; no one in leadership was there. All of them gone, leaving only a few men left who ran in fearful obedience to the horn's ringing cry.

"Why? Why is it so important? Where are Donald and Rhiada?" she pressed, horrid anxiety rising in her throat, guessing why Angus might be so distressed.

"'Tis Rhiada." Angus' blue eyes swam in tears. He let go of her arm while his fingers slipped down to take her hand gently in his. "He's dying."

~ 25 ~

RHIADA

NAE! *This cannae be! This mustnae be!*

The snowy world came to a swirling standstill. Fiona stared at Angus in horror. "Ye're nae jesting wi' me, are ye?" she managed to get out at last, her voice barely louder than a whisper. Her throat was thick; she could not swallow through the lump forming there. Her eyes smarted, burning her.

"Fiona, why would I jest like tha'?" he returned, his voice weak. "If only it *was* a jest," he added, gently guiding her to a hastily erected tent.

She followed him mutely like an unresisting bairn, lacking the strength to force her feet to move on their own. They both ducked as they entered the tent, finally out of the rising wind. But the respite meant little. Rhiada was dying.

A dim lantern hung from the main tent pole, providing the only light. Rhiada lay on a pile of tartan blankets, his cloak wrapped around him. A darkening stain slowly spread from his chest, and his breathing was harsh and rasping.

Donald knelt by him, his arm in a rough sling, a thick bandage about his chest visible through his shirt. He stood as they entered, momentary relief crossing his face. "She's here," he said to the dying harper. Then he left the tent, beckoning Angus to do the same, leaving Fiona and Rhiada alone.

She stepped closer and sat down next to the man who had been her guide since he had arrived at the castle of Caerloch, who had faithfully and patiently advised her in the days following until now.

"Fiona?"

"Aye, I'm here," she answered in a calm voice that surprised her; the emotions warring inside of her were at the point of breaking.

"I am so sorry fer wha' has happened. Drummond's betrayal—h-he came and tried to kill both of us, but escaped to lead his men against ours.... I should hae been more careful, we all should hae—" He broke off in a fit of choking. "Our time is short, Fiona, so listen closely. If Donald and his men manage to escape south, he must gae wi' his sons and other chieftains and gae to Cymru."

"Cymru?" she interrupted in astonishment, wondering why the old subject was so important to be brought up now.

"Aye. They must gae to the High King and ask fer help." He reached out with his hand and laid it on her shoulder, his lips trembling with pain. "'Tis our only hope. We cannae win without them." He was silent, trying to regain his breath.

She said nothing, not trusting her voice to speak. Tears slipped down her face and she made no effort to brush them away.

"Fiona, I hae greatly enjoyed the time I had to teach ye and help ye along in this very difficult time of yer life. I ken the shame ye hae wi' yer father marrying a Danish woman to bring peace to the land... but the Scots mustnae blame ye fer tha'. Ye are no' responsible fer the acts of yer father. Many still remember him as the first to fight back the enemy."

"But he still lost in the end." Her voice was barely a whisper.

His hand slipped from her shoulder and rested on her fingers, holding them gently in his own. "Aye, but we cannae change the past. We can only move on." He paused once more, trying to regain his breath that rattled in his throat like a cart led over rough stones.

Then Rhiada's breathing quickened and he tightened his hold on her, clinging to her wrist like a drowning man. "Promise me—" he gasped, a trickle of blood appearing at the corner of his mouth. "Promise me, Fiona, tha' nae matter wha' happens, ye will ne'er surrender to the Danes."

Fiona nodded, choking back the sobs that threatened to break. "I promise," she forced out at last, her voice sounding odd and strained even in her own ears. If she said anything more, she knew she would burst into tears and not be able to stop. Speaking through the lump in her throat pained her almost as much as the knowledge of what was soon to come.

She heard someone enter the tent, a burst of cold wind coming with them, bearing the sounds of conflict beyond; but she did not turn to see who it was.

Rhiada eased back, and a shadow of a smile passed over his scarred face. "They say tha' a man speaks truth on his deathbed. Hear ye now what I must say, Fiona. Though it will be hard in the winning, the Scots will triumph in the end..." He closed his eyelids and inhaled deeply, his breath catching in his chest. "Godspeed to ye, Fiona. I wish ye well in the days tha' come."

"Nae, Rhiada!" she cried out desperately, a sob escaping her lips. "Ye mustnae leave me. Who will guide me in wha' to do?" Tears fell down her cheeks, spilling onto his hand that still held onto hers, his last stay against the shadowy gate of death. "Ye hae been a father to me when my own failed me. Ye mustnae leave me!"

His eyelids flew open, though he could not see. "Och, Fiona, I cannae control tha'. I gae the way of the Warrior's Road, as all men must.... Farewell, fair lass. Ye will overcome this storm, I ken ye will. Donald will guide ye as—" He broke off, coughing, and more blood trickled down the corner of his mouth, a dark stain in the dim lantern light. "Farewell..."

Then he was dead, the fingers around her wrist loosening in the release of death.

Fiona rose to her feet, numbing pain coursing through her veins, tears falling silently from her face. She no longer had the strength to cry. Her heart was bursting with grief, and yet she felt empty, as if all life had been drained away with Rhiada's passing: a hollow weight as heavy as the earth.

A hand rested on her shoulder, a sudden warmth against the cold daze that had swept over her. She lifted her head to see Angus standing there, his blue eyes dark with sympathy.

Fiona turned and flung her arms about his neck, releasing the pent-up grief and crying into his shoulder much like he had done to her when Duncan had died. And he, like she had done to him then, comforted her, saying nothing but simply holding her, letting her grieve unstopped.

A horn sounded the retreat in the distance, high and clear in the winter air, though muffled by the tent's walls.

Angus unclasped her hands from around his neck and said,

"Come. Father has sounded the charge. He means to rush down the Pass and escape south if we can. We must gae if we are to survive."

"But we cannae jist leave him here," she whimpered, her voice dull. "Rhiada deserves better than tha."

"I am sorry, truly, but we hae nae other choice. We need to leave now." Angus reached down and picked up the bag that contained Rhiada's harp. Then he took the princess by the hand and led her outside as she followed like an obedient child.

The wind was cold, swirling snow blowing about, less than there had been before. The ground was covered in white, reflecting the blurred light of torches. Men and horses rushed past them, assembling in rough formation, one last attempt to flee for their lives.

Donald McCladden saw his son and the princess standing by the tent and he slowed his pace, a grim, sorrowful look crossing his face. "He's gone, then?"

Angus nodded, shifting the harp bag over his shoulder.

"Find yerselves a horse and get ready wi' the rest; we'll charge within a few moments. Malcolm is wi' me, so donnae worry about him." Then he turned away, shouting some command to one of the chieftains who passed him.

Together, Fiona and Angus mounted the first abandoned horse they found, one of the Scots' but not one they knew. Angus rode in front of her, taking the reins, as she clung to him from behind.

The horncall sounded for the last time, the final note ringing in the air with triumphant defiance. It rang in Fiona's ears, searing its way into her memory.

With a hoarse cry, the Scots charged. Angus spurred the horse forward, the ranks riding out of the camp towards the Pass. The wave of horsemen overwhelmed the startled Danes, many of whom were trampled in the Scots' wake. Then they were through—what little remained of the Lowlander war host—leaving the dead behind.

Fiona McCurragh leaned forward, her head resting on Angus' shoulder, and closed her eyes as freezing tears spilled helplessly down her cheeks.

The wind was bitter, gusting into their faces, nearly blinding them with snow. Around them, men on horse fled south, fleeing death, fleeing the Danes, fleeing whatever torturous punishment their enemies might inflict upon them were they caught.

A heaving cry escaped Fiona's lips and she closed her eyes, unable to see against the swirling snow. She was overcome with cold, not having her cloak nor a dress to wear over her clothes to provide further warmth. That was all left behind, back in the caves of the Pass and the camp now being destroyed by vengeful Danes, the fires of destruction and merciless blades destroying those unable to escape and their last hopes for freedom.

Even if the Scots managed to safely return to the Lowlands, they would have to swear a surrender. There was no hope of fighting back the Danes now. She wondered what the terms would be, whether she would lose her life after all, whether the leaders of the rebellion would be put to death. She had already lost Rhiada, her mentor and guide; she could not bear to lose more. Not Angus, not Malcolm.... What would the price be for failing to achieve freedom?

Rhiada had said they would win someday, but that day was not now. She wondered whether she would live to see that day, whether any of them would.

Freedom always would be costly.

But Fiona feared that the price was too high for them to pay.

~ 26 ~
DEATH BEFORE DISLOYALTY

IT was nearly two weeks before the survivors from the Scottish war host finally arrived at their homes.

As each league passed from Carbinenth toward An Dùn, the place that had birthed the valiant band of warriors, the remnants of that small army shrank even further. The chieftains separated to their own chiefdoms and glens, promising to meet again to discuss what would happen since they had lost the war: terms of surrender, what the Danes would demand, and how they would answer...but that was not for Fiona to think about.

She remembered the journey back dimly, the only things clear to her being the cold and the sleeting rain that almost never stopped as it washed away the snow, leaving freezing mud in its heartless wake. All were miserable and only stopped when they came within sight of a homestead or village willing to feed and house the men and their horses.

The only other thing she remembered besides the rain and the cold was Angus, his steadiness and patience, never speaking to her but letting her grieve in silence, giving her food when they had it and fresh water from the burns they passed, riding with her, sleeping near her, almost never leaving her side.

She felt numb, the shock having yet to wear off, and the world around her appeared unreal and distant, like a nightmare that she seemed unable to wake from.

Even Malcolm kept his distance, watching her with sad, tired grey eyes. Only Angus dared to come close to her, to never leave her alone, to protect her from falling into the void of grief. For he understood the pain she was going through—because he had once endured the same.

It was a handful of men who finally reached the fort of An Dùn as darkness fell over the world and the sleety rain began again with a vengeance. The gates opened in silence to let them in, no calls of greeting, no cries of welcome, only a cold understanding of what had happened, a sense of hopelessness that was worsened by the winter weather.

Bidding the last of them goodbye and leaving their horses at the stables, Donald McCladden led his two sons and the Scottish princess down the muddied chariotway to their home. Rain pelted from the skies instead of soft, feathery snow, the last remnants of the storm gusting about the roof eaves. But the light that fell around Annag as she stood in the doorway of the McCladden croft was warm and welcoming to the weary travellers.

Malcolm immediately ran into her embrace, burying his face in her shoulder and sobbing.

She held him closely, kissing the top of his head, and then spoke to the others. "Come inside," she greeted in a gentle voice. "There is porridge waiting, and fresh bannocks. I ken ye all must be starving."

Malcolm did not need to be told twice. Wiping away his tears, he dashed inside and was seated at the table, swiftly proceeding to fill up his empty stomach.

"Where are Duncan and Rhiada?" Annag questioned with a worried look on her face as the rest of them entered the warmth and safety of the croft. Her eyes were dark with fear, her face pale as she noticed the missing members of their company.

Donald did not answer, wrapping her up in his arms and running his hand up and down her back as the devastating truth hit her. She clung to him, clenching the folds of his shirt and plaid as if to cling on to reality before she lost it completely. Without a word, Donald led her to the upper story of the croft, where they remained for some time.

Angus jerked his head in the direction of the table, and Fiona sat down with him and his brother as they began to eat in silence.

The food was warm, an edge of sweetness on the thick porridge that she had missed while on the war trail. The blazing hot fire seemed to nearly melt their frostbitten hands and faces. Though they had been given warm food before and slept beneath roofs and by fires, there was something different about this one. A feeling of rest and security, of finally being home, settled over them.

And yet it was not the home they had left. There was the loss of Duncan, but for Fiona, it was the deeper pain of missing Rhiada, his quiet, steady presence, the surety that if she needed to ask for advice or encouragement, he would readily give it. But he was no longer there in the place where he used to be; he was gone, and nothing would bring him back.

She swallowed the porridge through the lump in her throat and blinked back the tears. She could not stay focused on her own grief; a good leader was concerned with the needs of others, not themselves, as Rhiada would say. But all the same, the numbness was wearing off and the pain, still sharp, was nearly unbearable. Yet she did not wish to ruin the homecoming for the McCladden brothers.

So she shoved down the swirling storm with another bite of porridge, glad to be warm and safe, if only for a little while.

Who knew how long this brief reprieve would last, or whether worse things were in store for them in the future.

Fiona found it difficult to sleep that night. She was dry, being clothed in spare garments from Annag since her own dress had been left behind at Carbinenth and it wasn't seemly for her to always wear her brother's clothes. She was properly fed for the first time since they had left An Dùn what seemed like years ago. And she was comfortable for the first time in weeks, but rest refused to come. The shock following Rhiada's death was now gone entirely, and the harsh reality of the world crept in, cold fingers trembling at the edges of her consciousness. An awful lump sat in her throat, one that she could not swallow, and she felt a terrible ache in her chest, heavy in its emptiness.

Thrusting aside the blankets, she sat up against the wall and peered out into the chilly dimness of the room. The faint forms of the sleeping occupants could be seen, just as it had been when she was here a few months ago, though there were fewer of them now. The hearth stones were beside her, embers burning, a faint glow against the dark. Lost in memory, she brushed over the stones with her hand.

They were still warm.

Like a flash of lightning, she could see the firelight shadowing the scars on Rhiada's forehead and the hollows of his missing eyes. With the clarity of a cold mountain burn, she heard his voice in her mind from weeks before, when he had spoken to her, encouraging her despite her fears.

As quickly as it came, the vision faded, leaving her in lonely darkness.

Fiona pulled up her knees and buried her face in her arms, muffled sobs shaking her frame, the last bitter dregs of sorrow overwhelming her. And more than that, she was afraid. Rhiada had been something to hold on to as her world had changed from a prison to a war. His steadiness and words of advice had been beyond value to her ever since he had mysteriously showed up at Caerloch in the beginning of autumn. And now he was gone.

She knew that Donald would do his best to stand in the harper's place, but it would not be the same. And soon Donald and his sons would also be gone, leaving for Cymru in hopes of reinforcements against the Danes. Who would guide her then?

Unexpectedly warm, strong arms clasped around her, and she heard a familiar voice whisper, "There now. 'Tis gang to be all right."

"Nae—it isnae." It was hard to speak smoothly when sobbing.

"Och, Fiona, death always grieves people. Ye are nae the only one who is grieving o'er Rhiada's death." Angus sat down beside her, still embracing her gently.

"It doesnae—seem like it." She raised her head as the tears continued to spill down her face, leaning against him and closing her eyes.

"Why do ye say tha'?"

Words failed her, so she only shrugged, sniffling hard.

He held her closer, resting his head against hers. "Does it seem like nae one is visibly grieving over it?"

She nodded, not trusting her voice to speak.

"Fer one thing, all of us are exhausted. Either we crack down or we donnae." He hesitated, as if thinking through his response.

"Mother...well, she is grieving most o'er the loss of Duncan. She was never close to Rhiada like the rest of us were, so she will ne'er lament his loss like the rest of us will. Father is grieving o'er the loss of yet another of his sons and his adviser, but he doesnae like to make his sorrow kent to jist anyone. And Malcolm is too young to really appreciate wha' Rhiada was to us." He paused again, before continuing in a softer tone. "I am glad if death doesnae hurt him so deeply because of his youth. There is enough darkness in this world without needing to destroy his innocence."

By this time, her sobs had gradually calmed, and only an occasional sniff broke the silence. "Angus," she began but stopped.

"Aye?"

"Did ye hear about the plans Rhiada told yer father before he died?"

She heard him swallow. "Something about us gang to Cymru?"

"Aye."

"Tha' was all I heard before I was sent to find ye." She did not answer so he continued, "But, Fiona, Rhiada wouldnae like to see ye in such distress about it. I jist ken he wouldnae."

"Nae, he wouldnae. But I still cannae gae on like nothing has changed!" Though they spoke in whispers, her voice rose to nearly a normal tone before she stopped, afraid to wake anyone else.

"Nae, and he wouldnae expect ye to. But the time fer healing will come, and it will be all right someday."

"When?"

"I donnae ken exactly, but I do ken tha' the healing always comes after grief, always.... Now, ye must get some rest before dawn. We all need our rest, especially ye." Holding her tightly for one last moment, he rose to his feet and returned to his own straw-filled mattress that rested beside Malcolm's, leaving Fiona to stare at the ceiling until, at long last, she finally fell asleep.

It was some weeks later, during preparations for the midwinter fires, when the High Chieftains met again in An Dùn. The skies were grey and the air was biting and damp. Snow lay in thick drifts around the buildings of the fort, but inside the Council Hall, it was warm and dry. A large fire burned on the centre hearth, the earthy smell of peat permeating the place.

Besides the chieftains, McCladden sons, and Fiona herself, there were also some of the warriors of An Dùn, many of them fathers, interested in knowing what was to be discussed. Official terms of surrender had been sent by the Danes for the Scots to agree to, but no one yet knew what those terms were. And there was, of course, Rhiada's dying request to be spoken of as well.

Fiona glanced at them all as they were seated, noting the familiar faces—even the unnamed ones who lived in An Dùn—and noticing the new chieftain in their midst, who had taken Jamie McBride's place.

Hamish McLairdun boasted a shock of sandy-blond hair and grey eyes that were serious and stern, the sort that Fiona imagined would soften if he smiled. He was much older than Jamie had been, about the same age as Donald McCladden, though it was hard to tell for certain.

Once they were all gathered, Donald rose to his feet and signalled for silence. "As most of ye ken, this latest attempt to overthrow the Danes didnae end well."

"'Twas a disaster," interrupted Bryce MacClydno, his fingers lightly drumming on the table they were all seated at.

"We were no' ready," added Alastair McThraedan, his mouth set in a firm line.

"Aye, we were no' ready," repeated Donald. "And when the day comes when we rise to fight again, we mustnae make the same mistake. But tha' day isnae here yet. And we hae more pressing matters to attend to. Lady Nuith has sent us a set of terms fer surrender, which are here before us now." He laid his hand for a moment on the papers before him, written first in the rigid runic script of the Danes and then in the rolling Celtic lettering of the Scots, though they looked stiff. "They ask fer a complete and total surrender, giving them our weapons, and our best warriors when they call on them."

A wave of grumbled complaints rose and swelled nearly to a breaking point at this, but he raised his hand to quiet them.

"But the worst of it is..." He sighed heavily before continuing, looking down at the terms before him as if simply staring at them long enough would make them disappear. "They wish fer us to hand over our princess and swear an oath to ne'er rise up against them again." Donald sat down, his forehead creased in worry, glancing at each of their faces in turn.

The wave, though leashed from breaking, now shattered upon release, a shocked silence settling over the room.

Fiona felt as though she had been struck in the heart. A cold blade of fear wedged between her ribs.

Angus, beside her, placed his hand on hers beneath the table for a moment, his face as pale as she imagined hers to be.

"We cannae accept such terms, even were we driven to such dire straits," Eachann MacDonald said softly, speaking for the first time. "'Twould be a dishonour to all those who hae died in the struggle fer freedom, nae to mention nothing short of betrayal to our princess here." His gaze flickered towards Fiona and he bowed his head slightly in acknowledgment of her position.

Her cheeks flushed, but she dipped her head towards him in recognition. She was still reeling in shock from the terms. But of course, the second war had failed, and Lady Nuith yet thirsted for revenge. It was as it had been months ago, except the Lowlanders had too few men to defend themselves now. Yet would she be so abandoned? Did they have a choice? Was there still a chance they might win?

"Indeed, it would be a dishonour and betrayal, but we cannae jist ignore them!" Bryce grunted. "They will come after us, and we will be unable to stop them. We ken wha' they will do—burning our homes, slaughtering our animals, salting our fields, slaying our finest men and enslaving our women and bairns.... We hae seen it before. We hae nae choice but to accept, whether we like it or no.'" He cleared his throat and ran his fingers through his thick, greying beard. "Perhaps there is a way to accept some of the terms and nae all of them, but wha' difference does tha' make? None of them are pleasant to me, nor—should I expect—to any of ye."

Murmurs followed this, but no one raised their voice to speak, whether to add to his defence or to argue with what he said.

"We must accept them, or at least feign to," Donald said at last. "Otherwise they will overrun us. Whatever we decide, we cannae give up our princess."

A chorus of agreement replied, and Fiona felt somewhat relieved knowing that, even in defeat, the Scots would defend her with their lives. Perhaps Lachlan had been wrong all along: she was indeed loved by her people. Still, she wondered how the Scots would ever manage to keep her away from Lady Nuith. She knew firsthand how relentless Nuith could be once she set her mind to something.

"We cannae give up our princess, aye, and we cannae give them our best men. They already took that in blood," Bryce snarled. Though his face remained passive, his black eyes glittered in fierce fire.

"Then wha' are we agreeing to?" Hamish asked, his voice burring at the edges, like the rumble of a discontented bear.

A moment of silence fell. The fire continued to burn away the crumbling peat, torches flickering in their brackets above those seated at the table.

As if guessing their thoughts, Donald said, "We can swear a surrender and an oath to ne'er rise up. They willnae make us do it by the ways of our people, and therefore it willnae be truly binding. As fer men, they hae already taken tha', as Bryce said. We can hide away our weapons, and if they demand them, say we need them to fight against the Saxon menace.... They may no' like tha' so much, but we hae nae choice. And we cannae give them our princess. Whether we pretend she has died of fever and hide her away until we are ready or find some other means of keeping her safe, she must no' fall into their hands." His voice was grim, fiercely determined, and Fiona found some of her courage return to her.

"When will we e'er be ready to fight again?" Alastair asked with a heavy sigh, voicing the question they were all thinking.

"Before he died, one of my closest friends and advisers, Rhiada ap Derlyn, made me promise something." Donald paused before continuing. "Several times in the past—and many of ye here might remember him mentioning this last time we met here—Rhiada suggested gang to Cymru to ask fer help in defeating the Danes. Unfortunately, there was nae time to send fer help, but now tha' is the last choice left to us. We donnae hae enough men on our own, but wi' their forces and allied strength, we may hae enough to finally drive the Danes back into the sea."

"But wha' good would tha' do? The Danes mean nothing to them," Eachann interrupted. "The Saxons are their main threat."

"'Tis wha' I thought as well, but Rhiada confirmed tha' the Danes do attack them from the sea. Besides, Rhiada had ties to the royal family of Brenin ap Brynmor, having married his daughter. He said tha' Brenin would be more than happy to help us as it will eliminate one of the biggest threats to their country."

"Can anything be gained by this alliance besides more men and support?" Hamish questioned.

"The Cymry are excellent archers and are kent fer their skill at bow-making," Donald replied. "We cannae make many bows here due to lack of ash and yew trees. And as we hae said before, they can provide more men than we hae. I think it is an alliance that will prove beneficial to both sides, but does anyone else agree?"

Murmurs and nods of agreement sounded around the table.

"And Fiona McCurragh, do ye object to this?"

"Nae," she answered steadily. "'Tis in my heart tha' this is a wise thing; I only wish we had been able to do it sooner." Indeed, for then she might not have lost Rhiada, the McCladdens may not have lost Duncan, they all may not have lost so many fine, irreplaceable men.

"Then we are agreed," Donald said, a slight smile on his face. "But it yet remains wha' to do about the terms."

"I agree wi' wha' ye said earlier about the swearing, but I wish fer the rest to be done as well," Alastair stated. "We keep our princess and our weapons; we hae nae men to send them fer we need those to help wi' the fieldwork and keep our people from dying out. And methinks the rest of us are one on this thing as well."

"Then I will write out our terms and send them back. And let us hope they hae mercy," Donald concluded grimly.

"Who will gae to Cymru and when?" Bryce demanded, ever a man of action.

"I will, wi' my sons and a few of the warriors tha' can be spared. If ye wish to come, or to simply send yer men as well, tha' is fine. But they must be well-trained. We must show the Cymry tha' we are worthy to be treatied wi'. And I hope to leave when the weather warms in spring, when the planting begins. Unfortunately we cannae help wi' tha', but if this plan succeeds, then it will be worth it after all."

Emptiness hollowed itself in Fiona's chest at the thought of having to say goodbye to Angus and Malcolm. Though it was yet months away, that day would come all too soon. She glanced at the McCladden brothers, who met her gaze briefly. Perhaps they shared her sentiments, but she was sure that at least Malcolm was excited by the prospect of it all. The light shining in his eyes at his father's words could not be mistaken.

"I will send men wi' ye," Hamish spoke up, disturbing her thoughts, "wha' can be spared."

Several others nodded in agreement.

"But wha' of our women and children? How will we keep them safe from the Danes?" Nairn, one of the men who lived in An Dùn, questioned, speaking for the first time. "Especially the heir, or is she gang wi' ye?"

A flicker of hope rose in Fiona's chest and she glanced at Donald's face, at the way the grey daylight reflected in his blue eyes. Did that mean no separation after all? But his next words dashed her hope to pieces.

"Fiona is staying here. I intend tha' she and my wife, Annag, will gae to Caerdun Castle. 'Tis safer fer them since 'tis farther from the Danes, and out of all such places in the lands I govern, 'tis the most defensible place and easier to hide away in. Those ye wish to gae wi' them may do so, but I wish fer some to remain here. Wi' the princess gang, the Danes may nae longer see this place as dangerous but merely another village tha' dots the countryside."

Fiona bit her lip and looked away. So a goodbye after all. But so it must be, if they were to have hope of freedom. And at least she would be safe. Yet that did not console her much.

"Any other questions?" There was no answer, so Donald concluded, "We hae survived these last few months on the war trail, and while we hae no' returned victorious, we still hae a chance to fight should the time come again. But we must prepare. Until we return, all men of fighting age in yer chiefdoms must train relentlessly. We must breed and train horses fer battle. And we must keep an ever-watchful eye on the doings of the Danes. We must prepare so tha' when we return to fight—and return we will—we will win."

"Death before dishonour," Eachann murmured into the silence that followed.

"Death before disloyalty," came the reply from the rest.

With that oath came an echo of the past, when it was first spoken in Fiona's hearing. She knew it would haunt her until it was fulfilled, or her death and the destruction of their country and all they knew and loved rendered it void.

Nonetheless, in the bitterness of memory and fears of the future lay an ember of hope that could not be quenched. It would burn far into the night until morning came again for Scotland. But perhaps that was what they needed: hope, however small, to last them through the coming darkness until the new day dawned.

They may yet fight another day.

~ EPILOGUE ~
THE COMING STORM

A warm breeze whispered gently among the winding streets of An Dùn, bringing with it a hint of spring. Grey skies thinly veiled the sun, parting at times to reveal the glorious blue of the heavens beyond. And outside the gates, the drab colours of winter began to turn green amid the patches of slowly melting snow scattered on the moorland.

Fiona McCurragh stepped lightly from the McCladden croft and walked down the centre of the fort, along the chariotway muddied from recent rains. The air was cool and clear, as refreshing as the azure skies that sometimes shone above her, and while she wore a cloak against the cold, she welcomed the early heralds of spring—except for the one thing that made her wish it was still the deep heart of winter.

For with early spring had come the snow's thawing. Since the mountain passes into Cymru were clearing, the embassy could leave An Dùn and head south. Even now, the Scots finalised the preparations for the journey. Most of the activity was happening near the south gate, where the chieftains and their best warriors gathered to depart.

Fiona looked among the men assembled in their vivid tartans, their spears glittering in the grey dawn. She saw Donald McCladden talking to a couple of the leaders, Bryce and Eachann, but Angus and Malcolm were nowhere to be found among them.

Hearing the sounds of horses and familiar voices coming from the nearby stables, she strode to the large, timbered building and entered, greeted almost immediately by the sweet smells of hay and horse. It took a few moments for her eyes to adjust to the dim and dusty light, but when she could see clearly, she caught sight of Malcolm leading two saddled horses out of the stables. He grinned as he passed her, the slight breeze toying with his messy hair.

She flashed a smile in return and walked deeper into the stables, finding Angus, who latched shut the doors to the now-empty stalls.

Once finished, he strode towards her, adjusting the folds of his cloak over his shoulders. "Well, there's tha.'"

"How many are riding?" Fiona asked, inquiring since many had spears with them, which were difficult to hold while managing a horse for the many leagues that lay ahead.

"Only the leaders, I think. The rest of us hae to walk to Cymru, something I donnae think Malcolm is gang to relish much," he finished, chuckling.

Fiona laughed with him, but her lightheartedness faded when she remembered the reason they were there at all. "Yer mother is coming to see ye all off," she said softly.

He did not reply, and the silence hung heavy between them.

"I wish ye didnae all hae to gae." She spoke at last, gazing down at the fodder-strewn floor, scuffling some loose strands of hay with the toe of her boot.

"Aye, I ken, but we must. Besides, 'tis nae like we are gang off to fight. We will come back.... The only question is whether the treaty-making will gae well or no.'"

"Rhiada said tha' it would." Her gaze flickered up to meet his, a stab of fear piercing her thoughts. Might it all come to nothing anyway?

"Jist because he said, doesnae mean it will," he replied. "Brenin might no' be the king anymore. After all, he was old when Rhiada last saw him, and tha' was how many years ago?"

Angus' words did not console her in the slightest; rather, the opposite.

"True, but 'tis the only hope we hae left!" she returned desperately. "Tha', and tha' ye all return safely," she added in a softer tone, her cheeks burning.

Angus nodded, not catching sight of her blush—to her relief—as he was staring out the open doors of the stables. "Fiona..." he began, his voice trailing off like a dying breeze.

"Aye? Wha' is it?" she prompted, regardless of her racing heart. Why did she care so much about what he would say?

He did not answer immediately, turning his gaze away from the open doors and reaching up to unclasp something around his neck. He withdrew a slender cord on which hung a simple yet elegant silver knot, usually hidden beneath his shirt collar. "My mother made this fer Sioned before he went off to war, but Sioned gave it to me for safe-keeping." He placed it gently in her palm, his fingers brushing against hers, a wave of crimson flaming his cheeks. "I want ye to keep it fer me until I come back." His voice was soft and gentle, a timid whisper.

Fiona fastened the cord around her neck, slipping the pendant inside her dress. The metal was warm against her skin, warm with his warmth. "I will keep it fer ye, then, until ye return," she said solemnly. She met his gaze, seeing the fear melt away in his deep blue eyes.

He smiled. "Thank ye, Fiona. Oh, and Malcolm insisted tha' ye keep this in his stead," he added, raising his eyebrows and procuring the pine knot that he had made several months ago in the Pass of Carbinenth. The pine needles were now dried and would forever remain in that knot until it was broken or burned.

She laughed. "I will keep it fer him then," she answered, taking it and placing it within her brother's pin beneath her plaid.

Angus opened his mouth to say something else when his father called from the entrance to the stables, "Angus, we are heading out."

Pinching his lips in a firm line, Angus nodded and turned away from the princess, walking towards his father.

Fiona followed him out into the brightness of the silver morning, greeted by the gentle spring breeze. She caught sight of Annag and moved to stand next to her as Donald gave some final instructions to the men staying behind. Fiona watched the men waiting to leave, some already mounted, others leaning on their spears. Malcolm chattered to his brother, but Angus gazed at the ground, his brows knit in deep thought, though perhaps not over Malcolm's words.

Having finished speaking, Donald walked to his wife and embraced her; and, as if no one else was watching, he kissed her farewell before he mounted his horse.

Annag McCladden held Malcolm fast to her, the ginger-haired lad squirming in an attempt to escape. When she finally let him go, he side-stepped and squeezed Fiona tightly in farewell, daring to kiss her cheek before running off, laughing, to join the others leaving An Dùn.

Fiona watched him go, her cheeks burning, uncertain whether to lose her temper or laugh with him. It had caught her off guard, yes, but Malcolm was now too far away for her to do anything about it.

She turned, watching Angus embrace his mother, the two of them whispering to each other as Annag clasped him closer to her, as if afraid to lose yet another son. But she let him go at last, her soft eyes brimming with tears.

Angus gazed at Fiona for a moment before wrapping his arms around her with a tightness as if he meant to carry her off with the embassy headed south. She closed her eyes, trying to put the feeling to memory, something whispering deep in her heart that it would be a long time before she saw any of them again. When he released her, though he remained silent, his eyes told the farewell he seemed not to trust himself to speak.

It nearly broke her heart to see him so close to tears, knowing she could not help him this time, for it was something he had chosen, and only he could bear the burden—and bear it alone.

Then he was gone, intermingled with those departing and out of her sight.

Annag took Fiona's hand in hers, and together they ran up one of the stairways that led to the battlements upon the wall. They watched the small troop of men and horses as they followed the chariotway south, which would eventually bend westward, crossing another trackway that would lead them, in the end, to Cymru.

Annag watched them slowly disappear into the distance, a worried expression on her face, unusual for her calm and steady nature. "I jist hope they return safe," she whispered to no one in particular.

"They will," Fiona answered in as brave of a voice as she could manage. "And we will be waiting fer them when they come back."

Annag smiled sweetly despite the grief in her eyes. "Aye, ye're right. But come, we must prepare to gae to Caerdun." She turned and headed back down the stairs, her skirt billowing in the breeze, but Fiona still lingered upon the wall, watching as the group of warriors marched away, gradually disappearing into the dark, misty horizon—perhaps it would rain soon.

Rhiada had once spoken of another storm that was coming, a storm that had not yet broken. The Scots had to prepare against the time that storm would break over the land so when the Danes came again, they would be able to defeat them.

Fiona inhaled deeply.

Until then, there was much to be done.

Angus McCladden glanced over his shoulder at the fortress town of An Dùn, watching as it vanished into a tiny speck in the north, smoky grey against the greener braes. They were climbing a slight rise now, and he knew that beyond it, his home would no longer be visible.

A bitter wave of homesickness rose within him, an absinthian longing for his mother and the fiery-haired lass that was Scotland's princess. Still within sight; and yet so far away. He wondered when he would see them again, knowing it could not be soon enough.

Yet he hoped that this last chance would be worth it. That the Cymry would agree to this treaty—this alliance, that their combined strengths would be stronger than previous loyalties, strong enough to defeat the Danish tyrant and regain a stolen crown. It was the only thing he could console himself with now.

Angus heard a heavy sigh beside him and turned to see Malcolm's shoulders drooping as though bearing the weight of the world.

"Wha' is it?" he asked kindly, wondering if perhaps his younger brother also shared his sentiments. But any expectations he might have had were dashed by the answer.

"Och!" Malcolm cried. "I'm so hungry!"

Glossary

Athair-cèile - Scots' Gàidhlig for father-in-law

Bannocks - a variety of flat or any large, round article baked or cooked from grain. Also known as oat cakes, barley cakes, etc.

'Bout - about

Brae - hillside

Burn - stream

Cannae - cannot, can't

Couldnae - couldn't, could not

Cymraeg - Welsh word for the Welsh language

Cymreig - Welsh word for something pertaining to Wales, i.e. Welsh harper

Cymru - Welsh word for Wales

Cymry - Welsh word for the Welsh people

Didnae - did not, didn't

Dìlseachd - Scots' Gàidhlig for loyalty

Donnae - do not, don't

Fer - for

Gae - go

Gang - going, gone

Gearran - Scots' Gàidhlig term for a small, sturdy horse

Ghaists - ghosts

Glen - valley

Hae - have

Haggis - a traditional Scottish dish made up of sheep intestines and finely chopped herbs boiled together with oatmeal inside a sheep's stomach

Isnae - is not, isn't

Jist - just

Ken - know

Kenning - knowing

Kens - knows

Kent - knew

Loch - lake

Muckle - much/more/a lot

Nae - no, not

No' - not

Och - oh

Sabhal - storage building, usually used for grain

Shouldnae - shouldn't, should not

Teulu - Welsh term for family; can also refer to close companions or bodyguard

Tha' - that

Wee - little

Wha' - what

Wi' - with

Wouldnae - wouldn't, would not

Ye - you

Yer - your

Ye're - you are, you're

Yerself - yourself

Yerselves - yourselves

ACKNOWLEDGEMENTS

THIS book was born out of loneliness. At a time when I was going through a season of change, I wanted loyal friends, wanted to belong somewhere, wanted a place to set down roots when everything around me felt uprooted.

I know that not every reader will like this story. That's not why I wrote it. I didn't write it for the sales or algorithm rankings. I wrote it to fill a void in my life, writing about characters my age, writing about them going through difficult circumstances and emerging out the other side, still holding on to hope.

Yet God is good. And along the way from me finishing the first draft to publishing the final draft some six years later, He gave me steadfast friends and precious memories of times spent with them, almost to an equal measure of what Fiona, Angus, and Malcolm experienced. (Though, perhaps, not so many brushes with death, thank goodness!)

They say it takes a village to raise a child. In the case of *Dìlseachd - A Stolen Crown*—as with any great enterprise—it took an entire clan. And to them I owe my eternal thanks.

To Alpay B., Bekkie H., and Mason C., who read the first few chapters I ever wrote and told me you were intrigued: thanks for giving me the encouragement I needed to continue past chapter three.

To my English teacher, Mrs. Feia, to whom this book is also dedicated. If it wasn't for you giving my story a chance and telling me it needed to be published, I would not be where I am in my writing career. Thank you for pushing me to excel in my writing and being the first to tell me my writing was worth pursuing.

To Victoria S., a.k.a. Sariyah Starsong, for being the first to read the entire rough draft. Your energetic texts and squeals gave me hope others would enjoy these characters as much as you did. (Also, thanks for coining Fiangus!)

To my mom and my sister, Cayli—yes, you're in my acknowledgements now. You're practically famous. Thanks for the criticism. I know I didn't like it at the time, but it helped me become aware of my weaknesses as a writer and begin to work to make this story what it was meant to be. Thanks for being the first to cry over my writing and forming Malcolm's fan club. I'm sure he'd be thrilled to know about it.

To Josiah M., Bailey G., and Verity B., for reading this book on Wattpad.com in days long ago and for telling me what I needed to fix. I hope the villains are clear enough and Fiona is properly respected. ;)

To my first band of beta readers, Grace J., Allison R., Lydia F., Hannah W., Ethan W., and Brianna D., for giving me your time and insight into this book. Your feedback was invaluable.

To Faera Lane, for making that trilogy set of covers just for fun. Seeing what my books may become someday was inspiration that words cannot describe.

To my grandparents, who suffered me making changes and telling them they needed to go back to the beginning and read the newest version. This is the final draft; I promise I won't interrupt your progress again. ;)

To my first editor, Victoria L., for helping me fix the last major content changes and smooth out the worst wrinkles.

To my final band of beta readers: Alissa J. Zavalianos, Robin Degan, Hannah Yu, Rachel R., Rebekah, Alexus Wiebe, Janice Verhoog, Nicole, and those who wished to remain nameless. Thank you so much for your feedback, both critical and also from a reader's standpoint.

To my main editor, Brianna De Man, who started as my beta reader and has over the years become one of my best friends and now my editor. Thank you for all you've done in polishing this story into the book I've always envisioned it to be. I can't thank you enough.

To my copyeditor, Deborah O'Carroll, for catching all the last few errors and mistakes. Working with you is always a delight!

To Jess a.k.a. jessthebluestocking for all your help with Gàidhlig translation and for putting up with my sudden and random messages regarding pronunciation of something. *Tapadh leat!*

My eternal thanks to Susan L. Markloff who helped me format this story. If it were not for your aid with this, I might have chucked my laptop out the window and called it quits, so close to the finish line. Thank you times infinity!

Thank you also to Hannah W., who volunteered to proofread the .pdf files and caught the very few last mistakes I had missed.

To all my readers and future fans of this story. Thank you for giving my work a chance. Hold fast to hope!

And lastly, I wish to thank my Saviour who used this story to teach me so much, and Who is my Hope and Light in the darkness. Thank You for letting me tell this tale.

THIS STORY WILL BE
CONTINUED IN

BOOK 2

OF THE

PRINCESS OF THE HIGHLANDS
TRILOGY

ABOUT THE AUTHOR

Cheyenne van Langevelde is a young author and musician whose greatest passion is weaving tales through story and song. When not struggling to attempt the most metaphorical prose, she enjoys composing and recording soundtrack pieces for books, practicing calligraphy and Irish dance, and studying the Welsh language. She occasionally emerges into the real world to restock her chocolate supply, of which she hoards like a dragon would his gold.

You can follow her on her website and social sites listed below:

Website: https://www.thedancingbardess.com
Instagram: @thedancingbardess
Twitter: @dancing_bardess
Goodreads: Cheyenne van Langevelde

9 781736 758762